JOHN R. MAXIM

"MAXIM KNOWS HOW TO PULL READERS IN WITH WILD PLOT TWISTS."
Chicago Tribune

HAVEN

"Top-drawer entertainment."
Kirkus Reviews

"Maxim does a great job . . . An entirely believable story of international espionage . . . An intriguing thriller that keeps you guessing until the end."
Providence Journal-Bulletin

"Elizabeth Stride and Martin Kessler make quite a pair . . . Readers will come to care about them . . . [Maxim's] plot moves along swiftly with plenty of ups and downs to keep the pages turning. And he handles dialogue as well as Stride handles her bloody knife."
Denver Post

. . . puts a smart spin on this tense, clever new thriller . . . In Elizabeth and Kessler, Maxim has created vivid characters . . . This high-octane thriller stands out from the pack."
Publishers Weekly

"Maxim constructs a complex plot, juggles numerous characters, and pulls it all off with a cinematic, breathless pace . . . There is something here for everyone—plus good writing and real page-turning suspense. Highly recommended."
Library Journal

Books by
John R. Maxim

Novels

THE SHADOW BOX
A MATTER OF HONOR
BANNERMAN'S LAW
THE BANNERMAN EFFECT
THE BANNERMAN SOLUTION
TIME OUT OF MIND
ABEL BAKER CHARLEY
PLATFORMS

Nonfiction

DARK STAR

Coming Soon in Hardco

MOSAIC

For Howard Morhaim
. . . whom I've never thanked enough

One

The men of Abu Shatt had never stoned a woman.

A few had seen it done in the land of the Saudis, but because they were visitors they had not taken part. The sins of those women were against their own villages and it was up to their families to expiate their shame. To join in would have shown bad manners.

That in mind, this night's stoning seemed very strange indeed. The woman to be killed was not of this village, nor were those who had brought her. As if that were not enough to make the men ill at ease, they were told that the stoning would be recorded on videotape. The old sheik, their holy man, had said that this was all the more reason that the stoning must be done correctly.

Their village was a small one. It had always been poor. It lay eighty miles to the southeast of Cairo, though the distance could well have been measured in centuries. Its name, in Arabic, meant Father of Rivers but the village was a dry and dusty place. Not even the sheik knew how it got such a name. But the sheik had said that soon the name would have meaning because copies of the tape would flow from it like rivers and the faithful would know how things are done in Abu Shatt.

The sheik chose six men, three young and three old. The six would prepare the pit. They worked most of the night at the place he selected, lit only by the flame of a single tin lamp. The place was a small and rocky field that God

1

must have cursed because not even millet would grow there. It seemed a good place for an adulteress to die.

Some of the men argued that first she should be lashed because adultery was said to be but one of her crimes. Fifty lashes to her back and her buttocks. Fifty more across her bared breasts. But their sheik said no, this was not in the law because the woman's other crimes were unproven. Her accuser, moreover, was a friend of this village and he had asked that she not be beaten. He had asked that she be given a chance to repent. After that it would be enough that she be stoned.

The sheik, because he was old and feeble, needed two men to hold him as he stepped off twelve paces. That would be the width of the ring. Returning to its center, he scratched a mark with his cane. There would be the hole in which the woman would kneel. The two men who had held him began to dig. The others were sent to gather stones.

The gatherers had no lamp, only light from the stars, and yet the stones were chosen with care. There should be none so large that it would kill too quickly, none so small that it would merely torment her. They were to be arranged in four separate piles, one hundred and one stones in all. The odd stone would be placed before her where she knelt. It would be thrown by her accuser. The sheik had heard of no man, much less a woman, who had ever survived more than thirty or so. But by law each would have to be thrown.

The pit was finished not long before dawn. Her accuser, who had come in a big white Mercedes, was asked if he was ready to proceed. This man, named Bandari, looked over at the Englishman who had set up the lights and the video camera. The Englishman nodded, then yawned. Her accuser had also brought a third man with him, an American, tall and thin with cold eyes. The American and Bandari both wore dark suits and ties. The Englishman was known to always wear white from his shoes to his floppy canvas hat. The hat was pulled down over stringy blond hair that seemed ever in need of being washed. They had arrived from Cairo well after midnight and had brought the woman in the trunk of their car.

The old sheik was not pleased that two Christians were present. But the Englishman was needed because he would do the taping. Also he was the one who had tracked down the woman. It was said that he found many others like this one and grew rich from the bounties he had been paid. The sheik knew nothing about the American, only that he was a friend of Bandari, the accuser, and wanted to see the adulteress punished. Very well, he could stay, but he would have to watch from the car. The sheik gave the signal for the woman to be brought out.

She was dressed head to toe in a black abaya. A mask, called a burka, covered all but her eyes. A single length of cord bound her arms to her sides and it coiled very tightly from her shoulders to her hips. The old sheik frowned when he saw this. To bind her so was immodest. The cord should have been tied beneath the abaya so that the garment could hang freely and conceal what it should. This way it revealed the shape of her body and caused her breasts to thrust forward. Although most of the men kept their eyes on the ground, a few were already stealing looks at her bosom. These were the same ones who wanted her lashed, first her back and then her bare breasts.

But the sin, the sheik decided, was hers and not theirs. It was she, the adulteress, who put lust in their hearts. He urged the men to quicken their pace so that her body, all the sooner, would be hidden from them. In any case dawn would soon be upon them. This had to be finished before morning prayer.

A burst of brilliant light caused the woman to falter and the men to raise their hands to their eyes. A few of the men held back for a moment because they knew that the lights meant the camera was running. Not all were so happy about being on tape. Some had argued that they should cover their faces because stoning had been outlawed for several years now. They could end up in Cairo's Kanater Prison and how would their families survive if they did? But the sheik would not permit them to cover their faces. God's work, he had said, should be done in the open.

Now the woman could see the hole that had been dug and her chest began heaving in fear. Her burka blew out with each breath she exhaled and sucked back with each new breath she drew. She tried to resist by bracing one heel but she could find no footing in the hard-packed earth. Her shoes had already been taken from her and she wore only black cotton stockings. Next she fought them; she refused to walk. She twisted away from the men who were escorting her and threw herself to the ground. They saw that they would have to carry her.

Two men picked her up, taking care to touch only her forearms and elbows and not to touch any bare skin. A third looped a cord around her legs, being careful not to bare them, not even with stockings, fastening them together at a point below her knees. Holding fast to the cord, he pulled her legs up behind her. In this manner they carried her to the edge of the hole and lowered her body into it. The two held her steady as the third used a shovel to pack dirt and rock into the spaces around her.

A man being stoned is buried to his waist. A woman must be buried to her chest and this was done. But the shape of her breasts showed even more clearly now because the dirt was pushing them up. The sheik gestured to the man with the shovel. He wanted the dirt piled higher. As this, too, was done the woman's eyes darted from the face of one man to the next. They knew that she was searching for the face of her accuser. At last she squinted into the lights and made a sound like the hiss of a cat. She called out the name of Gamal Bandari.

"*Gamal!*" she shouted. It was more like a croak. She swallowed hard and called again, this time more clearly. "Gamal, for God's sake, don't do this."

When no answer came from behind the lights, she turned to the men of Abu Shatt. "I swear before God, I am innocent," she cried. "Don't you see what that murdering bastard is doing? He is using you. He is using Islam. He is—"

Her bad language brought gasps, but from some it

brought sneers because they knew that this adulteress, not Bandari, was the murderer. A young man named Mahfouz strode into the pit. He was one of the four who gave evidence against her, but the only one born in this village. He bent and struck her with the back of his hand. The blow silenced her but it tore off her burka. Mahfouz wiped the hand against the sleeve of his robe as if to show that merely touching her had made it unclean. It was bad enough to touch a woman not of his family, but worse to touch one who soon would be in hell.

The sheik was speaking. He was quoting from the law.

It was hard to hear, because his voice was not strong and because the woman was shouting again. Not pleading, not praying, but staring past the lights and calling out to the man named Gamal. Also some of the men were not listening to the sheik because now they could see that the woman was beautiful even with a smear of blood on her mouth. One was heard to mutter that she didn't look so evil and that maybe this could wait another day, another week. The sheik, hearing this, stopped quoting the law and began lecturing them instead about women. All the trouble they caused when they didn't know their place, and how women, all women, had Satan inside them.

The young man named Mahfouz looked over at Bandari and saw that he, too, was perhaps losing his resolve. Bandari's face was perspiring greatly and he seemed to be arguing with the American. The American was supposed to have remained with the car but now he was up behind the Englishman's camera.

"Bandari, let's move this along," he was saying. "Get out there and ask her to sign."

"Not yet." Bandari was trying to hush him. "Soon. Very soon. When she is frightened enough." Bandari wiped his face with a handkerchief.

The American looked past him at the woman in the pit. Her chin was now trembling, her eyes wide with terror, and her voice had become a hoarse rasp. She was not yelling now; she was trying to breathe; she sucked air in great shuddering gulps.

"Frightened." He snorted. "She's going into shock. Make your offer, Bandari. Make it now while you can."

"Mr. Tarrant . . . I have told you. This must be done correctly. The sheik must first finish reading his fatwah."

The American shook his head as if in wonder. "Where do you find these people, Bandari?"

"You would not understand, Mr. Tarrant."

Mahfouz did not know what to make of this American. The Englishman's eyes were shining with a sickness that Mahfouz understood. This man hated women; their suffering brought him pleasure. Right now, he had an erection. He had even asked if he might throw a stone. Bandari, who detested him, almost said yes because he knew that the sheik would have ordered his throat cut before the stone that he threw had stopped rolling.

Tarrant, however, showed no emotion at all. Like all Americans he loved only money. To him this woman might as well have been a bug. But Mahfouz shared his view that they had better proceed before the sheik noticed that Tarrant had disobeyed him. He walked to the sheik and knelt by his ear. It was time, he suggested, for Bandari to come forward and give this woman her chance to repent. The old sheik only shrugged and fell silent. Mahfouz stood up. He waved Bandari forward.

Behind the bright lights that stood on a tripod, Gamal Bandari balled his hands into fists so that no one could see that they were shaking. He was a man nearing fifty with thinning black hair and a body, always stocky, that lately had gone to fat. His dark suit from Italy no longer fit him. His jowls spilled over the collar of his shirt.

Bandari told the Englishman to shut off the camera. This part was not to be recorded. The Englishman, named Pratt, was about Bandari's age and he had a pot belly but from drinking, not eating. Cyril Pratt turned the camera so Bandari could see that the little red light had gone out. That done, Bandari took a final breath and stepped beyond the tripod mount of the lights. He walked slowly to the edge of the pit. He seemed not yet able to look into the eyes of the woman who had been his brother's wife. He looked instead at the single jagged stone that had been left for him, her accuser, to throw. On an impulse, he bent to pick it up. Perhaps showing this stone to Leyna, he thought, would help persuade her to do as he would ask.

She raised her chin slowly as she saw him approach. Such wonderful eyes, thought Bandari, even now. Big like a deer, just as soulful and dark. But now they were glazed. All he saw in them was fear. Bandari had to steel himself to keep his heart from melting. He lowered himself to one knee.

"Leyna." He showed her the stone in his hand. "Even now it is not too late. You do not have to die in this terrible way."

Her lips moved slightly but no sound came from them.

He lowered his voice so that no one else could hear him. "You must sign the papers that I have brought with me. I ask only for what is mine by right."

Still no answer.

"You must also give up your daughter, my niece. Or else tell me where Aisha is hidden."

Tears welled in Leyna's eyes. She took a breath and let it out. A moment passed before she could speak. "If I tell you, what will you do with her?" she asked.

Bandari answered as if he had taken offense. "You think I would harm her? She is my blood. How could I harm my own blood?"

It was the wrong thing to say, and her eyes flashed contempt. He knew that she was thinking of her dead husband, Avram. "Gamal," she repeated, her voice gaining strength, "I asked what will you do with my daughter."

"I will bring her home where she belongs." He now raised his own voice so that the villagers could hear. "Next year, God willing, if she's kept herself pure, I'll arrange a good marriage for her. I will see that she's prepared to make a good Muslim wife."

"Prepared?" Leyna blanched. "Does that mean she'll be sewn? I will never give you Aisha if you'll have her cut and sewn."

Bandari realized that he'd made still another mistake

but he could not retreat with the whole village watching. "You should have done it yourself before you sent her away. What man will have her if he cannot be sure that she's saved herself only for him?"

Now Leyna's tears spilled freely, wetting her cheeks. She lowered her head in an effort to hide them.

"And me?" she asked weakly. "Am I still to be stoned?"

"The sheik . . . is prepared to show mercy."

She dropped her eyes and went limp with relief until she realized that these last words were spoken in English. She took a few seconds to gather herself. "You're lying, Gamal. He can't and you know it."

"He can and he will," Bandari insisted. "Confess and repent and sign the damned papers. Do that and a lashing is the worst you will get. You'll survive it," he assured her, "with just a few stripes. These will be all on your back, none in front, that I promise. After that I will take you into my house. You will have every comfort, you'll have Aisha with you, but your days of running around loose will be over. That's unless . . . I mean . . . if your attitude improves. . . ."

Her eyes locked on his. She said, "Say it, Gamal. What else will you want of me if I agree?"

"I will . . . treat you as generously as you treat me." He said this in English as well.

She began to weep. Bandari's hopes rose.

"Is . . . that the real reason why you had Avram killed?" she asked this as if her heart had been broken. He realized too late that she had switched back to Arabic. "You murdered your brother because you wanted me?"

Bandari sucked in a breath. He glanced toward Mahfouz and a man called Faisal, another who had come to bear witness against her, but neither man seemed to have heard. Leyna, however, had followed his eyes. It struck her, although wrongly, that these men had done more than swear falsely. She thought these were the men who, three weeks before, had cut down her husband as he walked from his car to his office in Suez. But they were not. The two who shot Avram had been hired by Tarrant. They were thugs from West Cairo who themselves were in hell by the time the sun set that day.

"Murderers," she shouted at Mahfouz and Faisal. "What did he pay you to murder my husband? What lies did he tell? Don't you know he'll betray you as he betrayed his own broth—"

A chopping blow cut off her words and whipped her head to one side. Gamal gasped as he realized that he had struck her with the rock. It tore the flesh of her lovely face from the side of one eye to her chin. When he saw what he'd done, a wail of remorse rose up in Gamal's chest and the bloody stone fell from his fingers. At that moment he wanted to pull her from the pit and speed her to a clinic two villages away. But she wouldn't shut up. Once more her tongue lashed at him.

"This man spits on your prophet," she cried out to the villagers. "He mocks your faith, he buys you with money he gets from the Jews." The words came slurred from a mouth filled with blood; broken bones in her jaw ground together. "This pig sleeps with boys," was the next lie she shouted. "Have you not wondered why he has no wife? It's Gamal who plays the wife when he sleeps with young boys and for that God has said he must die."

Bandari felt his face growing hot. He could hear rising murmurs from the circle of men. They seemed so loud that they almost drowned out Leyna's vengeful and desperate lies. With a shout of "Whore!" he snatched up the stone again and brought it down hard against the top of her skull.

"Liar! Devil!" He struck her once more.

"Whore!" He hit her again and again. He thought he must have gone faint because the next thing he knew, Mahfouz was prying the rock from his hand and Faisal was pulling him out of the pit.

Mahfouz led him away from the others of the village. He guided him back toward the Englishman. Bandari, whose eyes were dull and unfocused, did not notice that the Englishman moved to block the machine lest he see that the red light was glowing again. Mahfouz said he must stay there, he must say nothing more, then Mahfouz returned to the pit.

He squatted before the form that had once been Leyna Bandari. He tilted her head back and felt for a pulse with his fingers. He looked up at the sheik and shrugged sadly.

The sheik threw up his hands in a gesture of disgust. He lifted his eyes toward the stars for several moments, then nodded as if to acknowledge instructions.

The stoning, he said, would proceed all the same.

Two

The men of the village had no heart for it now.

Some had worked themselves into an enabling rage, but only a sickened confusion was left. They cast their stones at the body, all one hundred that remained, but most were thrown indifferently and missed. Some were merely bounced in her approximate direction. As each pile was depleted they split off in small groups and faded away toward the lights of their houses. At last the sheik himself was helped up. He, too, walked away, with the help of two men. Only Mahfouz and Faisal had stayed behind. Faisal remained because he was not of this village. He worked for Pratt, the English bounty hunter. Mahfouz remained to try to comfort Bandari and to salvage from this what he could.

Mahfouz had not seen the things that he'd sworn to. He had never been inside that hotel in Alexandria where the other three, Bandari, Pratt and Faisal, had said they'd caught the woman giving sex to a man in return for false papers that would get her out of Egypt. She had schemed, they said, to run off to America where family means nothing and all virtue is lost. This they said was her crime of adultery—her husband only three weeks in his grave.

"But how is this adultery if she is a widow?" he had asked.

"She was and remains my brother's wife. The condition of my brother is irrelevant."

"But you said that she murdered him. Why not charge her with murder?"

"The law is . . . more difficult for murder."

Mahfouz understood. To charge this woman with the murder of his brother, Gamal would have to name the killers she was said to have hired. But even that was not really the problem. The sentence of death was not mandatory for murder, but it was mandatory for adultery.

But to charge her with adultery was also not so easy. To convict for adultery, four men had to give testimony that they had witnessed the act of penetration. Even a simple farmer like Mahfouz had to ask how this could ever happen. Could four men be hiding under the bed on the chance that a wife was unfaithful? Did four men find a way to sneak into her closet and leap out when the bed springs started to squeak? Yet he and Faisal had sworn that they, with Bandari and the Englishman, had burst into that hotel room at just the right moment to witness her sin.

Mahfouz did not feel right about this, but Bandari had been a good friend to this village.

One year ago he gave this village a mosque. It was only of cinder blocks and the carpets were not new but the sheik now had his own mosque nonetheless. This year Bandari gave the village electricity. The cables had not yet reached Abu Shatt but Bandari had promised that they'd be coming very soon. Waiting, meantime, was a large new refrigerator and also a TV and videocassette player. The old sheik had asked for the videocassette player so the men could watch sermons from all over the world. The men smiled at this because some knew how to get tapes that were not so religious. They could watch them after the sheik fell asleep.

"I will not try to fool you in asking this favor," said Bandari, who had looked Mahfouz straight in the eye. "Yes, it is usually a sin to swear falsely but it won't be a sin in this case. Yes, it's true that swearing falsely can get you eighty lashes, but no one's going to call you a liar. You'll be swearing only to what my eyes have seen unless you think it's me who is the liar."

"I believe you," Mahfouz had answered, although he had misgivings. "But it's not the same as knowing."

"Mahfouz . . . my friend, who knows better, you or me? More than that, who knows better, you or God?"

Mahfouz had to agree with this last, of course. And as for the first, he would take Bandari's word. If swearing falsely is a sin, the sin would be Bandari's. As for God, if Bandari had lied about her sin, surely God would not allow her to be stoned.

To help the old sheik in making up his mind, Bandari had added a long list of crimes. This Lebanese whore had seduced his brother. Like all lying whores she tricked him into marriage and then, helped by lawyers who he knew to be Jews, spent the next fifteen years robbing him of all that he valued. But Gamal was never blinded by the wiles of this whore. He went to Avram, his brother, with proof of her crimes and Avram had been about to divorce her. But the whore found out and before he could act, she quickly plotted his murder. "As terrible as this is," Bandari told the old sheik, "who among us should have been surprised that it happened? Poor Avram Bandari, good man that he was, was ten times a fool to have married a Christian, even if she swore to convert." A chorus of agreement rose up from the men.

Now Bandari added the charge of apostasy. This woman had, he swore, converted to Islam as a condition of marrying his brother. But then she reverted once he was in her grasp and this also was a sin worse than murder. This in itself was enough to condemn her. The woman, however, had loudly denied it. Her husband, she said, could have asked her to convert but he loved her and took her as she was. She was, and remained, a Maronite Christian and therefore this sheik had no right to judge her. All that got her was a gag stuffed into her mouth.

Maybe she was still a Maronite Christian but here in this village that was hardly a defense. To the sheik, if you marry a Muslim, you're a Muslim. Her apostasy was plain for him to see. Leyna, to begin with, had been educated in the West. There, already, was the sin of pollution. She had sent her daughter abroad as well, from the time she was eight years old. Now there were two generations of sinful pollution.

Most damning of all was Leyna's suitcase that they had brought from Alexandria to show him. In it was nothing but Western clothing. Not a single abaya, not even a head scarf. Instead there were dresses that showed bare arms and legs and one that revealed the top half of her breasts. The sheik beat it with his cane when they showed it to him.

Also in the suitcase were birth control pills, although these, Mahfouz suspected, had been put there by Pratt. The pills, by themselves, told the sheik all he needed to know. They showed him all her jewelry and her money in dollars as proof of the way she robbed Avram. They showed him her new tennis racquet from Prince, as proof that all she cared about was games played half naked, but the sheik didn't know what tennis was. They showed him the counterfeit Italian passport and a visa for a visit to America. These two documents revealed the new name she had taken.

''Monica Blye?'' The old sheik read it, squinting. ''What kind of name is Monica Blye?''

''A name that's not Muslim. A name as false as this woman.''

What annoyed the old sheik even more than the alias was that a woman was allowed her own passport. An Egyptian passport was not issued that way. It does not show the name of the woman. An Egyptian passport would have simply identified her as the wife of Avram Bandari. An unmarried woman was shown on a passport as the daughter of so-and-so, sometimes even as the sister of so-and-so. That was the right way to do it, thought the sheik. A passport should show her place in the family. To show her own name was immodest.

This, too, would have been enough to convict her, especially before the sheik of Abu Shatt. This sheik had once banned sunglasses on the grounds that God meant the sun to be bright. This sheik had ordered that the vaginas of all girls be sewn shut lest they tempt some man into sin. For that reason, Mahfouz had been pleasantly surprised when the sheik had agreed to accept a refrigerator. He had expected him to say that God meant food to rot.

Mahfouz approached Bandari, who was shaken and pale. He was wetting a handkerchief with Evian water and washing the splatters of blood from his face. The blood also stained his fine Italian shirt. The Englishman, Pratt, was taking down his tripod. The American was pacing, still shaking his head in the manner of a man who was thoroughly disgusted. Mahfouz took Bandari to one side.

It is true, Mahfouz told him, that this was not done well. But he would talk to the sheik and the men of the village. He would urge them to speak of it better than it was. Nor should he be troubled by those bad things she said. No one would believe such poisonous lies from a woman whose soul has been lost. No one would believe that Bandari sleeps with men or that he had insulted the Prophet. All the same, Mahfouz told him, the tape of this stoning would now be of no use. A few extra gifts for the people of this village would help them forget what they had seen. He then asked Bandari, "What time is it now according to the beautiful gold watch that you wear?"

Bandari, glumly, took the Rolex from his wrist and offered it to Mahfouz. Mahfouz made a show of speechless surprise as he clutched the watch to his heart.

But Bandari, by now, cared nothing for the watch. Drained, feeling sickened, he stared back at the pit. With the lights turned off it was hard to tell his brother's wife's head from the stones. It had also been covered with a piece of old burlap. Later, when it was light, Mahfouz would dig her back out. They would take her to the clinic two villages over. There, he'd get a paper that was proof of her death. Mahfouz was right, this had been done very badly. But at least the main impediment was out of the way. He was one big step closer to getting control of all that his brother had owned. Now there was only the girl.

Damn his brother, thought Bandari. Damn his soul to

Satan's fire for driving him to this. Avram had left all he owned to his wife and daughter. That in itself was a crime against Islam—the largest share should have gone to a brother. He didn't need Avram's money—to hell with the money—what he needed were two things, control and respect, not to mention the keys to a certain warehouse that Avram owned in Suez.

Avram knew this full well. It was why he wrote a will that would thwart him, shame him. Men would ask, "How can Gamal be the head of the family if his own younger brother did not think him worthy?" Bandari's hope had been that none would ever know this. His hope was that Leyna would sign it all over if she wished to see one more sunrise. And she would tell him where she had hidden her daughter, so the daughter could never make a claim on that inheritance. After that he would be able to get into that warehouse and dig out what was under those bags of cement. The watch and the few other gifts to this village would be a small price to pay.

Tarrant had asked him, "Where did you find these people?" His answer should have been that it wasn't so hard although it was true that most sheiks couldn't be bought. Most were wise and compassionate. But there were always those few who had the heart of a cockroach. That this one was sick and confused was even better. All that mattered was that this one was the law in Abu Shatt. And God's law was whatever he said it was.

Like it or not, such men and such sheiks ran more of the country than did Cairo. The whole south of Egypt was already in their hands and Cairo was content to let them have it. It would not be long, he was more and more sure, before the rest of Egypt went the way of Iran, or Algeria. But the real war would come when they rose against the Saudis, the Saudis who had so much from their oil but wouldn't share. When they won, the West would come hat in hand although first they'd try to come with their tanks.

Mahfouz, like Bandari, was ready to teach the West a lesson. Soon the Egyptians would rise against the Saudis and this time it wouldn't be like Iraq. This time the war would come home to their cities. New York and Washington would become graveyards. Deserts where not even a scorpion could live for the next two or three thousand years. And the Americans would have Lawrence Tarrant to thank, because of what was buried in that warehouse. Lawrence Tarrant and his secret partners, all thieves, who would like all the oil for themselves.

First things first, however. First there was Aisha.

He suspected that Pratt already knew where she was. They'd sorted through Leyna's belongings in the hotel room, with Leyna lying on the floor bound and gagged with silver tape, unconscious from the drug Pratt had injected in her neck. It was then that Pratt had found the false passport and visa. Bandari was more surprised than offended that she had taken a Western name.

"Monica Blye?" he asked. "An Arab woman named Monica Blye?"

Pratt mocked his surprise. "Take your eyes off her tits and look at that face. She could pass for Italian or French with no problem."

"Save your filthy talk for your pubs," Bandari told him.

Then Pratt exclaimed, "Aha! Airline tickets!" He tore the folder from the lining of a tote bag. "No, just one set." He scowled, disappointed. "There's no ticket here for the daughter."

He read aloud what was written on the one. "*Ms.* Monica Blye . . . first class," he said. "Cairo to London and on to Miami . . . with a connection from Miami to Savannah."

The Savannah destination caused the Englishman to blink. He mouthed the name of that city. "No ticket for the daughter means she's meeting her in London? Or does it mean she's already in Savannah?" He was asking these questions of himself.

"This place, Savannah. It's in Florida as well?"

"In Georgia," Pratt answered. "In fact it's almost not in Georgia. It's almost in South Carolina."

At this Pratt's eyes narrowed. For several long seconds he stared at the ticket and he stared at the new tennis racquet from Prince. Tennis . . . Savannah. Together they seemed to have meaning. At last Pratt struck his forehead with the heel of his hand.

"Well?" asked Bandari. "What has it told you?"

"This new name, Blye." Pratt was thinking aloud. "The daughter, of course, would use it as well . . . is probably using it already."

"Do you know where she is?" Bandari felt his pulse racing.

"I might," Pratt answered. "Yes, indeed, I just might."

Mahfouz nudged Bandari's arm, interrupting his thoughts.

"Will the Englishman now go to this Savannah in America?"

"I suppose. If that's where the girl is."

"The sheik will speak well of you. This I *think* I can promise."

"Think? What is 'think'? You did promise."

"I will try. It will be said in every mosque within many days' travel that Gamal Bandari is a man to be honored. At least it's my hope that it will."

"Mahfouz . . . no more bargaining. I gave you my watch."

"It is a wonderful watch, but what would please me even more—"

"The watch and also the money in your pocket."

"For these I am grateful. I should ask nothing more. But there's a thing I have dreamed of since I was a boy. I would like very much to ride on an airplane."

"Mahfouz . . ."

"If the Englishman is going to this place called Savannah, I would like to go with him at least part of the way. I would like to ride an airplane to Miami."

"Miami is Jews. You won't like Miami. Besides, you don't have the papers."

"A deputy minister can't get me the papers? How can I convince them of your value as a friend if you can't even get me some papers?"

"I will think about this. Now shut up."

*   *   *

The first wink of sun had broken the horizon. The three men had gathered at the trunk of the Mercedes where Pratt was stowing his camcorder and lights. Pratt reached into the tote bag he always had with him and withdrew a small bottle of Gleneagles scotch whisky.

"You brought alcohol here? Are you crazy?" hissed Bandari. He looked to see if any from the village had seen. Pratt answered by offering Bandari a swallow, hardly a generous gesture. Bandari, whose personal preference was rum, was being mocked for a hypocrite and he knew it.

"Put it away." Tarrant added his voice. "Let's not get our throats cut before breakfast." This reminded Pratt that he'd had nothing to eat. He reached into his bag for a package of crisps that Bandari, to his horror, saw were pork rinds. Tarrant told Pratt to put those away as well.

Lawrence Tarrant, having witnessed his first so-called stoning, was annoyed that he'd wasted his time. If a head cracked open was all he had wanted to see, it was done in West Cairo every night of the week with considerably greater efficiency. Now the woman was dead, they had nothing to show for it and time was working against them. All he had gained was a heightened resolve to be rid of Bandari as quickly as possible. And especially that foul little Englishman, Pratt. He resolved that when this transaction was completed he would make certain that neither would embarrass him further.

"She did lie, you know," Bandari muttered to Tarrant. "I do not sleep with boys or young men."

"As you wish." Tarrant shrugged. "Except what was that she said about you playing the wife? That did seem to get their attention."

Pratt, who had sneaked a large swallow of Gleneagles, answered for him after wiping his mouth. "That woman, give her credit, knew what buttons to push. Say the Muslims catch two fairies going at it. The one pitching gets off with a hundred lashes but the one being butt-fucked gets burned alive. Nothing makes these people squirm like the thought of a man who will take a big dick up his ass."

Bandari would have slapped Pratt had not Tarrant stepped between them. He said, "Enough . . . Mr. Pratt, that will do. Bandari, what happens now?"

The Egyptian took a breath and then another to calm himself. "This . . . one must go find my niece. Aisha is now the sole heir."

"Bandari . . ." The American rubbed his eyes wearily. "Help me to understand why we're wasting our time with this. All we need do is break into one warehouse and deliver the goods that we've promised your friends. Why must that warehouse be legally yours?"

"I have already told you. It's a question of honor."

Tarrant grunted. "Ah, yes. You did say that."

"Yes, honor!" spat Bandari, who heard a snigger from Pratt. "It is honor and it is respect." But the Egyptian knew that he had wasted those words. You can't explain honor to a man such as Tarrant or to any American for that matter. You can't make him grasp that a man in our culture is disgraced if he cannot control his family.

The Libyans are Arabs, they know about honor, they know that Avram had cut him out of his will and they saw Leyna slap him at the funeral. He had seen in their eyes what they expected him to do to her. The Libyans, however, expect their shipment as well. They will wait but not very long.

Bandari turned to the Englishman. "When will you bring me the girl?"

"Soon, I think," Pratt replied but he was looking at Tarrant. "How grateful would you be if I had her in a week?"

"He's paying you what, fifty thousand?"

Pratt nodded.

"He'll double it," said Tarrant. He raised a hand to keep Bandari from speaking. "But he'll halve it if it's longer than that."

"Done," Pratt said eagerly. He offered his hand. Tarrant ignored it. He looked at his watch.

"Today is Monday, March 12th," Tarrant told him. "Your deadline for the bonus will be this coming Sunday."

Pratt nodded and smiled. He sipped from his bottle.

"Savannah," said Tarrant, "is not Alexandria. How will you find her so quickly?"

"She's not in Savannah," Pratt answered, "but near it. I'm pretty sure that I know who's been hiding her. It's all I'm going to say for the moment."

Tarrant was frowning. "You're being coy. Why?"

The Englishman cocked his head toward Bandari. "One hundred thousand is fair for his daughter and you'll have her by then if I'm right. But there's another woman. She'd be at this same place. That woman is worth a cool million dead to a client of mine in this region."

"Forget it," Tarrant told him. "One job at a time."

"Oh, I'll take the niece first. You can count on that much. But this woman is my chance for the payday of a lifetime."

Tarrant's frown remained. He didn't like this at all. More than ever, he wanted it over.

"What help will you need?" he asked Pratt.

"I need only Faisal. He has lived in the States. I'm damned, by the way, if I'll be stuck with Mahfouz."

The Egyptian was not comfortable with sending Mahfouz either but he needed Mahfouz to speak well of him. "All he wants," Bandari told him, "is to ride in a plane. You can leave him in Miami until you're finished."

"Whatever," said Tarrant. "But you'll use my men, too. I'll be flying to Washington by week's end myself for a meeting I had hoped to avoid. In the meantime I will leave you some numbers. You will call a Mr. Loomis when you've located the girl but make no other move until he says so. Mr. Loomis will arrange to have a plane waiting. You can have her back in Cairo that same day."

"This Loomis is a pilot?"

"Mr. Loomis is a fixer. What we have here is a problem that needs to be fixed."

A scowl from Pratt. "He won't give me an argument when I show up with this woman? I will have the girl but I do want this woman."

"Just remember your priorities, Mr. Pratt."

*   *   *

Bandari, disgusted, and now shut out by Tarrant, had wandered away from the car.

Part of him felt greatly relieved that this business might soon be concluded. He was relieved, not least, because Tarrant would be patient. He would not hire thugs to break into the warehouse and kill the four guards who were still standing watch. He would not see what Avram had done with their shipment. Avram had fixed it so that no one could move it. They would need a jackhammer to even get at it and if someone got careless there would be no more warehouse. More than that, thought Bandari, there would be no Suez.

He was concerned that when they jackhammered through the cement in the warehouse, Tarrant might see that two containers were missing. The deal was for six but instead the shipment had included eight, because that's how these weapons were packed. Bandari had taken the two extra containers on the day Avram found them. He took them before Avram could post those armed guards and before he could cover them with tons of cement. Those two were now hidden aboard the *Alhambra*, the yacht that he kept on the south coast of Spain. It was crewed by men who were fugitives themselves, but these men didn't know what was under their feet.

It was good that they didn't. If they did there would soon be no Tel Aviv either.

Three

A few miles north of Savannah's airport lies the South Carolina state line. Turn east toward the ocean for another thirty minutes and one approaches a group of barrier islands, the largest of which is called Hilton Head. That island is a barrier in more ways than one.

Long inhabited largely by slaves and their descendants, flattened by hurricanes every century or so, the island eventually caught the eye of developers. It had splendid beaches and a tropical climate that was cooled by a steady soft breeze from the sea. In the clamdiggers' shacks that lined those beaches the developers saw opulent oceanfront homes. In fields that once produced the world's finest cotton they saw golf courses waiting to be sculpted. Lining these, tee to green, they saw tree-shaded lots waiting to be snatched up by northerners with money who would see the island as a gentle escape from all that was harsh about their cities. In its hurricane season they saw an incentive to build and sell houses as quickly as possible before the inevitable happened.

But the island's luck held. The odd hurricane threatened but it always veered north, and a stream of white Anglo-Saxons moved South. As the value of real estate rose, the black population sold out and moved elsewhere, except those who stayed to work as builders and landscapers or to staff the several resort hotels. True southern accents were infrequently heard, replaced by the almost indistinguishable accents of the upper Midwest and, increasingly, those of Europe as well.

Those who moved to the island came for many different reasons. Some came to retire, often quite young, and enjoy the fruits of their industry or luck or divorce settlements. Some came to find work in the shops and restaurants and the many other businesses needed to serve the residents and restaurants that opened to accommodate the tourists. Some came to feel safe for the first time in years. And some came to escape their pasts.

For those seeking safety, the island of Hilton Head seemed nearly ideal. All but its more modest homes and villas were located within gated communities called Plantations. There were nine such plantations to choose from. In the wealthiest of them all visitors were screened. Others were considerably more hospitable to tourists but all were patrolled by private security forces. State and county police watched the rest of the island. The many fine homes, often unoccupied for months at a time, would seem tempting targets for any burglar who gains access pretending to be a tourist. Crimes against property were nonetheless rare and crimes involving violence were virtually unknown. More so even than the police, the primary disincentive to criminal activity was the single bridge that connected the island to the mainland. That bridge could be blocked and the island sealed off within minutes of an alarm being given.

For those who came seeking to escape their pasts, whether criminal or merely unhappy, Hilton Head Island was equally ideal. New arrivals often speak of feeling reborn, a sensation due only in part to the Edenesque nature of the lush, subtropical setting. The larger part is something else. An ethos characteristic of most such communities is that residents don't much care how a newcomer earned his or her living before crossing that bridge. The question "What do you do?" is no longer relevant because it no longer serves to define. The answer to "What *did* you do?" asked idly if at all, is almost never questioned.

To Elizabeth Stride, this factor played no minor role in

her decision to return to this island. After this, she was determined, there would be no more running. This was the place where Elizabeth would settle and begin to rebuild her life.

A full year had passed since she came here to stay. More than reborn, she had begun to feel cleansed. She had kept her real name, which might have been foolish, but she changed almost everything else. Before crossing the bridge she had stayed a few days in nearby Savannah where she took a scissors to her long straight hair and bleached out the dark brown with which it had been dyed. She colored it again with a Clairol shade that seemed close to her natural auburn. She took out for the last time, but did not throw away, the tinted contact lenses that had darkened her eyes and had allowed her to pass as an Arab.

When her natural hair did eventually fill out she was pleased that she found no gray. Although still a young woman, not quite thirty-six, she had somehow expected that all she'd been through would have left her hair gray if not white. As it grew, she tried it in several new ways, finally settling on a short, flattering cut that her hairdresser called a *stack*. The look, said the hairdresser, was soft and feminine. It framed her face nicely and it brought out her wonderful eyes. Elizabeth's only misgiving was that the cut reduced her peripheral vision somewhat. She would never have worn it so before. But "soft" and "feminine" were the words that convinced her.

Those "wonderful eyes" took a bit of getting used to. Even as a young girl she had thought they looked odd. Their color was closer to amber than brown. A boy back in Texas whom she'd dated in college had likened her eyes to limpid puddles of beer. Normally, he'd said, they were exactly like Coors, but they became more like Heineken at night and like Guinness whenever she was angry. Years later, although she should have known better, she told Martin Kessler what the young man had said. It was when she was still convalescing and he saw their natural color for the first time.

Martin disagreed; he said the boy was no poet. The boy

could at least have said pools, not puddles. Martin said
her eyes were more like a cat's. A graceful and beautiful
cheetah, perhaps. That imagery, she thought, was a considerable improvement and it would have been fine if he'd
left it at that. But the first thing anyone had to learn about
Martin was that he never knew when to leave well enough
alone.

"Not so much a cheetah at rest. A cheetah who has
spotted an unwary gazelle."

"Um . . . I think I like limpid pools better. Even puddles."

"But it's true. You have the eyes of a stalker, Elizabeth. All that's missing is drool on your chin."

"You do have a gift for saying just the right thing."

"They are exactly the right eyes for Elizabeth Stride.
With you, 'eyes to die for' is not a cliché."

Martin was the first thing she changed before coming
here.

After her hair came her clothing. She had taken almost
nothing when she left him. Only half of the diamonds,
enough to last a few years, and the contents of a small
blue duffel. She spent her first day on the island just looking, noting what the full-time residents wore. She eventually asked a few where they shopped. She spent the next
day in those stores. She chose whites and bright colors,
pastels and pinks. She bought a few complete outfits right
off the store mannequins that matched her perfect size 8.
She bought nothing black—she'd had enough black—not
so much as a sheath for the evening. The only black things
she still owned these days stayed packed in that duffel, a
bag she hoped never to open again. She purchased three
pairs of designer sunglasses, in part to cover those damned
cheetah eyes. And she bought jewelry, most of it fake—
bought it with glee by the bagful. She bought jewelry that
dangled and jangled and glittered day or night. She would
not have done this before either.

Within a week of her arrival, having spent just two days
with a capable broker, Elizabeth selected a house. She
offered the seller full asking price if the seller would va-

cate within two weeks' time. The house was exactly what she'd hoped to find. It was a small U-shaped ranch on a private road well away from the streets that were traveled by tourists. The house was located in Sea Pines Plantation and set on a quiet lagoon.

She shared the lagoon with a young six-foot alligator that occasionally sunned in her yard. Two graceful egrets and a single blue heron had a prior claim on her property as well. They would sit for hours at water's edge, motionless, watching for a careless fish to swim by but always keeping one eye on the alligator.

The grounds were parklike, beautifully landscaped, with mature plantings of azaleas and camellias, and dotted with graceful palmettos. The house was shaded by massive live oaks. Their limbs were draped with strands of Spanish moss. A family of whitetail deer lived nearby. They came through Elizabeth's yard at dawn every day, pausing to nibble before moving on. Her property was just off the Harbour Town Golf Course and within a short walk of Harbour Town itself. The beaches were a five-minute bike ride away. She felt sure that she could be happy here. It was all so wonderfully green and blue and the nights were cool and nearly silent. So unlike the Mideast. So unlike any place she had known.

Even while painting and papering her house, Elizabeth set out to make friends. It was not easy for her to let down her guard but she had no intention of becoming a recluse. The Welcome Wagon pointed the way. It provided details on dozens of activities through which one could meet people with similar interests. There were Women's Club luncheons with tables for ten. This meant that within the space of two hours nine new acquaintances could be made. The community theater needed help building sets. Theater people, according to the Welcome Wagon lady, tended to be interesting and pleasantly eccentric. She also joined an aerobics group and signed up for an oil painting class that met weekly. She bought a bike, wide tires, no gears. There was no need for gears on this island. She signed up for lessons in tennis and golf after not playing either for almost fifteen years. But they came back quickly, especially tennis, which had been her best sport in college.

She told those who asked that she was a widow, her husband having died in a rock-climbing accident out West. This was less to elicit sympathy than to discourage speculation and to help other women be more comfortable with her. Americans, she noted, still seemed more at ease with widows than with women who had never been married.

Elizabeth was by no means disinterested in men. A hunger, in fact, had been growing for months now. She had not had sex in nearly a year, not since her last night with Martin. More than once she had considered driving to Atlanta, checking into one of its better hotels. There she could pick out a partner for the weekend, some traveling executive whom she'd never see again. But she'd never done anything like that before and feared that she might do it badly. Or that the man might get . . . she didn't know . . . too forceful. The calming effect of this year notwithstanding, she still could not be sure what she might do to him. Better, she decided, to stick to the island. Better to be patient. With luck she might meet a good and gentle man who enjoyed quiet dinners and long walks on the beach.

Two months shy of her first anniversary on the island her patience was finally rewarded. She had arrived at the lesson tee of the Harbour Town Golf Course just as another man's lesson was ending. Her pro introduced her to Jonathan Leidner. She guessed him to be in his late thirties. He'd been hitting very nicely before she approached but his swing fell completely apart after meeting her. He picked up his clubs and went off toward his car where, he later admitted, he spent twenty minutes trying to get up the nerve to come back. He watched her hit and then after her lesson asked her and the pro if they would join him for lunch. His eyes begged the pro to say yes.

He was shy, unlike Martin, and rather nice looking in a quiet sort of way. Martin was anything but quiet. Jonathan's face was the sort people trust at first meeting. She learned over lunch that he was new to the island, that he lived in the nearby Shipyard Plantation where he shared a rented house with one other man and that he had never been married.

"But I'm not . . . I mean . . . the guy I share the house with is just . . . I mean there's no special reason why I've never been . . ."

"He wants you to know he's not gay," said the pro.

He called her that evening. He said every man should be entitled to make an ass of himself once upon meeting a beautiful woman. He asked her if she'd care to see a movie with him. They did and the day after that they played golf. Within a week they were, as it happened, taking long moonlit walks on the beach. After a level of comfort was reached, he turned out to be a man she liked talking to. He had not traveled much but he was quite well read and could discuss a wide range of subjects. These included a few that she knew all too well but about which she thought it best to feign ignorance.

Jonathan was also the much better cook. His specialty was Northern Italian—he made the best Osso Bucco she'd ever had in her life—and he further surprised her by beating her at tennis. He had all the essentials as far as she was concerned. Where Martin could be kind when he rose to the occasion, Jonathan was kind all the time. Where Martin's general conduct bordered on the deranged, Jonathan was the soul of stability. Besides, he thought her eyes looked like jewels.

"Elizabeth . . . this man is dull," Martin would have said.

"You'd say that about a serial killer."

"Speaking of killing, could this man protect you? How would he behave if there was trouble?"

"Not that I'll tell you where I'm living now, Martin, but the biggest trouble here is a sand trap."

In truth, Jonathan *was* a little bit dull . . . but she now aspired to dullness. She also, however, aspired to a sex life and that was her one and only problem with him. The flesh on both sides was willing enough but Jonathan Leidner was a doctor, not only a doctor, but a surgeon. He would know bullet wounds if he saw them.

He had already felt one through her blouse while they were dancing. She told him she'd been stabbed there by a ski pole. She said that it happened years ago when she collided with another skier at Vail. That explanation seemed to satisfy Jonathan; he reacted with a sympathetic wince. But she didn't know how she would explain the others unless she claimed that all four ski poles had managed to skewer her. There was one scar directly beneath her right breast, a second where a bullet had bounced off her rib cage and a third to the left of her navel. That one was now just a lumpy little slit but the bullet had exited near her spine, where it had left an ugly indentation. That was the one he had felt. It was also the one that tore up her insides. It would keep her from ever bearing children.

The wounds were also an issue, she supposed, because she was privately vain about her body. She had always worked hard to keep it in shape, and her skin was otherwise virtually flawless. She had a few light freckles on her nose and hands and one other thin scar on her forehead. But that one hardly showed at all with the hairstyle she'd chosen. In years long past, she'd enjoyed turning heads. Turning heads, these days, was the last thing she wanted.

No . . . no. That wasn't quite true. The absolute last thing she wanted these days was to see Martin Kessler show up on this island. And now he had. He had found her after more than a year.

She would have to make him understand that it was permanently, irrevocably over between them. She had women friends now who asked her to lunch. They laughed and joked with her. They asked her to ride bikes with them, to go to the beach with them. There was no one who hated her, no one who feared her. She had changed her life entirely and she would not let Martin Kessler change it back to what it was.

"*But what if I've changed?*" he would ask.

"*You can't. It isn't in you.*"

"*Let me stay for a few days. I might surprise you, my darling.*"

"*Out of the question. No.*"

"You're more beautiful than ever, you know. I love what you've done with your hair and your wardrobe."

"Martin . . ."

"But so much junk jewelry? You might as well wear a cat collar with bells."

"I should have blown that bridge the day I crossed it."

"What difference can a few days make, Elizabeth? At least I'll know you're all right."

What difference, indeed. An invasion couldn't do to this island what Martin Kessler could do in two days. And Martin would never, ever change. Before long, ten years will have passed since the German Democratic Republic ceased to exist—and the Stasi along with it—and he still thinks he's Reineke the Fox.

That was what they called him then. His East German bosses had actually published a comic book about him. It was an idea they'd borrowed from the KGB, which had been doing comic book propaganda for twenty years, showing how their agents had routinely outwitted the agents of the decadent West. The name Reineke came from Reineke Fuchs—Fuchs meaning Fox—a wily character in a medieval German fable.

Martin always claimed to have detested the idea. "What use," he asked, "is an agent who becomes a celebrity? Does he say, 'Yes I'm spying on you but you should be honored? I'll give you my autograph and we'll call it even?' "

Elizabeth felt that he protested too much. The Stasi, she'd heard, had to give him two secretaries just to handle his fan mail. East German women named their children after him. He probably sired a few of them himself. And Martin even looked the part of a comic book hero. He was not movie-star handsome exactly. His features were rugged rather than classic. He had thick curly hair and a let's-make-trouble grin and a V-shaped scar at the corner of his right eye. The scar, for some reason, drove certain women wild. And a serious agent would have had it removed.

On the whole, however, she was forced to agree. The comic book's value as a propaganda tool did not, in her

mind, compensate for making him a target for retribution
by the West or the object of petty jealousy by certain of
his superiors in the East. That jealousy—and the suspicion
that he might have been playing both sides—might well
have played a role in getting her shot. Still, he had saved
her life. And he had avenged her.

It might have ended there but it didn't. Martin, not content with revenge, also took the time to loot them. Looting
their loot would be more precise. In consequence, the two
of them were hunted in return. For seven more years,
throughout Europe, this was their life together. Martin
would say, ''They have found us, Elizabeth. We need to
move on.'' A time finally came when enough was enough.
For her, it was time to come home. She would try, she
thought, to rediscover the person she had been before hatred turned her soul to ice.

Martin came with her. They went to New York first,
where he sold a few diamonds and they bought an RV.
He said that for a while it was best to keep moving and,
besides, he had always wanted to see more of this country.
Somewhere in it they would find their place.

They headed south. They bypassed Washington because Martin knew that city well. He had spent two years
there with the GDR embassy and was reluctant to take a
chance on being spotted. They explored the entire south-
eastern coast from Virginia all the way to New Orleans.
One of many stops was Hilton Head Island. She thought
it so serene and dreamlike that they stayed a week longer
than they'd planned. But Martin was eager to push on.
He wanted to work his way west to Texas and the city of
Houston in particular. He wished to see the city in which
she'd grown up and hear all about her childhood and boy-
friends and proms. It might also, he said, be good for her
to get acquainted again with such things.

All it did was make her sad. She had no living relatives
there—her father having died when she was nineteen and
her mother two years later—and they were not, in any
case, her real parents. Richard and Hannah Stride, nearing
fifty years old and childless, had bought her from the war-

den of a Saudi prison. Richard was a geologist with Mobil Oil and Hannah was a registered nurse. They were nearing the end of the three-year tour with Aramco in Saudi Arabia.

They had been housed in the walled American compound at Dhahran, a segregated community that had been designed to resemble a Texas suburb. It had split-level houses with tennis courts and pools and a golf course, although the golf course was made totally of sand. The compound had Western-style supermarkets. They sold no alcohol of any kind but the makings of bathtub wine could be bought and the Saudis pretended not to know it. They even sold pork but it was labeled as veal and bacon was simply called ''strips.'' Women, as long as they remained within the walls, were free to drive cars, sunbathe by their pools, and dress, within reason, the way they dressed in the States. Outside they went covered and always in groups.

Hannah first saw the child who she would adopt at a clinic in downtown Dhahran. The Saudi nurse had fallen ill and Hannah had volunteered to fill in for her. A baby that had no name was brought in, an infant barely two months old and sick with a rash and fever. Hannah saw to the treatment of this fair-skinned child with hair that was then almost blond. Struck by the baby's large and unusual eyes, Hannah presumed that she had been born to another foreign worker. She was shocked to find out that the mother was an unmarried convict at Az Zahran Prison and that the infant was soon to be sold by the warden. A coffee merchant from nearby Bahrain had offered him two thousand dollars for her.

Hannah knew what this meant. At worst the merchant was a dealer in slaves, an activity then legal in Bahrain. At best the child would be raised a Muslim but not be otherwise educated. She would, in all likelihood, face a lifetime of servitude. Hannah knew what sort of servitude a pretty young blond would face and could not bear the thought of it. She spoke to her husband and brought him to see her.

Richard had serious misgivings about this. They were

no longer young. And the infant, after all, was the child of a prisoner who might be a prostitute, maybe even a murderess. The warden, who had raised the price to three thousand, assured them that neither was the case. He said that the child was of good European stock and would therefore make a perfectly normal American. Both parents, he said, had university degrees, both were definitely Christian, absolutely not Jewish, and no, they were not Catholics either.

Hannah was not about to take the word of this man, but some Saudi friends whom she trusted volunteered to look into it for her. They were able to verify what the warden had told her. They said that she'd be better off not knowing the specifics, but the mother was no criminal in the usual sense. The offense for which she had been imprisoned would not have been a crime in most countries. The best news was that they prevailed upon the warden to forgo any payment in exchange for this child. That same day the child was brought to the Aramco compound where she was christened Elizabeth Stride. At the end of their tour, they moved back to Texas where Elizabeth grew up and went to school, all the while knowing nothing of her earlier circumstance.

When she was ten years old, her parents had told her that she was adopted. By that time, it was obvious that her genes were not those of Richard and Hannah. Her features, her coloring, her interests and athleticism seemed to owe nothing to them. They sat her down and told her the lie that they had rehearsed in anticipation of this day. Her birth parents, they said, were an American couple who had been in an accident before she was born. The father had died in the accident. The mother lived long enough to give birth. Neither had any close relatives, at least none that the consulate was able to find. Hannah, who had assisted in the birth, took care of her from that day on and Richard soon fell in love with her. In this sense, said Hannah, they had been her only parents from the very moment she was born.

Elizabeth had accepted the story. She adjusted very

quickly to knowing she was adopted. In her heart she supposed that she had known all along.

Elizabeth and Martin did get to Houston. They drove by the house in which she'd been raised and near it the high school she'd attended. They visited the graves of Richard and Hannah. Martin brought flowers. She thought that was sweet of him. Then he took a long walk because she wanted to talk to them alone for a while. There was much that she needed to tell them.

Their tour of Houston ended abruptly when Elizabeth ran into a classmate who said that two men with foreign accents had been to the neighborhood just the day before asking whether anyone had seen her. They said it was because she'd inherited some money. She knew the hotel where the two men were staying because they, said they would pay a reward to anyone who could make their search easier. Martin, being Martin, did not want to leave.

"Let's go and collect the reward ourselves. We'll teach them a lesson while we're at it."

"We're leaving. Right now," she told him.

"But I haven't seen the Astrodome yet," he protested.

This last remark, it struck Elizabeth, said all one needed to know about Martin Kessler.

Martin argued but he yielded. As much as he liked a little excitement he loved traveling in the RV even more. From a bulging file of maps and brochures he had compiled a list of over one hundred sights which he wished to see in America. It took all of the next two years. The child in Martin Kessler could not get enough of Disneyland, the Grand Canyon or any roller coaster or water slide within a hundred miles' journey. The darker side of that child, however, still longed for the days when he was Reineke the Fox, when he could start a buzz just by entering a room.

So when water slides would no longer serve he would seek out other forms of amusement. He would, on occasion, provoke brawls with local bullies in seedy redneck bars. This was harmless, he argued. A means of staying fit. All he did was oblige the occasional piece of human waste who was looking for someone to humiliate. He said he never harmed anyone who was not overdue. Further, he denied ever picking a fight. He simply sat at the bar, lit a small cigar, and ordered a drink. He claimed that he never said a cross word to anyone.

This was true. The small cigar, however, was a brand called Swisher Sweets—a name that intrigued him since the day he first saw it. He thought that it must be a cigar for gay men. So pretending to be one of them he would mince into saloons in the worst parts of town, lay his pack of Swisher Sweets on the bar, order a banana daiquiri and wait for the inevitable. Elizabeth saw this herself when one night she followed him. And then had to extricate him. She was forced to destroy the knee of one bruiser who was advancing on Martin with a pool cue.

She told him once again that enough was enough and that she'd seen enough water slides as well. They would either find a place to settle down and live quietly or she'd leave him and do so by herself. Martin promised to behave. They were back on the road that same night. She threw his Swisher Sweets out the window.

Martin, a skier, suggested Colorado. They visited Aspen and Deer Valley but they knew that they couldn't stay long at such places. Too many celebrities, too many cameras. Instead they chose Boulder where Martin sold another diamond and rented a house on the side of a mountain.

During the winter that they spent in Colorado, Martin had taught her to ski. Martin was a wonderfully fluid skier as well as an excellent marksman. Put the two sports together and he was world class. In fact, he had competed in the biathlon during the 1980 Moscow Olympics, where he'd narrowly missed winning a medal. Elizabeth was pleasantly surprised to learn that this was true. She had always assumed it to be the invention of Martin's comic book editor.

The sojourn in Boulder came to an end after Martin, once again, slipped into his Reineke mode. He assaulted a stockbroker who had solicited him by phone and urged him to invest in a limited partnership which very soon proved to be worthless. The loss was relatively minor—the equivalent of perhaps one small diamond—and Martin would have dismissed it as the price of an education about the downside of the capitalist system. But then he mentioned his loss to his favorite bartender. Martin knew bartenders everywhere.

The bartender completed his education with considerable personal bias. Brokers, he said, were no better than thieves. The surest way to lose money, he told Martin, was to buy any stock recommended by a broker, the one Martin used in particular. He told of an aunt whose life savings had been decimated after she had put her trust in this man.

Martin could accept that he'd done a foolish thing but he could not accept being cheated by some weasel who preyed on the gullible. On the following morning he intercepted the broker outside his office on Canyon Boulevard. The broker said, "Ah, I was just going to call you. I have a new issue that can't help but double but I can only let a few people in."

Martin broke all his fingers. He told him, "Don't worry, you can dial with your nose," but then as an afterthought he broke that as well. The incident drew several police cars but it also drew applause from the gathering crowd when they learned why Martin had done this. One of the bystanders alerted the media, who were waiting in force when Elizabeth arrived to post bail. The reporters photographed both of them. The wire services picked up the story. On the day Martin's face appeared in the newspaper, he jumped bail and they left Colorado. They spent their last night together parked at a truckstop in Kansas.

"I'm leaving you, Martin," she told him the next morning.

He was not altogether surprised. He had seen it in her coldness when he tried to make up with her, when he tried last night to make love to her. He did not argue because he knew what she would say. "I care for you, Martin, and I owe you my life but you're not ever going to change. I've got to get away before you get us both killed."

Instead he asked, "Where will you go?"

She looked away. She would not answer.

Sadly, he reached into his pocket and produced the leather pouch which held the remaining diamonds. He poured them on the countertop and began sorting them, dividing them into equal piles. There were more than thirty stones in each. Few were less than two carats in weight. Elizabeth knew then that he'd seen this coming. He had taken them from their hiding place while she showered.

"Those diamonds are yours," she told him.

"Don't be foolish," he said. He swept her half from the counter to his palm and poured them into her purse. She nodded, resigned, but her eyes were grateful.

He watched as she snapped her purse shut and began to gather her belongings. She reached under the cabinet where the diamonds had been hidden but stopped and threw him a questioning glance.

"I've disarmed it," he said.

She reached once again and drew out the device which Martin had built. It would have shredded the hands of a thief. She placed it aside and found her blue canvas duffel. She opened it on the countertop and started emptying it of its contents. Kessler saw the Ingram machine pistol that she'd purchased in Florida, the silencer that the Israelis had given her and the curved Moroccan knife which she had owned as long as he had known her. There was also a thick manila envelope in which she kept private papers. She put that to one side. Next came a bundle of clothing, all black. This bundle was wrapped in an Egyptian abaya, similar to a chador but with slits for the arms. He knew what it contained. Shoes that were soft and silent. A head scarf and an assortment of veils. A pajamalike garment, almost a jumpsuit, that was meant to be worn underneath the abaya but sometimes by itself when she worked at night. All these she dropped in a trash basket. She slid the weapons toward Kessler.

"I won't need them," she said.

She refilled the blue duffel with her toilet kit and with the items of clothing she'd selected. Nearly all were lightweight. Very little for winter. On top she put her thick manila envelope. She zipped the bag shut.

"Will you drive me to an airport?" she asked him.

Kessler rose from his seat and reached for her hand. He brought it to his lips and kissed it. She did not resist him. She did not relent either. He kissed it and held it against his cheek before sighing and letting it go. He picked up her Ingram, and her curved knife, and retrieved the black bundle from the trash. He opened her duffel and placed them inside it.

"I don't want those things, Martin," she told him.

"A bus would be better. No metal detectors."

"Did you hear me? I'm not going to need those things."

"Don't be foolish, Elizabeth," he told her once again.

Several times during the year that followed, Elizabeth had wanted to discard that blue duffel. With each month that passed, its contents seemed more and more alien to her. They belonged to a person she no longer knew.

Until Martin Kessler found her. Until he reminded her.

But Martin also brought news for which she was thankful. No one was looking for her anymore. He had seen to it that she was thought to be dead.

The dead, however, should be allowed to rest in peace. If only Martin would let her.

Four

The reunion had left Kessler considerably depressed.

He had allowed himself to hope, he supposed, that she might actually be a little glad to see him. She might not leap up and down like a welcoming puppy but she could have said more than a "Damn it, Martin. How did you find me here?"

Maybe a *"You're looking good, Martin. Have you lost a little weight?"*

Even a *"You're a pain in the tush but I've missed you a little."* That would at least have been something. Maybe add to that a smile. A peck on the cheek. Most women, if you've given them a million in diamonds, will at least offer to make you a sandwich.

As for how he found her, he had never lost her. He had seen her eyes when they first toured this island together. So many times she would just stop and stare, longingly, dreamily, reluctant to move on.

It did not take a genius to know that she would come back here. A good clue was that she took no winter clothing. Better ones were in that manila envelope that she kept stashed away in her duffel. Of all the places they'd visited together, it was only on Hilton Head that she'd bought— and kept—those little souvenir books that they sell in all the drugstores. Plus postcards, plus a map of the island, plus two books of real estate listings. He peeked once while she was out.

That trouble in Boulder gave her the excuse, but he had

HAVEN
41

known that it was only a matter of time. All during their travels she kept her hair and eyes dark when the sensible thing would be to change her appearance. He told her, "Wear eyeglasses, get yourself a blond wig, maybe stop working out and put on thirty pounds." She answered, "I'll change but not now." On the evening of that last night she sat for a long time staring at herself in a mirror. Her contacts were out; she was fingering her hair. It was then that he knew. She was ready to try to walk away from herself, and a big part of that self was him.

He wished, he supposed, that they'd stayed here in the first place. He would not have caused trouble in such a setting if Elizabeth had said let's make our life here. Like a bird he would not have fouled his own nest, not even if that nest was in a lousy location.

To begin with, thought Kessler, this island is flat. The nearest pimple of a mountain is two hundred miles away. They call it the "Low Country" to try to give it some charm but what it is really is flat. One wave from a hurricane and it will be even flatter. Shoot a rifle in any direction and the nearest thing you'd hit would probably be a high rise in Savannah.

This was only a slight exaggeration. Those who built this community had done a good job in creating the opposite effect. Their bulldozers made rises and falls in the landscape where none had existed before. Winding roads were shaded by pines and huge oaks. The oaks blocked views which weren't there to start with. This island gave no reason to ever look up except to watch lightning or the flight of a golf ball. If you looked out toward water, you often saw swamp, or what the realtors more picturesquely termed "marsh."

Worst of all, this island was an island. The only way on or off was a bridge. That's unless you kept a boat or a small plane handy and Elizabeth did neither. It was not like Elizabeth to be boxed in this way. The old Elizabeth moved about like the wind and could vanish as if she were a ghost. She would not have chosen jewelry that was worse than wearing wind chimes. The Elizabeth he knew would not buy a house and put her name on the mailbox.

Nor would she, God save us, list her name in a telephone directory.

The phone book gave her address at number 30 Marsh Drive. God forbid that an assassin should be inconvenienced. This way they wouldn't even have to waste money on plane tickets. They could stay home with their children and send letter bombs. And just so there was no confusion she could maybe put a sign on her door. The sign would say, "Yes, I am that Elizabeth. The Black Angel to you. I dress in whites and pastels these days but don't let my new outfits fool you. What do you think of my hairdo? It's a little like the blinders they put on a horse but, hey, it's the style. It's okay if you don't like it because the head it's attached to is still worth a million. Here's a list, if you need it, of those who will pay. I'll start with the Muslims and work my way down to the Communists."

And look, by the way, who she'd picked for a boyfriend. A doctor, no less. A man who she has said she might marry. It would be interesting to hear how she explained all those holes in her body. He must have seen them by now. But perhaps he has not. Perhaps this doctor doesn't even exist. Her announcement came too quickly on the heels of his own. That he, too, was soon to be married.

"You're kidding," was her doubting response.

"Her name is Maria. She's a widow with two little girls."

"Um . . . where is this widow now, Martin?"

"Better you don't know, Elizabeth."

"But not here. You're not marrying someone here."

"We will live in South America. I came only to say good-bye."

"So . . . now you'll be leaving?"

"I'm to join her at the end of this month. She's attending to some business of a personal nature."

"Well . . . I'm almost engaged myself."

"Oh? To whom?"

"To a nice quiet man. A doctor. We've . . . talked about adopting."

Elizabeth, he was becoming convinced, was as big a

liar as he was. But at least his lie was not spur of the moment. For the past month he'd been spreading it all over Europe along with the news that poor Elizabeth was dead. Dead now for almost a year. She collapsed while pedaling an exercise bike. A fragment of bullet that the surgeons overlooked had worked its way to her heart. So terribly tragic and also ironic. After ten years, that same gunman's bullet had killed her after all. Those who've been hunting her finally had their revenge. He took her ashes back to Houston and sprinkled them over the graves of her parents. This, at least, was the story he'd told, and the Europe crowd seemed to believe it.

By the time she had arrived on this island he was already there waiting for her. She took longer than he did because she had taken the bus. This meant that she had kept her blue duffel. He stayed out of sight, watched her shopping for houses. He stayed until he saw that she was settled in safely and then left to give her the time and the distance she needed.

After that he went back across country to Aspen where he did a few weeks of spring skiing. From there he kept moving and touring. For a week or so here, a week or so there, he had managed to find female companionship. But all these women did was make him miss Elizabeth. He drifted back to Europe where at least he had friends. That was how he spread the story of her death and of his own plans to settle down on a ranch in South America. "Forgive me if I don't tell you where," he had said.

But the man to whom he had told this had said, "Why bury yourself on a ranch? No one is looking for you anymore. Reineke the Fox is ancient history."

This bit of news was not all that welcome. Truth be told, it wounded his pride. The dealer in information had seen this. He had said, "That is not to say that you're out of the woods, Martin. There are many who would like to get their hands on the money you took. They would go looking for this new wife of yours and grab her to extort a few million from you. But not the ones who were hunting you before. Those boys are back in power. The communists everywhere are getting re-elected. Not only do they have all of Eastern Europe to loot once again but on top there's American aid.'' He had said, ''Believe me, they have no time for vengeance. Not even for those two who you stuffed down a sewer in Geneva.''

Kessler tried not to show his surprise. Those two were alive the last time he saw them. And what was this reference to extorting a few million? All Kessler had taken was that one bag of diamonds. Someone, and he thought he knew who, had given him far too much credit.

The important thing, however, had been the last thing this man said. ''With Elizabeth dead, God rest her soul, I think you can drop your guard and relax. With her it was the Muslims. They never forget. They could never forgive what she did to so many.''

Okay, thought Kessler. So he cracked a few heads and broke a few fingers. And for this, Elizabeth left him. She said, or as much as said, that it destroyed the serenity of the life she was trying to find. This might sound almost reasonable until one considers who was talking. This was the Black Angel, Elizabeth Stride, deciding that she wanted to be Ozzie and Harriet. Also, not to be selfish about this, but what about his own serenity? For him, serenity would have come easily. All it would have taken would be to hear, just once, the words, ''I love you, Martin.''

Not ''Thank you for saving my life. Now good-bye.''

Not ''You've been very good in bed, Martin. So much more tender, more giving, than those guards in my Saudi prison.''

And not ''I might even love you,'' followed by ''*but* . . .''

Just a simple ''I love you, Martin Kessler.''

If he'd heard that . . . just once . . . he would have needed nothing else.

Martin had booked a suite at the Hyatt Hotel on the beach of Palmetto Dunes. In the lobby shops he bought all new clothing so as not to stand out from the tourists. He also rented a second car because Elizabeth had already seen the first. He would use the new rental to follow her about and perhaps get a look at this fiancé of hers. It was childish and he knew it but he had come a long way.

Over the next two days, however, he saw her only with women. With some she went shopping and with some she had lunch. This in itself was remarkable. Unlike the tourists these women were all tanned and they dressed pretty much like Elizabeth. With these women Elizabeth was actually laughing. With these women Elizabeth was *chatting*. It is easier to imagine Joan of Arc making small talk or Lucretia Borgia making jokes. It was good to see all the same.

In the week that followed, her doctor turned out to be real. But in that whole week he saw Elizabeth with this doctor only twice. Both times were in restaurants and both times were for lunch. Not once did he see the man's car in her driveway or her car in his. Some romance, he sniffed. Some engagement.

The first of those lunch dates was at a restaurant called Reilley's, located near the main gate of Sea Pines Plantation. Kessler watched as her car—a Ford Bronco of all things—turned into the restaurant's rear lot. He saw a man wave to her from the restaurant's entrance but he couldn't get much of a look. Doctors, he reasoned, do not take long lunches and so he decided to wait. After forty-five minutes they came out together, her smiling young doctor first holding the door for her and then walking her over to her car. He opened the Bronco's door for her as well; his reward was a kiss on the cheek. He grinned like a schoolboy as he watched her drive off.

This doctor wasn't much, Kessler grumbled to himself. His last name was German, but that was all one could say for him. What, he wondered, could they possibly talk about? Does he tell her at lunch between bites of his sandwich of the hernia that he repaired that morning? Does he draw on a napkin his technique for resecting a bowel? If so, Kessler had news for him. She's probably resected more bowels than he has. She could teach him a few things about throat surgery as well.

Their second lunch was much the same. Even the same

restaurant, same kiss on the cheek, but this time he was
so bold as to give her a squeeze in response. Having witnessed the replay of this sickening scene, Kessler decided
that he could do with a drink. He waited until they both
drove off and went into Reilley's himself.

The lunch crowd, now thinning, consisted of middle-
aged men, most of whom were dressed in golfing attire
and had already played a round that morning. Golf was
also a part of the decor. Clubs and golf caps, photos of
foursomes. Autographed pictures of pros. But another big
theme was Ireland. Just outside the entrance was a sort of
calendar whose only function was to count down the days
that remained until the next Saint Patrick's Day. Reilley
was said to throw a wonderful parade. The doors to the
rest rooms said "Fir" and "Mná" which he presumed to
be Gaelic for "Men" and "Women." This last was a
little too much for Kessler. He found a place at the bar
and ordered a good German beer.

Nearby was a photograph of another golf foursome.
Kessler found himself drawn to it. There was a man,
standing second from the left, laughing at whatever the
photographer was saying. The man seemed familiar. And
he seemed out of place. Kessler tried to return to his
thoughts of Elizabeth but the face in the photo seemed
determined to intrude. He waited until his beer was served
and asked if the bartender knew who that was.

"The one who's laughing? I think he's Tom Reilley's
cousin or something."

"You don't know his name?"

"Um . . . Jimmy . . . Jimmy Flood."

"And is one of these Reilley?"

"On the left. Next to Jimmy. Are you new to the island,
Mr. . . . ?"

Kessler chose not to fill in the blank. But implicit in
the question was that everyone knew Reilley. Well, Martin Kessler didn't. And he couldn't place Jimmy Flood
either. He sipped his beer and resumed his brooding.
There was a time when everyone knew Elizabeth as well.

Five

She was already famous when he met her. But her notoriety was limited to the Middle East back then, just as his was largely limited to Europe. Their paths, in fact, should never have crossed. He first saw her name when it appeared on the guest list of an embassy reception in Bucharest. Representatives of several countries had been invited and everyone pulled dossiers on everyone else.

This was nine years ago, almost ten. She was only twenty-six at the time and already worth a million dollars dead. If her killer was a Muslim he would get the million now plus a guaranteed acceptance into Paradise later. Non-Muslims had to settle for the money.

The Israeli delegation, of which she was a part, had come to buy Jews from the Ceausescu regime, which would let their Jews emigrate for a base rate of four thousand dollars a head, twice that amount for doctors and scientists. He, Kessler, was there buying ethnic Germans from Saxon Romania who wished to emigrate to the German Democratic Republic. For them, the price was much lower. That they wanted to move to East Germany at all, thought Kessler, reflected how bad it was for them in Romania.

The reception was at the Hungarian embassy because the Hungarians were buying ethnic Hungarians. At this rate Romania would have soon been empty except that there were certain Romanians who the Ceausescus couldn't afford to free—their stories would have been too embarrassing. The Hungarians thought it might be useful if all the buyers got together and swapped notes on where some of these people might be found. This was the point of the reception.

Elizabeth's presence with the Israeli delegation was all the more interesting because it seemed that she herself had been bought. Her dossier made fascinating reading. Her story, told briefly, was this:

To begin with, she wasn't a Jew, but had been raised Presbyterian. She grew up knowing she was adopted but not that her biological mother had been a convict in a Saudi prison. She learned that only after her adoptive mother's death when she sorted through some family papers. A year later, she traveled to Dhahran with the intention of learning who her birth parents were.

She engaged a Saudi lawyer who learned the name of the warden of the prison, who was now a police official. He said he would try to arrange an interview. Instead, he notified the official that this young woman could be an embarrassment if certain of his sideline businesses came under scrutiny. Elizabeth was arrested the next day. Drugs and other contraband were "found" in her hotel room. She was imprisoned for eight months, kept in isolation and brutally interrogated. Kessler assumed, although Elizabeth had never really spoken of it, that she'd also been repeatedly raped. In the Middle East, rape and sodomy had long been a means of intimidating female prisoners. Elizabeth had simply been given to the guards.

At the end of eight months they apparently concluded that Elizabeth had gone out of her mind. She was taken from her cell and thrown in a truck that was part of a convoy bound for Jordan. After a twelve-hour ride without food or water—locked up in what amounted to an oven—she was dumped half naked, no money, no passport, just past the last checkpoint of the Saudi-Jordanian border.

Some goat-herders found her, delirious and emaciated, and brought her to a woman they knew. This woman, named Rada Khoury, ran a literacy program through a local mosque. They thought she might speak whatever language poor Elizabeth was babbling. She took Elizabeth into her home and after two days managed to get her stabilized. She fed her liquids one sip at a time until Elizabeth could hold a cup by herself. She oiled her skin where the sun had baked it and bandaged her eyes with wet towels. When Elizabeth could speak and it was learned that she'd been in prison, Rada became afraid that the Jordanian police might treat Elizabeth as a criminal who had entered their country illegally.

Rada called the American consulate in Amman and asked them to send someone for Elizabeth. No one came—the consulate officer didn't want this headache either. So Rada Khoury took Elizabeth to another woman, a doctor, who ran a nearby clinic and was trying to teach peasant women that not all pregnancies are the will of God and that most can be prevented. The doctor's name was Nasreen Zayed. Martin had read dossiers on Khoury and Zayed, as well, but that was a whole other sad story. For the next several weeks these two women cared for Elizabeth until most of the physical damage was repaired. The damage to her psyche ran much deeper.

They finally had to move her because the clinic was attacked by rock-throwing men to whom family planning was heresy. Teaching women to read was almost as bad. Nasreen and Rada were severely beaten but Elizabeth was spared because they had hidden her down the clinic's well. Now it was Elizabeth who had to care for them, although she was clearly no longer safe there. When Nasreen had healed sufficiently, she and Rada drove Elizabeth to Amman. Not trusting the American consul, they took her to the office of Amnesty International. They left Elizabeth under that organization's protection and said their good-byes.

During Elizabeth's stay with Amnesty International, she was debriefed by two visiting investigators and treated by a psychiatrist. All three, it turned out, were Israeli agents. The Israelis had no real interest in Elizabeth but rather in who else she had seen in that prison. But they were with her when word came back that Rada and Nasreen had been murdered by fanatics. Perhaps they saw the cold hatred in her eyes. Perhaps they saw that she had possibilities. They offered to help her trace her parents and suggested that in the meantime, she would benefit from some training in the ways of the Middle East. That was how the Israelis recruited her.

She eventually learned that her real father had been a soccer player on the Romanian national team and her mother was a medical student who traveled with the team as a therapist and masseuse. When the mother got pregnant, she knew that they would never be permitted to marry and that the child would almost certainly be taken from her because that was the practice in Romania. They decided to defect while traveling to a game in Saudi Arabia.

They slipped away from their hotel in Riyadh, she in a stolen abaya, and made their way to the British embassy, but were caught en route by the Mutawain—the Saudi religious police—who had spotted him holding her hand in public. They were beaten, then the father was turned over to the Romanian authorities, who drugged him and flew him to Bucharest. He was executed a few days later as an example to the rest of the national team. The mother was tried in a Mutawain court on a charge of having sex outside marriage. The warden of the prison at Dhahran learned of her conviction and had her transferred to his custody. The baby, once weaned, had been promised to a merchant from nearby Bahrain but then the baby got sick. That's when Hannah Stride saw her and offered to double what the merchant had agreed to pay. In the end, however, no money changed hands because not all Saudis were like the warden and some friends of Hannah's made it clear they'd see him in prison if he didn't turn over the baby.

Elizabeth's mother, according to the Israelis, served only one year of a ten-year sentence. The warden, it seems, had a taste for fair-skinned European women and he raped her repeatedly until one day she resisted so violently that she beat her to death.

Kessler knew this story from Elizabeth's dossier and from details which she filled in much later. But he was never quite sure how much of it was true. It had come, after all, from Israeli Intelligence and they had used this account to recruit her. Months later they smuggled her back to Dhahran where, hidden under an abaya and wearing a niqab—a veil that covers the entire face—she stalked the former prison warden until she caught him having lunch at a sidewalk table. She approached him from behind. As he raised a cool orange fizz to his lips, she reached under his arm and slit his throat.

She had been trained to go for the carotid artery. Once it is severed, there is no more blood pressure to the brain. Loss of consciousness, then death, is almost instantaneous. But Elizabeth missed the carotid. She did so deliberately. She wanted to watch as he lurched to his feet, knocking tables and chairs aside, trying to close the wound with his hands. It was then that she lowered her veil and looked into his eyes until she was certain that he knew who had killed him. Two days later, she found the lawyer who betrayed her. She did not kill that one. She only cut off his hand.

This last even stunned the Israelis. The Mossad, Kessler assumed, had its own reasons for wanting the police official dead. In the end, the Mossad was thrilled. They loved the idea of a veiled female avenger wandering at will through Arab capitals, carving up Israel's enemies and then vanishing like a ghost among thousands of women who all looked exactly the same. From that day Elizabeth became the Black Angel. The Israelis, of course, came up with the name.

As for cutting off that man's hand, Kessler had understood this to be the standard Koranic punishment for thieves. Elizabeth, he had assumed before this, had merely stretched that particular point of law. Actually he wondered why she bothered. If the lawyer had it coming, why not kill him and be done with it? A footnote on her dossier provided the answer. It seems that it's considered an insult among Arabs to touch someone using the left hand. The right hand must be used for touching, eating, accepting a gift—doing anything polite—because the left hand is reserved for unlovely purposes such as aiming to piss and wiping one's ass. To be forced to use the left hand is to be constantly humiliated for the rest of one's days. Elizabeth, clearly, knew what she was doing.

She stayed on in Israel because her life as an American now seemed totally foreign to what she had become. To hear the Israelis tell it, she cut dozens more throats in Iraq, Lebanon, Saudi Arabia, Syria and even Kuwait. In Kuwait, a few years ago, a new law was passed, preventing women from driving a car while their faces are covered with a veil. The Israelis liked to call this "Elizabeth's Law." It was rushed into passage after one of her visits.

Elizabeth denied the stories. She said "dozens" was nonsense. She said she only went out a few times more and mostly into Lebanon in response to attacks against Israeli civilians. She said one such attack was against a busload of children that left five of them dead and several maimed. The Israelis say she evened the score for those five and for each of those who lost limbs.

As for Kuwait, she says she's never even been to that country. That might be true. But *someone* was. And the Israelis let it leak that the someone was Elizabeth.

Elizabeth had asked to go along on the Bucharest mission—the ransoming of Jews—because she hoped that during her few weeks in Romania she might learn something more about her roots. Martin's own mission involved a lesser ransom, but he hated the assignment all the same. He despised Ceausescu and his regime. (Marxist solidarity meant nothing to them. Nor did the Marxist ethic. They took money wherever they found it. As just one example, with their left hand they took money from the CIA for informing on terrorist activities while, with their right hand, they took money from Iran to train Hezbollah fighters on Romanian soil.) The Marxist ethic meant nothing to Ceausescu.

People would mock him, Martin understood, for some of his views on Marxism. They'd ask him how he could ever have believed in it. Well, he did and he didn't. It had become a racket for those at the top, but that wasn't Karl Marx's fault; his philosophy was nothing if not humane. Marx believed in the dignity of the working man, who in his day had none. He argued for the violent overthrow of their governments because he knew that peaceful protest would only get them killed.

People spoke of Karl Marx as if he were the anti-Christ. They'd quote Marx's famous dismissal of religion as the opiate of the people. But those who quoted that single remark were ignoring the rest of Marx's observation. "Religion," he wrote, "is the opiate of the people. But it's the heart of a heartless world."

But Communism was now unraveling. And a part of Martin Kessler cheered its promise.

It was Elizabeth who made Martin's stay in Bucharest bearable. She was stared at wherever she went, even by those who knew nothing of her reputation. You couldn't miss her. She always wore black. Jumpsuits by day, Paris fashions by night. Dark hair that shined like a raven's wing. Black eyes that could show you heaven when she smiled and a glimpse into hell when she did not. At the time he still thought the black eyes were genuine. If only a tenth of the stories were true she was still an extraordinary woman. Elizabeth, however, on meeting him, was considerably less impressed. She said, "Ah, yes. You're *that* Martin Kessler. I believe I've read about you in the funnies."

By mid-evening, however, things began to take a turn for the better. He'd seen her in a prolonged whispered conference with her Israeli colleagues. Whatever they were saying was making her angry. The conference ended and the anger was replaced by a smile. The smile was directed at him. His heart soared. This, he felt sure, could mean only one thing. The Israelis had urged her to encourage him in the hope of compromising or even turning him. Kessler was all for it. It would give him more time to win her over.

To this end, after meeting for dinner a few times and showing her around Bucharest, he gave her the addresses of a few more Jews—all scientists—whom the Romanians had no intention of letting emigrate. They happened to live in Timisoara, up near the Hungarian border. Elizabeth brightened. That region, she said, was also where her birth parents were from. Her mother had gone to the medical school there.

They drove north to Timisoara where they managed to find the several Jews, one of whom remembered her soccer player father and the girl, the medical student, who had sometimes traveled with the national team. He gave them the names of some relatives who still lived in the area.

Elizabeth tried to meet with a few. They were afraid to speak with her, however, and only hours later, Elizabeth and Martin were forced to leave Timisoara because demonstrations had erupted over the arrest of a popular priest. There had already been round-ups and considerable shooting. Two Hungarian journalists had been murdered, and Kessler and Elizabeth thought it best not to linger. The trouble had not yet spread to Bucharest. On their second day back, he and Elizabeth walked out of their hotel together and a car roared up. Two men wearing ski masks were inside. The one on the passenger side raised an automatic weapon. Kessler shoved Elizabeth to one side and jumped to the other as he clawed for his pistol. But the gunman was already shooting. Kessler heard bullets slapping flesh. They lifted Elizabeth and slammed her backward. Kessler emptied his pistol at the fleeing car but he hit only metal and glass. The gunman raised a fist as the car sped off.

Elizabeth was ten hours in surgery. Her wounds were not fatal but two were extremely serious. The bullet through her abdomen was the worst. As he paced the hospital's waiting room he tried to think who could have done this and whether he, not Elizabeth, had been the real target.

As it turned out the Romanians had in fact been watching them. They became convinced that the two of them must be somehow involved in the Timisoara uprising.

The secret police could not arrest them because they both had diplomatic passports. So they did the next best thing. They told their Hezbollah guests that the notorious Elizabeth Stride, enemy of God, was staying at the Hotel Excelsior.

Retribution, however, would have to wait. Once Elizabeth's condition was stable, Martin and the Israelis had hijacked an ambulance and gotten her across the border into Hungary. He stayed close by her side for two weeks. She never whimpered, never complained. This was when he fell totally in love. But he left her in good hands and returned to Bucharest, where the Israelis were already hunting the men who shot her. By the time he arrived, the uprising against the Ceausescu regime had begun and the Ceausescu family was fleeing. All of Bucharest was in chaos.

The Israelis had kidnapped the secret police major who had served as liaison officer with Hezbollah. They caught him trying to leave Bucharest dressed as a worker and carrying a rucksack crammed with Swiss francs and brought him at gunpoint back to the Excelsior. Kessler joined them there. Under less than gentle questioning, the officer claimed that he had been personally against the arrest of Elizabeth's Jews, but the approval had come directly from Nicolae Ceausescu's brother, Martin Ceausescu. This was Kessler's first hint that the Timisoara Jews had been imprisoned after he and Elizabeth left them. The major then named several Hezbollah guests who "might" have been the assassins. Kessler took the major's rucksack and poured the Swiss francs out a sixth-floor window of the hotel. When a sufficient crowd had gathered below, he threw the major out as well.

That done, Kessler wanted to get to Vienna. He and two of the Israelis drove all night to get there while the others stayed in Bucharest to hunt down the Hezbollah gunmen. Kessler was less interested in the actual triggermen. He wanted Martin Ceausescu. He was too late. Martin Ceausescu, who was known to be his brother's bag man, had already been tortured and hanged by members of his own embassy staff. They wanted the numbers of Nicolae's Swiss accounts where Martin had stashed many millions for his brother.

Much of that money was from the sale of emigrating Jews and the few ethnic Germans from Saxon Romania. Some was the money paid by Iran for the training of Hezbollah fighters. The Israeli agents made it clear that their country was entitled to the bulk of it. At the very least, they said to him sternly, it is not to be thrown out of windows. They pursued the torturers to Geneva, where, equipped with photographs of the embassy staffers, they found two of them leaving the office of Credit Suisse, each carrying a briefcase so heavy that it had to be held with both hands. The Israelis intercepted them, disarmed them and guided them toward the car where Kessler was waiting.

The bags contained seventy kilos of gold bullion and several small bags of diamonds. Their pockets contained bundles of cash in three different currencies plus cashiers checks and letters of credit totaling more than thirty million American dollars. One of the Israelis put a bag of diamonds to one side and then wrote out an inventory of the rest. That done, he asked Kessler to sign it as a witness.

"What about those other diamonds?" Kessler asked.

"Call them a finder's fee. Take them, they're yours."

Kessler never asked what happened to the two Romanians. He assumed that the Israelis had let them go because there was no real point in killing them now and because they didn't need trouble with the Swiss. He learned much later that he, Reineke the Fox, had put a bullet in each of their heads, stuffed them down a sewer in Geneva and kept all that wealth for himself. And Elizabeth learned that it was she, the Black Angel, who had tracked down and executed those Hezbollah gunmen who shot her. The story was that they did not die easily. Dressed in her veil and abaya, she had slowly and deliberately cut off their heads with her famous Moroccan knife, leaving them conscious as long as she could. Needless to say, this came as a considerable surprise. He did know, however, that those suitcases were returned to the Israeli treasury because Elizabeth, after he had nursed her back to health, was later able to confirm it.

Kessler, even so, was not pleased to hear this. The Israelis had obviously found the two gunmen and had, more than likely, put bullets through each of their heads just as they did with those two in Geneva. But the Israelis, being a tricky lot, decided that they might as well milk their avenging Black Angel routine for all its worth. The problem was that the price on Elizabeth's head, to say nothing of his own, would now approach the payoff on most national lottery tickets. It seemed a good time to retire. Elizabeth was inclined to agree.

Three months passed before they first made love, and one more after that before she was able to travel without pain. The lovemaking was not all that he might have hoped for. He had fantasized, he supposed, that a day would come when she realized that she loved him just as much as he loved her. But when she did take him to her bed it seemed more with a sense of resignation than of passion. Gratitude mixed with a sense of inevitability.

There was no question that she liked him. And she'd grown to trust him. But the bedrock of it, he felt sure, was that she realized he was pretty much all she had. Elizabeth was all Kessler had as well because there was nothing for him back in Germany. The two Germanys were being reunited and anyone who had worked for counter-intelligence was marked as either a Stasi informer or a party bully.

So together they wandered through Europe together, as their larger-than-life reputations—and the bounties on their heads—drew ever more attention. They had two close calls, one in Paris and the other in Amsterdam. Both were kidnapping attempts. In the first, Elizabeth took a knife slash along her hairline before opening up the man who cut her. In the second, it was he who had to kill again. It was time to leave the continent. It was time to try America.

So, thought Kessler, this is where he ends up.

Forty-two years old, no friends, no family, nothing even to believe in anymore. Sitting in a bar called Reilley's, his third beer in front of him, listening to old men talk about golf.

Kessler took a breath and let it out with a sigh.

"Hello, Martin."

Elizabeth was suddenly in the seat next to him. He didn't know how long she had been there. He answered with an embarrassed nod. Caught, he dared not look at her. But Elizabeth placed both her hands on his shoulder and rested her chin on top of them.

"I know that you use two cars, Martin," she said into his ear, not unpleasantly. "You've done that as long as I've known you."

He could only shrug.

"And now you're sitting here sulking because a nice normal man is finally interested in me."

Finally? she said. What was he for nine years, her chauffeur? Also, hundreds of men have been interested in her except that half were too afraid of her and the other half wanted to kill her. But the approach of the bartender spared Kessler from pursuing the subject.

"Sir, that's Tom and Mr. Flood over there," the young man said.

"Ah . . . who?"

"You were asking about Tom Reilley and his cousin. That's them. They just came in."

Kessler followed his eyes toward two pleasant-looking men, both in their late fifties, who were now moving toward the bar. The owner, Reilley, waved greetings to several patrons. He stopped at one table where he shook one man's hand and introduced him to the man named Jimmy Flood. Kessler now saw this Flood in profile. This man looked even more familiar than before.

"I lied about Jonathan," said Elizabeth, who was still at his ear. "We're good friends, nothing more."

Kessler blinked. "That's your doctor's name? Jonathan?"

She closed one eye, skeptically. "You've been here a week and you don't know that? You haven't followed him home?"

"Who? Me? Why would I do that?"

"You haven't broken into his house? Checked the bedroom? Sniffed his pillows to see if you could smell me on them?"

"Certainly not," he hissed at her.

"Now tell me about Maria."

"There's nothing to tell."

"Hmmph!"

"What's hmmph? I'm not entitled to a private life?"

She took his hand and lightly bit one finger. "Martin," she said gently, "I know that I was not very nice to you. But you're being just a bit of a jerk."

Kessler made a face. This once, he told himself, she is not going to have her way. She is here for one reason only. She wants to know that he will not . . . who knows . . . buy more Swisher Sweets and blow smoke in her Jonathan's face. Or twist his stethoscope around his neck. Or, worse, tell him a few things about his lady friend.

"Martin . . . we need to talk. But not here."

"There's no need. I won't bother you again."

"Martin . . . listen. It's not that I don't have feelings for you."

At this, this minimization of feelings, all he wanted to do was get away from her. The bar was becoming more crowded. More men had come in from more golf games and on many their sweat had not dried. It was as if they were gathering just to hear Elizabeth throw him another such bone. He was about to pull his hand away and get up from his stool when the door from the parking lot opened again. A man entered Reilley's who was not like the others.

This one was dressed in tennis whites. He wore a white floppy hat made of canvas and he carried a bag that said Nike on the side and it had a pocket that was made to hold two racquets. The hair beneath his hat was blond and stringy but his clothing was still fresh and his skin was still pale. A tennis player who had not yet played tennis. He looked for a seat at the bar and found the one remaining vacancy at a place three stools away. An Englishman, thought Kessler. The English have not yet discovered shampoo. And now, sure enough, he is asking the bartender for Gleneagles, neat, without ice. His accent was British Midlands. Elizabeth, however, paid him no attention.

"Martin, let's take a walk, okay?"

"Wait," he answered. "Wait just one minute."

Kessler knew that man. He was sure of it. The name was hiding in the back of his mind but this man had once been pointed out to him in Europe. Sprat? . . . Splat? It was a name like those.

Elizabeth signaled the bartender. She wanted Kessler's check.

The name remained just out of reach. But Kessler did know him. And he knew how this man made his living. At this his brain made one other connection. He suddenly realized why the cousin of Reilley had seemed so familiar to him. Kessler turned to Elizabeth. He brought his lips close to her ear.

"Listen to me," he said quietly. "I want you to get up from your stool and say good-bye to me. Say it as if you don't know me very well. Then walk straight out the door."

"Um . . . Martin, what's going on?" She turned her head to see his eyes.

"Please do it, Elizabeth. Do it now."

Her eyes bored into his. She could see, as he'd hoped, that this was no game.

"There's a bank out the front door," she whispered in his ear. "That's where I'll be waiting. I'll be watching the door." She picked up her purse and slid from her stool. "Gotta go," she said cheerfully. "Nice meeting you, Fred."

Kessler had a strong feeling that her life on this island was finished. But this time, at least, she could not blame him.

Six

Kessler watched the eyes of the man dressed for tennis. They did not so much as flicker at Elizabeth's parting. He did, however, reach into his bag. Kessler thought that he might have a signaling device but all he produced was a leather-bound notebook which he placed on the bar before him. He opened it to a place that was marked by a folded map tucked inside it.

Kessler waited and watched. The man seemed less and less aware of his surroundings. Every so often he would rub his chin thoughtfully, jot a notation, then take another sip. At one point he unfolded and studied the map. Kessler remained alert all the same.

That this man never looked in Elizabeth's direction meant little in itself. A professional would hardly have sat gaping at her. That he did not follow her meant even less. If he had come for Elizabeth he would already know where she lived. But also, Kessler realized, he would not be alone. An associate might well be outside at this minute trying to drag her into a van. The thought of this caused his stomach to tighten but he fought to stay calm and deliberate. Elizabeth Stride, he reminded himself, would not be so easy to drag.

Kessler left a ten-dollar bill on the bar and languidly slid from his stool. He moved toward the exit in a path that took him directly behind the man in tennis attire. He would try for a look at whatever he was writing. Failing that, thought Kessler, at least he would see how the man reacts.

There was nothing subtle about his plan. There was also nothing useful because, as he passed, Kessler could make out nothing at all, not in the one or two seconds that the notebook was in sight. But he did see enough of the map to know that it was not a map of this island. The man made no attempt to cover these things. Nor had the hair on the back of his neck gone up. That alone was encouraging. It suggested that this Englishman did not know him by sight or else he was a very cool customer indeed. Kessler continued past the rest rooms and out the side door, not the door that Elizabeth had used. He would rather have waited for the Englishman to leave but he needed to see that Elizabeth was all right.

To his instant relief, he saw her Ford Bronco and Elizabeth sitting at the wheel. She was waiting perhaps fifty meters away, with one arm out her window, her fingertips tapping against the roof in a gesture of bored impatience. Kessler spread his hands and cocked his head questioningly. The gesture, he hoped, asked if anything was amiss. She spread her own hands and added a shrug. *"Like what?"* her own gesture was asking. He signaled that she should stay where she was, then he took a long moment to scan all the cars that were parked within sight of the door. This was meant to tell Elizabeth to watch them as well.

He climbed into his own car and, with a moment's apprehension, turned the key in the ignition. The engine spat but it did not explode. Putting it in gear, he steered directly toward Elizabeth's Bronco. As he approached her, he was pleased to see that her eyes were still locked on Reilley's rear exit. Good girl, he said in his mind. This island has not yet turned your brain to pudding. He pulled partway into the space next to hers, stopping at her open window.

"It's clear behind you," Elizabeth told him. "What am I looking for?"

"You saw the man in tennis whites, blond hair in need of a washing?"

"Of course I did. Who is he?"

"He's a bounty hunter, Elizabeth. An Englishman but his name eludes me. Years ago he tracked dissidents, sometimes for the Stasi. Last I heard, however, he has a new specialty. He hunts Muslim women who have run."

Her eyes narrowed. "Would his name be Pratt?"

"That's it. Cyril Pratt." Kessler slapped his head.

Her eyes went cold. "You're sure about this?"

Kessler nodded vigorously. "And I'll tell you something else, Elizabeth. You saw the man named Jimmy Flood who came in with the owner of that restaurant? The last time I saw him he was Ian McShane."

It was years ago, fifteen at least. Kessler was still with GDR counter-intelligence. McShane was IRA. Not one of the bomb-throwers or ambushers but he ran the security force that protected the leaders of Sinn Fein, the political wing of the IRA. Such a job would only be offered to a man of unquestioned loyalty. Ruthlessness would also have been a prerequisite and it would need to have been demonstrated. There were stories that he worked his way up over the bodies of informers and of British agents who tried to infiltrate Sinn Fein. Also, Kessler wondered, who knows about Reilley? Do we think that he's only a restaurateur? Do we think he sits around waiting for his sign to tell him Saint Patrick's Day has come? He's probably an IRA gunrunner himself. Kessler said all this to Elizabeth. Her expression was now one of blinking confusion.

She asked, "Why do I even listen to you?"

"Okay, not a gunrunner. A fund-raiser maybe."

"Martin . . . get real here. How do *you* know McShane?"

"We tried to recruit him. We hoped to use him against the British. But I never met him face to face. It was all through intermediaries. In any case he wouldn't take our money or even our weapons. He didn't like us any better than he liked the British."

"Okay, now stay with me. What in God's name does this have to do with Pratt?"

Not much, he supposed. Except it was possible, of course, that Pratt had come here for McShane. McShane, like themselves, still had a price on his head. Sedition was the least of the charges against him and Pratt, perhaps, had gone back to working for the British.

"Or else," said Elizabeth, "Pratt followed you from Europe."

Her tone was accusatory. But Kessler doubted it strongly. The route he had taken back after spreading the story of Elizabeth's death was so labyrinthine that surveillance would have required a dozen men. And why would they have been so patient? That many could have taken him along the way. They could have tortured him until he told them where Elizabeth was if they thought she was alive after all.

"So in short you don't know if he's here after me," she responded.

"You want me to go back in and ask him?"

"What I want is for you to . . ." She didn't finish. She threw up her hands. "Damn it, Martin. Everywhere you go, you bring trouble. Just when I've—"

Kessler glared at her. "Elizabeth . . . go home."

She realized that she'd been unfair but she was stubborn. "First it's wait. Now you tell me to go home?"

"Elizabeth . . ." He spoke quietly but he showed his teeth. "In ten minutes I have identified a potential ally and a more than potential catastrophe which you would never have seen coming. In those same ten minutes—"

"The ally is who? McShane?"

"Why not? You have both made new lives. You've both chosen this place to begin them. You both have something to protect."

"Martin . . . I have no wish to—"

"And if you both chose this place, how many more fugitives might have done so as well? Keep your eyes open, Elizabeth. You might be surprised who your neighbors are."

"Are you out of your mind?" This was the last thing she wanted to hear.

He raised both his hands. "As I started to say . . ."

"Martin, I have no intention, damn it, of forming a

mutual defense league with every island resident who's wanted for something.''

"As I started to say," he repeated, speaking quietly, "in those same ten minutes you have done nothing but patronize me, insult me, and blame me. I will now say good-bye to you, Elizabeth."

He slid his gearshift into reverse and allowed the car to coast backward.

"Martin . . . wait."

"I've *been* waiting. No more."

"Damn it, Martin, here comes Pratt. He just came out of Reilley's."

"He's all yours, Elizabeth. Enjoy your new life."

Kessler backed his car all the way out. He slapped his transmission into drive and steered for the parking lot exit. There he paused and looked into his rearview mirror. Her car had begun moving as well but she was not coming after him to say she was sorry. She was moving in another direction. So be it, he decided. Good-bye for the last time, Elizabeth.

But why, he wondered, was she moving so slowly? Suddenly, he realized what she was doing. Her eyes were locked on the cars behind Reilley's. She was going to follow Cyril Pratt. Kessler muttered a curse. In her stupid Ford Bronco, a red one no less, she intends to conduct a surveillance. Her brain had turned to pudding after all.

Kessler cut his wheels sharply, he tapped his horn twice. She saw him. She waited. Kessler let her see the anger on his face and he showed her a fist through his windshield. But then he opened the fist and showed her two fingers plus a thumb that he pointed at himself. She nodded that she understood. Now he pointed at her car and made a series of gestures. Again, Elizabeth nodded.

The Englishman's car was a white Toyota Camry. Kessler watched as it exited the complex of restaurants and made a right on the island's main thoroughfare. It proceeded toward Sea Pines Circle. Elizabeth fell in two cars behind. Upon reaching the circle, Pratt could go one of three ways. Elizabeth would follow if she understood his gestures but only for the first turn Pratt made. When he turned after that, she was to break off and Kessler would pick him up from there.

Pratt entered the circle but left it at once. He turned east on Pope Avenue and continued straight ahead. That was good, thought Kessler. In the direction he took there was only a Holiday Inn and some shops. After that there was nothing but beach.

A half mile later Pratt signaled a turn at a road called Cordillo Parkway. That road as far as Kessler knew led only back toward the East Gate to Sea Pines. Pratt was turning, perhaps, to see who might follow, but Elizabeth was obedient for once and kept going. She gave no hesitation, no glance to her right that a man being followed would be watching for. Kessler followed Pratt onto Cordillo.

There was another hotel after all. Kessler had never noticed it before because it was set back and hidden by trees. An easy-to-miss sign said this was the Players Club. Pratt's Toyota pulled in and turned toward the parking lot. Kessler kept going for another fifty yards. He turned into the driveway of a group of condominiums and waited. The Toyota did not reappear.

Kessler needed to be sure of where the Englishman was staying but he was reluctant to drive onto the Players Club grounds. The only entrance he saw was too easily watched and there was too little traffic at the moment. Before him, near the pool of the condominium complex, he saw several unattended bicycles. He considered borrowing one of these on which to explore the grounds at leisure. But if he should need to withdraw quickly, the image of himself pedaling furiously was too far beneath his dignity to contemplate. Instead he went in on foot.

He saw Pratt's car but no sign of Pratt, and the parking lot was busy after all. Two small jitney buses had arrived. They were white with darkened windows and were now disgorging some thirty boys and girls, all dressed for tennis as Pratt had been, all with racquet bags over their shoulders. Their matches, by the look of them, had already taken place. Each jitney also carried two adults beside the driver. Nearly all of the children were white but all of the adults were black men or black women. Some of the blacks were calling out to the children, reminding them to be on the drill court at four. The adults all wore jackets that said "Van Der Meer" on the back.

Ah, yes, thought Kessler. The Van Der Meer Tennis Center. He'd read of it in one of Elizabeth's brochures but he'd never entered Sea Pines by this route. The brochure, as he recalled, said it was known the world over as a place to send your child if you think you have a prodigy on your hands. The Van Der Meer Center seemed clearly allied with the Players Club. Kessler took a moment to survey the layout. On the far side of the parking lot was a large swimming pool flanked by two residential units of three stories each. On the outskirts of these were at least a dozen tennis courts, including one with a grandstand and two that were covered by a tent in case it rained. The Players Club, off to his left, was a building all to itself. A ramp climbed up to the entrance where a sign on the front said *Reception*. There might be residential units in there as well but much of the building housed a restaurant and bar. As Kessler stood making these mental notations he suddenly saw the head of Cyril Pratt.

Kessler had almost missed him entirely. He was up on that ramp near the entrance to the club and stood largely concealed behind shrubbery. At his eye was what looked like a video camera and he seemed to be recording those jitneys. He was panning over those sweaty boys and girls who were breaking off in pairs and heading, one assumed, for the pool or the nearest cool shower. He seemed to lock in on one pair of young girls who to Kessler looked the same as all the others. But now he swung back to the black men and women and lingered on each one by one. Kessler's impression had been that these adults were merely chaperones but now it struck him that there was something off-center about them. He could not put his finger on what.

Whatever Pratt's purpose, he had finished his taping. As he stepped away from the shrub that had concealed him, he placed the camera in his tennis bag from Nike and turned as if to enter the Players Club. But he paused at the doors and looked off to his right. He was looking at an open-air bar. The bar changed his mind. He walked back down the ramp to a table and sat. Kessler watched until a waitress approached. This seemed a good time to take a look at his car.

The Englishman's Toyota had Georgia plates and had probably been rented at the airport in Savannah. Pratt had also rented a cellular phone. Kessler did not see the phone but the manual for it was lying across the front seat. Other than that the car told Kessler little except that this Pratt was a slob. The well of the back seat was littered with bags he had emptied of junk food. There were two blister packs which had once held batteries and tapes for the camcorder and a paper bag that had a piece of cardboard sticking out of it. The cardboard was the sort of divider liquor stores put between bottles when you buy more than one. Given Pratt's line of work, Kessler said to himself, he seems to drink more than is good for him.

Partly hidden by the bag was a map of the island. It was not the same map that Pratt was reading in the bar. The location of the Players Club was marked with red ink. Kessler could see all of Sea Pines on the rest of the part that showed. He saw Marsh Drive where Elizabeth lived but it was not marked in any way. Nor was Reilley's for that matter. Also on the floor was a photograph of a cabin. It seemed very old, very rustic, and not in the best of repair. There was swamp grass behind it and a body of water. Whose cabin it was, he had no idea, but printed on the margin was the name Bluffton Realty.

Kessler scanned the debris for visitors' passes. Such passes were cards, perhaps six by eight inches and of all different colors, for the various destinations within each plantation. Most were good for one day only. Once obtained, they were to be kept on the dashboard. Every car of every tourist had at least one, usually several. A slob such as Pratt would surely have crumpled them when their dates had expired and thrown them over his shoulder. There was none, however, in this car. This suggested that Pratt had not visited Sea Pines. Nor had he visited Palmetto Dunes where the Hyatt Hotel was located. He felt sure that Pratt was not here as a tourist but there was also no sign that his reason for coming had anything to do with Elizabeth. Or with himself. Or even with Ian Mc-Shane.

Wishful thinking, perhaps. And on the thinnest of evidence. Pratt's reason for coming, if Kessler had to guess, had something to do with those black men and women. Or perhaps with the children who got out of those jitneys. If his specialty, however, was hunting Muslim women, Kessler had seen no one who fit that description. The chaperones could certainly be Muslims, he supposed, but if so they were American Muslims. Their accents, moreover, were distinctly northern and the ones who called out didn't even sound black. Speculation, however, was wasting his time. This seemed to be none of his business.

He would try to find out what name Pratt was using. Perhaps the bartender would know. He would then do a little more looking around and after that he would meet with Elizabeth. He would give her his report and let her make what she pleased of it. After that she would be strictly on her own.

"It's not that I don't have feelings for you, Martin."
Well, how nice of you to say so. Good-bye.

He had backtracked for less than a quarter mile when the red Ford Bronco appeared in his mirror. Elizabeth had been waiting for him. She tapped her horn, then pulled out to pass him, and beckoned him to follow as she did. She led him through the East Gate of Sea Pines and, in a roundabout way through streets not familiar to him, eventually back to her house on Marsh Drive. This, he presumed, was in case they had picked up a tail of their own. Once there, she told him to come inside. She would put on a fresh pot of coffee, she said. They could talk about this in her kitchen.

Kessler declined to get out of his car. He left the engine running. He took less than three minutes to tell her what he had seen. He told it simply and professionally, only what he had observed and learned; he offered nothing in the way of speculation. Except, he told her, Pratt's not here to play tennis. He's not even here as Cyril Pratt.

Her eyes clouded over. This last had dashed the ridiculous hope that even bounty hunters take vacations. "What name is he using?" she asked.

"Harry was all his bartender was sure of. He thought the last name might be Wheeler."

"Is there anything else?"

"That's the sum of it," he said. "From here you can do as you wish."

"Martin . . . will you stop this and please come inside?"

"Thank you but I'll say good-bye from right here. I'll be gone from your island in the morning."

Kessler didn't give her a chance to speak again. He left her standing alone in her driveway.

Seven

Elizabeth wanted to turn away. She did not want him to look back and see her standing there watching him go. But she did watch him go and he didn't look back. Not when he made his left turn off Marsh Drive and not when she saw him again through some trees as he sped down the road out of Sea Pines.

What she wanted to feel was relief that he was going. She felt only sadness. She wished that he had at least come in for coffee. There were things she would like to have said to him, things she'd started to say at that bar.

She drank the coffee by herself. With the mug in her hand, she began to wander through the rooms of her house. It suddenly seemed so quiet. For the first time since coming here she felt empty and alone. She berated herself for that feeling and Martin for bringing it on. To be free of him was, after all, what she wanted. Free of Martin and his lunatic adventures. She was well rid of him a year ago and just as well rid of him now.

She returned to her kitchen and opened the drawer in which she kept her telephone book. She found the number of the Players Club and dialed it. She asked for Mr. Harry Wheeler. She broke the connection when the switchboard rang his room. So that was definitely the name he was using.

"*You know him?*" Martin had asked.

"*I've heard of him,*" she had answered.

But she never quite believed that he had come here for

her. He specialized in hunting women, it's true, but not the sort of woman who could hurt him. The women he hunted were already scared to death and were strangers in a new land. Those who ran often ran with female children. This sort of quarry was far less lucrative than someone like herself, for example, but more numerous and easier pickings. There are men all over Europe in that line of work and some in this country as well. She had first learned about them from women they had found. Women who would never see their children again. These were women she had met in Az Zahran Prison. And they were some of the luckier ones.

Among her sister convicts in the Saudi prison were several who had fled to the New York area, where they hoped to get lost in one of its several largely Muslim communities. They had all been betrayed by the same bounty hunter, a Lebanese who worked as a cab driver by day. This one man had found, kidnapped and returned more than eighty fugitive Muslim women and at least that many children at an average bounty of seven thousand dollars per head. Later, long after she got out of Az Zahran, she had asked the Israelis to find this man for her. They said they would and came back later to say, "Forget about the Lebanese cab driver, Elizabeth. He already got what was coming to him."

They told her that he had been a boastful man and like all boastful men he was careless. He had tried to grab one woman too many and that one, for a change, had male Muslim friends looking out for her. They stuffed him in the trunk of his taxi and rolled it off a Hudson River pier.

She accepted what they told her but she knew they may have lied. The Israelis had other work for her. Their plans did not include wasting her training on some cab driver thousands of miles away. The Lebanese, having made himself rich, had more likely returned to the village he came from where he's living like a prince to this day.

But even if they didn't lie, his death would not have helped the eighty women. Those women, some of whom surely met terrible deaths, had run for many reasons. Most, like the women she met in prison, were from the educated and affluent classes who had traveled to the West in the past. The poor would not have had the means. People wonder why women in the Gulf states buy so much gold jewelry if it's hidden under yards of black cloth. It's mostly in case their husbands divorce them and they need to pay a lawyer to get them their due. But that gold is also the stuff of dreams. Dreams of becoming teachers or scientists or writers or athletes . . . whatever has been simmering inside them. Dreams they would never be allowed to pursue if they stayed. They give much of their gold to the men who get them out and then hope that these same men don't decide to cash in twice by collecting the reward that is usually offered by husbands, even brothers, who were shamed by their escape.

But still they try. They flee in an ever-growing stream from countries where the fundamentalists are in power or where, as in Egypt and Algeria, they will probably soon take control. They flee countries where their right to practice family planning, to keep custody of their children in the event of a divorce, to receive alimony, to keep any wealth they inherit, even to step out of the house without their husbands' permission have been stripped away by recent laws. They flee men who believe that the right to beat them—the duty to beat them—comes directly from God. Some flee to avoid being given in marriage to men they have never met, or men who repulse them, or men whom they fear. Mothers flee with their daughters to keep them from being given in marriage on the day when they reach the permitted age of nine. Others flee with daughters who, on the day they turn eight, would be sexually mutilated if they stayed. That's the day when their daughters are due to be circumcised.

These mothers are women who know their Koran. They know that there is nothing in Islam, nothing in the law, which requires this barbaric procedure. And yet it is done in many Muslim countries because it is thought to keep their women chaste. The practice predates Islam by hundreds of years. But some Muslim countries have kept it alive because the men have reasoned that if a woman can be kept from enjoying sex she is less likely to tempt a man into sin before marriage or to commit adultery after. Never mind that the Koran is very explicit about the right of a woman to take pleasure in sex.

To their credit, she knew, a few Muslim countries had outlawed the practice of genital mutilation. Even the Saudis, the most oppressive of them all, have seen the absurdity of this logic. But such butchery was the rule in many others and women resisted at their peril. To resist brought shame upon the family. It meant that no suitable husband would ever be found for a woman who had not been made pure. All that was left to such a woman, the family would feel, would be to go to the city and become a prostitute. Better by far to kill her. Some mothers, a few, took their daughters and ran. But most saved their lives in an easier way. They tied them down and cut them.

If a family was not poor, this was sometimes done by a doctor. Even Nasreen, the doctor who had cared for her, had performed these operations. Nasreen detested the practice but she sometimes did the surgery because the alternative, she realized, was a razor blade in a filthy shack followed by massive infection and a lifetime of pain. Nasreen had told her what was involved. And Rada Khoury showed her. It had been done to Rada herself.

The operation, in its mildest form, involves the removal of part of the clitoris. More drastic than that, and more common, is an excision which removes all of the clitoris and all or part of the vaginal lips. Finally, there is infibulation—a horrific procedure which few doctors will perform—involving the removal of all genital parts and the sewing together of the two sides of the vulva. This left an outlet for urine and blood that was about the width of a pea. It stayed that way until a bride's wedding night when the groom, if he was kind, brought a doctor to open her. If he was not, he ripped it open with his finger.

Elizabeth set down her cup.

This was not good, she thought. She could feel the old hatreds welling up inside her and she knew what might happen if she allowed them to fester. Her need, she realized, was to talk to someone and that someone could only be Martin. She thumbed through the pages of her phone book once more and found the number of the Hyatt Hotel. She began to dial it, then stopped herself. The Hyatt was at least fifteen minutes away. Martin had not had time to get there.

All those women. All those little girls.

How many, she wondered, had Cyril Pratt found in the more than ten years he'd been at it? She had learned about him from the Israelis as well. They had kept a file on him but only because of his earlier career tracking dissidents. After Pratt switched to hunting Muslim women the Israelis might have felt a measure of sympathy but they said it was none of their business. Elizabeth couldn't blame them. They had enough on their plate just to keep their own people alive.

She remembered, however, expressing surprise that Muslims would trust such a mission to a man who cared nothing about their faith. She had assumed that his blond hair had something to do with it. A runaway woman looking over her shoulder would be watching for darker complexions. The Israelis explained that as well.

These hunters, they said, are not all in it for the money. There are many who believe in what they're doing. Unlike the taxi driver from New York, some will only take expenses. Some of these will even try to be decent about it. They will track down the runaway and try to persuade her to return because, after religion, there is nothing more important than family. They will offer to mediate, to help her reach some sort of compromise with her husband. They will guarantee her safety if she agrees to go back. Some, a few, won't take her back at all. Some will leave her in peace as long as they can see that she is living a good Islamic life.

This, therefore, is why they'd use Pratt. Men like Pratt do not mediate. They wouldn't care what kind of life a woman was leading. They wouldn't shrink from finding women whom they knew might be killed within days of their return or young girls who were sure to be maimed. But Pratt, said one of the Israelis, was the worst of the lot because he wasn't in it strictly for the money either. He was in it to indulge a sickness. With Pratt it was the

pleasure of seeing them tremble as he told them what was
in store for them.

"Elizabeth . . . put him out of your mind."

Martin's voice. In her mind she heard it.

"Go take a hot bath. It will do you good."

"A bath is not what I need."

*"What, then? To go use your knife on Cyril Pratt?
Forget him. He's not here for you."*

She didn't answer. But she'd thought about that knife.

*"Also, where would it end, Elizabeth? Will you carve
up every Muslim who shows up on this island?"*

*"Martin . . . I do not hate Muslims. Some of my
best—"*

She stopped herself, but too late. A smile lit Martin's
face in her mind.

*"Were you actually going to say it, Elizabeth? That
some of your best friends are Muslims?"*

"I did have Muslim friends, Martin."

*"Sure. Two women. It's the other billion or so you
despise."*

"That isn't true."

"It should not be, my darling. But it is."

The Martin of her mind was now standing in her
kitchen. He approached her from behind. She could almost feel his hands as they reached for her shoulders and,
as they had done so many times, began massaging the
muscles that had tightened there.

"I will tell you what is true," he said gently. *"This
has nothing to do with Islam. Every religion has its fanatics, its bullies and its hypocrites. The men who hurt
you just happened to be Muslims and if there's a hell,
they're now in it. Let it go, Elizabeth. It's time you let it
go."*

She could feel the warmth of his body. It caused a
shudder from deep inside her and her chest began to rise
and fall.

"Oh, Martin," she sighed to the man who wasn't there,
"if only you weren't such a pain in the ass."

His smile disappeared. *"Well don't let it trouble you
further,"* he said. *"I'm gone for good this time. There is*

nothing for me in your little island paradise.''

The shudder inside her turned into an ache. Old feelings were rising. And this was dumb. She was doing it to herself because Martin was leaving her. She'd left him first but that was different. What she'd left was not so much Martin but rather that part of her life. She left him because she was known to be traveling with a man with a German accent. And a scar near his eye. A man being hunted by God knows how many but who didn't know how to lie low. But here was Martin; and he was leaving her, and not for those sensible reasons. He was leaving because . . . Oh, God, this was childish . . . because he simply didn't like her very much anymore.

"Martin? If I came to the Hyatt . . . if I knocked on your door . . ."

"Elizabeth . . . what would be the point?"

"I don't know. I don't want to lose you and yet . . ."

"And yet you don't want any more trouble. Don't worry, Elizabeth. I'll fix that before I go."

"Um . . . wait a second. What does that mean?"

"It means Pratt. I'll take care of him for you tonight."

"Damn it, Martin. Not on this island."

"Be well, Elizabeth."

"Martin!?! Don't you dare. You come back here."

But Martin was gone. She was alone in her kitchen. And she cursed herself.

Here she was, having a totally imaginary conversation with a man who was probably sitting on a bar stool at this moment trying to charm some divorcee out of her pants. He wouldn't go after Pratt. He couldn't care less about Cyril Pratt.

Go ahead, Martin. Have a few beers, pick out some vapid liposuctioned twit and spend your last night on my island screwing your brains out. Nine years we've been together and that's all I've meant to you. Well, good riddance, damn you. Good-bye and good riddance.

But the thought of a bar led to thoughts about Reilley's. Reilley's was on Martin's way out of Sea Pines. Reilley's was where he might stop. Once again, she saw Martin in her mind. He had walked up to Reilley's cousin and put an arm around his shoulder.

"*Listen, Jimmy, you might remember me. Think back to when you were Ian McShane . . .*"

Oh, my God, thought Elizabeth.

"*I was in here today with Elizabeth Stride . . . Yes, that Elizabeth, the very same . . . In any case, Elizabeth and I were talking about a problem that the two of you might have in common . . . Cyril Pratt . . . Ah, you know of him . . . Anyway, I was thinking that as soon as it's dark you and I might drop over to the Players Club and see about nipping that problem in the bud.*"

"Oh, my God." This time she said it aloud. "Damn you, Martin. Oh, my God."

Eight

It was morning the next day, a Thursday.

Kessler could live to be one hundred, he decided, and he would still not understand Elizabeth Stride. Anyone who thought that her head was on straight needed only to have seen her last night.

There he was, in his room, he was packing. He had driven away from her, never to return . . . well, perhaps . . . and went straightaway back to the Hyatt. In the lobby he turned in his second car, went up to his room, and laid all his clothing out on his bed. He packed everything but his toiletries kit and the clothing that he would put on in the morning. Suddenly came a knock at the door and there was Elizabeth. She was breathing hard as if she had been running. She asked if he had made any stops coming back here. She walked in before he could answer.

"What stops?"

"Never mind."

"What's wrong?"

"Never mind."

By now she was checking the rest of the suite to determine that they were alone. She looked even in the closet and behind the shower curtain. Who she thought she might find he could only guess. Perhaps she had decided Maria was real.

"Where were you going to go when you finished packing?" she demanded.

"Ah . . . maybe to get a bite to eat?"

"Fine. Let's do that. We'll have dinner together."

This was not the most gracious of invitations but it was clear that the subject was not open for discussion. They took the elevator down to the restaurant where they found that they would have to wait to be seated. At this point he glanced toward the bar. His thought was that they might have a drink in the meanwhile but Elizabeth tugged on his arm.

"They're not your type, Martin," she said to him coldly.

"Ah . . . who are you talking about?"

"Those floozies. They're just not your type."

He looked over again. Sure enough there were women there. One sat with a man who was clearly her husband because she had little to say to him. Two others, both matronly, sat with each other. These two were sipping wine and there was a shopping bag on the floor between them. One was showing the other some things that she had purchased. The one who hadn't gone shopping had probably spent the day by the pool because her face and arms were seriously red. These are floozies? he thought. What would make Elizabeth say such a thing?

"Never mind," she said when he asked.

And so they had dinner. Or he did at least. Elizabeth pushed a few scallops around her plate and told him that she didn't hate Muslims. As proof she told of the women in prison who had comforted her and taught her some Arabic and the other two women who had nursed her back to health. He had heard all these stories ten times.

"So you don't hate the women. I believe you."

"And I don't hate the men. Not the good ones."

He must have raised an eyebrow at this because it set her off on an effort to prove that she was not totally pathological. She didn't much care for Kuwaitis on the whole; they lived one of the most indolent, gluttonous lifestyles on the planet and that war was fought for cheap oil, nothing more. The Saudis, she said, were a very close second. She threw in a few more details about Kuwait that convinced him she had been there after all. She had no use, in fact, for any Arab government but she surprised him by saying she admired the Palestinians.

The Palestinians as a group, she said, were highly educated, resilient, took one wife, and—the PLO aside—didn't try to use Islam as a billy club. She said if there were any two peoples who should have found a common ground, it was the Palestinians and Israelis. Both were stereotyped as being clannish, aggressive, pushy, and obsessed with educating their children. They were the professional caste of the Middle East, running newspapers, hospitals, construction companies, banks and often the executives are women. They are women who can vote and who can dress as they please.

"Ah . . . where is the part where you like Muslim men?"

She lowered her eyes. "Rada Khoury respected them. A few must have earned it."

"I see."

She looked at him. "Have you taken up golf?"

The nonsequitur made Kessler blink. "No, I haven't. Why do you ask?"

"That jacket you're wearing. It's a golf jacket."

It was the jacket he'd been wearing all day. Why was it suddenly significant? "It's not just an everyday windbreaker?" he asked.

"It's for golf and it's also too big for you. You kept it on even up in your room. Are you carrying a pistol under there, Martin? Is that why you bought a jacket that full?"

"Elizabeth . . . eat some of your scallops."

"I'd like an answer. Are you carrying a gun; if so, why?"

"Please eat. After that, please go home and relax."

"I'm not hungry. I would like to take a long walk on the beach."

"Then do. By all means."

"You don't want to walk with me? After more than nine years you won't even walk on the beach with me?"

This was from the same Elizabeth who wanted him to get lost. Best proof, he thought, that all women are deranged.

*   *   *

They walked, shoes in hand, for a mile or so. They passed a few other couples. Most of those couples had their arms around each other. They were lovers but also they were cold. Hilton Head Island in March, especially at night, was not yet such a tropical paradise. The afternoons could be sunny and pleasant but after dark you wanted more than a golf jacket. Elizabeth suddenly seemed to feel the chill. She said "Brrr" and put her arm around his waist.

What is this? he wondered. Is she feeling for that gun or is this her Israeli training? The Israelis would have said don't stand out in a crowd. If the crowd is all lovers then you should act the same even if it was only Martin Kessler you were with.

"Elizabeth, we had better start back," he told her.

"Martin . . . will you let me stay with you tonight?"

"Stay where? In my suite?"

"Don't say no to me, Martin." She gritted her teeth before adding, "Please?"

"If that's what you want . . . then of course."

"What are you saying? Are you saying you don't?"

At this, Kessler wanted to scream. In the whole week he'd been here he had yet to say a single thing that Elizabeth thought was right. He would, however, give it one more try in the hope that this would be the exception.

"You can have the bedroom. I'll take the sitting room. There's a couch in that room that folds open."

She looked away. "You're a rat."

"Don't say no, you ask. So I don't and I'm a rat?"

"I'll take the couch. You can keep your damned bed."

Kessler thought that he must have screamed after all because faces on the beach turned and looked. Elizabeth grabbed him. He thought she would punch him. But instead she threw her arms around his neck and she kissed him hard on the mouth. He wished she had been just a little less impulsive, at least to the extent of first dropping her shoes so the soles didn't clap against the back of his head.

He didn't know how he should respond so she showed him. She let go of her shoes and she reached for his right arm, which was hanging limp and befuddled. She placed that arm around her waist. She repeated this procedure with his remaining arm, except that one she placed around her shoulders. She reached one hand to the side of his mouth and shook his cheek until his lips parted. That done and with everything now just so she kissed him again, but more gently. She kissed him more tenderly. More sweetly.

"Elizabeth . . . listen . . ."

Again her fingers came up to his lips and her eyes beseeched him not to speak. Her next kiss wasn't sweet. It was a hungry kiss. She probed for his tongue with her own. He felt a thumping that came from low in her belly as that part of her body pressed hard against him. He felt himself rising to meet her.

"Just love me, Martin," she said into his chest. "Please don't say a word. Just love me."

And love her he did. Three times that night. The first time he did all the things that pleased her, one of which, in this case, was not speaking. She gasped and she writhed and she called out his name. She gave up all control of her body and mind and threw herself into the moment. It was as if she'd been someone who was starving to death and then discovered an unguarded buffet. She had not, he was certain, gone to bed with her doctor or with anyone else for that matter. A hunger this great was a whole year in building. Exhausted at last and glowing with sweat, Elizabeth fell asleep in his arms.

That was the first time. On the second he awoke when he felt the touch of a warm and moist wash cloth wiping his abdomen. Elizabeth said, "Shhh" and continued to bathe him. When she finished she did things that had always pleased him. After that she lightly tickled his chest. She said, "Go to sleep," and kissed his forehead.

The third time was just after sunrise. He had called to have breakfast sent up and Elizabeth had said to tell them not to hurry. The third time was the best of them all in its way because this time it was not done in darkness. He could see on her face that she was glad to be with him, not just for the sex but specifically with him. Still, however, she would not let him speak.

Afterward came a quiet knock on the door. She waited on his terrace as he signed for the room service breakfast. He brought the tray out to her. She was standing at the railing, looking out at the sea, dressed only in the comforter she had taken from the bed. He had put on a white terry robe with the emblem of Hyatt Hotels on its breast. He poured and mixed her coffee the way that she preferred it. He broke her croissant and sweetened it with honey.

"Am I allowed to observe that it's a beautiful morning?"

"Every morning is beautiful here," she said softly. "Look out there. See the dolphins?"

Kessler saw them. A school of seven or eight. They were snaking through the water in the wake of a shrimp boat that was returning with its catch. Gulls and terns swooped and dove all around them.

The morning air still held the night's chill. The comforter had slipped from one of her shoulders as she sipped with both hands from her cup. He kissed the bare shoulder and then covered it. She thanked him for that with the kind of smile that she must have had as a girl. He reached to arrange the hair at her forehead that had been pushed back and flattened as she slept. He fixed it so it covered her scar. She helped with the back part, feeling the strands at the base of her neck that were still cool and damp with perspiration.

"I think I could use that hot bath you mentioned," she said, reaching and squeezing his hand.

"A hot bath I mentioned? When did I say that?"

Her smile became sheepish. "Never mind."

He refilled her cup as she tasted her croissant. She seemed in no hurry to leave. Whatever her reason for coming last night, whatever her reason for wanting to stay, her eyes said she had no regrets.

"Martin . . . ?"

But here goes Elizabeth, he said to himself. When she let herself love there was little confusion. This was also true when she hated. With Elizabeth, confusion only came when she thought.

"Martin, I just need time," she said quietly. "And I need you to give me that time."

"Well, you'll get it because I need to move on."

"You're still leaving," she said, as if to herself.

"We both know there's nothing for me here."

Elizabeth frowned. He tried not to smile. Elizabeth always frowned when he failed to say his lines in the way she'd already rehearsed them.

"I'm nothing?" She looked up at his face. "Last night and this morning were nothing?"

"Last night and this morning were wonderful," he answered. "But this is the cold light of day."

"What's that mean? All cats are gray in the dark? Were you pretending that I was this Maria?"

"Your life," he said gently, "is here, Elizabeth. You've found yours and I must find mine."

He stepped in from the terrace and called the front desk. He asked that they total his bill.

There was no understanding Elizabeth, thought Kessler. There was only attempting to stay one step ahead. If he'd said to her, "Elizabeth, I've decided to stay," she would have told him why he must go. And he had no intention of going just yet. What man in his right mind would leave a woman like Elizabeth especially after spending such a night in her arms?

He knew that she could never have asked him to stay. She saw vacillation as weakness. One did not survive as she had survived without a focus that approached obsession. The most she could do was what she did upon parting. She asked him to admit that Maria was a phantom and to say where she could reach him if she needed to talk. He had satisfied neither request.

He would give her the time that she needed, he said. Maybe a year, maybe less. But she should, he told her, remain celibate in the meantime. If the night they'd just shared was to be the result of a year of unfulfilled needs, there was much to be said for annual visits. Her eyes, however, became glazed at the prospect. It took her a while to see this as a compliment and not, say, deserving of a knee to his crotch. Instead she only bit his ear a little and after that she kissed him. He had walked her to her car door, which he opened for her as her Jonathan had, and he handed her a flower that he'd plucked from a bush. These acts left Elizabeth unable to speak. She kissed him again, she kissed him long and deeply, before managing to whisper a tender "Damn you."

Her Jonathan would have died for such a "Damn you."
Her Jonathan would have died for such a kiss.

He did check out of the Hyatt Hotel because Elizabeth would soon call there to see if he had. He drove from the Hyatt to the island's small airport where he turned in his first car at the Avis counter and rented still another from Budget. He chose a white Camry exactly like Pratt's because similar cars can be useful sometimes. From the airport he telephoned the Players Club Hotel and booked himself a room for three nights.

He had known, he supposed, why Elizabeth had come to him. No part of it, clearly, was to catch him with a floozy. Nor was it to break her sexual fast with a man who wouldn't question her scars. Oh, her passion and affection were genuine enough. She was certainly hungry for physical contact but the offer of her body had begun as a tactic. What gave her away, as if he'd had any doubts, was that business with his gun-hiding golf jacket. What did she think? That he'd go and shoot Pratt? On an island where slamming a door is big noise? Where a rabid raccoon becomes front-page news? Where a man found shot would get almost as much press as a rationing of Chardonnay wine?

No, he wouldn't shoot Cyril Pratt. He would merely look in and try to see what Pratt was up to. After that he just might smash his kneecaps.

Nine

Mahfouz was thrilled to have ridden in an airplane. He was even more glad to have survived it.

The plane came back down through lightning and thunder and the bouncing had brought up his lunch. And he learned to his amazement that time stood still when an airplane has crossed an ocean. The clocks in Miami said the time was much earlier than the time on his new gold watch. The Englishman had said this was because the watch was cheap but he would buy it all the same for twenty dollars. Twenty dollars seemed too little for a gold watch with diamonds. It seemed too much for a watch that didn't work. But a man on their next flight, the one to Savannah, showed him how to make the watch tell good time again.

Cyril Pratt would not let him stay in Miami. Miami, he said, was too filled with Jews and the Jews would just get him arrested. Where they're going, he said, there are plenty of beaches and the only Jews living there are no longer Jews. There is also Faisal, who was already there waiting at the cabin he rented near this place known as Hilton Head Island. Faisal speaks good English and can show him around and can keep him from getting into trouble.

Faisal showed him much in the next two days and Mahfouz was troubled by all of it. He had never imagined that such a place could exist without needing to die first to get there. Why, he wondered, should so much beauty be given to a people so corrupt. Why give them a place so green and so rich, a place that is so much like heaven.

"Just wait," said Faisal, who had claimed to be Hezbollah. "It won't be so long until we make this a hell."

But Faisal, he had learned, talked like that all the time. He was tough and he was mean and he was also a braggart. In his wallet he carried newspaper clippings that he opened and showed to Mahfouz. In one a car was blown up in New Jersey and Faisal said, "See that? That was me." In another a building burned down in Miami and Faisal said, "See that? A building full of Jews. That was us." God forbid that a hurricane came to this island. Faisal would probably say that he seeded the clouds. What made Mahfouz doubt him more than anything else was the photo of him standing with Yassir Arafat.

There was Faisal, holding up a Kalashnikov, while he hugged a man who was definitely Arafat. But the photo, he knew, meant nothing at all. Arafat must have posed for a thousand of these. To get such a picture is easy. All you do is dress up in old army fatigues, borrow someone's Kalashnikov and have a camera ready when Arafat comes to give one of his harangues. You work your way to the front of the crowd and yell out, "I am ready to die for you, Yassir. I am ready to knock on the gates of paradise with the skulls of the Jews I have killed for you, Yassir." You don't have to mean it but you'll get your picture. Also, if you don't watch out, you'll get a wet kiss on your mouth to go with it.

Mahfouz had his doubts that Faisal was Hezbollah. He would not be the first to make such a claim just to puff himself up. Every Muslim community had men like Faisal who always came asking for money. They told those who were pious that it was used to build mosques and those who hated Jews that it was for Hezbollah. Or Hamas or Jihad or Egypt's Muslim Brotherhood to equip more brave fighters like himself. Someone once told him that it was like the Italians. The Italians have their own Christian gang called the Mafia. He said, "It's the same. You can't find an Italian who doesn't have an uncle who he claims is a fighter for the Mafia."

But none of this answered his question. Why should Americans have a place that looks like heaven?

He had known all his life what heaven would be like. It was described in the Book which was not to be doubted and Mahfouz had memorized every verse that spoke of it. "It is a place where there are lush green gardens watered by running streams . . . The faithful shall dwell in these gardens where rivers will roll at their feet . . . Reclining there upon soft couches, they shall be decked with bracelets of gold and arrayed in garments of fine green silk and rich brocade. They will be shaded by palm trees and by fruit trees that stay heavy with fruit no matter how much is picked."

They will eat, the Book said, those fowls which they relish, which must mean there would be plenty of chicken. Never again would they work or get covered with sweat or have to break plows against rocks. Never again would they cough desert dust from their lungs or blow globs of sandy snot from their noses.

This much about Paradise was certain. "They shall be served with silver dishes and with beakers as large as goblets . . . They will drink from cups always filled to the brim with water that is flavored by ginger . . . They shall be attended by boys who are graced with eternal youth and who, to the eyes of their beholders, will seem as sprinkled pearls . . . They will drink a delicious wine that will neither dull the senses or befuddle them . . . They will sit with bashful dark-eyed virgins as chaste as the sheltered eggs of ostriches . . . And each man will be wed to a dark-eyed houri more beautiful than an angel and the houri will give him endless pleasure." This, too, was in the Book which was not to be doubted. All this and more had been promised.

Mahfouz, for one, could hardly wait. He was curious, also, to see what awaited women. Surely good Muslim women would end up in heaven but the Book said nothing about them. Their husbands on earth all get houris in heaven but what becomes of their wives and daughters? If dogs go to heaven—and the Book says they do—God surely has made some arrangement for women. Mahfouz would find out when his time came.

But meanwhile, here he was, still on earth, in a place that was very much like heaven. There were palm trees and fruit trees and fountains of water and shops that sold nothing but chicken. Here the men never worked. They did sweat here but only at play. And the houris were every place you looked. They floated by on skates that were like tiny bicycles and were otherwise practically naked. Only little short pants that didn't cover their navels and a top that barely held up their bosoms. They lay on the beach where they wore even less and a man could look at them as long as he liked. And there was no sin for looking. In sins of the flesh, as the old sheik had taught, the blame was not on you but on the temptress.

But how could all this exist? Mahfouz wondered. These people will surely go to hell when they die but why should they first have heaven? He could only have faith that God knew what he was doing. Maybe it was just to make hell all the worse by comparison. In hell, says the Book, garments of fire awaited their arrival. Scalding water would be poured on their heads, melting their skin and that which was in their bellies, and they would be lashed with rods of iron. Even this, thought Mahfouz, was too good for these people. It was surely too good for that woman who hid here, the one who Pratt wanted even more than the girl. But the girl was young and she still might be saved if her virtue, God willing, had survived.

"We move soon," the Englishman, Pratt, said at last. "Tarrant's men and their seaplane will be here in two days. Faisal has my map. Your route to the cabin is marked on it. You and Faisal will take the jitney and he will practice driving that route. Drive it until both of you know all the landmarks. Make sure you can find that cabin at night."

"I, too, may drive? In Egypt I have driven a tractor."

"Don't even put your hand on the wheel," said Pratt.

"Then I may have a gun? Faisal has a gun."

"Ah, but you have that lovely new watch from Bandari.

You will use it to record how long each trip takes. In the meantime, you will kindly stay out of sight and stop leering at teenagers' tits. You will also stay the hell off that beach.''

Mahfouz did not like this request. It was rude in its form. It was also unfair because this Hilton Head beach was for everyone. Faisal, who read English, translated a sign that said this was so. ''But,'' Faisal told him, ''this time of year this beach is mostly for prostitutes. It's too cold for swimming—See? Not one of them swims—but warm enough for them to show off their wares. That's why only prostitutes would lie upon blankets when the sun's arc is still so far south.''

This was a good thing to know, thought Mahfouz. Tomorrow, perhaps, when there was nothing to do except drive back and forth, he and Faisal would strike a bargain with one.

''You won't like them,'' Faisal had told him already. He touched his hand to his crotch. ''Too much hair down below, not smooth like our women. Down below they look almost like men.''

That may be, thought Mahfouz. But hair or no hair he was twenty-five years old and he'd never once been with a woman. He had never even touched the bare skin of a woman who was not of his family. Here men and women touched all the time. He had watched them and it wasn't just shaking their hands. On the beach one young boy spread some sort of ointment all over the shoulders of two different girls and the girls made no effort to resist him. At a store where they stopped to buy food for the cabin a woman touched cheeks with a man she encountered just because she had not seen him for some time.

Mahfouz knew that he himself should wait until he was married, and there was one in Abu Shatt he had his eye on. But her father and brothers had not yet said yes so he was not bound by a betrothal. Tomorrow, therefore, he would choose one of these so that he'd know what to do on his wedding night. Her price should be low because it wouldn't take her long. She would only have to walk from the beach to the jitney where a mattress from their cabin would be waiting inside.

Tomorrow, thought Mahfouz, would be a good day. He would get a little taste of what awaited him in Paradise.

Ten

Cyril Pratt's white Toyota was still in the lot when Kessler drove its clone to the Players Club. Pratt himself was nowhere in sight.

He had determined that Pratt's room was in Building 100. It was up on the second floor facing some tennis courts. Kessler had asked for a room there as well. Building 100 and Building 200 flanked a large swimming pool which was crowded with guests. Elsewhere were Building 300 and so on. No poetry was wasted in naming these units.

He found them not unattractive, however. Each of the units was prettily landscaped and each room had a terrace of comfortable size. Kessler registered and took his bag to his room.

His room, unlike Pratt's, looked out over the pool. From its terrace he could see almost all of the parking lot and also the outdoor bar. The clerk had told him he was lucky to get it because a guest of long standing had moved out that morning and had rented a time-share instead. The room, when he reached it, was still being cleaned by two maids whom he noticed were dressed more like nurses. They wore long-sleeved white smocks and white stockings and shoes, and their hair was tucked under starched caps. He said, "Don't mind me. I'll just leave my bag."

The maids smiled politely but they kept their eyes down. Neither spoke as one finished making his bed and the other began dusting furniture. Both were women in

their forties, dark eyes, olive skin. He suspected that they
spoke little English. The one who was dusting paused to
peel a decal from the surface of a table near the window.
The decal was in the shape of an arrow and it seemed to
be pointed at nothing in particular, just a spot on the unit's
east wall. The maid saw him looking at it. She shifted
slightly to block his view. In moving she revealed a sheet
of Players Club stationery that had been taped to the table
near the arrow. He got only a glimpse before she snatched
that up as well but he saw, written in longhand, yesterday's date followed by a series of four-digit numbers. The
numbers, he felt sure, were five times of day written out
in the military fashion.

Kessler had seen such sheets and such decals before
this but only in hotels of the Middle East countries. There,
the arrow would point in the direction of Mecca and the
sheet of five numbers would be the five times for prayer
depending on the time of sunrise. The previous occupant,
Kessler concluded, could only have been a Muslim.

Muslims, he marveled, everywhere you turn. He stayed
just long enough to wash his hands and to make sure that
he'd left his bag locked. He had more exploring to do.

Kessler walked down the hall and paused at Pratt's
room. He heard no sound but did not try the lock. That
would come later when he knew where Pratt was. The
room Pratt had chosen, away from the pool, faced only
the courts of the Van Der Meer School where dozens of
students seemed to practice all day. It seemed, to Kessler,
the least desirable of rooms. All one would hear all day
long was the whopping of tennis balls and the slapping
of sneakers on clay. What it was good for, however, was
watching those students. Pratt's interest in the students
was already clear. Kessler found Pratt himself at the Players Club bar, not the one on the outside but inside. The
Englishman was alone, and he was drinking his lunch.
Kessler waited and watched to see what he'd do next but
Pratt drank there for more than two hours.

Kessler was puzzled. He was also disappointed. Even
a drunk does not drink on a mission. Therefore, he reasoned, there is either no mission or else Pratt is simply

killing time. Once again, Pratt was dressed to play tennis and again he showed no sign of actually playing. This in itself seemed to argue for a mission. If one stays at a tennis resort, there is no better way to become almost invisible than to dress all the time for tennis.

''Sauce for the goose,'' muttered Kessler to himself.

He walked from the bar to the Van Der Meer Pro Shop, where the salesperson helped him to select a new wardrobe. He purchased a blue warm-up suit by Adidas and a racquet plus two cans of balls. He bought shoes that promised he would play like Pete Sampras and a bag for his racquet that was similar to Pratt's. Elizabeth, he thought, should have one of these. On the outside it had a pocket of canvas that could completely encase two racquets. That pocket could easily encase her Ingram, fully loaded with a thirty-round clip. She could even keep the silencer attached because it would go in the part that zips over the handle. Cyril Pratt, no doubt, had been attracted by this feature as well.

Kessler carried his purchases to his now readied room, where he changed into the warm-up suit and shoes. The pants of the suit had elastic cuffs and above them the fit was baggy. Perfect, he decided, for an ankle holster and better than a golf jacket even. He strapped on his Walther P88 and pulled the elastic cuff over it. Next he stripped all the tags from his new tennis racquet. He would carry it with him to complete the illusion. The final touch was a pair of dark glasses, aviator style, and a Velcro sun visor on his brow. Now, all but invisible, he would go and check up on the Englishman again. If Pratt showed no sign that he'd be leaving the bar soon, Kessler would test his lock-picking skills and see what he could find in Pratt's room.

But the Englishman was no longer in the bar and not at the one outside either. Kessler went to see if his car was gone but he saw him before he reached the lot. Pratt was standing up by the main lobby entrance, near the spot where he'd stood on the day before when he was holding his video camera. No camera today but again he was watching the parking lot. Kessler chose a shaded spot and waited. Twice in ten minutes he saw the Englishman look at his watch. Kessler guessed that he was waiting for those jitneys filled with children and with blacks who seemed somehow out of place.

At last one such jitney came into view but it didn't look quite like the others. It was white like the others with the same darkened windows but no Van Der Meer logo on its door. He saw two men in front—or rather their outlines—they might or might not have been black. Kessler could not tell more precisely because the sun made a glare on the windshield. This van did not stop. It entered the parking lot, turned, and went out again. He looked up at Pratt who once more checked his watch. Kessler checked his own. The time was twenty minutes after three.

Whatever this meant, Pratt was finished. He turned from the entrance and walked in the direction of his room, his key already in his hand. So much for trying his lock, thought Kessler. But now, at least, he could take another look in Pratt's car. His own was parked two spaces away. He took his own keys from his pocket and held them in his hand as he walked.

There was really no confusing Pratt's car with his own because Pratt's was so awash in debris. Candy wrappers had been added. Milky Ways, Mars Bars and a package of M&M Peanuts, now empty. The map that he'd seen, folded open to Sea Pines, was still in the rear well, more covered than ever. It had the look of a thing that was no longer needed once Pratt had found his way to the Players Club. But now he noticed that there were new maps since yesterday. They were on the console between the two front seats. The top one was a map of Beaufort County, which included this island, and it had been opened and used. The two beneath it seemed identical to the first except they were in pristine condition.

Why three? he wondered. Why three all the same? To give to others was the obvious answer, which would mean that he was working with confederates. Kessler memorized the cover of the top one. Its colors were mostly green and blue. He had a hunch that if he were to go to a drugstore and buy a copy of that map, somewhere inside, on one of the folds, he would see the same area that Pratt was studying while he sat at the bar at Reilley's. What help this would be was another question. However, one thing at a time.

"Sir? Can I help you?"

He glanced up to see two black men approaching. They were about his own age and they wore the dark coveralls he had seen on the maintenance staff. Their names were embroidered over logos on their chests. The one who spoke was named Roy.

"Not now, I think," Kessler answered. "Now I see why my key doesn't work." He looked behind him at his own white Toyota and grunted in the manner of a man who feels stupid.

"Are you a guest with us, sir?" the second man asked. This one, said his patch, was named Sam.

"I'm a guest," answered Kessler, patting his pockets. He located his room key and showed it.

"Thank you, sir," said the one named Roy. "You say this is your car over here? They do all look alike. Perhaps you'd better check to make sure."

Kessler shrugged and complied. He climbed in and started it. Now of course he had to actually drive it. "Could you tell me where I could find a drugstore?" he asked.

"Go out, turn right on Cordillo," said the man named Roy. "Turn right again on Pope. You'll see the Circle Shopping Center."

"Ah, yes. I have passed it. Thank you both."

As Kessler cut his wheels and backed out, he saw that both men had visibly relaxed. He waved and drove on. They waved in return.

This place, thought Kessler, gets more curious by the moment. First we have those drivers and chaperones. Something about them struck him as odd although he couldn't say why at the time. Now we have these two, Roy and Sam, dressed essentially as laborers and just as well-spoken as the others. Take away their coveralls, dress them in business suits, and they could be . . . what? Perhaps military? Policemen? No, he decided. Not policemen. Policemen who were posing as maintenance workers would know to stoop over a little and walk with a shuffle. They would know that a maintenance man doesn't challenge a guest and would at least pretend to show deference. They would know not to speak as if they graduated from Harvard. They might also try to sound a little bit southern, the better to blend in around here.

Kessler proceeded to the shopping center where, in the Revco drugstore, he found the map he was looking for. Opening it, checking each of its folds, he found the section which Pratt had been studying. As he'd thought, it was not on this island. It showed an area of inland waterway, sparsely populated, much of it swampland, about ten miles to the south and west. Beyond that, it told him nothing. But it was, perhaps, a piece of the puzzle.

He drove his car back to the Players Club. The original jitneys, the ones he'd seen yesterday, had returned in his absence and again disgorged children. The last ten or twelve were just walking away. This time, however, they were not dressed for tennis and most carried an assortment of shopping bags. Today's trip, he realized, must have been to the mall. One of the black chaperones, a woman, called out to them as they dispersed.

"Twenty minutes, kids," she said. "Drills start at four o'clock sharp."

Kessler scanned the immediate area, expecting to see Pratt lurking somewhere with his camera. The Englishman was nowhere in sight. Kessler didn't wish to be caught gawking either, especially by the vigilant Roy. Without breaking stride he walked up the ramp and in through the Players Club entrance. The lobby was empty except for a well-scrubbed young woman at the desk. Kessler smiled as he passed her and turned toward a dining area that was off to the right of the lobby. That area, not then in use, was actually the upper level of the Players Club bar. From there he could look down and see everyone at the bar. Several people were there watching sports on TV. The English bounty hunter was not one of them.

He stepped to the back of that second-floor room where the windows looked out on the tennis courts. Pratt, Kessler realized, would have much this same view from his room in Building 100. Kessler opened a window and looked to his right. Indeed, he could see the Englishman's terrace; it was about fifty meters away. Kessler walked down to the bar where he ordered a beer and brought it back up to a table by the window.

Students began appearing on the practice courts. They were now dressed for tennis but in outfits of every description. Most wore shorts that were anything but white and T-shirts of the kind sold in tourist shops. There were several adults directing them, dividing them into groups. One woman seemed to be in charge of the girls. She was tall and lean, built rather like Elizabeth, breasts somewhat less generous but the same erect carriage. Her hair, like Elizabeth's, was a lush reddish brown although a good deal more curly and thick. Her skin color, however, allowing for suntan, seemed closer to that of the maids. Kessler guessed her age at about forty. She carried a clipboard and she, too, wore a souvenir T-shirt. ''Unless you're the lead dog, the view never changes'' were the words inscribed across the back. He heard one of the students call her Nadia.

She formed the girls into two lines, one at either end of the court on the right, where they began some sort of round-robin drill. A girl in one line would hit to the girl at the head of the other. That girl would return it and then run on so that the girl behind her could hit next. Kessler watched them do this, barely pausing, for a full fifteen minutes. The boys were doing a similar drill. The boys had both male and female instructors. One of the men, a black man, seemed familiar. It took Kessler a minute to make the connection because the man wore dark glasses and a white floppy hat like Pratt's. It was the man from the parking lot, the one named Roy. Very curious indeed, thought Kessler. We have maintenance men who are security guards who are also now tennis instructors.

Back on the girls' court, standing near Nadia, was a second woman who seemed to be an assistant. She was shouting at the girls, calling several by name, urging this one to ''Get down ... Bend those knees,'' or saying,

"Racquet back" to that one. This woman was black as well. Kessler recognized her as the one from the jitney who called out that they had twenty minutes. It surprised him, he supposed, to see two black coaches in a sport not known for attracting black athletes. Not one of the students was black. Most, in fact, had blond hair. All were tanned, some were dark, but none black.

"Nice, Cherokee. Nice," called the woman named Nadia. "That's what I like to see."

Nadia's accent seemed vaguely European. She also had wonderful legs. But his attention was drawn more to a girl she called Cherokee. She was darker than most of the others. She could well be the Indian that her name implied. Her hair, black and lustrous, was held in place by a white terry headband with a blue egret feather stuck in it. A single long braid ran down her back and was tied at the end with a ribbon. She had answered her coach with a pump of her fist and a grin that seemed impossibly wide. Her eyes were enormous as well. She was fourteen, maybe fifteen, Kessler guessed, and he knew that one day she would be beautiful. There was a radiance to her, a joyousness to her, that few of the others displayed. The others might curse if they mis-hit a ball or sneer when they bested another. What they were doing was only a drill but they played, rather fought, as if their futures were at stake. Not so with this Cherokee. Like her coach she would even encourage the others. She could laugh at herself if she hit a poor shot but her poor shots were rare; most could not be returned.

So captivated had Kessler become that he almost forgot about Pratt. Once again he eased his head out the window until he could see Pratt's terrace. The first thing he saw was a pair of pink knees protruding through its vertical slats. Pratt's elbows were resting on top of the railing. He was holding his camera to his eye. It was pointed first at the woman named Nadia but now it swept left to the court used by the boys. His fingers could be seen working the zoom. From this angle, Kessler could not track his line with precision but he seemed to be focused on the black man named Roy. The camera was still for ten seconds perhaps before panning back to the girls. He was now, quite clearly, zooming in on the woman named Nadia. Kessler was sure of it. When Nadia appeared to glance up in his direction Pratt pulled his camera back in. But Nadia was only checking a clock.

So, Kessler wondered, who is Nadia? Could she be Pratt's quarry, a runaway Muslim? This seemed somewhat unlikely to him. He could understand women who ran off to become doctors or teachers or poets but did this one run off to be a tennis coach? Kessler would bet that in the whole history of Islam not a single Muslim woman had ever been consumed by a desire to teach tennis to the children of the rich. Her accent, in any case, was all wrong. It leaned closer to French than to Arabic. Her features could be Middle Eastern, he supposed, but one saw faces like hers all throughout southern Europe. He took another peek at Cyril Pratt's terrace. He no longer saw the bony pink knees. He leaned out further. Pratt was gone.

Kessler left his beer and walked back to the lobby. From there he could keep an eye on Pratt's car and be ready to follow if Pratt left. And as long as he was waiting, he decided, he would see what he could learn from the young lady at the desk.

He said, "I was watching the tennis . . . there's a woman called Nadia . . ."

The girl smiled. "Yup. That's her," she replied.

"Ah . . . that's who?"

"Oh. Sorry." The smile became a grin. "I thought maybe you recognized her. Our guests do that all the time."

"Nadia, I take it, is famous?"

"That's Nadia Halaby."

Kessler must have looked at her blankly.

"Nadia Halaby," the girl repeated. "She won the French and the Australian in doubles. And she made the finals at Wimbledon twice. And in singles she's three time French national champion."

"Ah, she *is* French," he exclaimed. "I was trying to place the accent."

"Well, kind of. She's Algerian by birth but Algeria used to be French."

Interesting, thought Kessler. "I noticed her assistant. Please don't think me racist but I couldn't help noticing ..."

"That she's African American? We have several on staff. The assistant was probably Jazz. She's cool."

"Jazz? What kind of name is Jazz?"

"Just a nickname. It's short for Jasmine."

Most interesting, indeed. First an Algerian, very likely a Muslim, and now a black American who has a Muslim name. "There is also a Roy. I thought he was a handyman but he coaches as well."

"Roy does a lot of things. Mostly he looks after the kids. Nadia hired all the coaches and chaperones and she pretty much runs the security system."

"Security," Kessler repeated. "A tennis coach is in charge of security?"

"Oh, not for the hotel. Just for the program. Parents send their kids here, sometimes for as long as two years. And you know how kids are when they're feeling their oats. The parents want to know that we keep them on a leash."

"Two years, you say?"

"Except when they're home for the holidays. Most also go to school here at Hilton Head High."

Kessler had other questions but he put them on hold because suddenly, outside, there was Pratt. He was standing directly in front of the door. He was looking out over the parking lot, more toward the main entrance off Cordillo. His posture suggested that he was waiting for someone. Kessler moved to a rack of tourist brochures—boat trips, factory outlets and the like—and pretended to be making a selection. No more than two minutes had passed when a woman on a bicycle turned into the lot. She wore shorts and a windbreaker much like his own and a wide-brimmed straw hat held on with a scarf. A big round pair of sunglasses covered her eyes. Although only a fraction of her face could be seen, Kessler recognized Elizabeth at once.

He had no idea what to think about this. He watched as she slowly circled the lot, his eyes darting constantly between her and Pratt. Pratt was watching her as well, but he did not seem in any way surprised or alarmed. Could Elizabeth have come here to meet him?

She circled the lot one more time. Twice now her bike went by Pratt's car—and his own that was parked there as well—but she paid no particular notice to either. Nor did she look up in Cyril Pratt's direction. He could have no doubt that she'd seen Pratt there. Pratt stood in plain sight, even framed by the entrance. Now Elizabeth steered her bike toward the path which led to the restaurants and rooms. She paused there but did not dismount. She scanned the layout of the place as he had, then turned and pedaled slowly toward the exit. Cyril Pratt, to his relief, was no longer paying the slightest attention to her. Within seconds she was out of his sight.

"*Elizabeth*," he asked, when at last he could breathe, "*what was that all about, pray tell?*"

But no answer came because even as he wondered that same unmarked jitney appeared. Pratt had seen it approach. He then looked away after glancing at his watch. He pretended, thought Kessler, not to notice it. But the jitney stopped and the driver tapped twice on his horn. Pratt tried or pretended to ignore this as well. The jitney lurched forward and again the horn bleated. Its driver, still only a silhouette to Kessler, spread his hands as if asking Pratt a question. Blood now rose to the Englishman's cheeks. He looked toward the heavens as if in despair. His right hand flicked out in a *Go away I don't know you* sort of gesture. But once more came the bleat of the horn. Pratt seemed to be fuming. He glanced left and right, and then toward the lobby but Kessler had backed out of sight.

Now Pratt gestured more urgently, angrily. The first part of it clearly said, *Go, damn you, go*. In the next he moved his hand in a circular motion. He seemed to be saying, *Keep driving in circles* or *Go away and come back* or some such. The driver, not pleased, threw up his hands. He jabbed a finger at his wristwatch as if to say, *Look at the time*. Pratt showed him a fist. It said, *Go now, or else*.

The driver stubbornly folded his arms but the man at his side was now urging him to leave. The driver turned on him angrily. Kessler saw, when he did so, that he seemed to be bearded.

Suddenly Pratt had enough of all this. He stormed down the ramp, his shoulders hunched up and both hands now in fists. The driver saw him coming. Still defiant, he revved up his engine and slammed it into gear. He seemed ready and eager to run over Pratt. But the man in there with him was slapping at his arms. The driver aimed a swipe at his passenger's head but the passenger blocked it and was shouting at him now. The Englishman had almost reached the driver's side door. Facing an imminent assault on two fronts, the driver gunned his engine and cut his wheels abruptly. His tires now screeched as he aimed for the exit. They squealed again as he sped from the grounds, nearly running down several more tourists on bikes.

Pratt stood for a moment fairly trembling with rage. At last he turned away in the direction of his room. Once there he climbed into his bottle. Kessler knew this because when he emerged two hours later, he was already weaving from too much Gleneagles.

During that time Kessler nearly called Elizabeth.

"Why were you here?" is what he would have asked. *"You can't stand not knowing, am I right?"*

"Why am I? Why are you?" would have been her reply.

"Never mind that. Just listen to what I've found out."

I know some of it's guesswork, so don't start your picking. Just shut up and listen because here's what I think.

Pratt *is* on a mission, he *does* have confederates, and I think his confederates are Muslim. He is here to kidnap a woman. The woman, I think, is one Nadia Halaby, an Algerian teacher of tennis. The plan is to drag her into a jitney that looks like a Van Der Meer jitney. They will take her to a place some ten miles off this island. What they'll do after that I don't know.

Why this woman, you ask? I don't know that either. She is hardly the typical runaway. But she and this place are certainly guarded. The guards, I suspect, are all Muslims as well and all of them happen to be black. No, the men are not bearded and the women are not covered and in fact they all seem to be Americans. Trust me, however; they're Muslims. And so, by the way, are at least some of the maids. Did I mention the arrow I saw in my room showing which way to face when you pray?

The attempt, he would have told her, might happen tonight. He'd have said this only because Pratt seemed so frantic and because there was so much activity today. The Englishman, however, had emerged from his room already three sheets to the wind. He went to his car and drove directly to Reilley's where he sat at the bar and had the fish and chips special, washed down with three more Gleneagles. He met with nobody, spoke with nobody—no, not McShane either—and was lucky to get back without being arrested. It would not be tonight after all.

His mission, all the same, had some urgency to it. True, this was only a feeling. But his team had the look of being quickly slapped together, not one that had worked as a unit before. The men in the jitney did not like taking orders. This alone offered proof that they were probably Arabs.

"Why didn't you follow them?" Elizabeth would have asked.

"Because my team is me. Who would watch Pratt if I followed the jitney?"

"But you know where Pratt lives. What you don't know is where the two others are staying. Wherever that is, that's where they'll take the woman."

He had thought of that of course. But Pratt would have seen him if he ran to his car. If he walked, they'd be too far ahead of him. Even if he did catch up to the jitney they would surely have seen him through their rearview mirror because they would have been watching for a white Toyota Camry. They would have thought it was Pratt coming after them, maybe planning to shoot them for trying to run him down.

"Or simply making sure they went home," she would have said. *"They might have decided to behave. Isn't this*

why you always rent duplicate cars? You could have fol-
lowed them almost to their doorstep, Martin. All they'd
think they were seeing, if you kept your distance, would
be Cyril Pratt's car turning back.''

There's Elizabeth for you, thought Kessler.

There's no pleasing her even in his head.

Eleven

The more that Mahfouz saw and heard of Faisal, the more he was convinced that this man was no fighter. A crazy man, maybe, and a bully for certain, but fighters took orders and maybe complained but they didn't try to run down the man who was paying them.

"No more," the raging Faisal had insisted. "Back and forth, back and forth while you stare at your watch. Ten times back and forth is enough."

"It is true that we now know the way well enough. On this I agree with you, Faisal."

"No more back and forth. No more stupid orders. Tomorrow we stay in this cabin and sleep."

Sleep? thought Mahfouz. His one time in America and he spends a day sleeping? He wanted to go to the beach tomorrow. He wanted to go there with a mattress in the jitney and buy sex from a girl with blond hair.

"Forget girls on the beach. I should not have agreed. Nine out of ten are diseased."

"But for that the clinic near my village has a powder. They don't even write down your name."

"Shut up about girls. Go make us some supper." Faisal folded his arms and turned away to show that the subject was closed. But if Faisal could be stubborn, Mahfouz could be sly.

"Pratt told me to watch out for you," Mahfouz sniffed. "Pratt told me you don't keep your word."

This led to another ten minutes of ranting. To be called

without honor by a man such as Pratt was more than even this criminal could bear. But he still insisted that they should stay here and sleep because, unsaid, he was actually fearful of Pratt and because tomorrow would surely be the night.

"As for sex with some kid, if that's all you want, you can have it with the girl while you're guarding her here."

The suggestion made Mahfouz gasp. "Sex with Aisha Bandari? How can this be allowed?"

"What difference would it make?" Faisal tossed a hand. "Bandari will probably have her sewn up; that will make her a virgin again. And don't you think Pratt will be having his fun first?"

Mahfouz was now horrified. Nothing had been mentioned of this before now. All the Englishman said was that they'll keep her tied up until just before dawn. Then they'll take her to the seaplane in the little boat outside.

"I cannot permit this," said Mahfouz, rising. "It is too great a sin."

"Oh, shut up. Go fix supper."

"Pratt must not touch the niece of Gamal Bandari. He can have all he wants of the Algerian."

"All he'll have of that whore," said Faisal, "is her head. Her head packed in ice goes back with the seaplane. The rest of her goes to the alligators."

But Faisal, as he ate his lamb shanks and hummus, was envisioning Pratt's bare white ass on that girl. The thought of it threatened to bring up his supper. Pratt's breath by itself could well gas her to death. He slowly came around to Mahfouz's way of thinking. They should none of them touch her, especially not Pratt.

"Not with so many more on the beach," Mahfouz added. "All with bodies as firm as Aisha Bandari's but with these there's no sin because they're all whores."

"I told you. Forget about the beach," snarled Faisal.

"No beach? Why no beach?"

"Because Pratt said we can't and I want to get paid. Give him an excuse and he'll cheat us."

"Pratt said we can't? What are we, his dogs? When he told us to shave off our beards, did we do it?"

"Our beards are our beards," said Faisal.

"And are we his children? He says only drive, all day back and forth, back and forth to this cabin full of bugs that are trying to eat us alive."

Faisal frowned for a moment but then only shrugged. "After this you'll have money. You can do what you want."

"After this Pratt says I must go straight back to Egypt because my papers don't permit me to stay. But you have better papers because you lived in New York. Let me go with you to New York."

Faisal started to say a definite no. But Mahfouz showed his fingers and rubbed them together, an offer that a bargain of some sort might be made. Now a slyness crept into the eyes of Faisal.

"New York is expensive," he said, leaning forward. "There is much there to cause a man's juices to flow but the thing is it wouldn't be cheap."

"I'll give you a tenth of the money I get."

"Not enough," said Faisal. "Make it half."

"Two tenths and no more," Mahfouz countered. "Don't forget I have parents in Egypt to feed."

"You can feed them with your half and give me the other."

Mahfouz looked at his wristwatch. He did so with longing. He waited for Faisal to notice.

"That watch," said Faisal. "That watch and two tenths would be fair."

"Hah! A robbery, you mean. This watch is the finest one made by the Swiss. The diamonds alone are worth half. Even Cyril Pratt wants to buy this watch. He has already made me an offer."

This had its effect. Faisal twisted his lips in a sneer. "The watch and one tenth, then, and this is a gift. It is only so that pig doesn't get it."

"The watch and one tenth. But only after you take me to New York. Plus tomorrow we go to the beach."

"Maybe the beach. But for one hour only."

"I agree to one hour. But you can't count the time I spend striking a bargain."

"Agreed," said Faisal.

"You have robbed me," said Mahfouz.

He picked up their plates and walked to the kitchen. He did this lest Faisal see his smile. Faisal knew guns and he knew how to bully but in bargaining the man was an infant. In New York, Pratt had told him, there's a place called Canal Street where the twin of this watch is sold on the sidewalks. He would find such a twin for Faisal. On Canal Street, says Pratt, it cost only ten dollars, which was why Cyril Pratt offered twenty. Pratt must think he's a fool. This watch is a Rolex, made by the Swiss. Would Bandari wear a watch that was only twenty dollars? This watch was easily worth fifty.

Twelve

It was well past noon of the second day, Friday, before Kessler understood what was different this time. What was different was that Pratt wasn't drinking.

Pratt had spent the morning on his terrace as before. He sat sipping coffee from a room service thermos, watching the students and instructors at their drills. He seemed to have no further need of his camcorder.

When the students took their lunch break so did he. Pratt took a table at the outdoor restaurant where he pretended to study a book about tennis. He ordered more coffee. No Gleneagles, no beer, not even a Bloody Mary. Another thing different was the bulge in his pocket. Kessler thought at first that it might be a weapon, but then realized it was his cellular phone. It rang as the waitress set a salad plate before him. A salad, for this man, was different as well.

Pratt rose from his chair with the phone at his ear and turned his back to the neighboring tables. He nodded his head as he listened. Abruptly he returned to his table and opened his book about tennis. Tucked inside, Kessler saw, was the blue and green map of the place that was not on this island. He opened the map to a different fold and traced a finger over one section. The finger stopped and he nodded again. He spoke a few words of acknowledgment as he marked the spot with a pen. It was clear from Pratt's manner that he was receiving instructions. But from where Kessler stood, the place that he marked seemed not to be on dry land. It seemed like the middle of a river or sound. Kessler memorized the look of that fold.

Pratt broke the connection and dialed again. He paced and snapped his fingers as it rang. At last someone answered. Now it was Pratt who was giving instructions, but he seemed to be getting an argument. It didn't take much for Pratt's color to rise, his skin was so pasty and pale. Kessler saw that it was rising again now. He was hissing at whoever had answered. It was Kessler's hunch that the voice on the other end could belong only to the driver of that jitney. The one who had wanted to run Pratt down. The one with the short Muslim beard.

The lunch break ended at half past one. The students were filing back toward the courts. Kessler heard some of them talking as they passed. One girl asked another if she wanted to go play some miniature golf. The other said no, she was going Rollerblading instead. She asked still another. She said, "Cherokee? Wanna go?"

"Not today," came the answer. "I think that I'm going to ride my bike to the beach."

Pretty girl, Kessler noted as he had the day before. Her voice was a regular teenager's voice but her diction seemed unusually precise. He didn't know why that surprised him a little. Did he think that all Indians sounded like Tonto?

From the way all the students were talking, thought Kessler, this was to be a short day. But it was Friday, he realized. Soon the students would be off to do what teenagers do, which meant their instructors would have free time as well. He wondered how Nadia spent her free time. Did she stay pretty close to her Roys and her Sams? Or did she get careless? Cyril Pratt, he suspected, knew the answer to that question already.

The drills lasted two hours more. At the end of that time the students were gathered and Nadia read several announcements. Most had to do with the weekend's activities, a special exhibition of some sort that evening and a tour of historic Savannah on Sunday. They ended with a reminder that those having dinner elsewhere on the island were bound by a nine o'clock curfew. The announcements concluded and the students dispersed. Kessler kept one eye on Pratt who had once again pulled out his phone. He tapped out a number and waited.

No answer, it seemed. Again he dialed and again he waited. Again there seemed no answer. And once more his color was rising. He stood for a moment, slowly shaking his head, angry lips revealing his teeth. At last, with a curse, he snapped the phone shut and stormed off in the direction of the parking lot. Kessler followed but kept to a distance.

Without looking back, Pratt started his car and drove out through the Players Club entrance. But now he turned right, not left to Cordillo. To the right was only the road to the beach. Kessler was reluctant to follow him now; there was not enough traffic that way. But Pratt's mind, he hoped, would be on where he was headed and not on who might be behind him. Kessler followed in his own white Toyota.

Down the road was a circle, called Coligny Circle. To the right was a Holiday Inn. To the left was parking for the public beach. Pratt's car pulled into that parking lot. He found the nearest place and stopped. He opened his door and stood up on his runner in order to give himself height. He was scanning the hundreds of cars and RVs when Pratt's head jerked to a sudden stop and he banged an angry fist against his roof. Kessler followed his eyes. He was not much surprised where they settled. The jitney was parked four rows over.

Kessler quickly found a space of his own. Pratt in the meanwhile had walked to the jitney and was peering through the darkened glass windows. Whatever he saw in the rear of that vehicle made him throw up his hands in despair. Kessler had no time to see what it was because Pratt was now headed across to the beach. Again, Kessler followed at a distance.

The beach was quite crowded for this time of year because the temperature had reached the low seventies. Of those sunning themselves, a few were adults but most were young people in their teens. Only the hardiest had entered the water which had not yet been warmed by the flow from the tropics. Kessler heard a burst of laughter from his right. He traced it to a group partly blocked by a dune. From the sound they all seemed to be girls. Pratt heard it as well but had trouble locating it because he'd been scanning the beach to his left. One hand had formed a visor at his brow. Kessler shifted his position out of Pratt's line of sight but where he now had the source of the laughter in view.

There on a blanket were four young girls, the oldest no more than sixteen. All four of their faces looked up at two men who were standing with their backs turned to Kessler. They were dressed in dark slacks, white shirts and street shoes. Kessler knew at once who these two men were and that one or both men had short beards. The girls looking up at them had a range of expressions from stunned disbelief to high humor but none showed any real sign of alarm. The four huddled briefly then burst into laughter. The taller of the two men was already fidgeting. He reached for the arm of the other and began to try to pull him away from the blanket.

All at once, there was Pratt. He came stomping through the sand as he shouted a name. It sounded like ''Fooz,'' or perhaps he called them ''fools.'' Now the big one was dragging the other in earnest, but Pratt moved to cut off their retreat. He lurched through some flotsam at the line of high tide and tripped on a tangle of seaweed. This allowed the two men to gain a few steps but it added all the more to Pratt's fury. Kessler wanted to watch this and to hear what he could but he saw no good place of concealment. It was best, he decided, to get back where they parked and where he could be ready to follow. He retreated to the edge of the Holiday Inn and picked out a line to his car. Just then, in Pratt's voice, he heard the word ''Shit!!''

Kessler glanced back. Pratt had caught the two men and had each by the neck. Only the bigger one struggled, and only until Pratt said something in his ear. At that the two bearded men tensed. They stood as if frozen and all three were averting their faces. Kessler's first thought was that maybe they'd spotted him but now he could see what had alarmed them. Coming in from the road was the tennis school student named Cherokee. She had changed her clothing. She wore cut-off jeans over a blue one-piece swimsuit and a wide straw hat of the cowboy variety with a cluster of those same blue feathers in the band. The Englishman must have feared that his whites would draw her eye, that she might remember seeing him at the club, that she might wonder who the two bearded men could be and might mention to someone that she'd seen them. But the girl never looked in their direction. She pedaled on past them and stopped at a rack where she paused to lock up her bike.

For Kessler, this was a good time to leave. He crossed Forest Beach Drive to the parking lot where he entered his car and sat low. He adjusted his mirror and watched as the three men approached. Cyril Pratt was practically frothing. Of the two bearded men, the smaller one cowered visibly while the bigger one first tried some bluster of his own but ended up blaming the one known as Fooz. The big one's English was heavily accented but Kessler felt sure that he'd heard the word "mattress." And indeed he had because Pratt now repeated it and once again began frothing.

"*That's* what that's for?" he shouted at the big one. "You let him bring a fucking mattress along? You could have cost me a million fucking dollars, you ass. It's a wonder they didn't call the police. If they did the cops would have clubbed your cocks flat if you'd waved them in front of those girls."

To Kessler this was an interesting image but the mention of a million was what held his attention. This was the same bounty that was offered for Elizabeth, yet Elizabeth was clearly not the object of his visit. Could Nadia Halaby be worth a million dollars? If so, why and to whom? He would have to find out but the question at hand was whom to follow. In his mind he urged Pratt to go back to the Players Club. Give these two a kick in the ass if you like but then send them packing and quickly. I want to see where on that map they end up and I bet it's that cabin I saw pictured in your car.

Except for the kick, Pratt did as he hoped. On exhausting his supply of invective, Pratt pulled out his phone and held it so both men could see it. Kessler could not hear all the words but he had little doubt of their meaning. Pratt was saying that he would be calling them often to be sure that they stayed where they should. One more stunt like this and they're finished, he said.

The jitney pulled out onto Forest Beach Drive and turned toward Coligny Circle. Pratt walked to his own car still fuming. He reached for his key but he hesitated. He looked once in the direction the jitney had taken and then turned and walked back toward the beach. Damage control, surmised Kessler. Pratt would now go and talk to those girls on the beach. He would tell them, most likely, that he was just passing by when he saw those two tourists annoying them. He would say that he's now going to call the police so no action on their part is necessary.

Kessler could not wait until Pratt reached the dunes before pulling out after the jitney. He could not risk a high-speed chase to catch up. But catch up he must if he wanted to know where they intended to take Nadia Halaby.

Elizabeth, as usual, was right, he reflected. They would see this car following. They would lead him straight to their door. Kessler wished that he'd thought to buy a white floppy tennis hat. They'll be watching for a white floppy hat.

Thirteen

She was on her screened porch enjoying the sunset when her kitchen telephone rang. She would have bet half her diamonds that the caller would be Martin.

"You're still on the island, aren't you," said Elizabeth at the sound of his voice. It was more an accusation than a question.

"Not exactly," he answered. "But I need to come see you."

"Is this your idea of giving me time?"

"Nag me later, my darling. There are things you should know. And don't be alarmed when a white Toyota Camry pulls into your driveway. That's not Cyril Pratt. That's me."

"License BVT228?" she asked dryly. "Your left rear tire needs air."

"Cute, Elizabeth. You want to be cute? Your bike chain could also use oil."

That had always been one of their problems, thought Elizabeth. They knew each other too well. There was no use in saying that she didn't want to hear it. He knew that she needed to know what he was up to and whether it affected her life here. If it didn't involve her he knew that she'd say, "This is interesting, Martin, but it's none of my business so get off this island right now." And therefore she was not going to say it.

He knew that she'd say, "Make it quick and then go."

So therefore she would fix him some dinner.

He smelled veal chops cooking when he entered her home. He saw that her table had been set for two. He asked, "Is this where you say, 'Don't count on dessert because you won't be staying that long'?"

"Just shut up and open the wine," she told him.

She listened without speaking as he told her what he'd seen. Pratt with his camera, the two men with beards, the cabin where the two men were staying. He had followed them nearly all the way there. He broke off when they turned down a rural dirt road. He then hid the Camry and went in on foot.

"You went skulking through the woods in a warm-up suit and sneakers?"

"Let's talk about fashion some other time."

"If they thought you were Pratt who had followed them home, what happens if they mention it to Pratt?"

"Also save your critique until I'm finished," he told her.

He said he spotted the jitney a quarter mile in and scouted as close as he dared. In the back was all swamp with just one narrow channel that led to open water farther out. A boat was tied up to a small wooden dock. It was sitting in the mud of low tide.

"And you think they're here to snatch Nadia Halaby?"

"For a million-dollar bounty. I'm sure of it."

"But she's not in hiding. She hardly sounds like a runaway wife. All she is, is a tennis instructor."

"Just as all you are is a widow who plays golf?"

He told her of the guards who pretended they weren't guards, all of whom for some reason were black. He told of chambermaids who dressed very modestly like nineteenth-century nurses. He told her of the prayer arrow he saw in his room, used by the last guest who was also a woman. Elizabeth kept her eyes on the floor of her kitchen.

"So what's going on there?" she asked quietly. "Do you know?"

"You would know better than me," he answered.

"Martin . . . the Van Der Meer School is very well

known. I think there are branches in Europe as well. Are you trying to tell me it's all just a front?''

"Not a front. It's legitimate. But there's a sideline, perhaps."

"You . . . think it's a safe house of some sort, don't you."

"I think all I've seen is not just to protect Halaby. I think maids dress like nurses because they can't walk around in traditional . . . what is that called, again? What Muslim women wear?''

"You mean long skirts and head scarves? Hijab."

"And I think all the blacks are American Muslims who have learned in northern cities how to handle themselves. I think that they do, for scared Muslim women, what your two Muslim friends did for you."

She still had not met his eyes. "Martin . . . I will not get involved in this."

"Who's saying you should? I just thought you should know."

"And you won't go near Pratt. Will you give me your word?''

"If you wish. But after you've slept on it."

"Martin . . . damn it . . . that won't make any difference. What did you expect me to say?''

"I expected you to say this is none of your business. You won't mean it but that's what you'll say."

"You can go to hell, Martin."

"Do I still get my veal chop?''

"I cooked it. You'll eat it. But you're right about dessert.''

She served Kessler first then filled her own plate. She sat, staring thoughtfully, not touching her food. She got up abruptly and went back to the kitchen. She returned with a newspaper, *The Island Packet*, which she opened to the editorial page.

"If you're looking at tide tables, I've already checked them," said Kessler between sips of wine.

"The boat was on mud. When was that? About five?''

He nodded. "High tide is about two hours from now. The next one is ten tomorrow morning."

"And that call Pratt took on his cellular phone. You think it was to set up a rendezvous point?"

"With a bigger boat probably. Maybe even a seaplane."

"Two hours is too soon. They'd need to have taken her already."

"They haven't. I checked that as well. Right now she's playing in an exhibition match that won't be over until nine. After that, there will be a reception."

"A fugitive who goes to receptions," mused Elizabeth.

"I know," agreed Kessler. "It seems very foolish. Next thing you know she'll put her name on her mailbox."

Elizabeth chose to ignore this last. "They won't try her tonight, not with so many people. Do you know what her habits are in the morning? Does she, for example, go jogging on the beach?"

Kessler had no idea. He could only point out that no one set up a rendezvous unless the time to use it was at hand.

Elizabeth studied him. "Martin . . . why haven't you warned her? Why didn't you call her and tell her about Pratt?"

"Without consulting you first? It's your island, Elizabeth."

That was not the reason and she knew it. He could have warned the Algerian and gone on his way. But if he had, coming here would not have been necessary. Martin, she felt sure, wanted more than a veal chop out of this. He even wanted more than to bed her again, to make her want to keep him occupied again. What he wanted was the game. And he wanted her to play on his team.

"I'll warn her myself," said Elizabeth abruptly.

"An anonymous phone call from here?" he protested. "What if she has Caller ID? And even if she doesn't you'll only upset her. Instead, why don't we drive out to

that cabin. We can ask those two Muslims what Pratt is . . .''

"Don't even dream of it," Elizabeth scolded. "And a hotel's front desk won't have Caller ID."

Once again she stood up and went into the kitchen. She consulted a pad on the wall by her phone and tapped out a number. Kessler noted with interest that she had written it down before this. The phone rang several times before the desk of the Players Club answered.

"I need to leave a message for Nadia Halaby," said Elizabeth to the clerk. "I believe she's playing in an exhibition right now but it's urgent that she gets it right away."

The reply caused Elizabeth to frown.

"Canceled? Then where is she now, do you know?"

The frown deepened.

"No . . . thank you . . . never mind. I'll call later."

Slowly, reluctantly, she placed the wall phone back in its mount. She turned to the entrance to the dining room. Her eyes were strangely distant. Kessler asked her what's wrong.

"A girl . . . she's fourteen . . . is missing. The adults are out trying to find her."

Kessler narrowed his eyes. "A diversion, perhaps? Or simply a kid who lost track of the time." But before she could answer his expression turned pained and he slapped the side of his head.

"I've been very stupid," he told her.

"A girl?" asked Elizabeth. "Pratt's come for a teenage girl?"

Kessler threw down his napkin and rose to his feet.

"Answer me, Martin," she said, her voice husky. "Are there young Muslim girls in that school?"

"There is one who could be." He reached for his car keys. "Thank you for dinner, Elizabeth."

"Give me a minute. Don't go."

She turned toward her bedroom, removing her bracelets and earrings as she walked. She was back in what seemed only seconds. In one hand she carried a pair of soft boots. The other hand held her blue duffel.

"Are you armed?" she asked him.

"The Walther." He gestured toward his ankle.

"You'll drive," said Elizabeth, slipping out of her dress. "I want you to show me that cabin."

Fourteen

It was two in the morning, Cairo time, when the phone woke Bandari from a terrible dream.

In the dream he was in his office at the Ministry of Development and the Libyans had come because they'd run out of patience. They picked up stones from a pile on his desk—a pile that he'd never noticed there before—and began smashing his face but not too hard yet because they wanted the money they'd already advanced him. He screamed, "Tarrant used it. It's already been spent. If only you'll give me just a few more days . . ."

This made them beat him all the more.

Standing and watching from behind them was Leyna and standing next to Leyna was Pratt. Pratt was taping all this with his video camera. Leyna was ignoring what the Libyans were doing because she seemed to have eyes for no one but Pratt. Her face was all healed and more beautiful than ever but what she was doing was disgusting. She was reaching inside the Englishman's pants and was rubbing her breasts against his arm. This horrified Bandari even more than the Libyans who by then had decided to cut off his hand. He was begging the Libyans, "Give me time, give me time," and he called out to Leyna to help him. "No more time, no more time," was the Libyans' response. Pratt and Leyna took up the same chant. The chant blended into the ringing of his phone, which he groped for and knocked to the floor.

"Bandari?" It was Tarrant. "The girl has been taken."

He heard these words through a Valium haze and was afraid that he might still be dreaming.

"Did you hear me, Bandari? Pratt has your niece. My man, Loomis, will pick her up in a seaplane. You will have her by sunset tomorrow."

Bandari's heart soared. He could scarcely believe it. Tarrant added details that whirled in his mind. An island called Hilton Head, near to Savannah, something else about a center for tennis. "There's no harm in telling you now where she was. It's a place run by Muslims and very well guarded but Pratt seems to have snatched her from under their noses."

A thought stabbed Bandari. "You won't let Pratt . . . touch her."

"Pratt won't be a problem. Forget him."

But Bandari was still seeing the Pratt from his dream and the things he was doing with Leyna. "How soon will this Loomis come and take her from him?"

"At first light. Bandari . . . shut up and listen. I'm calling you now from my plane. I'm on my way home to take care of some business. This plane will bring the girl back to Cairo. I'll be back myself on Tuesday at the latest. By the time I get there you damned well better know when our friends can expect their shipment."

Bandari could see these friends in his mind. Some had no faces because they were the bankers whom Tarrant had never allowed him to meet. The others were the Libyans who had come in his nightmare. They were getting ready to cut off his hand while Leyna stood playing with Cyril Pratt's cock. Leyna, alive, would never do such a thing. She would throw up at even the thought of it. Leyna's ghost in his dream was behaving this way in order to drive him insane.

"Well?" snapped Tarrant. "What may I tell them? For your sake don't let it be more than one week."

"You can tell them five days." His voice was now strong. "Tell them *they* should be sure that they're ready to pay."

"Make it a week to be safe. I'm going to ask them to

transfer the funds. You'll deliver as soon as I have confirmed that the balance is in my account.''

"One week is next Saturday," Bandari said boldly. "Bring me Aisha tomorrow and I guarantee Saturday."

Bandari wanted to dance through his house. He wanted to wake up the servants. He wanted to tell them he was going to be rich with his share of twenty-five million dollars. Even more important than that was the part of the shipment that he'd hidden away for himself. It could make him one day even richer than Tarrant. It could make him the biggest man in Egypt.

In forty-eight hours plus a few more at most, he and Aisha would stand in front of a judge who had already been given a generous gift. The adoption papers would be signed in five minutes. At a stroke all that Avram had owned would be his, most of all one sealed warehouse on a dock at Suez. This judge would not say, as the last one had said, "Come back when you can show me that your brother's will was forged and that you are his true heir by right." And the Libyans would not say what he knew they must have thought when Leyna slapped his face at the funeral. It's a pity he couldn't show them her last moments on earth. It's a pity he couldn't show at least parts of the tape because Pratt had already erased it.

He has done so much for the Libyans already, one would think they would have known that they could count on him. They have hundreds of millions, thanks to him more than Tarrant, now safely invested in Red Sea resorts and in hundreds of gas stations all over Europe. All this was money the West would have seized as part of their sanctions for Lockerbie. Yet to hear them talk, all this was nothing compared to what sat in that one container in a warehouse that Avram hadn't visited in months.

What made Avram go there on that day of all days, Gamal couldn't even imagine. But it wasn't bad luck that made Avram curious, it was more the stupidity of the former Russian army major who shipped it from the former Republic of Ukraine. "Machine Parts for Tractors" is how it was labeled. "A Gift From the Children of Muslim Ukraine to Their Brothers and Sisters in Egypt.''

The warehouse foreman had called Avram and said, ''This consignment here in your brother's name . . . since when has Ukraine become Muslim Ukraine? And do children give gifts of machine parts for tractors?'' But worse, far worse, than that ridiculous ruse were the safety instructions that the foreman had found inadvertently taped to one drum. The instructions were in Russian but the symbol for hazardous materials was not. And the instructions came complete with illustrations on the dangers of radiation poisoning and the kind of protective clothing to be worn.

Even with that Avram needn't have died. He could have just said, ''Get it out of here now, I don't want to know what is in it.'' But instead he got righteous and asked too many questions. He asked by what right this was stored in his warehouse and what stupid scheme was his brother up to now. You don't talk that way to your older brother who by right is the head of the family. You don't start giving him the third degree, and then when he swears that it's for doing God's work, you don't call him a fool and a hypocrite. And on top, Avram lectured him. He cited the Koran.

He said, ''It is written . . . 'Do not make God, when you swear by him, a means to prevent you from dealing justly and from making peace among men.'''

He said, ''Gamal, you'd do well to remember these words. God will surely, one day, remind you of them as he kicks your dumb ass down to hell.''

Some nerve Avram had quoting from the Koran. This is one of the verses he cited all the time when he was asked why he shakes hands with Jews. Bandari could have told him what was also in that book and even on the very same page. It said, ''You shall not wed pagan women or idolaters unless they embrace the faith.'' Are Maronite Christians idolaters or not, with all their little crosses and statues? Who, he could have asked, is the hypocrite here?

The Book said much more that Avram chose to ignore although Bandari didn't know about his will at the time. It said all those who die leaving any kind of wealth should distribute it equitably to kindred. Did Avram do this? It says that a male got twice as much as a female. To this, did Avram pay the slightest attention? Even their parents had tried to teach Avram that a younger brother should remember his place and not be so much better at school. And at games. And at catching the eye of the prettiest girls.

Seeing this, they tried to arrange a good marriage for Avram. They found him a nice quiet girl of good family who had never read a book that was not about religion. Avram wasn't so interested but he ruined her anyway by teaching her to drive his car. Then even their parents changed their tune when Avram started to make lots of money building houses, not only for the rich but for the poor. Everybody said what fine parents they must be to have such a wonderful, hardworking son. And how dutiful he was to secure for his brother a nice steady job in the Ministry of Development. And how fair he was in his dealings with Christians, even though he was a little too fair with the Jews.

On top of all this there was Leyna. Gamal would have given anything he owned to have Leyna look at him . . . even just once . . . in the way she looked at Avram all the time.

It is true, God forgive him, that he always hated Avram. But even on the darkest nights of his torment, knowing that his brother was lying with Leyna, he might in truth have wished Avram dead but God knows he would never have killed him. Tarrant knew that as well. And so Tarrant had it done. This was after Avram padlocked the warehouse and put guards there until he could arrange to dispose of the container. He was going to have it loaded onto a boat and dump it in the Red Sea a thousand meters deep.

"You'll recall," said Tarrant in that icy way of his, "that our friends have certain interests in that area."

"This is a time to talk about resorts? What has one thing to do with the other?"

"And you recall, of course, the World Trade Center bombing? If those fools had added to their fertilizer bomb a fraction of what's in just one of those drums, do you understand what would have happened?''

"The whole building comes down?''

"The whole financial area of New York City—one square mile of the most valuable real estate on earth—would have been uninhabitable for the next hundred years.''

At this, Bandari whistled. At last it was clear why the Libyans were so eager to get what the former Russian major was selling. The drums contained radioactive cobalt-60 and iodine-131. But even these were not the real prize because they could have been acquired elsewhere and because they needed a bomb to disperse them. The real prize was in a single lead-lined case the size of a child's coffin. Inside were eight warheads for artillery shells, but not the actual shells. He had known that the warheads were nuclear warheads but at first he had wondered what use they could be because Tarrant had said they had no arming device and couldn't make a nuclear explosion.

But they could, Tarrant told him, be made to contaminate. It was a simple two-stage thermonuclear device in enhanced radiation warheads. The radiation, once released, would go through every building within a half mile and down into subways and tunnels. The cobalt and the iodine enhance the effect. The combination also created a bomb "signature" that couldn't so easily be traced back to Russia. Each warhead meant a city that would become like Chernobyl. They would have to be abandoned for decades to come.

But there wouldn't be eight. There would only be six. Bandari would keep two, hidden and safe, against the day when the radicals came to power. He would show them how to keep the West at bay when the West made its threat to send armies to crush them. They would say to the West, "You should read the Koran so you know who you're dealing with. You should read where it commands us on pain of sin to 'Make wide slaughter in the land of the infidel.' But if you don't bother us, we won't bother you so don't make us teach you a lesson." For this, the radicals would be grateful indeed.

It was lucky he took the two when he did. Avram had guessed that he'd try to get them out before Avram could bury the whole lot at sea. And so on the day before he was killed he had his workers stack hundreds of cement bags on top of the container and wet the whole thing down with sea water. Bandari thought it better not to tell Tarrant and certainly not to tell the Libyans. They would sneer at him, say his brother outsmarted him, and call him a fool for not renting a storage place of his own. But try to find such a place in all of Cairo where thieves didn't break in the moment you left or where soldiers with their hands out didn't start sniffing around. They'd get their shipment, just a little bit wet—although it might take a day or two of chipping at cement. But first, however, there was Aisha.

He might treat her decently when all was said and done, unless she'd been totally ruined. She might now be a beauty. She already had her mother's eyes and would soon have a body like Leyna's as well. Perhaps he wouldn't find her a husband after all.

Fifteen

When Nadia Halaby learned that Cherokee was missing she was more annoyed than alarmed. It was not the first time that a student had missed curfew.

Because they were teens and because none had a car, there were only so many places they could go. The first place she'd look was usually the beach and that, after all, was where Cherokee had said she was going. A few hours at the beach often led to new friends who by evening were reluctant to part. Well after sunset they'd be sitting on their blankets and someone might be playing a guitar. They'd have gotten a pizza from Coligny Plaza and, when the sun went down, they would often sneak a dip in the Holiday Inn's heated pool.

Nadia found Cherokee's bike right away. It was parked in a rack with a half dozen others. She knew it by its green canvas saddle bags on which Aisha had stitched the name "Cherokee Blye." Greatly relieved, she rehearsed in her mind the severe reprimand that the girl now called Cherokee had coming. Never mind that she'd never missed curfew before.

But the girl was nowhere in sight.

Nadia still, at this point, was not frightened for her. She would probably find Cherokee just a block or so away in Coligny Plaza itself. The plaza was a sort of open-air mall with dozens of shops, bars, and restaurants and one movie theater, all catering largely to tourists and teens. Its centerpiece was a flood-lit lagoon with a large restaurant terrace abutting one side and tree-shaded walkways lining the other. Teens went there to meet other teens at the places selling burgers or ice cream or pizza. Or they sat on the grass feeding popcorn to the ducks and geese that roamed freely and begged at the tables.

She wandered through Coligny for nearly an hour. Twice she called the center on her cellular phone to suggest other places where the male guards might look. Two of them were already walking the beach for a mile in either direction. Nadia would stay a while longer, she said, at least until the movie at the Island Theater ended. Perhaps Cherokee was in there. More than one student had gone to a movie and had fallen asleep after a hard day of practice. Nadia, on second thought, chose not to wait. She got the manager to take her inside with a flashlight. Cherokee was not in there either.

First time or not, this was now unforgivable. She tried to control her rising concern lest concern give way to panic. What would she do if the girl had been taken? How could she live with herself if that happened? She knew that she should have kept a tight rein on Cherokee but that would have only caused the girl to ask why. She almost wished now that she'd told her the truth. That, no, she was not at all like the others. That her father had been murdered four weeks ago in Cairo and that her mother should have been here two days ago. That now more than ever she should not leave the grounds without an escort of at least one armed guard.

She had justified not telling her because Cherokee could never have kept it to herself. She'd made too many friends among the other boys and girls. They would know that something was terribly wrong. Cherokee would surely confide to at least one of them. In doing so she'd have told her real name. And why she was here. And why, by extension, those other six women were here. The ones who were assistant tennis instructors but who seemed to know little about tennis. Grown women who cleaned rooms but who looked and behaved as if they'd had servants themselves all their lives. Women who vanished at odd hours of the day as they looked for a quiet place to pray. But these had been secondary reasons for not telling her. She simply could not bear to break that sweet young girl's heart.

The chirp of her phone caused her stomach to flip. She clawed it from her purse and answered.

"Nadia, it's Jazz," said the female voice. "We know where she is. She's shook up but okay."

"Well, where, for God's sake. And what happened?"

"She was leaving the beach. She had trouble unlocking her bike. Two kids in a pickup gave her a ride but then they tried to get into her pants. One of them held her down on the floor and drove her way the hell off the island. They took her to some ratty old trailer, broke in, and then started to rip off her clothes. She kicked one in the nuts and ran into the woods. She hid there until they quit looking and left. She made it back to the road and walked to a farmhouse half naked. That's where she is now. The farmers, some old cracker and his wife, wanted to call the cops. I asked them not to do that; it would only shame her more."

"Did you talk to her? How is she?"

"She was in this man's bathroom when he called. His name is Floyd Wiggins. Wiggins's wife was in there with her, trying to clean up her cuts and find her something to wear. She's hurting, Nadia. I could hear her crying in the background."

"Is he going to bring her back here?"

"Wiggins says he would but she's afraid to get into another car. He says she asked him to tell you how sorry she is and please don't be mad at her but she asks if you'll drive out and get her."

"What's the address? I'll leave now."

"You still at Coligny? I can pick you up there and go with you."

"No, you call him and tell him I'm coming, then bring all the others back in. How do I find this farmhouse?"

"Man gave me directions. You writing this down? It's way past Bluffton on Route 46 but you can be there in about thirty minutes."

Nadia Halaby groped for a pen.

*   *   *

On the day when Pratt rented the fishing shack he scouted the Wiggins farm as well. The house had stood empty for almost a year with a real estate firm's sign in front. Floyd and Sarah Wiggins had moved up to Richmond to be near their only daughter and her children. They left the house sparsely but adequately furnished at the urging of the listing agent. A local charity was permitted to farm it in return for a promise to keep up the grounds. All Pratt would need do to make it seem occupied would be to remove the real estate sign. When the time came to use it he would simply break in and turn on a few lights and a radio.

He knew that his plan to lure the Algerian could go wrong in no end of ways. But if he could get her to come by herself, or even with one other person to drive her, he would have her the moment she knocked on the door. They would leave her car, with most of her in it, under a few tons of straw in the barn. Months might go by before anyone found it. A companion, if any, would also be left headless just in case there's a price on the companion. If it went wrong this time round then so be it. It was too sweetly simple not to give it a try. If she showed up in force or if she sent the police—an option that he very much doubted she'd choose—he would take her the next day, or else the next week. But take her he would in the end. With the million she'd fetch he might even decide to settle down as a gentleman farmer himself.

The shack where he now held Bandari's niece was a bare quarter mile from the farm. Taking her had gone smoothly, a plan just as sweet, with the added advantage that she was not on her guard. It was simply a matter of jamming her bike lock and being on hand when she struggled to open it. Faisal tapped his horn and she turned to see a jitney that looked just like one from the center. That was all that was needed to make her come running. Far from suspicious, she had actually smiled upon seeing the face of the pleasant old Brit who'd been watching her play these past days.

She was inside the door and saying hello when she

realized that a man she'd never seen before was driving. Her eyes had just focused on Faisal's scruffy beard, and the truth began to dawn on her that something was wrong, when he, Cyril Pratt, knocked her senseless with a sack filled with sand. He had hog-tied and gagged her. He had to stun her once more when she woke near the bridge and had freed one leg and tried to kick out a window. The next thing she knew she was inside the shack handcuffed to the post of a bunk bed. She woke up to see that same pleasant old Brit setting up his camcorder and tripod.

He had plenty of footage of Aisha playing tennis. Her arms, head and legs were all immodestly bare. He had footage of Aisha at the pool with her friends. Her suit was more modest than many of theirs but utterly lewd by the standards of the people who'd be viewing the tape. He had footage of her leaving the Van Der Meer jitney in the company of godless American children, one of whom, a boy, had put an arm around her shoulder, an intimacy that in itself would serve as proof of her ruin.

It would all make a very nice video indeed. On second thought he would edit out the boy because he also had a sequence in which Aisha was holding the hand of a girl. The sequence was brief, not more than two seconds, but freeze-framed he could use it to damning effect. It would serve as more evidence that the Halaby bitch ran a place that turned good Muslim girls into lesbians.

But now it was time to tape the finale for which he would need a few props. He reached into his bag and pulled out a folder in which he had a number of eight-by-ten photographs. One was of Aisha at the age of six, dressed in her first little veil and abaya, a red one, a gift from her Uncle Gamal. The effect was not as sober as he would have liked—she looked like a girl having fun playing dress-up—but the photo would do to show how far she'd fallen. The next was of Aisha at about thirteen. In this one she was dressed in a cowboy hat and jeans and no trace of piety or virtue remained. She looked into the camera, her eyes bold and bright, with a grin that was nearly as wide as her face.

The third was of Gamal Bandari himself holding Aisha,

then an infant, in his arms. Avram and Leyna stood at his side clearly wishing that they could be elsewhere. It was the standard sort of photo in which the head of the family shows off the latest addition. Bandari's expression was self-important as usual but the arch of his brow also managed to convey a sort of unspoken apology. The addition, after all, was only a female. "Next time," his expression seemed to be saying, "my brother will try to do better."

Pratt could imagine what else he was thinking. "My brother, after all, is not a man such as I. If Leyna were mine I would have made two strong sons in the time that my brother made only one daughter."

Pratt pinned each of these photos to the side board of the upper bunk. He would pan them in close-up and then zoom slowly back to reveal the lower bunk where Aisha was lying in a fetal position. But she had turned away from the light he'd set up and her body was shaking with fear. He needed her facing the camera. He needed her gathered up close to the headboard so that he could squeeze into the frame alongside her. And he needed the duct tape removed from her mouth.

Pratt checked through the lens and made some adjustments. He then pressed a button and left it to record automatically.

"Turn this way, young lady. Look, look, watch the birdie."

That only made her press her face down more deeply. See? That's what you get when you try to be friendly. He stepped to the bunk and seized her long braid. With his free hand he felt for one end of the duct tape and peeled it very slowly from her skin. She squealed and she kicked as he did so.

"Stop complaining," he told her, enjoying her pain. "You should see what nice color it brings to your cheeks."

She tried to twist and bite his hand. He gave a few more yanks on her braid. Too much spirit, he realized, could send the wrong message. So he reached for his sand sock and aimed a measured blow at a spot just behind her right ear. The girl stiffened as if shot, then went limp.

Still holding her hair, he reached over her body and turned it so it now faced the camera. He lowered himself to one knee alongside her and turned his own face to the lens and the microphone.

"I am the one called the Englishman," he said. "This is the lesbian, Aisha Bandari. She is the daughter of the adulteress, Leyna Bandari. Her father was a good man, Avram Bandari, but his slut of a wife had him murdered. The slut has now answered to God."

At this the girl's eyes began blinking back to life as if the reference to her parents had cut through the fog. But the eyes were still dazed and unfocused. Pratt gripped her hair tighter and forced her to look at the camera.

"With sadness I tell you that this girl has been ruined. In this place where she thought she could hide from God, many boys have defiled her as well. But as God is compassionate, as God is all merciful, how can her uncle be less? You all know her uncle and all should respect him. He is the honorable Gamal Bandari. It is Gamal who has sent me to find this girl. It is Gamal who, God willing, will cleanse her of the sins that have so polluted her soul."

Pratt glanced at his watch. He was pleased with himself. The scene had been done in one take. It would be twenty minutes, at the very least, before the Halaby woman could possibly find that farmhouse. He and Faisal would be there to meet her. Mahfouz would stay here to watch over the girl.

Outside, Elizabeth was only a shadow. Kessler watched as she made her way to the cabin, silent as the breeze that blew in from the swamp. At times he couldn't see her at all.

He had taken a position from which he could cover the front and left sides of the cabin. Elizabeth had already located the jitney. They had driven it into a juniper forest until its outline could barely be seen. But the white Toyota had been left out in front as if it would soon be needed. The two bearded men waited near it.

Of the two, one was definitely armed and on guard

although his manner was less than alert. He sat leaning on the fender of the Englishman's Toyota, a cigarette glowing at his lips. Slung from his shoulder but carelessly worn was a small and clunky automatic weapon that looked like an old Czech Skorpion. Kessler had expected the trademark Kalashnikov that every Arab in the world seemed to own. The Skorpion was a decent enough weapon, he supposed, but no match for the Ingram with which he was covering them. With the Ingram's suppressor he could take them both out without Pratt even knowing he was now all alone.

The smaller of the two men did not seem to be armed. He was also by far the more nervous. He was pacing back and forth while biting his fist. More than nervous, he seemed almost anguished. Now he was speaking to the man with the Skorpion. The tall one seemed to answer, "Don't bother me. Relax." The smaller one, however, could not. Abruptly he walked down the side of the cabin to a window where a dim light was showing. He stopped to look in. From the way he was crouching, the shades must be drawn and he was trying to peek underneath them. Now he's waving to the other, come look, come look, but the other tried to calm him with a settle-down gesture and tapped a finger to the watch he wore on his wrist. He seemed to be saying that there wasn't enough time.

Kessler heard a rustle of leaves to his right. The sound, he knew, was deliberately made. Elizabeth was announcing that she was about to materialize. He heard the beating of her heart before he saw her.

"She's there," she said huskily. "That piece of shit's with her. He's making a movie of his catch."

Too much emotion, thought Kessler, frowning. This is always the danger with Elizabeth.

"What could you see of the layout?" he asked her.

"Two rooms." She took a deep breath before continuing. "Front room has an open kitchen on the left as you enter, a couch and two chairs on the right. The door to the bedroom is in the middle. Go through it, you'll see a small bathroom on your left and the sleeping room straight ahead. That room has double bunk beds on each side with a table and chairs in between. Pratt's camera and tripod are set up on the table. The girl's in the lower left bunk. She's cuffed to the post. She's alive. I saw movement.''

''There's a back door?'' he asked.

''Middle of the room, opens onto a deck. But be careful. The deck's badly rotted. And watch out for alligators at the edge of the swamp. I almost walked into a big one.''

Kessler grunted at the possible consequence of that encounter and then took a moment to visualize the interior. He gestured toward the two men who were now both in front. The two men were arguing in whispers.

''How thick are the walls?'' he asked.

She knew what he meant. She shook her head. ''Any bullets that miss will go straight through that cabin. All three must be out here and clear of the girl.''

''Or if these go back in,'' said Kessler. ''Then we take them.''

''Martin . . . just make sure they're clear of the girl.''

They waited together in silence.

Pratt had gathered the photographs that he'd pinned to the bunk and replaced them with two others from his bag.

Both of these were of Nadia Halaby. Neither was recent. Her dress in the first was suitably Islamic at least to the extent of a head scarf. She stood at a lectern before a group of reporters. Pratt knew of the occasion at which it was taken. She was part of a committee that was formed to protest Algeria's Family Code Law. That would make this a 1984 photo. Under that code, the women of Algeria lost the right to marry whom they wanted, to divorce, to retain custody of their children or to have any say in where they lived. Bad for the women, thought Cyril Pratt, but quite good for him. Hundreds fled to France within weeks.

He knew that five other panelists had appeared with Halaby. Four had been killed within a few days. Two of the four were killed by their husbands and two, so they say, took their own lives in prison. The fifth was shot only recently after many years in hiding. Oddly, however, she was killed by chance in that the killers didn't know who she was. They simply saw a house with a satellite dish on its roof. A satellite dish meant Western TV and Western TV meant pollution. They broke in and slaughtered every person who lived there, not even sparing the servants. They shot out the television receiver as well.

The second photo of Nadia Halaby showed her in tennis attire. This one was actually a magazine clipping which he'd found in an old tennis program. There were several to choose from but this one was best. It showed her crouched and awaiting a serve, full face looking forward, directly into the camera that took it. He could see in his mind the scene it would make when he posed for the video record of her death. He would hold that photo aloft in one hand and her dripping head in the other. That tableau would make for a splendid credential.

His eyes fell on the backs of Aisha's long legs, firm and supple, not a blemish or a ripple on either of them. She wore short cut-off jeans pulled over a swimsuit. A pity that he didn't have time for her now but at least he could finger the merchandise a bit. He reached under her waist and opened the snap of her jeans. She bucked but he managed to pull down the zipper. He placed one knee over both her calves and gripped the ragged hem of her cut-offs. He pulled them down over her tight little bum and then down over her knees. Holding her down with one hand on her neck, he reached for the back of her swimsuit. He tugged it, by inches, gradually baring the muscles of her back. Smooth muscles. Young muscles. Pratt felt himself rising already.

"This is bad," croaked Mahfouz, who had entered the shack. "This is not to be done to this girl."

"Mahfouz . . . go away." Cyril Pratt didn't bother to turn.

"Faisal, did I tell you?" Mahfouz shouted toward the front of the cabin. "Faisal, come and help me make him stop."

The so-called fighter came into the room. He glanced

at the girl, then at Pratt with disgust. "Enough," he told
Pratt. "There's no time for this anyway."

"Look at him. Look there," said Mahfouz, turning red.
His finger took aim at Cyril Pratt's crotch. It had developed a conspicuous bulge.

"Get out," said the Englishman. "Get the fuck out."

"I'll make you a bargain," Faisal said to Pratt. "You
can play all you want with the Halaby woman." He
picked up a sheet that had been kicked from the bed. He
shook out its folds and he used it to cover the girl, head
and all. But a mortified Pratt had already seized Mahfouz
by his shirt and thrown him against the back door. He
snatched at the knob and pulled open the door. He threw
Mahfouz bodily onto the deck. The sodden boards split
and collapsed from his weight.

"Enough," said Faisal. "Let's go to the farmhouse. Do
you want a million dollars or don't you?"

Mahfouz heard these words as the door slammed shut
but he no longer cared about the woman who taught tennis. His hand came to rest on a long splintered board still
held by bent nails to the deck. He rolled to his knees and
pried it loose. He would use it to smash that foul Englishman's face if he once more put his hands on that girl.

As he thought this he felt someone helping him rise. A
part of his brain said it must be Faisal. An arm had
reached under his chin from behind and a hand took the
board he was holding. But the arm was too tight and it
choked off his breath. It made his face start to swell. His
eyes could not see because a thousand little lights began
jumping and spitting like the sparks from a fire. This was
all that he saw before his eyes rolled back in his head.
And yet his ears were still working. As if from a great
distance he heard Faisal's voice.

"Mahfouz? Come back in now. We're leaving."

But Mahfouz could not move. The jumping lights
faded. He felt himself floating away.

Kessler lowered his man, now unconscious or dead, and,
kneeling, drew his Walther from the holster at his ankle.
His body partly shielded by the one he'd just taken, he

waited for the man who had called to him. The door was pulled open and the taller one stepped through. He saw the legs of one man and the head of another. In the darkness it must have confused him. But now he saw the pistol that was aimed at his face. Kessler warned him with gestures to make no sound, to place both hands on the top of his head and move to one side of the doorway. The taller one considered his options and obeyed. Kessler would now have a clear shot at Pratt when he came out to see what was keeping these two.

But when Kessler swung his pistol toward the open door, the tall one made a stupid move. He dropped both his hands to the weapon that hung from his shoulder. The fingers of one sought the bolt of the Skorpion. This told Kessler that a round had not even been chambered. He shook his head no but his advice was ignored. The man didn't call out; he didn't try for cover. Instead he chose this insalubrious moment to familiarize himself with his weapon. Kessler had no choice but to fire. The shot caught him cleanly through his open mouth. Kessler thought for an instant that he'd missed. He fired again. The second shot put out his eye.

The man was still falling when Kessler heard the girl squeal. He also heard sounds of feet moving quickly. He had swung his sights back onto the doorway waiting for Pratt to appear. But he heard Pratt say "Jesus" and then back away. Pratt had seen Faisal's body or he saw blood and brain, some of which would have spewed through the door. Next came the roar of a pistol inside, so loud that the windowpane rattled. Four shots in succession and four holes in the wall where the slugs from Pratt's gun splintered through it. If Kessler had been standing he would have been hit.

But he couldn't stay down, he could no longer wait because Pratt would surely take the girl as a shield. He jumped up and he dashed to the far side of the door where he had wanted to go in the first place. It was the side that would give him a clear view of the bed. Sure enough, Pratt had reached it and had aimed a hard kick at its post. He was frantically trying to break it apart in order to free

the girl's handcuffed arms. He had wisely concluded that
this was no time for keys. The girl was now screaming
from under a sheet and the bedpost was yielding too
slowly. He turned and he snapped two more shots at Kessler whom he now could see crouching outside. Kessler
rolled to the cover of the taller one's body and Pratt saw
this as his chance. He dashed for the door firing wildly.

"Bad mistake," muttered Kessler as he lined up his
sights on Pratt's head. But there suddenly came a metallic
chatter and Pratt did a dance like a puppet. The front of
his tennis shirt blew out from his waist and the spray from
his insides traced an arc on the deck. He yelped and he
flailed and he staggered to the door frame, which he
reached for and tried to hold on. Insanely, he looked out
at Kessler, his eyes wide and questioning, as if Kessler
might explain what had happened to him. Then he turned,
looking first toward the bunk as if thinking it was somehow the girl who had done this. All he saw was her head
still covered by the sheet, all he heard were her terrified
screams. He did not see the shapeless black ghost floating
toward him or the soft black boot coming up at his face.

Pratt was slammed through the doorway and onto the
deck. Kessler had to leap out of his way. Back inside, the
girl's screaming was nearing hysteria. For a moment Elizabeth paused in the doorway, looking back toward the
half-collapsed bed. Kessler knew that she wanted to go to
the girl and tell her that the danger was over. That's how
you get killed, he wanted to shout, because Pratt was still
gripping his pistol. As if she could hear him Elizabeth
turned, but Kessler had already pinned Pratt's hand with
his heel. He looked up at the veil that showed only her
eyes. He noticed for the first time that she wore her dark
lenses. Those black eyes looked wild, they looked cruel,
almost mad. Now they darted from Pratt to a place behind
Kessler. The Ingram came up and she fired once more.

Kessler spun to follow her line of sight. He saw the
man he had choked do a staggering dance before pitching
forward on his face. This time she had aimed to kill

quickly. The Ingram then vanished beneath her abaya and her curved Moroccan knife appeared in her hand. She glanced one more time back into the cabin before closing the door quietly behind her.

Sixteen

Nadia Halaby heard shots from her moving car. They seemed well ahead and off to her left but the sounds were so muffled it was hard to be sure. She reminded herself that she'd heard shots before while driving this road after sundown. The locals were known to hunt deer out of season and to shoot alligators for their tail meat and hides.

She eased off her gas pedal and listened again. She heard only night birds and the distant hum of trucks. Nothing else seemed out of the ordinary. The farm she was looking for, as near as she could tell, was as much as five minutes away on back roads. The shots, she decided, could not have come from there. They could not have carried so far. And yet the hum of those trucks was coming from the Interstate, a road even farther away.

Nadia wished that she'd waited for Jasmine. It had been foolish to come out here alone like this. There was always the chance that the call was a ruse; she had not, after all, actually spoken to Aisha. But caution was one thing, paranoia was another. Aisha was out here and she was terribly frightened. Right now she was probably more frightened of the paddling she might get than she was of the two bums who grabbed her. And fourteen or not, she just might get one for going to that beach by herself.

"Nice of you to show up," Kessler hissed at Elizabeth. "Did you stop to admire the decor?"

"He was too near the girl." She, too, kept her voice low. "I had to wait for my shot."

"He was *kicking* that bed, not trying to climb in."

"I needed to wait," she said stubbornly.

Elizabeth could probably write her name with that Ingram. The truth was that she had wanted Pratt down but alive and above all she wanted him conscious. Never mind that Pratt, meanwhile, had been shooting at him.

Pratt was conscious, all right, but that was all one could say. He had raised himself into a reclining position, not knowing or caring who shot him. All he wanted to know was how bad his wounds were. He made odd mewing sounds as he probed with his fingers. The sounds turned to whimpers as he found each new hole in a line from one hip to the other. But they need not be fatal and he probably knew that. He had likely seen men who were gut-shot before, men who lasted for hours, even days, in great pain, but could survive if they got to a surgeon on time.

Kessler picked up Pratt's pistol to move it out of his reach, then he knelt at the body of the second man she had shot. The man's eyes stared at nothing and his throat had no pulse. At this he was doubly annoyed. He had only intended to put this one to sleep, this one who carried no weapon and who, for whatever reason, had tried to keep Pratt from raping that child. He would have preferred to have two men to question so he'd know much more quickly the truth from the lies.

"You're Loomis?" gasped Pratt as he looked up at Kessler.

Kessler raised an eyebrow. It gave Pratt his answer. Whoever he was, his name was not Loomis.

"A doctor . . ." Pratt no longer seemed to care. "Get me to a doctor. I'm hurt."

"You don't know what hurt is," came Elizabeth's voice, "but I'll teach you, you son of a bitch."

The Englishman blinked at what he'd thought was a shadow. Only now did he remember that there had to have been two. Only now did he recall the similar shadow that had kicked him just after his belly exploded.

"Who's . . . that?" he asked, his eyes growing wide.

The shadow approached him and lowered itself. It seemed to melt into the deck. From where Kessler was standing she looked like a nun who knelt to say prayers at the bedside of the sick. But Pratt, he felt sure, made no such assumption because the thing in her hand was no rosary. What color there was drained out of Pratt's face as she drew her curved knife from its scabbard.

"My name," she said coldly, "is Elizabeth Stride. And you're now going to die, Cyril Pratt."

He raised one hand as if to cover his throat. He tried to push backward but his legs wouldn't function. The effort caused blood to seep out through his pants. More bleeding, thought Kessler, was not what he needed. Already he was down half a liter.

"Ah . . . excuse me," said Kessler, his hand touching her shoulder. "I think we should do this away from the cabin and I'd like a few minutes alone with him first."

Her black eyes flashed up at him through the slit in her veil. Their message was *"Martin . . . Butt out."* But Kessler had indulged her enough for one evening. Abruptly he reached for Cyril Pratt's hat, which had somehow remained on his head. He jammed the hat into Pratt's gaping mouth to keep him from screaming for the moment. Next he grabbed a fistful of hair with one hand and snatched up one ankle with the other. He lifted the thrashing man clear of the deck and half carried, half dragged him in the direction of the dock.

Elizabeth had abandoned her praying-nun pose and was following after him, furious. Kessler set the Englishman down and moved quickly to block her approach. "What the hell are you doing?" was barely out of her mouth when he lifted her bodily over his shoulder and carried her away from both Pratt and the cabin. She punched at his back with the hilt of her knife. He had to trust that she wouldn't reverse it. He counted twenty paces to a stand of pines. To go further would be pushing his luck.

He set her down roughly and seized both her arms, alert for a possible knee to the groin. "There's a girl in that cabin scared out of her wits. She does not need to hear that man screaming.''

''That *man*, as you call him, was undressing her, Martin.''

''And for that he will pay—but he'll talk to me first.''

''I'll just cut his dick off while you're having your chat. You don't know this man, Martin. You don't know what he's done.''

He shook her. ''Elizabeth . . . *think*. Look around at this mess. We'll either come up with a way to contain it or the new life you've made here is over.''

The mention of leaving, of running again was as good as a slap in the face. Her eyes, through her veil, drifted over the carnage. Sounds of squeaking and banging came up from the cabin where the girl was still trying to tear herself free. They could leave her, she supposed, tied up just as she was. They could finish off Pratt, call the school from their car, tell the Halaby woman where to find her. But meanwhile the girl might hurt herself badly. She was already half crazy after what she'd been through.

The worst of it, however, was what would come later. When the school people saw this they'd call the police and might well have done so already. By morning this place would swarm with reporters, by evening all the networks would carry the story. A young girl is kidnapped from Hilton Head Island, where nothing like this ever happens. She's a Muslim, maybe a runaway princess. They'll make her one even if she isn't.

The three men who took her, one a known bounty hunter, are found shot to death by a mystery pair who came out of nowhere then vanished. The tennis school claims to know nothing about them and no one believes them, of course. The two dead Muslims will be labeled as terrorists and that brings the FBI into the picture. This was just too delicious, Elizabeth realized. It was fodder for tabloids all over the world. The police, the reporters, would never stop looking. It would only be a matter of time, perhaps days, before someone's computer kicked out the names of every island resident with a past.

"You're right," she said, wilting. "I'll have to move on in the morning."

"No," answered Kessler, "you can't do that either. The first thing they'll watch for is people who leave."

"Martin, look around you. If you think we can contain this, you're dreaming."

"We can give it one day. We can try."

"What are you thinking? Get rid of the bodies? The girl in that cabin still knows they were shot."

"The girl," he corrected her, "knows nothing of the sort."

To begin with, he told her, Pratt had knocked the girl senseless. By the time she came to she was scared half to death and her head was under a sheet. It's true she heard shots and crashing and moans but she can't know that anyone's dead. Never mind the two bursts from the Ingram she heard—an Ingram sounded more like a sewing machine than a gun. Nor would she be able to say where she'd been. Pratt would hardly have allowed her to memorize road signs and this shack must be one of hundreds just like it.

"Put yourself in the place of whoever sent Pratt. If these three simply vanish, what would you think?"

"What I'd think is they're worm food, Martin," she answered. "And I'd think that those people at the tennis school killed them."

"But you'd also assume that at least one must have talked first. That leaves you with something to worry about."

"That we . . . that whoever did this might hit back?"

Kessler nodded. "So the person who sent him is left with two choices. He can send more like these or he can call it a bad job and quit. This really could end here, Elizabeth."

She took a deep breath. He could see her misgivings. But he also saw a glimmer of hope.

"Let me clean up the mess. You go see to the girl. Calm her down and take her back home."

"If I take her home, Martin, she'll know what I look like."

"In your veil and abaya? How can she?"

"I'm to drive her to Van Der Meer wearing this all the way? This is Hilton Head, Martin, not Yemen."

"So dress down. Drive her home in your jumpsuit. Make a mattress of blankets for her in the trunk."

"That's how you'd keep her calm? Say everything's fine, now curl up in my trunk and relax?"

"You might try a somewhat more delicate touch."

"Then you go do it. I don't know about kids."

"Do you want her to hear a German accent? You don't think that might narrow us down just a little?"

"Well, then give me some words. What do I say to her?"

"You're stalling, Elizabeth. Get going."

Nadia Halaby had found the farm. There was a light on inside but in only one room. She saw no cars in the driveway. She flashed her high beams and gave a tap on her horn. No curtain moved. No one came to the door. She opened her cell phone and tapped out the number of Jasmine's.

"House is white with green trim? Says Wiggins on the mailbox?" asked Jasmine when told that the place looked deserted.

"I've got the right house. She's not here."

"Then you've been set up. Get out of there now."

The Algerian was tempted but not without Aisha. "That number they gave you? Call it right now. Then call me back here. I'll wait."

"Don't you get out of that car till I do. You keep that car moving, you hear me?"

Nadia drove her car forward, up on the front lawn. She saw in her headlights that the door was intact. No sign of forced entry. No locks shot off by those shots she heard earlier. That was something at least. But what she wanted to hear most was the sound of a telephone ringing inside. She heard nothing but crickets and frogs.

Her own cell phone rang. It was Jasmine again.

"No answer," said Jasmine.

"Then the number was a phony," Nadia felt her voice trembling. "The whole story was a ruse. Jazz, I think Aisha's been taken."

"Then the ruse was for you. Get out of there, Nadia."

"I'm going. You call the state troopers."

Elizabeth knocked before entering the cabin. It was stupid but that was what she did. Martin was right once again. She was stalling.

The bunk had collapsed under Pratt's frantic kicks and the girl's own attempts to get free. The post to which she was shackled had held but she had managed to kick off the sheet. The top of her swimsuit had fallen away, leaving her nude to the waist. The shorts Pratt had pulled down had been kicked free as well. They lay on the floor with the bedding. Her wrists were chafed raw by the handcuffs that held them. Her eyes had started to discolor and swell; Pratt had hit her with a sap more than once. She jumped at the sound of the opening door and gasped when she saw the black figure that entered.

"Oh, no. Oh, please," she cried out. She kicked with bare feet to keep Elizabeth away.

Elizabeth realized what the girl must have thought on seeing a veil and abaya. She had told Martin, damn it, she'd be no good at this.

"It's all right," she hushed. She tried to sound soothing. "No one will hurt you. I'm taking you home."

But those words, far from calming her, caused her to panic. "No!! You can't take me back. I'm not going with you. I have to wait here for my mother."

"Your . . . mother's coming where? You don't mean to this cabin?"

The girl answered by trying to kick her again. "You can't make me leave before she comes. I won't go."

For a moment there she'd wondered if the mother had sent Pratt. But no, she must be coming to visit. "Stop kicking and listen. I'm not with those men; I did not mean back *there*, wherever that is. I meant back to Van Der Meer, Cherokee."

At this the girl trembled, part relief but part doubt. "Those . . . men. Where are they?"

"They're gone. They can't hurt you."

"No, they're not. I heard them outside."

"What you heard . . . they shot at us but then they ran. They ran down the road to their car."

The girl now understood all those deafening sounds. "Who are you?" she asked. "Is Nadia with you?"

"Nadia is waiting for you to get home. I'm going to help you get dressed now, okay?" Elizabeth reached to untangle her suit and fitted it over her breasts. Cherokee tensed but she allowed it to be done.

"Can't you take off these handcuffs?" the girl asked as she zipped her. "Let me up and I'll do this myself."

Elizabeth might have freed her if she'd thought to get the keys. It was better that she hadn't, she realized. "I need to find a key that unlocks those things. And I need to make sure that those men don't come back. You'll be safe where you are until I'm finished."

"On this bed?" she asked, blinking. "Please don't leave me like this. Can't you shoot off the chain or something?"

"That . . . really only works in the movies," said Elizabeth. "But there's someone outside standing guard with a gun. No one can get in here but me."

As Elizabeth spoke she was scouting the room. On the far bunks, unmade, she saw folded blankets and towels. A garment bag of the carry-on type had been left just inside the rear door. This had to be Pratt's; he must have checked out of the Players Club. Pratt's other bag, the one he'd had with him at Reilley's, had been knocked to the floor in his scramble to shoot Martin. His camcorder and tripod were lying nearby. Near them she saw a large roll of duct tape and a jumble of clippings and photos. A bottle of scotch had rolled out of the bag and had stopped against one of the girl's sneakers.

"I see your shorts . . . and your tennis shoes. What else were you wearing when they grabbed you?"

"That means . . . you're really going to take me

home?'' She had not fully believed it until that question was asked.

''Just as fast as I can. What else did you have?''

''Just my hat.''

''What's it look like?''

''It's straw. It has feathers. I think it fell off when he hit me.''

''Then it's where? In the jitney? I'll find it,'' she promised. It would not do to leave it. Nor any of the photos that were pinned to the bunk. She shook out one blanket and approached the bed with it. The girl recoiled once again.

''I won't cover your head,'' said Elizabeth quickly. ''This is only to warm you until I can free you. But that brings up another problem I have.''

''You . . . don't want me to see what you look like?''

Elizabeth covered her up to her shoulders. She reached to brush the girl's hair from her eyes. ''I don't want to blindfold you. I know that would scare you. But we'll have to figure out something, okay?''

''Yes, but why? I mean, if Nadia knows you . . .''

''Cherokee, honey, it's better for both of us. I guess I have to ask you to trust me on that.''

Elizabeth leaned over and kissed her head lightly. That kiss, that touch, and the use of an endearment seemed to do more to calm her than all her assurances. Elizabeth could not remember in all her adult life the last time she used an endearment. Or the last time she comforted a child.

Seventeen

Kessler had heard the girl's voice shouting "No!" and pleading with Elizabeth not to make her go back. Her reaction to Elizabeth hadn't surprised him. She looked like she just had flown in from Riyadh.

More interesting, however, was the look on Pratt's face. For an instant he seemed to forget his own pain and his eyes opened wide in disbelief. Kessler could see that Pratt was now thinking the same thing the girl must have thought. That Elizabeth must be a bounty hunter, too. And that he, Kessler, had not come to rescue the girl in that cabin but rather to steal her from him.

"That son of a bitch," Pratt cursed, spitting blood. "That son of a bitch, I'll kill him."

Kessler refrained from asking whose life he was threatening because Pratt clearly thought that he already knew. He shrugged and told Pratt, "I can't say I blame you," in hopes of eliciting more indignation.

He left Pratt to fume and hold on to his belly while he went back and dragged the two dead men to the dock. He emptied their pockets and took off their watches. These he left in a pile a few feet from Pratt.

Pratt, still in a fury, began coughing up blood. This was not a good sign, thought Kessler. The trouble with shooting a man in the hips is that fragments and bone go every which way. His mind still seemed clear as long as it was focused on whoever was the object of his rage. Even so, he would not last much longer. Kessler wasn't sure how long he dared wait to start getting some answers from this man.

To move things along he walked up to the cabin and returned with a pair of concrete blocks that were used to prop the corners of the rotting old deck. He stripped the belts from the two dead men and ran one through the holes of each block. The belt of the smaller dead man was cheap plastic but it seemed strong enough for his purpose. The clothing this man wore was also cheap cotton and yet his watch was a Rolex. Kessler wondered about that but he could ask later. He went back to the deck for a third heavy block which he set down at Cyril Pratt's side.

"Wait . . . what are they for?" the Englishman asked.

"They're to weigh down your bodies," Kessler answered distractedly. "We can't have you bobbing around in the swamp."

"You're going to kill *me*? What for, for Christ's sake?"

Kessler didn't answer because what had distracted him was the Rolex that was suddenly missing.

"Let's have it," he said, "the watch you just took."

"It's mine," Pratt answered. "I was letting him use it."

"You have holes in your belly and you need to know the time? Give it back or I break both your arms."

Pratt surrendered the watch, now smeared with his blood. His face was twisted with hatred. Kessler rubbed his thumb over the back of the watch where he saw an inscription in Arabic.

"Your watch, you say? That's not what it says here." The only Arabic Kessler could read was how to tell men's rooms in Middle East airports but Pratt, he assumed, would not know that.

"So he told you to get it?" the Englishman sneered. "That bugger-ass bastard even told you to bring back his watch?"

"Which bugger-ass bastard would that be?" he asked as if he knew but was toying with Pratt. But before Pratt could answer he looked up toward the cabin and froze. He saw the black shadow approaching again.

Elizabeth came bearing a stack of old blankets. The Englishman's tennis bag hung from her shoulder. She dropped one blanket near each of the dead men and a large roll of duct tape between them. She tossed a third blanket at the Englishman's feet and two worn terry towels as well. She stood for a long moment glaring at Pratt. Her eyes seemed to promise that her time with him would come. She bent to pick through an assortment of keys that Kessler had taken from the Englishman's pockets. As she lowered herself Kessler saw in the bag what looked like the neck of a bottle of Gleneagles. He reached in and took it.

"Why waste it?' he asked her in response to her scowl. "Also leave your Jambiya. I'll need it.'' Elizabeth was reluctant to part with her knife but she did in the hope that he would find a good use for it. She turned and walked off without saying a word. She did not go back to the cabin.

His moment now gone, Kessler showed no more interest in the watch or its owner. He picked up the towels and tossed them at Pratt. "Press these tight against your belly. You won't lose so much blood.''

Pratt snatched at them eagerly. He seemed greatly relieved. He saw the gift of the towels as a promise, perhaps, that they don't want him to die after all. Kessler rolled the Gleneagles toward him as well. "This might take the edge off the pain,'' he said.

"The woman,'' Pratt asked, "is she going for a doctor?''

"Elizabeth? Why would she want to save you?''

"That's not Stride,'' said the Englishman, suddenly defiant. "Stride's been dead and in hell for a year.''

Wishful thinking, thought Kessler. He answered, "As you like.''

"Anyone can put on a set of black rags. You can buy that damned knife in any souk.'' At this, his eyes widened as another thought struck him. "Oh, Christ. That's Halaby, isn't it?''

"Not Halaby. I can assure you.''

"No.'' He relaxed. "No, it couldn't be, could it. You're

here after Halaby too." He managed to open his bottle and drank deeply before adding, "But don't try to tell me that's Stride."

Pratt's doubt, Kessler knew, was more than denial. A year doesn't go by without some woman turning up and claiming to have been the Black Angel. The Black Angel shows up in some European tabloids as often as Elvis Presley. Kessler didn't bother to argue the point. He opened a blanket and shook it out over the body of the man he had shot. The man's papers said his name was Faisal Amini. He rolled this one up in it forming a shroud which he secured at both ends with long strips of tape. He considered attaching the cement block to his neck but that could wait, he decided, until they were out in the swamp. Hauling these three men into the boat would be hard enough without dragging their anchors as well. This one's belt was leather but of discount store quality and his boots looked like army surplus. No surprise—Kessler had already concluded that Pratt doesn't go top dollar for his help. As for Pratt, his shorts had no belt, just elastic. For Pratt, he would have to use shoelaces.

"And you. Who are you?" demanded the Englishman. His voice had more strength now thanks to the towels and a swallow of scotch but it sounded squeezed out more than spoken.

"Martin Kessler," he answered. He cut off some more lengths of tape with the knife.

The Englishman snorted. "My ass."

"I know," sighed Kessler. "Anyone can speak with a German accent." He gestured toward the trademark scar at his eye. "And you can get one of these bumping into a door."

"Kessler walked off with millions. He wouldn't touch this. That's how you got hired? You claimed you were Reineke?"

Those millions again. The Israelis again.

"But you damned sure didn't tell him that cunt with you was Stride. No Muslim would hire Elizabeth Stride."

True enough, thought Kessler. But he wondered what—if anything—this man would believe. Did he think these other two were only taking a nap? That the pain in his gut was indigestion? He added more tape to the first of the men, then started on the one whom the other called Mahfouz. The blankets were good thinking on Elizabeth's part. At low tide their bodies will be harder to spot, even if their feet should float up to the surface. The tape, however, was far from ideal. It was silver and shiny. He'd have much preferred cord.

"Bandari . . . that shit," the Englishman muttered.

Kessler noted the name but showed no reaction. "Business is business," was all he could think of to say.

"But I *had* her, for Christ's sake. I already had her. She was as good as on a plane back to Cairo."

Kessler shrugged. "There is more at stake here than that girl."

All Kessler intended was a vague provocation to keep the dialogue moving along. Pratt reacted, however, as if the words gave him hope.

"So you *are* here for Halaby. Well, you'll never get near her. But I know where she is right this second."

Kessler saw what was coming. Save me, we'll share Halaby. To encourage that subject would only waste time. "More even than Halaby," he answered.

Pratt looked at him, stunned. He coughed up more blood. As Kessler looked on, a cold building rage pushed the pain and the fear from the Englishman's eyes. Kessler wondered what it was he'd just said.

"That *fuck*!" Pratt exploded. "You're working for Tarrant. That's how you knew to come straight to this cabin."

"A smart man hedges his bets," answered Kessler.

This brought on a whole new string of obscenities aimed at the person named Tarrant. Not an Arabic name like the other, thought Kessler. British, perhaps, or American. Kessler took this occasion to pick up Pratt's weapons and throw them out into the swamp. The splashes of the Skorpion, Pratt's pistol, extra clips, quieted the frogs for a moment. He stepped into the boat and tested the motor to make sure that he understood its workings. It roared to life instantly. The motor, for some reason, caused the frogs to croak louder.

Pratt still hadn't finished. "That bastard," he growled. By now he made bubbles as he spoke. "That bloody rat bastard, I'll ruin him."

This man and reality are strangers, thought Kessler. Here he is holding his intestines in place and he's plotting revenge for the future.

"The truth," Pratt demanded. "Did he tell you to kill me? Or just to make sure this got done?"

"You want my opinion? I don't think he likes you." Kessler laid out the last of the blankets near Pratt.

"That bloody rat bastard," the Englishman repeated.

"Ah, you see?" asked Kessler. "It's exactly that attitude that's his problem with you. I think maybe he knows you don't like him much either." He reached for Pratt's ankles to drag him onto the blanket.

"And he's right. Will you wait?" Pratt managed to grip a low post of the dock. "There's a way to get rich off of Tarrant."

Kessler released him. "How rich?"

"You said it yourself. There are millions at stake here. I can wreck this one deal he's got going."

"He knows that already. It's what's getting you killed. Why would I want to know the same thing?"

"Will you listen, for Christ's sake? I'm telling you millions. He'll pay just to stay out of prison."

Kessler folded his arms. "I'll listen five minutes or until your first lie," he said. "Make it good and I'll get you to a doctor."

Elizabeth had watched for a while from a distance as Martin played his head games with Pratt. She didn't like games. They take too much time. Nor did Pratt have much time for them either. Her guess was that he had ten minutes at best before blood loss and shock made it pointless to question him further. A few probes with her knife to the joint of his knee would have worked much more quickly than a few sips of scotch.

She went first to the place where they had hidden the jitney. She found the girl's hat on the floor between seats and also a map on which the route to the Players Club had been marked. Ahead, among the junipers, she could see a low spot in which water had ponded to a depth of several feet. Down there, she decided, it could go undiscovered for weeks, even months, and only then if some hunter came across it.

She took a minute to wipe the vinyl surfaces with handfuls of rotting wet leaves. Next she started the engine with one set of the keys she had taken. She put the jitney in gear and stepped out as it started to roll. She watched it settle, partly submerged, until the water caused the engine to sputter and die. She would rather have abandoned it far from this cabin but the jitney was too conspicuous to risk being seen in it.

She returned to the place where they had left Martin's car. She peeled off her veil and removed the abaya, then shook out her hair with her fingers. The dark contact lenses could stay in for now. She would hide her hair under a kerchief. Unless she could bring herself to blindfold the girl, that might have to do as a disguise.

Pratt's bag contained mostly surveillance equipment, several false passports, a vial of knock-out drops—chloral hydrate—and a single filthy syringe. She would dispose of these and also the camcorder. For now, however, she would take a quick look at the tape that was in the machine. Pratt's camcorder had an instant replay feature on a small external screen. She pressed *Rewind* and held it for several seconds. She released the button and pressed *Play.*

In the darkness the picture was as clear as a movie and the scene was of Pratt and the girl. Pratt gripping her hair, twisting her head, showing her off like a trophy. Yet she fought him every step of the way until Pratt brought that sap to the side of her head and the girl hung limp from his fist. A very brave girl, thought Elizabeth.

Aisha Bandari. Pratt had just said her name to the camera. Aisha Bandari . . . the lesbian daughter . . . of the adulteress and murderess Leyna Bandari . . . niece of the honorable Gamal Bandari. It's the uncle, she realized, who sent Pratt to bring her home. Father dead, according to this, and the mother apparently dead now as well. Uh-oh, thought Elizabeth. The girl didn't know that. She had said in the cabin that her mother would be coming to join her.

She played a bit more. Pratt's narration was in English but the idiom he used sounded Arabic. Elizabeth knew that to call one a lesbian could mean very little in that language. Conservative Arabs tend to use such terms loosely. The word "whore," for example, can mean any Muslim woman who shows more of herself than her eyes and her hands. It can mean any Western woman at all. It was a language in which style had more meaning than substance, more suited for imagery than rational discourse. It was why Arabs negotiated with non-Arabs so poorly unless agreements were reached in a third neutral language. "Murderess," however, usually meant murderess unless, of course, the charge was a lie.

Now came the part that she'd heard herself when she followed those first two through the door. Now she could see what he couldn't have seen then. First Pratt climbing in on top of the girl, pulling her pants down, now removing her suit. The smaller man shouting at Pratt. The other not as animated but objecting as well. Pratt throwing the first one out of the room, the second one covering the girl with a sheet. She knew all the rest because she'd seen it.

The tape counter said this was near the tape's end. She pressed *Rewind* again and let it run. She realized that this was no time to watch movies. There were spent shells to be gathered, trails left by dragged bodies to be swept and obscured, pools of blood to be covered with dirt. But she was curious to see whether she, herself, might possibly have been taped after all. Or Martin, perhaps. Or even that IRA crowd back at Reilley's.

The camcorder clicked to a stop. She pressed *Play*. The scene that came on was barely discernible. It was happening at night. A wide-angled shot of a large group of shadows approaching. But a floodlight blinked on. Men covered their eyes. She now saw that the men were all dressed in robes, all men except for one woman. The woman was garbed in a burka and abaya and her arms were bound at her sides. In the foreground Elizabeth saw piles of rocks. A chill ran up from the small of her back. She knew at that instant that she was watching a stoning.

Elizabeth moved the tape ahead. She watched at the jerky fast-forward speed as the men forced the woman into a pit and then packed rocks and dirt all around her. They withdrew but two more came to pile them still higher. The woman was moving her head left and right as if searching their faces or pleading with them. Now one man stepped into the pit and was speaking. Their sheik, perhaps. No, too young. Suddenly that one slapped her face hard. The veil was knocked loose. It flew to one side.

Elizabeth had to stop for a moment. She wiped silent tears that were welling in her eyes. She had almost decided to watch it no more when her own mind replayed the scene of the slap. It told her that the man who gave it seemed familiar. She pressed *Play* again and looked at the screen. The man turned toward the group and spread his arms wide. She did know that man. She'd just killed him. That was the one who had tried to stop Pratt. And a killing that she'd almost regretted.

The man taping this scene, undoubtedly Pratt, zoomed in on the face of the woman. It was no longer obscured by the veil. Once again a chill seized Elizabeth's spine. That woman had Aisha's big eyes.

Elizabeth pressed *Scan* to speed the tape forward. A man in a dark suit now entered the pit, a fat man who squatted before her with effort. Now the woman looked up, straight into his soul. Her eyes began flashing and so did her teeth. She wasn't afraid now. Her expression was one of contempt. Elizabeth's mind had barely formed this impression when the man brought a rock down hard against that face.

Elizabeth winced. That brave and beautiful face. It must have been shattered by the blow that she took but this woman . . . this Leyna . . . would not yield to it. She was speaking again, berating this man, berating the villagers who had gathered to kill her. The man cried out in fury or anguish . . . it sounded like both . . . and he raised the rock once again. He brought it down harder, with all his might, and while it was still in its arc Elizabeth knew that the woman's skull was about to be crushed. Her thumb pressed the *Pause* button just as it made contact, as if stopping the action might save the woman's life.

She stood for a moment, her eyes filling with tears, her face lit by the glow of the camcorder screen. The tableau before her was frozen in time yet it still seemed to flicker as if it were moving. She realized, slowly, that the lights she now saw could not be coming from Cyril Pratt's machine. She looked around her, then up, and a bit to the north. She saw strobes of red washing over the sky. She could not see their source, but there must have been several. Police cars, she realized. And they seemed to be only a few roads away.

Kessler got his five minutes but only just barely. The subject at hand was just getting interesting when Pratt raised one hand in a gesture that said, "Just a moment." He seemed to be trying to bring up a belch. What came was not gas but a great spew of blood. Pratt stared at this new mess for two or three seconds. Disbelief, even now, was still clear on his face until his eyes lost their focus and rolled back in his head.

Kessler felt for his pulse. It was weak but racing as if desperately searching for enough blood to make pumping worth the effort. Pratt's skin was also growing cool to the touch. Kessler dug his thumb into sensitive flesh under the hinge of Pratt's jaw. Pratt did not react to the pain.

"We have to go. Kill him," came Elizabeth's voice. She materialized wearing only her jumpsuit, no veil. She held the girl's feathered hat in her hand and used it to gesture toward some lights in the sky. Kessler had already seen them.

"It's police, but they're not coming here," Kessler told her. "They're going to a farm a few minutes away where Pratt says he hoped to lure Nadia as well. He was going to—"

Elizabeth cut him off. "If they do come we're trapped. There's only that one road back out."

"Then you go with the girl. I'll finish up here. If I see headlights coming, I still have the boat."

"They killed that girl's mother. They stoned her to death."

"Having falsely accused her. Pratt told me."

"Is he dead?" She jabbed him with the toe of her boot. "Tell me he didn't die easily."

"Elizabeth . . . trust me. Just go."

Again, she knocked and called out before entering. "Cherokee . . . I'm back. But my face isn't covered."

"Oh, come in. I won't look," the girl answered eagerly. She shut her eyes tight and turned her head to the wall as Elizabeth entered with Pratt's key in her hand. She moaned with relief when one wrist then another was finally freed from the handcuffs.

"Don't get up just yet," Elizabeth told her. She picked up the shell casings, Pratt's and her own, and spread still another blanket on the spray of blood and brains from the man Martin took with a head shot. She placed Pratt's luggage outside the back door where Martin would not overlook it. She added the very few personal effects that the two other men had brought with them.

"I said no blindfold so here's how we'll do this." She gathered the shorts and the tennis shoes next and added the hat she'd brought with her. "We'll walk to a car, you first, me behind you, my hand will be on your shoulder. You'll go where I steer you and you'll never look back at me. For most of the ride you'll sit on the floor with your arms folded over your head. Can you do that or will you be frightened?"

"Those men. You're sure that they're gone?"

"They won't be back."

"I won't mind, I don't think, as long as you're with me. Can I go to the bathroom real quick?"

Elizabeth took her by the shoulders and helped her to stand. The girl suddenly lurched and appeared to be turning but she grabbed the top bunk and held on.

"I'm sorry. My legs. They're like jelly," she said.

"Close your eyes. I'll walk with you," said Elizabeth gently.

She guided the girl through the bathroom door and put the rest of her clothing in with her. From outside she heard sounds of the toilet in use and then sounds of the girl being sick. She gave her two extra minutes to wash what she could and to put on the rest of her clothes.

"I'm coming out now. It's okay, I'm covered," said the girl before opening the door. She emerged with a towel hooding her head, one end held up covering her face. She wore it in the manner that Muslims wear head scarves. She kept her eyes shut, reaching out as if blind until she felt Elizabeth's touch.

"Keep them closed for a minute. Good girl," said Elizabeth who guided her toward the front of the shack and through to the gravel road outside.

"You can open them now, Aisha. We have to go through some woods. By the way, is it Aisha or Cherokee?"

"No one here calls me Aisha. Only Nadia and Jasmine know my real name is Aisha. My name here is Cherokee Blye."

"Cherokee, then. How's your head? Any dizziness?"

"Not too bad but my left eye's all blurred."

"That will clear. How's your stomach? Are you still feeling queasy?"

"A little, but don't worry. I don't think I'll get sick in your car."

She had a concussion, Elizabeth realized, but the symptoms seemed mild and not dangerous. She kept her talking to keep her from thinking as much as to keep her from being afraid. The girl, she noticed, had no single accent but rather a hint of at least three or four.

"Where was your schooling?" Elizabeth asked her as they neared where Martin had hidden his Toyota.

"Switzerland, mostly. The American School. Then the past two years here at Hilton Head High."

"I don't hear much Arabic left in your voice."

"Oh, my Arabic's still pretty good." She answered as if to assure another Muslim that she had not strayed too far from her heritage. "I read Arab poetry and stories all the time and a little of the Koran every day."

Elizabeth grunted at this without meaning to. "Your nationality is . . . ?"

"Egyptian, by birth." The girl rocked a hand. "But there's Lebanese, Greek, and some French in my family. I'm pretty much of a mutt."

Elizabeth would have guessed Saudi. But the village where that woman was stoned, she knew, could have been in a half dozen countries.

"Do I still have that much of an accent?" she asked. "Jasmine thinks I sound like a preppie."

"You sound more American than I do." Elizabeth said that more as a reflection than as an attempt to mislead the girl. There wasn't much Texas left in her either. She knew it was ludicrous to be prattling about accents but this was a girl who needed to talk about anything except what she'd just been through.

"Where did 'Cherokee' come from?" she asked.

"That was Nadia's idea. Lots of full-blooded Cherokees live in this state."

"And the other kids think you're what? A chief's daughter?"

"Uh-huh. Jazz told them I was. Where's your car?"

"Ahead and to your right."

"I see it."

Elizabeth gave her a comforting squeeze.

She had many questions she wanted to ask such as what made Cherokee worth all this trouble, who were all the others and how many, and whether this safe house was a permanent thing as opposed to one that might now move on elsewhere. She hoped that it would. But Elizabeth asked none of these questions because Cherokee clearly thought she was one of them and should know the answers already. It's better, she decided, to leave it at that.

They had reached within fifty feet of the Toyota. Elizabeth still saw those lights in the sky. "Close your eyes for a minute, just until you get in," said Elizabeth.

"So I can't see the license plate, right? I won't look."

Elizabeth squeezed her shoulder and smiled.

She liked this girl more than was good for her.

Eighteen

The boat, Kessler realized, was not built for four men, let alone when cement blocks are added. Only fifty meters out and the railing was nearly awash. He steered the boat into a patch of dense grass, taking care not to foul the propeller. He slipped the motor into idle and got down to business. He eased the taller one partly over the side. The block and the back of his head were submerged but the rest of him straddled the railing. Kessler reached for Elizabeth's Moroccan knife.

He cut through the blanket at the taller one's throat and performed a bit of crude surgery. This produced more blood that would attract hungry creatures but to do so was not Kessler's motive. The cuts were a kind that would confuse the authorities in the event that these bodies were found. This done, he eased the taller one over the side. The boat took water as he did so. He slid it back into gear and returned to the channel. Up ahead, where it branched, he chose another likely patch and repeated his work with the knife. He slid the second one in with less splashing this time.

Tying weights to their necks was the best he could do but it was not a well balanced arrangement. Their legs seemed likely to rise to the surface. He hoped, however, that the marsh grass would conceal them until the crabs and the alligators reduced them to bone.

This left only Pratt whose brain was quite dead but whose lungs still tried to suck air. The Englishman, he

knew, would feel nothing if they sucked in water ins.
Nor would he feel the knife as it probed for his tongu.
Kessler would wait a few more minutes all the same.

He spent those few minutes going through a white sock
in which he'd stuffed what he took from their pockets.
Pratt's wallet was first; it was filled with little notes and
with ID in three different names. Kessler kept it intact; he
would study it later along with the notebook he'd twice
seen Pratt using. That might be in the bag that Elizabeth
had left by the door.

The one called Faisal had a Newark, New Jersey, address and a temporary visa that was two years expired.
He was mostly an extortionist, according to Pratt, who
preyed on new Muslim immigrants. Pratt used him because he knew how to intimidate but mostly because he
worked cheap. Kessler tossed Faisal's wallet over the side
after first tearing all his papers to bits and strewing them
over the water. The pockets of the one called Mahfouz
held an emergency passport and visa. They were issued
in Cairo just three days ago, arranged through the influence of the Egyptian, Bandari. Pratt thought even less
highly of Mahfouz.

"Fucking useless," said the Englishman before his
brain shut down. By then he was slurring his words.
"Can't shoot, can't fight, can't read fucking Arabic, let
alone English. Fucking twit. You know what he did at the
beach?"

Pratt told how Mahfouz, with Faisal translating, had
tried to buy sex from a blanket-full of teens . . . offering
to pay with an Egyptian five-pound note, worth about
three dollars American and from which he expected to get
change. This was the scene Kessler witnessed from a distance. He knew that to listen used up time, but he was
reluctant to slow Pratt's momentum.

"Were you going to take him back? Or were you leaving him here?"

"And I still want that Rolex, by the way."

Amazing, thought Kessler. Here's a man only minutes
before his last judgment and he wants to steal a dead
man's gold watch. "I only ask because it's such a small

boat and your rendezvous point is quite a distance away.''

Pratt glared at him. ''So you know about the seaplane.''

Kessler, in fact, had doubted a seaplane. He saw in his mind the penciled spot on the map where the place of the rendezvous was marked. Given three men and at least one kidnap victim, he had assumed that a larger boat would be waiting there.

''I know seaplanes don't fly to Egypt,'' he told Pratt.

''They fly to Grand Cayman. From there back to Cairo on Tarrant's private jet.''

''Why didn't the seaplane come here?'' he asked.

''Too hard to find . . . too many cabins like this one. Hey, hold on. I never told Tarrant which cabin.''

Kessler cocked his head toward Mahfouz, suggesting that Mahfouz had been his informer. This caused Cyril Pratt to feel doubly betrayed; he nearly threw his bottle at the dead man's shroud until he realized that it wasn't yet empty. He took one more swallow and resumed his rant against Tarrant and also against these two who, Kessler now realized, had been destined to be left in this swamp from the start. The seaplane, it turned out, had only four seats. That was one for the pilot, two for Pratt and the girl, and one for this Loomis, a lieutenant of Tarrant's. No wonder the boat seemed unsuitably small. Only Pratt and the girl would have been using it.

That aside, the deployment of the seaplane was the answer Kessler had hoped for. This Loomis and the pilot would not come looking for Pratt when he failed to show up at their rendezvous point because they wouldn't know where to start looking. They would not spot a motorboat hidden in the swamp. They would not see the glint of aluminum duct tape on legs and feet swaying with the current.

''Now Tarrant,'' said Kessler. ''Bandari and Tarrant. What else are they up to and how do we get them to pay?''

Pratt had barely had time to warm up to this subject when he felt the belch that would kill him coming on.

*   *   *

Elizabeth drove very slowly for the first quarter mile, picking her way without headlights. Cherokee sat, her legs folded to her chest, in the well of the Toyota's front seat. Her body was twisted so that she could bury her face against the seat in a cradle she formed with her arms. She did not try to look out to see where they were, nor did she complain when the rough dirt road jarred her. But her knees began to tremble from the aftershock of her ordeal whenever there was too long a silence between them.

"I know you're uncomfortable," Elizabeth reached to touch her. "You'll be able to sit up very soon now."

"I'm okay," said the girl, a shudder in her voice. "But could you just talk to me, please?"

"Let's talk about tennis. How long have you been playing?"

"Since I was five. My mom got me started."

"In Cairo?"

A nod. "We had our own court. Nadia sent over an instructor from France."

"You knew her since you were a child?"

"My mom did. They were friends. They go back to before my parents got married."

Elizabeth's feelings were mixed hearing this. On the one hand at least Cherokee would have someone who was close to her. On the other, that made this a personal matter. Nadia will not leave this at getting the girl back. Elizabeth brought the subject back to tennis.

"So your goal, I take it, is to become a professional."

"Uh-uh. Not really. I wouldn't mind giving it a shot, I guess. But my real goal is college, preferably Stanford, if I can stay in this country. I'd like to get good enough to play tennis for Stanford."

"You will. What comes after Stanford?"

"A job that helps my people. And a family, I hope."

"A family?" Elizabeth remembered that Pratt called her a lesbian.

"Sure. If I meet a good guy."

"Um . . . a good Muslim? Or don't you much care?"

"I do care. I guess I can see myself loving a Christian. My mother stayed a Christian when she married my fa-

ther. The guy wouldn't have to be of my faith but he'd
certainly have to respect it. No . . . More than that. He
would have to let me teach him all that's noble and fine
about Islam. After that he could follow his conscience.''

"Didn't you . . . just see some parts . . . that aren't so
noble and fine?''

"No, I didn't,'' she said firmly, "because that wasn't
Islam. That had nothing to do with my Islam.''

Kessler hadn't known, when on the subject of Tarrant,
that Pratt's lights would go out in about sixty seconds.
Elizabeth said it. He's sometimes too patient. But Elizabeth's method, he reminded himself, would have stopped
this man's heart a lot sooner.

What he got, all in fragments, amounted to a fair bit.
Tarrant was Lawrence J. Tarrant. Lived in Washington
. . . owned or controlled several companies . . . wife came
from money but was said to be a frump . . . Tarrant wooed
her for her family's connections . . . doesn't need them
anymore because he's made his own money circumvent-
ing UN embargoes. Some arms smuggling here . . . some
spare parts there. Tarrant's interest in the girl was purely
in getting this over with. He has one big deal pending . . .
for which he needs Bandari . . . and Bandari can't go forward until he has his own house in order. That, at least,
is Bandari's excuse. He's also scared shitless, as the Englishman put it, because this is so much bigger than anything he's done with the Libyans before. They'll turn him
into dog meat if he cocks this one up. So will Tarrant and
his partners. They'll eat him alive.

"Who are these partners?''

"I don't know exactly. Some bankers.''

"What Libyans, then? Let's have some names.''

"I don't know any names. Just two colonels.''

"Okay, then how big?'' Kessler prodded. "What are
his plans and how do we wreck them unless Tarrant
makes us both rich?''

"Bigger than a fucking biblical plague. Worse than the
Black Death. You'll see.''

"We're talking what? Bacteriological weapons?''

"Not bugs. Bugs die out. This keeps killing whole cities."

This was when Cyril Pratt thought he felt a belch rising. These were the last words he said. Elizabeth came, Elizabeth went, and he finished wrapping Pratt in his blanket.

Now out in the swamp, with only Pratt left, Kessler felt for a pulse one more time. Still there. By a thread. Barely breathing. Close enough, he decided. Kessler cut him.

He eased Pratt's head with the concrete block attached over the side of the boat. The rest of him tumbled in after. Pratt was still leaving bubbles as he started the motor and turned the boat toward the shore. Once there he smashed a hole in the bottom and disconnected the fuel line. He turned the boat, its engine still sputtering, and sent it back out to the reeds. All that was left was a final inspection and then he would return to the island. Elizabeth can thank him for all his help and then ask, "So, Martin. How soon are you leaving?"

Kessler felt the weight of the Rolex in his pocket. He could, he supposed, ask Elizabeth to translate but it was already clear that the watch was Bandari's. It was foolish to keep it if he should be stopped. He threw it as far as he could.

"You want it so bad? Take it with you."

As for Pratt's story, for all its detail, Kessler didn't know what to believe. A plot to kill tens of thousands and then keep on killing? What for? For a businessman this is a business? Why did Pratt take so long to get to the point? And why, above all, would someone like Tarrant let an insect like Pratt know the least little thing about his schemes? The answer is that he certainly wouldn't. Pratt took so long because it took that long for a good enough story to pop into his head.

What then, Kessler asked himself, might Tarrant's game be other than frustrating UN embargoes? That in itself was a good way to get rich. He sold things to countries that couldn't get them legally and earned an indecent profit. Bandari seemed to be merely his middle man for a deal being made with the Libyans. The Egyptians have been laundering Libyan money since long before the current sanctions were imposed.

Kessler knew about embargo-busting as well. The former East Germany did that all the time. These days, he imagined, it was probably taught in business schools as a good way to triple one's profits. Before the UN imposed an embargo—on Libya and Iraq, for example—there were weeks of debate. While they were debating it made sense to stock up if it was you they were about to embargo. So your country, say Libya, made a mad dash to order all the spare parts it thinks it would need. They'll pay up the nose to get everything delivered before the sanctions take effect. Before that, it's legal. The next day it isn't. And banks . . . not just Arab banks, Protestant banks . . . will earn millions just for moving money around, staying one step ahead of the UN officials who are chasing it trying to freeze assets.

The UN officials would say, "What are you doing? Your government voted for this, where's your loyalty? Don't you realize we're trying to stop terrorism here?"

The bankers would say, "Hey, don't wave me a flag. The world turns on money, not politics."

As for Lawrence J. Tarrant and Gamal Bandari, they must have been busting embargoes already in place. For that they could both go to prison but they wouldn't. The worst that could happen was that their deals would fall through and they'd be out all the bribes they had paid. Whatever they were up to, Kessler didn't much care. All Elizabeth would want is that they do it somewhere else because the only border she cared about was the bridge to Hilton Head Island. And she was right. One's borders were not the lines someone has drawn. One's borders were whatever one will fight to defend.

Elizabeth knew that she was less than open-minded when it came to the subject of Islam. *"That wasn't Islam?"* she was tempted to ask Cherokee. *"There's a tape in my trunk that maybe you should see if you think your religion is so noble and fine."*

But she knew that she'd do no such thing. If anything

here was noble and fine it was this little fourteen-year-old girl. She was tempted to say, *"I'm Elizabeth Stride and you can take it from me . . . your religion doesn't deserve you."*

But she wouldn't say that either. What she'd do is keep her mind on the business at hand. She had seen only one police cruiser so far. It had passed her at high speed, ignoring the car she was driving. The long bridge to the island was directly ahead. She entered the first and the lowest of its spans, taking care not to exceed the speed limit by much. As she neared the crest of the second span she tensed at the glow of more strobe lights in the sky. She knew that there must be a roadblock ahead.

There was. But it was set in the outbound lanes only. The police were stopping cars that were leaving the island but were paying no attention to those coming in. Relieved, Elizabeth drove on.

"Do you play tennis?" Cherokee asked. "Or can't I even know that?"

"Um . . . I play. Not great, but I enjoy it."

"I don't believe you. I bet you're very good."

"Cherokee, honey, you'd blow me off the court."

"Not if you won't let me open my eyes."

Elizabeth laughed and reached over to poke her. She still had her smile as she drove past the Hilton Head Welcome Center. They were now on the widest part of the island. The girl probably knew that she'd gone over the bridge because there were no other grades within miles. Even so, she decided, she would try to disorient her. She veered off toward Spanish Wells Plantation and made several more turns before rejoining the main road from that direction. Now the girl might think that's where she'd been held.

"You can sit up now," Elizabeth told her. "Just remember, keep both your eyes glued to your right."

Cherokee groaned with relief as she pulled herself up and straightened her legs. She pulled her hat further down on her forehead.

"Will I *ever* get to see you? Or know who you are?"

Elizabeth hesitated.

"I know, I know," said the girl with a sigh. "It's better for you if I don't."

She said nothing more for several heartbeats.

"I've got to at least have a name," blurted Cherokee. "How about if I pick one myself?"

"You mean make one up? What good will that do?"

"Look . . . I won't forget you for the rest of my life but all you're going to be is a voice. I want to have a name that we both know is you even if it's only the two of us who know it."

Elizabeth blinked at the logic but she saw no harm in it. "Um . . . okay. Do you have one in mind?"

"Yes I do. You're Martina."

"Martina," she repeated. "As in Navratilova?"

Cherokee nodded. "You're strong . . . like she is. And you're kind . . . like she is. I thought about GiGi as in GiGi Fernandez because she's my idol and she's beautiful and I bet you are, too. But GiGi isn't an elegant name. You're more of a Martina."

Elizabeth felt herself starting to blush.

The car was approaching Sea Pines Circle. The tennis school complex was off to the left but Elizabeth chose to go straight, wind around, and approach the complex from the rear. Anyone now out looking for Cherokee wouldn't be looking in that direction. She went through the main gate of Sea Pines Plantation, waved through by the guards because she had Martin's pass on her visor. She drove well into Sea Pines before turning left at the riding stables and, to make doubly certain that she was not being followed, wound through several residential streets before making her way to the smaller gatehouse on North Sea Pines Drive. That gate, she knew, opened onto Cordillo Parkway and was less than a mile from the school.

"I'll get you very close," she said to the girl, "but I don't want anyone there to see me either. What I'll do is let you out about fifty yards short of it. I'll be watching you until you're inside. Go straight to either Nadia or Jasmine, no one else, no police, and tell them exactly what happened as you know it."

"Do I have to say that man was undressing me?"

"No, but listen. Tell them I said they should make up a story. There was never any kidnapping, it was a false alarm, maybe you got rebellious and did something stupid. Kids do stupid things all the time."

"Hmmph. Thanks a lot."

"You can live with it. Do it. We all want this to die down."

"Well . . . I guess," she said doubtfully. "But you know Jasmine and some of the guards here. They'll want to go after those men."

"Tell them I said . . . that they'd be wasting their time. Tell Nadia that I'll give her a call but only if I see that she's keeping this quiet."

"That . . . sounds like Nadia won't know who you are."

"No, she won't. Tell her not to waste time trying to figure that out either."

"But she'll know that you're from the Society, won't she? She'll know that you're from the Nusaybah."

"She'll . . . know I'm a friend," said Elizabeth.

Cherokee heard the brief hesitation. She almost turned her head. "Martina?"

"I'll pull over here. Are you ready?"

"Martina . . . you are from the Nusaybah Society, aren't you? You and the man who was with you?"

"Who said it was a man?"

"Okay, then. That woman."

"We're friends. And I'm your friend. That's all you have to know."

The car crept to a stop. Cherokee didn't move. She reached one arm behind her and groped for Elizabeth's hand. She found it and squeezed it.

"Could I give you a hug?" she asked softly.

"Cherokee . . . go."

"Couldn't I hold you? Just for a second? I promise I won't open my eyes."

Elizabeth reached for her shoulders and turned her. They held each other for a full half minute. Elizabeth kissed her. She tasted tears. She realized that some were her own.

Nineteen

Nadia Halaby had a story already, the one Jasmine had told the state troopers. Like it or not she was stuck with it.

But her mind was reeling with thoughts of this woman who had rescued Aisha and brought her back home, but had not allowed her face to be seen. Aisha felt sure that a man had been with her, not a woman as this . . . Martina . . . had claimed. His footsteps were heavier than those of the woman; she thought she heard a man's voice say the words "Bad mistake" but he had always stayed outside the cabin. Aisha said this reluctantly. She seemed to feel that it was betraying a friendship. This Martina had her reasons if she lied.

As for the farmer, the caller, Floyd Wiggins, Nadia knew who he must really have been. Blond hair, British accent, two bearded Muslims assisting, even a video camera. It could only be the bounty hunter, Cyril Pratt. Even Jasmine now realized that the man who had called her had a drawl unlike any she'd heard in the South and that, on reflection, it was faked.

The story she was stuck with was the one Pratt concocted. A couple named Wiggins had taken the girl in after two drunken youths beat her up. Nadia drove to the Wiggins farm, no one was there, she didn't know what to make of it so she called the police. But then the couple named Wiggins dropped Cherokee off. No, Cherokee couldn't describe them very well. The poor girl was in shock and still is. Just an old man and woman, their car was blue, maybe green. Why this couple didn't wait there, why they can't be found now, Nadia could not imagine. The two boys who grabbed Cherokee were both in their teens, they had brown hair or blond and they drove an old pickup that might have been red and she thinks they said something about going to Atlanta.

"Cherokee, how good an actress are you?" asked Nadia as she spread an ointment on her wrists.

"When I talk to the police? I can do it, I think. But I can't stop my knees from shaking."

"Shaking is good," said the black woman, Jazz. "If the questions get hard, you just get hysterical. We'll jump in and take it from there."

Nadia bandaged both wrists with thin strips of gauze and covered the dressings with blue terry wristbands. "This is simpler," she told Cherokee, "than trying to explain why two boys would have handcuffs and especially how the Wigginses got them off you."

"They're too clean; make them dirty," said Jazz.

Nadia reached for some soil from a plant and rubbed some into the bands. That done, she unbraided Cherokee's hair and arranged it with her fingers so that it covered much of her face. She felt sure that no newspaper would run her photo but at least two reporters were waiting downstairs. She would try to persuade them, as Cherokee suggested, that the worst those two boys had done was try to kiss her but one lost his temper when she jabbed him in the eye.

Jazz thought that scenario would play even better if Cherokee had the smell of beer on her breath. "There's no sin," she told her. "You don't have to swallow. Just one sip to rinse out your mouth."

"Will it make me sick?" asked the girl with a grimace.

"Sick's even better. They say Indians can't drink. I'll get Roy to bring up a bottle."

While Jazz made her phone call Nadia knelt at the chair and got back to the part that confused her the most. "This woman who rescued you," Nadia asked. "When she first walked in she was dressed in full niqab?"

Cherokee nodded. "A veil and abaya. Black gloves, soft black shoes. She had everything covered but her eyes. And when she sat on the bed I saw the hilt of a Jambiya sticking out."

"A Jambiya?" asked Jazz who had completed her call.

"It's a knife," Nadia told her. And then to the girl, "But you say you don't think she'd ever heard of Nusaybah?"

"She . . . isn't even Muslim, I don't think."

"And later you could have looked at her face but you didn't. Same thing with the man who was with her?"

"I never saw the man. I mostly heard sounds. And I heard what I think was a motorboat starting."

"But you can't tell us anything about where this place was?"

Cherokee shook her head slowly and shrugged.

"You're holding something back," said Nadia. "What is it?"

"I . . . don't think she wants you to look for that cabin. She wants me to think it was out by Spanish Wells."

"And we shouldn't look for those three men either," said Jasmine. "Why do you suppose she'd say that?"

"She said they won't be back. She said they can't hurt me."

Jasmine and Nadia exchanged looks. The girl noticed.

"You're thinking she murdered them. She wouldn't have done that. All she did was scare them away."

The man named Roy knocked and entered the room. "It's show time," he said, pointing over his shoulder. "Police and an ambulance want to see her downstairs." He produced a beer can from one of his pockets. Jazz took it and popped it and picked up a waste basket. The girl made a face but she sipped the beer gamely, nearly gagging before she spit it out.

"Kids do dumb things all the time," she muttered.

"Beg pardon?"

"Never mind."

"Cherokee, child," said the black man named Roy. "They're going to want a doctor to examine you. You sure none of them, like, did anything bad?"

". . . The blond man just hit me. That's all."

Nadia heard the brief hesitation and saw the hand that went to her breast as if to hold the top of her swimsuit in place. She saw that the girl was remembering.

"Cherokee, sweetie, you'd best tell us now. The doctor will know if . . . if anything's changed."

But that was not what Cherokee was remembering. In her head she was hearing the Englishman's voice as if from a distant dream. It was after he hit her . . . he was talking to a camera . . . using words like "slut" and even "adulteress" but why would he say such things about her? He said to the camera that she shamed her father . . . *"that good man, Avram Bandari . . ."* but don't worry about that any longer because, *"the slut has now answered to God."*

"Was that man going to kill me?" she asked quietly.

Nadia shook her head. "He was sent to bring you back. By your uncle, I'm afraid."

"Uncle Gamal? But what good would it do? The only way he'd have a claim over me is if both my parents were . . ."

"Cherokee . . . the police. One thing at a time."

Cherokee stared at her. Her cheeks became hot.

"Don't even think it," Nadia said quickly. "Your mother is fine; she'll be here very soon; we've already arranged for her tickets and papers."

"But my father. He's not coming with her?"

"Your father is . . . not free to leave yet. Your mother will explain when she gets here."

Cherokee looked at her, and then at Jasmine. She thought she saw something in Jasmine's eyes.

"The woman who saved me . . . I want to see her again."

"See her how? We don't know who she is."

"But she'll call you. She said so. I'll talk to her then."

"Well . . . we'll see." Nadia straightened. "But for now you need to put her out of your mind. There's no mystery woman, there's no Englishman, no cabin. There's only those two boys who grabbed you and the farmers who drove you back home. Cherokee, are you able to do this?''

"I'll do it. If I don't, she won't call.''

Elizabeth had returned to her home on Marsh Drive. It was getting quite late and there was much left to do. She tried to push Cherokee out of her mind.

She backed her red Bronco out of the carport and replaced it with Martin's Toyota. She took a few minutes to hose down the tires to clean them of off-island mud. Next, she used a spray cleaner to wipe the passenger seat area to dissolve any fingerprints the girl might have left. From the well of the back seat she took Pratt's Nike tote. Her own blue duffel was beneath it. Because of its color she almost failed to notice a piece of blue feather from Cherokee's hat band. She picked it up, fingered it, and put it in her pocket. She would flush or burn it with a few other things.

Inside, in her bathroom, she removed her dark lenses. She next changed her clothing to the dress she'd worn earlier and put all her dangley junk jewelry back on. She took Pratt's camcorder from the Nike tote and stuffed the bag into her duffel. It was foolish to keep it, especially those photographs, but she could not bring herself to destroy them just yet.

Martin, she knew, should be finished with his work and would be on his way back in Pratt's car. He would probably call her on the Englishman's cell phone and ask her to meet him somewhere on the island. He'd realize that Cherokee had described Pratt by now. It wouldn't take Halaby and the rest long to realize that her description fit a guest named Harry Wheeler who checked out of the club that same day. It would not do, therefore, for them to see Martin driving up in a car with the same plates as Wheeler's. It was enough that those two guards had already seen him showing an interest in Pratt's car.

What did Cherokee call them? The Nusaybah Society. The name had rung a distant bell but she hadn't been able to place it until now. It was a woman's name, but unlike Aisha or Fatima, it was one seldom given to daughters these days. The original Nusaybah was an early Muslim heroine who fought at Mohammed's side in several battles. She saved his life at least once. Had an arm lopped off by a sword but survived. Muslim men don't name their daughters Nusaybah for fear that it would sound insufficiently meek. And it did, thought Elizabeth, seem a militant name for anything so passive as a safe house.

Her bedside phone rang. It was Martin.

"Our friend arrived safely?" he said when she answered.

"Uh-huh. Where are you?"

"Long-term parking at your airport. That's where I'm leaving our other friend's car."

"Twenty minutes," she said and hung up.

She would fetch him in the Bronco and drive him back here, then have him take his own car and get over to the Players Club. She would like, this one time, to ask him to stay but he'd best get back and see what's happening there. She could do that herself, come to think of it. She could drive to the airport by way of Cordillo. If she were to see more flashing police lights she would seem to be just a curious passerby who looked in to see the reason for all the excitement. Martin won't mind waiting a few minutes more.

Once again she went out through the East Sea Pines Gate and turned onto Cordillo Parkway. Approaching the Players Club, she did see police cars but their strobe lights this time were quiet. She wet her lips and pulled into the lot. There were three cars in all, two of the state troopers and one of the Sheriff's Department. Near them was a van with the logo of The Island Packet on its side. A female reporter and a young male photographer were trying to question a deputy. The deputy said little. Mostly he shrugged. A number of guests who had taken a late swim were watching from behind the heated pool's hedge. A half dozen more stood nearer the police cars. Some were chatting with one of the troopers. More shrugs.

All at once two more troopers emerged from the entrance at the top of the Players Club ramp. They were talking to a woman whom Elizabeth recognized from the clippings she took from the cabin. She looked very tired but not overly distressed. In fact, just now, she managed a smile as she touched one officer's arm. The officer, who had chevrons on his sleeve, seemed more sympathetic than grim. He whispered something into Nadia's ear then walked down the ramp to where the reporter had been waiting.

Some nearby guests were craning their necks to hear what the sergeant was saying. Elizabeth could hear nothing from where she had parked but she could almost tell what was said by their manner. The sergeant made gestures that seemed to convey that some misunderstanding had occurred. The reporter shrugged and nodded as if to agree that nothing worth telling had happened. The reporter and photographer went back to their van, the photographer dismantling his lights as he walked.

Elizabeth watched the van drive off and approached a young couple who'd been listening. "What happened?" she asked. "Do you know?"

"Just some kid, some girl," the man answered. "According to the cop she was out drinking beer and got into an argument with some other girl. She got beat up and was afraid to come back here."

Elizabeth raised an eyebrow. "The press and three squad cars for that?"

"Well, she missed her bed check and that woman up there panicked."

The man's wife frowned, annoyed at his dismissal of a justified concern. "A lot of these kids at the tennis school are rich," she told Elizabeth, "so the woman in charge of them was afraid she'd been kidnapped."

"But the girl did turn up."

"They took her to the hospital a few minutes ago. An assistant instructor went with her. She didn't look bad, though. She had a nice pair of shiners but seemed mostly embarrassed. They'll check her out to be sure."

"Kids," clucked Elizabeth.

"We all did our share of foolish things," said the woman.

Elizabeth wished them a pleasant stay and returned to

her Bronco. She was just a bit startled by the story. As she'd hoped, there was no mention of the girl being taken or of anyone trying to lure Nadia off the island. But it didn't explain how an adolescent cat-fight led to the bridge being blocked and to police cars converging on a farm outside Bluffton. The police weren't stupid so there must be two stories, this one concocted for public consumption so as not to alarm the tourists. She would need to call Nadia, sooner rather than later, to find out how much the police had been told.

Nadia Halaby, quietly furious, had returned to her second-floor office. On the wall were a dozen framed photographs of women. Only two were still living; most of the rest had suffered terrible deaths as the price of trying to help their Muslim sisters. She wondered how soon her own photo might join them.

She sat at her IBM desktop computer and brought up the file marked ''Nusaybah.'' She typed out a message and selected the addresses to which it would go by e-mail. The message was short, it was only two questions. ''Are any of your people on or near this island? Do you know of a woman called Martina?'' She watched for ten minutes as the answers came in and crawled across the bottom of her screen.

''No one from here. What has happened?''

''Not us. Don't know a Martina. Do you need us?''

''Not from here. Have you checked with our sister societies?''

She replied that the matter was under control. She thanked them and called up a new group of addresses, two of which were in England and France. Their responses were similar. She sat for a while, drumming her fingers. At last she touched the keyboard and called up the file marked ''Bandari.'' She scrolled past Aisha's biographical data to the section relating to next of kin. Avram Bandari was the first name she saw. She had known for three weeks that he'd been murdered in Suez. Leyna, Avram's wife, her old friend, called and told her. She asked, however, that she say nothing to Aisha but to please be all the more vigilant. Leyna said she was coming. She'd tell Aisha herself. The healing will be faster if they wipe each other's tears. But she should have arrived by midweek at the latest. Nadia dreaded the thought that it might now fall to her to tell Aisha that neither of her parents would be coming. And that still another photograph would now hang on her wall.

Also listed was the number of Avram's Swiss lawyer. She thought about faxing him with her suspicions but that was pointless until she was sure. Further down, at the bottom, was the name of Avram's brother, Gamal.

"But forget about him," Leyna had told her when she first enrolled Aisha two years ago. "Don't ever call him as next of kin."

"Avram and his brother are not close, I take it?" It struck her that she had never set eyes on Gamal. No photographs of him in Avram's house, no visits, not even on Leyna's birthday one year at a party that half of Cairo attended.

"He is never to know where she is," Leyna told her.

Nadia answered that she had no wish to pry. "But you came asking us to provide a safe haven for Aisha. I need to ask; a safe haven from what?"

Aisha's mother took a breath that was weary and sad. "Gamal hates my husband for being what he isn't. He hates me merely for being Avram's wife but he turns into mush if I smile at him. He's corrupt and self-serving but that's not what makes him so dangerous. While he lines his own pockets in his government job he has also been playing the Islamist card by pandering to the worst of that bunch. Don't ever let him get his hands on Aisha."

"This is all the more reason I should know about him. Get me a picture so we know what he looks like. For now, let's start with his name and address."

Nadia, at the time, was not especially alarmed. The Mideast had no shortage of men like Gamal but, thank God, it had more men like Avram. The Gamals of that world were the predatory elite. They were men who were strictly out for themselves but they tried to hedge their bets against the Islamists coming to power. Some did it by squirreling money abroad and some by trying to reserve box seats at home in any new fundamentalist regime. She'd known men who each day rubbed their foreheads with sandpaper to develop the callus the devout got from praying. But for two years she'd given little thought to the brother, until Leyna called to say Avram had been killed. A week after that she got a call from the network to say that Leyna herself was in hiding. This was after an ugly confrontation at the funeral and especially after Avram's will was made public. The network heard rumors that Pratt had been hired but assured her that Leyna was safe. She had fled to Alexandria and would leave the country as soon as new papers could be brought to her.

Nadia's fingers were drumming again. In her mind was the image of Aisha's battered face and of the Englishman who must have been Pratt. A part of her blamed herself for what happened. She knew that she should have been more vigilant.

"Nadia? There's a phone call."

She had not heard Roy knock. "From the network?"

"From a woman. She says you'll know who she is."

Twenty

Elizabeth had called with Pratt's cellular phone as she drove Martin back from the airport. Martin had objected, he said let it go, but that was before she let him look at the tape.

"What exactly have you told the police?" she asked Nadia.

"Martina? Who are you? Who sent you?"

Elizabeth almost smiled at the use of that name. She ignored these questions and repeated her own. As Nadia answered she held Pratt's phone so that Martin could hear the story she had told, an account that involved drinking beer with two boys...who took her for a ride... wouldn't let her out of their truck...she poked the driver in the eye so he stopped and beat her up...no, they touched her but that's all they did. The police, said Nadia, were annoyed, they were skeptical, but inclined to leave well enough alone.

At this Martin mouthed, "*Good advice*," to Elizabeth. At the part of the story that spoke of a farmer who supposedly drove Cherokee home, she looked at Martin with a questioning shrug. Martin knew where that came from. He mouthed the word "*Pratt*."

"From a farm out near Bluffton?" Elizabeth asked Nadia.

"Yes, the Wiggins farm. You were there?"

"No, we weren't, but someone was hoping you'd be. I gather you're worth a lot of money."

"That someone . . . who called here . . . was he Cyril Pratt?" Nadia said the name as if she were spitting.

"*Was* is correct. He's gone now."

"There were two men with him. I hope you will tell me that they're all more than gone."

"I will tell you that the three are no longer a concern. Do you know about Cherokee's parents?"

The line went quiet. "Leyna too? How?"

Elizabeth told her what she'd seen on the tape, that her skull had been crushed by the uncle. She repeated in a mix of English and Arabic what had been said between the mother and the uncle. Her account was interrupted several times by soft moans. Nadia had to swallow before she could speak.

"Martina . . . if you'll meet with me . . . if we can just talk . . . I swear on my life that I would never identify you."

"How is Cherokee doing? Is she holding up well?"

"She is made of good stuff. She'll be fine. But she wanted to talk to you if you did call. She'll be very upset that she—"

"There will be no more contact." Elizabeth cut her off. "We'll be out of the country by morning. But if you let anything else happen to that girl, you might see me once too often."

Elizabeth broke the connection.

"Done with your usual sensitivity," said Martin. "What country, by the way, are we going to?"

"You're going, not me. To wherever your Maria is waiting for you."

"Maria would at least have let me finish my dinner. I left a full glass of wine on your table."

"Martin, is there a Maria or not?"

He hesitated, then sighed. "There is for me somewhere, I hope."

Elizabeth drove in silence staring ahead, past all the landmarks that were part of her new life. Nothing seemed to look quite the same. At a light she came up behind a blue Ford convertible like the one that her doctor friend,

Jonathan, drove. It was not his car, it had Michigan plates. But she wondered if she'd ever walk and talk with him again, have lunch with him again, play golf with him, go dancing with him or whatever. And at the moment, sadly, she didn't much care. What she wanted at this moment was a thing she couldn't have. She wanted to be with Cherokee Blye. To be there to hold her when she learned about her parents. To walk with her, talk with her, afterward. She wanted to be with a brave little girl who knows at some level what she's capable of and who thinks that she's wonderful all the same.

"Martin?" She touched her hand to his arm.

"Here's your knife, by the way. It will need a good cleaning."

She ignored the Jambiya that he placed on her lap. "If you'd like to stay over at my house tonight . . ."

"You'd best get some sleep," he told her.

"What I'm saying . . . there's no need for you to be in your room. No one will care now who's there and who isn't."

Kessler knew what this was from other nights in their past. He knew what it wasn't as well. And she confirmed it.

"I . . . would not be much good for you," she said staring at the road, "but if you'd care to stay I would have no . . . objection."

Kessler took her hand and touched it lightly to his lips. "I will tell you," he said quietly, "what is good for me tonight. What I want is to see you take that hot bath you mentioned and bring in your glass of wine with you. After that I want you to fall sound asleep. That's what would be good for me tonight."

Her eyes became moist. "I won't sleep, I don't think."

"Then I'll be there to talk. Or to maybe play chess or backgammon with you. When you want me I'll be lying out back in your hammock. I'll teach you the names of some stars."

She was silent again for several long moments.

"You're a good man, do you know that?" she said to him at last. "I mean, look at your life, all the things that you've done, and you're still a really good man.''

"Elizabeth . . .''

"What's wrong with me, Martin? Why do I keep hating?''

He didn't answer because she asked the wrong question. The question that was really in her heart was more like, ''Why do I have feelings for a young Muslim girl and how is it that a Muslim admires me of all people?''

There's no irony in this. It's a question of need. As for how to stop hating, the girl, Kessler feared, would not be much help in that either. This was even if to see her again was not out of the question. That girl was about to be told about her parents. She would learn to hate the way Elizabeth learned. With Elizabeth it began with murdered parents as well.

"You're better than you know, Elizabeth.''

"How am I better? In what way?''

"You'd better give me Pratt's cell phone and case. I'll throw it in someone's lagoon, not yours.''

"Answer me, Martin. In what way am I nice?''

He patted her knee. ''I'll tell you while I'm helping with the dishes.''

The call had left a chill down Nadia's spine. This woman, this Martina, was as cold as a grave and she had ended with a threat that Nadia resented even though she knew well that she deserved it. And tonight or tomorrow she must break Aisha's heart. Roy, whose true name was Ahmad, had listened. He came to her chair where she sat at her computer and he hugged her in a way that was not strictly Islamic, but the hug gave her strength all the same.

"Do you think she did kill them? All three?'' she asked him.

"Oh, they're dead. I just hope she hid the bodies real good. We don't want some dog digging up Pratt's body and trotting along with a hand in its mouth. But on second thought, she didn't have much time. Maybe she still means to do that.''

"Still do it when? She said she's leaving the country.''

Roy grunted. ''That *is* what she said.''

"Well . . . why do you doubt it? They've done what they seem to have come for."

A thoughtful frown. "If she's not from around here, not from the sisterhood and not even Muslim according to Aisha, why should she care what you told the police?"

"So she wouldn't get stopped at a roadblock?"

"Yeah, but why would that matter if nobody knows what she looks like? Ask me, she wants this to blow over."

Nadia stared at him. "You're saying she lives here?"

"I'm saying she might. Either way, she was here long enough to watch Pratt. If she knew where Pratt and the others would take Aisha, she must have had him under surveillance. She might have wanted Pratt for herself for some reason. But if that's true, why wait until he took Aisha and then have to bring her back here? Why wouldn't she just go out to that cabin and put a few holes in his head?"

Nadia wasn't sure she was following. But Roy and Sam—in their lives before this—had learned the workings of dangerous minds. That last was what Roy would have done.

"I don't know," she asked him. "Why wouldn't she?"

"Lots of people on this island. They come from all over. My guess, there's more than just you worth a bounty. I'd say she spotted Pratt and was keeping an eye on him. I'd say she wouldn't have bothered Pratt as long as it wasn't her he was after."

"But she did, Roy. Why?"

The big man shrugged. "This is reaching, I know, but I wonder if she didn't know Aisha already. I wonder if that's why she couldn't show her face."

The phone made her jump. Nadia snatched at it hoping that it was Martina again, calling to say she would meet after all. But the call was from Jasmine. She said that the doctor was finished with Aisha. She was fine and could come home but Jazz thought she should have an armed escort. She asked that Roy or Sam come pick them up.

"I'll do it," said the man whose Muslim name was

Ahmad. "I want to hear more about this friend of hers anyway."

He went out and Nadia was alone with her computer. On its screen, highlighted, were the names of Aisha's parents. Avram and Leyna seemed to pull at her eye; it was almost as if they were trying to speak. *"Take care of her, Nadia. Tell her about us but don't say we suffered. Tell her that we're both now with God and we're happy. But tell her that our spirits will be with her as well. Every day of her life she should know that we love her. Every night while she sleeps we'll stand guard at her bedside."*

She would tell her these things and hope they gave comfort. It was much like what Nadia's dear father had told her on the day when breast cancer took her own mother's life. But for now she did not need to talk to ghosts; she did not need to be haunted by names on a screen. She reached for the switch to turn the thing off when her eye found a name at the bottom of the list. The uncle, that bastard Gamal. At this moment he was probably waiting in Cairo for word that his niece and his dead brother's fortune were his to use as he pleased.

On an impulse that she knew was better resisted, Nadia picked up the phone at her elbow. She punched out "OO" and asked the operator who answered to connect her with Directory Assistance for Cairo. A few minutes later—fast service for Egypt—she had the number of his town house on the Nile Corniche and another for his office at the Ministry of Development. It was then that her better judgment took hold. It was, after all, not yet morning in Cairo. To call him, she realized, would serve no useful purpose. She had enough on her mind as it was.

But her mind taunted her with a picture of Gamal, his belly rising beneath silken sheets. In Cairo the chants of a thousand muezzins would soon be calling the faithful to prayer. Gamal wouldn't hear them. Those men never do. All their windows are sealed against the street din of Cairo. He'd wake when he wanted and rub his forehead until it was pink so that everyone would think he'd been praying on a rug and would know that he was a good Muslim. After that he would look into his mirror and

smile because he knew he was soon to have all that he'd
coveted.

Nadia's fingers, as if they had a will of their own, began
working the buttons of her phone. She listened to static
and the ghosts of other voices and then the harsh rasp of
an Egyptian phone ringing.

"Yes . . . yes?" came the voice. "What has happened?"

He had answered in English as if he'd expected the
caller to be speaking that language as well.

"You're expecting Cyril Pratt? Well, he's dead, you
coward, you miserable pile of shit."

"What? Who? What . . . what?" was all he could stam-
mer.

"They're all dead. All three. All three of them died
after telling us everything, you murdering hypocrite, you
sole of a shoe. We have people in Cairo who watch everything you do and they'll know if you send any more. But
you won't have time, you diseased and putrid pig, because
now it is you who will be hunted. Oh, we're not going to
kill you, at least not at first. First we will disgrace you
because we have the tape that shows you crushing the
skull of your brother's good wife. It convicts you out of
that brave woman's mouth and it tells how you stick your
limp cock up boys' asses. I think before we kill you we'll
cut that off first and the hand that murdered Leyna after
that. We'll let you live with a stump where your right
hand is now until it's time to send the rest of you to hell."

She heard only a squawk before she slammed down the
phone. Her heart was pounding. She needed time to catch
her breath. She had done a foolish thing and she knew it.
But then slowly she smiled for the first time that day. She
wished now that she'd said those things to him in Arabic.
Curses soar much more grandly in Arabic.

Kessler told Elizabeth what she needed to hear.

In fact a good deal of it was true.

She was certainly a lady; you couldn't have a better
friend; she was utterly feminine when she let herself be.
She could stand, however, to bite her tongue now and

then. He was tempted to say that what she needed was a puppy because people like Elizabeth needed something to care for. But that would have led to thoughts about the babies which a Hezbollah bullet had denied her. And that would have led back to thoughts of the girl, which was what put her in this mood in the first place.

Kessler filled her tub for her and added half a container of bubble bath which he discovered under her sink. The granules were purple, the scent was of lilacs. You learned something new about Elizabeth every day. He brought in a radio which he tuned to a station playing classical music and set a fresh glass of wine by the tub. She smiled when she saw the foot-high mound of bubbles and asked him to turn his back as she undressed. This, he knew, was not modesty in the usual sense. She did not like anyone, even him, to see her scars.

"Stay with me awhile," she said as she settled. "Why don't you go get your glass?"

He did, and he thought it was nice that she asked but he would rather have had time to himself. He wanted to make one more call on Pratt's phone before the phone took a bath of its own. He supposed that it could wait a little longer.

He had gone through Pratt's bag and especially his notebook while he waited for Elizabeth to come get him. The garment bag had yielded nothing of interest, just some changes of clothing and a toiletries kit. He had weighted it with rocks and tossed it in a bog near the airport. He was learning to appreciate this low country landscape. It slurped up whatever you dropped.

The notebook, however, was a mine of information. There were several pages of names, all women, whom Kessler presumed to be runaways. More than half were followed by the names of children who apparently were traveling with the mothers. Quite a few of these had already been caught. Pratt would scrawl the word "Done" across their listings and usually he'd write in a date. Most, however, were still at large. After many of these Pratt had added notations saying where they might be living now, what names they might be using, and who might be pro-

tecting them. Some of the assumed names were Arab-
sounding but many had adopted Italian names, Hispanic
names, or even common American names.

A considerable number were believed to be living in
New York City and under the protection of the Nasreen
Society. Nasreen, said Pratt's notes, was the name of a
woman who died a martyr's death some years back. The
Nasreens were mostly Sunni Muslims with male as well
as female members and quite a few American blacks,
most of whom were recent converts to Islam. Others were
clustered in Southern California. The group there was
called the Sisters of Fatima. Fatima, Pratt wrote, was one
of Mohammed's wives. The women in this particular
group were all Shiites and most had escaped from Iran.

The smallest cluster was on Hilton Head Island and its
group was called the Nusaybah Society. Pratt's notes
didn't say who or what was a Nusaybah. These, like the
group in New York, were Sunni Muslims and the two
appeared to be closely allied. Within that cluster were two
names Kessler recognized, Nadia Halaby and Aisha Bandari. Aisha was a.k.a. Cherokee Blye. Penciled in near the
latter was a ''Monica Blye,'' whom he knew must have
been the girl's mother.

Other pages dealt with sister societies that were head-
quartered all over Europe. His notes indicated that their
addresses kept moving because fear of reprisals was constant. Not all ran safe houses. Some were merely support
groups to help Muslim women get used to Western ways.
Some ran extensive underground railways to get women
out—Pratt had drawn crude maps of two of them—and
then provided free legal help afterward. But the act of
going to a Western court was, by itself, enough to call for
a death sentence. It meant that you'd gone over to the
infidel, and that was apostasy, and the punishment for
apostasy was death. So, even if you won in court you'd
have to enter some Muslim version of a witness protection
program.

Pratt also had some notes on the uses of a fatwah. Kessler himself had always supposed, at least since the Sal-
man Rushdie affair, that a fatwah was something like a

mafia contract. Elizabeth explained that it was nothing of the sort. A fatwah, she explained, was simply a religious opinion. You could, for example, ask your local sheik if a Muslim could ever eat pork. The answer would be yes, but only if he's starving and has access to no other food. Afterward, she said, he'd be expected to atone for it by feeding someone else who was hungry. Most fatwahs, she said, are meant to be helpful and, coming from Elizabeth, this was quite an admission.

Another example: say a Muslim needed to take out a loan. Islam forbade the paying of interest; the Koranic injunction was actually against usury, but most clerics read it to mean any interest at all. The religious opinion or fatwah might be that if someone gave you the use of his money it was all right to give him a gift in return. As long as it wasn't excessive and you called it something other than interest.

Pratt, of course, was not concerned about usury or whether it was lawful to have sausage for breakfast. His questions all had to do with killing. The Koran, or at least his reading of it, listed a great many offenses for which one should be killed. It ruled out the killing of unwanted children and discouraged the killing of other Muslims, but after that it didn't draw much of a line. It said that you shouldn't kill without a just cause but there was no guilt in killing someone who had wronged you. These seemed to cover a great deal of ground. But in order to make sure that there was no guilt attached, the trick was to find a sheik or a mullah who said so. What Pratt had learned was that if you didn't get the answer you wanted from one sheik, you could keep asking others until you did. That done, and especially if a reward was thrown in, it was no problem to find a Muslim who would do the killing for you because now it was not murder and he couldn't be blamed. On the contrary, he'll become a hero on earth and can expect to be rewarded in Paradise.

''A most convenient religion,'' noted Pratt in the margin.

Elizabeth, by the way, had also once pointed out that the Muslims hadn't cornered the market on fatwahs. She said Orthodox Jews issued fatwahs as well. She said that the assassin of Yitzhak Rabin almost surely had had the blessing of some militant rabbi. She said Christian fundamentalists were no exception either. Witness the justifications some ministers had offered for the murder of doctors who agree to do abortions.

You could say what you wanted about Elizabeth, thought Kessler, but you couldn't say she wasn't even-handed. Also, you could say what you wanted about Cyril Pratt but you couldn't say he didn't do his homework.

This applied to the activities of Lawrence J. Tarrant as well. Pratt's notes were cryptic; Tarrant was simply "T," Bandari was "B" and there were other notations that, given the context, must have referred to the Libyans. Whatever they were up to, Pratt seemed to have been excluded and this made him all the more curious. He deduced over time, via this or that clue, the nature of this thing that he said keeps on killing. It was a special kind of bomb, or at least the ingredients, that was designed to turn cities into ghost towns. Pratt's notes indicated there were several. Wherever they were, Tarrant couldn't get his hands on them and "A" was going to destroy them.

"A" stands for Aisha? No, it must stand for Avram.

Kessler had decided he would not tell Elizabeth. Not about Tarrant and not about this bomb. It would be no use upsetting her now that she was thinking that this actually might quiet down. Kessler wasn't sure that he believed it in any case. The Lockerbie bombing was certainly Qaddafy but that, at least in Qaddafy's view, was an act of retaliation for the raid on Tripoli that killed his infant daughter two years earlier. A Pan Am flight is one thing but a city is another. To attack a city would be an act of war. If one single finger pointed back to Qaddafy, Tripoli would cease to exist in a week.

There was no harm in Elizabeth knowing about Gamal because the uncle was in Cairo and out of her reach. Tarrant lived, however, in a suburb of Washington, a distance from Hilton Head that was temptingly accessible. Pratt's notes gave several numbers where Tarrant might be reached and even his home address. Elizabeth might decide to drop in on him one night to make him pay for his role in making Aisha an orphan.

But as for this bomb, she won't believe it either. Even if she did he doubted she'd care as long as it stayed off her island. Not that she'd entirely turned her back on the world but she knew that it was only a matter of time before something like this happened for real. The nuclear genie had been out of the bottle ever since the Soviet Union collapsed and everything in it was suddenly for sale. No Middle East country except maybe Jordan would pass up the chance to be a nuclear power. After countries come tribes, after tribes come gangs, until even Hamas has a nuclear car bomb which it parks outside the Knesset in Tel Aviv. It was good to be living on an island.

No, Elizabeth needn't be told about Tarrant. He was just one more dealer in death among many. He might or might not have had the girl's father killed; Kessler had only Pratt's word that he did and Pratt hated Tarrant. He did, however, pull the uncle's strings. By itself that made him worth a telephone call to give him a few things to think about. In the business he was in, in the town that he was in, his phone was quite possibly tapped and he'd know that. Kessler hoped that it was. The more ears that were listening, the more it would ruin his evening.

"Martin?" asked Elizabeth, her eyes getting heavy. "What are you thinking right now?"

"Not a thing. Just enjoying the scent of those lilacs."

"I know you. You're scheming. You squint with one eye when you're scheming."

"I do that? Who else knows it?" He feigned dismay.

"Come on, give." She poked him. "Tell me what you were thinking."

"That I . . . might stay on this island. For a while. Not long. Just to be sure that you're safe here."

She traced a finger through a mound of bubbles. She asked, "You were thinking of me?"

He nodded.

She fell silent again for another long moment. "Martin

. . . do you like me? I mean . . . don't say you love me. I really want to know if you like me.''

''I like you, Elizabeth. I like you very much.''

''Would anyone else? I mean, if they knew?''

You see? thought Kessler. Why bother her with bombs when her biggest concern is whether she seems nice? And he knew whom she meant by *anyone else*. ''Elizabeth, they'll move her. She's been compromised here. If they're smart they will move her tomorrow.''

''I suppose,'' she said sadly. ''That's what I'd do.''

''But she'd like you,'' he lied. He rose to his feet. ''What you've been wouldn't matter. Now soak.''

''Are you leaving? You don't have to. I'd like you to stay.''

''Pratt's phone. I'll get rid of it. After that I'll come back here and like you, Elizabeth. I'll like you to pieces, I promise.''

She threw foam at him as he backed out of range.

But she smiled.

It was good to see her smile.

Twenty-one

Lawrence Tarrant sat alone in the large Tudor house that his wife's grandfather, who had been a senator, had built in the suburb of Chevy Chase, Maryland. The house was in darkness and entirely silent except for the sound of wind-driven sleet as it peppered the leaded stained glass of his windows. A clock in the front hall chimed seven in the morning. Outside there was only the promise of sunrise, a slate-gray light that was a match for his mood.

Tarrant had not slept since he arrived home at midnight after his long flight from Cairo. Nor had he eaten, except for antacids. His stomach still churned with ineffectual rage as he waited for Bandari to call him again, this time on a scrambler and not his home phone, the damned fool.

A part of that rage was directed at his wife. She had fled their home in the middle of the night screaming curses at him as she ran down the driveway. He had slapped her, he had to, to clear the stupid woman's head. He needed to know, every word and exactly how much the German had told her. After that he had to slap her to make her shut up.

God knows where she'd gone by now, God knows who she was telling the things this man said to her. But she did leave on foot; she ran out in that storm. With luck she was still out there, dead of exposure. That would solve one of his problems, at least. It would help to contain this until he decided what action would have to be taken.

He was being driven home from the airport when the

call came. His plane, by that time, had refueled and took off again. It was bound for Grand Cayman where the pilot would wait until the seaplane arrived bearing Lester Loomis and the girl. It was done; he could relax; the sale could go forward. The inquisitive Cyril Pratt, by now, would be nourishing the fish off Florida's Gulf Coast.

At least that's how it seemed until Clarisse in her stupor answered that goddamned phone. That she'd been able to answer it was remarkable in itself. She had already taken her pills downed with vodka in order to be asleep so that she wouldn't have to greet him. But even drunk, even drugged, she should have known better than to speak on a phone that was probably tapped.

"Hello. Mrs. Tarrant? It's late, I know, but I'm afraid I must speak to your husband."

"He's not here," she'd said she'd told him. "And you're right. It is late."

"He's in Egypt perhaps? Do you know where I might reach him?"

Clarisse should have said, "Call his office tomorrow," and then she should have hung up. He had told that woman again and again to assume that their home phones were under surveillance by one federal agency or another. He had certainly spread enough money around to make sure he'd be warned if they were digging too deeply. But she told this man that he'd be home any time now and that meanwhile she was trying to sleep. Her words and her tone as much as announced to him that all was not well in their marriage.

"Let me tell you what your husband has been up to," he said. "You might want to write some of this down."

She didn't write but she listened and was still on the phone when his limousine pulled into the driveway. She was sitting there blinking—the phone to her ear—when he walked in and saw the shocked look on her face and he thought that there must have been a death in the family.

"He's here," she said dully. "You can tell him yourself."

He took the phone from her and a cheerful voice said,

"Ah, Mr. Tarrant. A good evening to you. Here is what I've been telling your wife."

He listened in horror as the voice informed him that the death in question was Pratt's . . . who died slowly . . . but he outlived his two Muslim helpers. Your pilot, he said, could now save himself a trip. That went for the pilot of the seaplane as well. Tarrant told this German that he had the wrong Tarrant, that he had no idea what he was talking about. He repeated this protest over and over for the benefit of any listening devices. But he couldn't hang up because the damage had been done and he needed to know how much Pratt had told him.

He'd felt sickened when this man said he knew about Bandari and he knew about their Libyan friends and the bankers and the bomb that turned cities into ghost towns. He knew, he said, why Bandari's brother died and why Bandari had his brother's wife stoned. What's more, he said, he had it all on a videotape "and you might mention that to Bandari." And he had Pratt's notebook which is where he found this number. The notebook contained addresses as well.

"It comes down to this," said the voice, turning icy. "You can do what you want in the rest of the world but there's one little part you must never come near. Not you, not your friends, not your hirelings. If you ever again bother a certain young girl . . . or, for that matter, a certain Algerian . . . I will personally pay you a call, Mr. Tarrant. I suspect I'd be doing your wife a great favor."

At that moment Clarisse, who was still in her night-gown, came to life and made a dash for the door. She paused to grab a fur from the front hall closet but it snagged on her golf clubs and slowed her. Tarrant shouted once more, "You have the wrong number," then slammed down the phone and went after her. This was when he had to slap her. And when she clawed at his face. After that the night only got worse.

He tried to tell Clarisse that it was nothing but lies, an attempt to embarrass him by God knows who, a competitor perhaps, or the Jewish lobby. Jew lawyers, he reminded her, keep trying to indict him for trying to help countries that they want to keep down. It was the Jews, not him, who ought to be in prison. It was the Jews who used PAC-money as a way to bribe Congress so they'd keep those embargoes in place. But he knew that he might as well have talked to a lamp. Her mind had been poisoned long before this by her family, that pack of society snobs who never in their lives had to try to make a dollar. Clarisse sat with her vodka, staring ahead, holding ice cubes against her swelling cheek. Her eyes grew heavy, she had seemed to be dozing, but all she was doing was awaiting her chance. It came at almost one o'clock in the morning when the telephone rang one more time.

The caller was Bandari who should have known better but Bandari sounded out of his mind. "They're all dead," he wailed, "and they're going to kill me. This woman . . . she called me . . . she *knows*."

Tarrant shouted, "Who is this? What the hell's going on here?" hoping that Bandari would take the hint and shut up. He wasn't sure whether he did or not because that's when Clarisse made her break for the door. He dropped the phone and he tried to stop her again but she was already running across the front lawn yelling "You miserable bastard, you fuck," back at him.

For this he had married into Washington society. He might as well have married a truckstop waitress who at least would know how the world worked.

"Now, you listen." He snatched the phone off the floor. "I don't know who you are or what you're trying to pull or who put you up to this sick stupid joke. If I find you I'll scramble your brains, do you hear me?"

"Wha . . . what?"

"I said I will *scramble* your brains."

"Ah . . . Oh, yes," Bandari managed. He was catching his breath. More importantly, he seemed to catch on and with that Tarrant broke the connection.

But six hours had passed and he was still waiting by the phone that had an electronic scrambling device. He felt sure that Bandari had not fallen asleep again, not in the state he was in. Bandari should have got out and gone

straight to his office because that's where the nearest
scrambler would be. It was Saturday, he realized, the
Muslim Sabbath. Bandari might have trouble getting into
the ministry. But the Nile Corniche was lined with foreign
embassies. Bandari could have asked to use one of their
scramblers, that is if his brain was still functioning.

Tarrant jumped at the sound of an electronic beep. The
green light of his scrambler came on. With a mixture of
relief and six hours' worth of anger he peered at the dig-
ital readout that crawled with the number of the compat-
ible device from which the incoming call was being made.
He knew that number. It was not in Cairo. That machine
was the one Bandari kept on his yacht. Tarrant now understood the six-hour delay. He snatched the phone from
its cradle.

"What the hell are you doing in Spain?" he hissed.

"I could not stay there," Bandari answered. He swallowed and dropped his voice to a whisper. "They were
everywhere, watching me. She said they were going to
cut off my hand."

"She? She who?"

"I don't know. A woman. A woman who knew Arab
ways."

"One call from a woman and you ran off to Spain?
Bandari, what about my container?"

"I don't know. I must think. How am I to get Aisha
with so much gone wrong?"

"Bandari . . . now you listen. I have had it with your
niece. I have had it with your sheiks and your judges and
your head of the family bullshit. You can pick up any girl
on the street and pay her to be your niece for an hour. I
want you back in Cairo tonight and in front of a judge
Monday morning. By noon I want you to have a truck at
that warehouse and—"

"But this woman. She knows. She knows everything I
do."

"Bandari . . . for Christ's sake . . . she had to have
called you from Hilton Head Island. She must be the
woman Pratt was talking about. She was bluffing, Bandari. Forget her."

"Do you know what Pratt did?" Now Bandari was whining. "Pratt left his tape running when he said it was off. She knows it was me who accidentally hit Leyna. She thinks it was me and not you who killed Avram. Why should I take the blame for something you did?"

These words caused the knuckles on Tarrant's fist to go white. Bandari, that weasel, was trying to distance himself. He was about to tell Bandari that he'd cut off his goddamned hand himself when the voice came back suddenly strong and defiant.

"Who is this insolent woman who makes threats?"

Tarrant was startled. "I told you, Bandari. It must be the woman named Nadia Halaby, the one who Pratt said—"

"Halaby? That's the Algerian slut? The one who breaks up Muslim families?"

"Whatever. Now, listen—"

"I know of this woman. She is long lost to God. I will send her to hell for what she has done."

It dawned on Tarrant that Bandari must be talking for the benefit of someone who'd just entered the bridge where he kept his satellite phone. "Who's on that boat with you?" Tarrant demanded. "Are you showing off for one of your hookers?"

"I have guests. They are men. You can trust them, don't worry."

Tarrant heard a low buzz of whispers in Arabic. Bandari was assuring whoever was listening that this man who had called was no danger to them.

"Bandari? Bandari!! I asked who they are. Are they more of those dimwits you've been pandering to?"

"Not dimwits. Brave men. These are fighters," he said firmly.

"Oh, for Christ's sake. Can they hear my voice?"

"Ah . . . no. Only me."

"What fighters are they and what are they doing on your boat?"

"One is healing from torture. Also praying and planning."

"I gather that someone asked you to hide them and

being a suck-up you couldn't say no. Get rid of them, Bandari. There's no time for this.''

"Oh, yes. Very brave. Also grateful to me.''

Tarrant gritted his teeth. He also now gathered that Bandari was saying that there was no way in hell he'd give up their protection. Tarrant answered with an exasperated growl but he wondered if they might be otherwise useful.

"Let's hear it, Bandari. Who are they?''

"These, too, are Algerians but not like your slut. They fight for an Islamic Algerian state.''

"Not Algerians. Tuaregs,'' came a voice in the background. "Algeria is only a word on map.''

"That's their leader?''

"That's Ozal. Very famous. Greatly feared.''

"Are you saying these are fighters who have actually fought?''

"You can ask do they fight? All three men are Tuaregs. No tribe is more fierce than the Tuaregs.''

"What was that about healing? What condition are they in?''

"Ozal has no fingernails and only one eye after the torturers finished with him. To my shame it's Egyptians who captured this man and did these terrible things. They did it to curry cowardly favor with the illegal and godless Algerian regime. So you see why I feel it my Islamic duty to—''

"Bandari . . . Bandari . . . give it a rest. What kind of shape are the other two in?''

"Young men and strong. In good health.''

"Now tell me . . . these three . . . do they have even one brain between them this time?''

"My good friend Ozal, the one who they tortured, has a university degree from America.''

"Is that true? In what?''

"He learned chemical engineering from Rutgers of New Jersey. He knows how to make thunder if you know what I mean. You remember the airplane they were going to blow up in the sky as it flew over Paris?''

Tarrant heard another low urgent buzz, probably Arabic

for shut the fuck up. This one had some sense after all.

"Who are the others, Bandari?"

Tarrant heard him ask, in English, "I can say?" The bomber, Ozal, seemed to have no objection.

"They were soldiers who were sent to take him back to Algeria. Instead they shot their captain and helped him escape. They are soldiers again but this time for God."

"I see. Now, Bandari . . . if you lie to me I'll kill you. Do they know what we have in that warehouse?"

"I've said nothing of that. This I swear."

"Ask your friend, right now, how he'd like to get his hands on a couple of Stingers."

"Stingers? What are Stingers?"

"They're missiles! Bandari, ground to air missiles. Never mind, let me speak to Ozal."

Bandari wished that he had refused. But when his guest, Ozal, overheard the word "Stinger" his eyebrows went up and they stayed there. He was near enough to hear Tarrant's voice when he repeated, "Did you hear me? Let me speak to Ozal." Ozal shrugged and reached out with his ten ruined fingers. Bandari had no choice but to hand him the phone.

Their discussion seemed to last a very long time although only a few minutes passed. The Tuareg mostly listened and grunted but a shine had come into his eyes. Bandari's heart sank when he heard his guest say in English, "For two Stingers maybe I'll go to Suez," and again when he asked, "This warehouse . . . how well is it guarded?"

Bandari mouthed, "*He's crazy. Say no.*" The Tuareg told Tarrant he would think about this but right now it was almost time for prayers.

"I said I would think. Let me think," said Ozal as they walked down the ramp and onto the docks of the marina. One soldier came with them. The other, who knew boats because his father was a fisherman, would stay on the yacht and stand guard. Ozal walked very slowly because still far from healed was his anus where his torturers shoved a metal-tipped stick as they do with almost every male prisoner.

They weaved through the alleys of Marbella's old quarter and up toward the mosque that was on the main road. The Saudi, King Fahd, had caused the mosque to be built for the use of all the Saudis who had built fine homes there. The Tuareg, Ozal, did not like using that mosque because he detested the Saudis. But he prayed there because a mosque was a mosque and because he detested pretty much the whole world. No use spiting himself just because Saudis built it.

On the way Ozal told him what Tarrant had proposed. Take this boat back to Egypt, make Bandari go with you, he'll show you a warehouse on the docks of Suez. There are probably guards so you'll need your two soldiers. Take care of these guards and break into the warehouse. Bandari will show you a container he's left there. Get in and get out and sail east toward Libya. Stay well out to sea, let me know your position, I will rendezvous with you somewhere west of Benghazi. Bring me that container and I'll give you two missiles with which you can knock any plane from the sky.

"A ridiculous plan," said Ozal as they walked. "Does he think the Mediterranean is a small mountain lake? Just to motor to Suez at full speed takes five days."

"Ah, yes. Very true," said Bandari, relieved.

Ozal knows what he is talking about because his father once had a yacht of his own until the government took away all that he owned. But Tarrant would realize how far it was as well when he cooled down and took time to think. He'd be calling back soon with a better suggestion but Ozal was already ahead of him.

"We could fly there, however," said the man with one eye. "You could charter a boat and get guns for my boys here. Can you get us into Egypt with no problem, Bandari?"

"You would take such a risk of them catching you again? You want them to start on your toes?"

"Two Stingers are two Stingers," Ozal answered.

Bandari groaned inwardly. He tried again. "I can, of

course, make arrangements. Even so, the risk is still great. You know Cairo these days with its spies and informers. They don't want Egypt to be another Iran.''

''Iran is a picnic compared to what's coming.''

''If they catch you this time they won't ship you to Algeria. This time it's a bullet and that's if you're lucky.''

''I'll show them more than bullets. Just wait.''

''Also Cairo is eager to show the Americans how they crack down on radical Islam. I think even my friends might decide to betray you. After all, these are men who made peace with the Zionists.''

''I might show the Americans a few things myself. Them and the scum-sucking Jews.''

Bandari wondered if he even liked Tuaregs. This man kept a shotgun on the bridge of this boat because he didn't like dolphins or seagulls much either. ''So it's settled. I'll take care of that warehouse in Suez by myself. Believe me, what's in it can wait.''

''What's there, Bandari? More Stingers?''

''No weapons. No rockets. Only certain machinery.''

Ozal gave a snort at this obvious lie.

''Okay, and some chemicals, some dangerous poisons. The Libyans still have a few scores to settle with those who won't let them sell oil.''

''The Libyans are idiots. They'll probably spill it and poison themselves. There are much better ways to get back at the Americans.''

''You should see Ozal's maps,'' said the soldier who was with them. ''Ozal knows all the ways to punish America. He knows how to—''

The Algerian silenced him by clapping his hands. The clap made the tips of his fingers turn red. It must have hurt badly because his eye became moist and a long moment passed before he could speak. He wet his fingers with saliva from his mouth and he blew on them to cool them.

''So tell me, Bandari,'' said Ozal when his pain eased. ''Why don't you want me to go to this warehouse? You think I might keep what I find there?''

Bandari gave him no answer at first because a new idea

was taking shape in his mind. The seed of the idea had been planted by the soldier when he spoke of punishing America.

"On this we need to speak privately," said Bandari. "We will do so but first I must pray."

"Pray for what? That you'll think of an answer to my question?"

"For guidance, Ozal." He did need time to think. "I have something on my boat that would teach the West a lesson. I need to ask God if that's how I should use it."

"Tell me what you have and I'll ask him as well."

"It's between God and me. Please be patient."

They paused at the fountain outside the mosque wall. They sat to take off their shoes and their socks and to bathe their feet before going inside. Ozal and his soldier reached into their pockets and took from them thick rolls of gray cotton fabric. Bandari watched as each man fashioned a headdress and then kept unwinding all the way to their necks. The face of Ozal was the first to be hidden so that only his one useful eye was left showing. Others who came there were watching as well. Some were grumbling, all were frowning but none dared complain. Bandari looked into Ozal's one good eye. Ozal was enjoying the discomfort he caused.

It did not surprise Bandari that they covered their faces because Tuaregs had done so since long before Islam. The Tuaregs were Berbers, they were fierce desert raiders. They veiled their faces—the men, not the women—so that their enemies could not see into their hearts. They kept their own customs when their tribe embraced Islam, even though the other Muslims thought their customs were heresy. The Muslims would say to them, "Your tribe has it backward. It's women, not men, who must cover. Also your women must stop being friendly with men to whom they are not related. We have seen your women laughing and joking with men. Some who marry are not even virgins."

The Tuaregs would answer, "Women are beautiful. They're not only for the bed and they don't end all friendships on the day they get married. It is you who are stupid in this.'' So the Muslims called them Tuaregs, which came from the Arabic and meant ''The Abandoned of God.'' The Tuaregs accepted their new name with glee. They saw it as a joke that they shared with God because God, of course, knew that they were right.

Bandari had often envied the Tuaregs. Of all the Arabs they were the only tribe in which men had always been at ease around women. Most Egyptians couldn't even watch *Love Boat* on TV without breaking into a squirming sweat at the mildest erotic suggestion. That is one reason that he offered his boat when Algeria's Islamic Salvation Front came to him and said it needed a place to hide a few of their men. They wouldn't react in a horrified way if he rented a blond model for a night or two. But what he was counting on now was that Ozal was different, a Tuareg who didn't like women any better than he liked anyone else.

Tarrant was right. He had been wasting his time, first trying to save Leyna's life and then Aisha's. And now, on top, there was the woman who had called who had Cyril Pratt's tapes to use against him.

Tarrant was right. He must end this. Now he needed them all dead.

Twenty-two

The men in dark suits had met at Fort Meade, not far from the Maryland home of Lawrence Tarrant. There were five men in all plus their aides. Fort Meade itself was a virtual city entirely surrounded by electrified fences. It was the headquarters of the National Security Agency, but the men represented other agencies as well. One man, named Charles, was on the President's staff. They played, for a third time, the recording of the calls that had so upset Lawrence Tarrant. Each man had before him a copy of a file containing what was known of Tarrant's history.

"The reference to Pratt," said the one who chaired the meeting, "is probably to this man." A computer screen showed Cyril Pratt's face. "He is . . . or was . . . a bounty hunter who finds Muslim women. We assume he was working for this man, not Tarrant." Another screen lit with a photo of Bandari.

"The second caller was definitely Bandari. The question before us is who was the first."

"The question before us," another dark suit corrected him, "is what's this about bombs that turn cities into ghost towns?"

"Well, we'd like to ask him that, wouldn't we?"

"You know at least that his accent is German. Have you cross-checked Tarrant's file with those of his competitors? Maybe this man is a German competitor. Maybe he's trying to queer whatever deal Tarrant seems to have cooking with the Libyans."

"We're looking at voice prints. No matches so far."

"And the wife, Clarisse, she was no help?"

"She came to us, she's still being interviewed. But there's not much she could tell us about her husband's activities that we didn't already know."

"Okay, then Bandari. He seems the weak link."

"Bandari has vanished. We know he went to Spain. We know he keeps a boat there, the motor yacht *Alhambra*, and that it seems to have a rather odd crew. But his boat left Marbella several hours ago. We're trying to locate it by satellite."

"You couldn't unscramble his call back to Tarrant?"

"Our computers are trying. They'll get some but not much. In the meantime, here's what we have."

He reviewed those portions of Lawrence Tarrant's file that concerned his association with Bandari. Their common ground was a Libyan connection that did not in the past involve weapons or terrorism. Tarrant's business was supplying embargoed materials and helping the Libyans to launder their oil money in ways to prevent seizure. The primary laundry appeared to be Egypt, specifically investments through their Ministry of Development with Gamal Bandari greasing the way.

In the past, two indictments had been brought against Tarrant. Both times they were quashed, he said, because we couldn't bring down Tarrant without bringing down Egypt's Ministry of Development. The Cairo government said to proceed if we must but they'd expect us to make up for any short-fall it caused in the revenues that now came through Libya.

"We're to cover their losses? Tell them they can shove it."

"Charles . . . get real. We need Egypt as it is. What we surely don't want is the alternative."

"So, let *them* sweat Bandari. Hang him up by his balls. Let them hear where the German says Bandari killed his brother and then crushed his brother's wife's face with a rock. You don't think they'll want to find out if that's true?"

''They'll say they'll look into it. That's where it will end.''

Another dark suit agreed. ''If they should decide that Bandari's an embarrassment we might hear that he's died in an automobile accident. They will tell us he's dead, nothing more.''

''If we can't stop men like Bandari and Tarrant,'' pressed the dark suit called Charles, ''what's the point of even having an embargo in place?''

''I'll remind you that there's also an embargo on cocaine, for all the good that it does.''

The man called Charles raised his hands in surrender to show that he realized his question was naive. An embargo was a palliative, a political sop. For every door it closed it opened ten more.

''Let's try to sum up,'' said the man who chaired the meeting. ''The assumption must be that a terrorist act is being planned against an American city. The call from the German came from a cell phone somewhere in the vicinity of Savannah, Georgia. That in itself doesn't tell us very much because the German might have called from a car passing through. If he uses that phone to call Tarrant again we'll be ready to pinpoint it much more precisely. In the meantime we'll be keeping a close eye on Tarrant and allow him to sweat out where his wife might have gone. We're expanding our efforts to locate Bandari on the chance that his boat's destination is relevant. Judging by the way he sounds, however, he's probably gone into hiding.''

One dark suit had said nothing thus far. He sat with his head cocked as if he were listening to a sound that was off in the distance. His eyes were squinting. He said, ''Play that tape one more time. Play the voice of the German.''

The chairman complied. The man listened closely. At its end he could only grimace and say, ''Damn, it's familiar. The voice, the droll manner. That accent, by the way, brings Leipzig to mind.''

''You say he's East German?''

''Leipzig . . . Halle . . . Dessau . . . he has the inflection one hears in that area. But my mind's trying to tell me that I heard it right here. In my mind I'm standing with a drink in my hand and I haven't had a drink in ten years.''

''Are you dressed in black tie? A reception, perhaps.''

''Could be. Could be. And you know something else? My wife is enjoying him. So am I, truth be told, but I think I'm a little bit jealous. I tell her this man is not even real and she answers that he's real enough for her.''

Some in the room rolled their eyes at this exchange but the chairman was less willing to dismiss it. ''Leipzig, ten years ago, means he'd be GDR. Why don't you go look at some dossiers, Peter?''

''I could try I suppose. I just can't see the face. In my mind, as I told you, he isn't quite real.''

''Give your wife a look at them, too,'' said the chairman.

Bandari's yacht had been at sea for two days. His heading from Marbella took him west past Gibraltar, then south to Las Palmas in the Canaries where he stopped to buy provisions and refuel. From there with good weather he could cross the Atlantic in five or six days at the most. Then, with the help of Ozal and his soldiers, he would settle this once and for all.

On the first of those two days Tarrant called on the scrambler. He said, as expected, that he hadn't been thinking, that going to Egypt by boat took too long. Bandari told Tarrant that it was too late to change plans, that his yacht was already at sea heading east. Tarrant then demanded to speak to Ozal. Bandari told him that Ozal and his men were en route overland to Suez. Arrangements had been made to smuggle them in; he would rendezvous with them in five or six days; tell the Libyans they'll have to be patient. Tarrant argued and cursed him but did not seem to doubt him. Tarrant's major concern was that Ozal shouldn't know what was in that container in the warehouse.

Bandari knew well that Tarrant would be furious when he learned that the boat headed west and not east. Even so, he felt a measure of peace for the first time since Avram looked inside that container. At sea he was safe, safe from Tarrant and the Libyans who must think by now that they have been cheated, if they know that he's vanished from Cairo. Above all he was safe from that Algerian woman. Now it was she who should be frightened if she knew what was in store for her and her island. But first he would have to talk sense to Ozal, who turned out to have ideas of his own.

Ozal, at first, did not want to come and help him. What he wanted was two Stingers to knock down two planes. It was then that Bandari told him that he had something better. He had a way to fix a whole island so that no one could ever live on it again. He told him that he had a device from the Russians that would poison the land for all time.

"Poison? What poison? A bacterial weapon?"

"This is a radioactive device. An atomic artillery warhead."

"Only the warhead, no shell?" Ozal asked.

"Who needs a big shell if you don't have a cannon? Anyway this little warhead is easier to hide in case we get boarded by Customs."

"And how many of these do you have, Bandari?"

"Only one. Just one," he lied.

"But I think more than one in Suez, Bandari. No wonder this Tarrant is willing to pay."

Bandari tried a stammered denial but he knew that his manner had given him away. Ozal let it pass with a gesture of dismissal. A device within reach was worth ten in Suez.

"This island is where? You mean the island of Manhattan?"

"No, this one." Bandari pointed it out in his chart book.

"Hilton Head Island? What is Hilton Head Island?"

"It is a place where the enemies of religion are gathered. It is a place where Muslim women go to hide out when they have turned their backs on their families and God. It's a place where young Muslim girls go to beaches and lie half-naked tempting men into sin. The men bribe them with hot dogs which are nothing but pork. It is a place where women have thrown off their veils and—''

''So what? Veils are stupid. They should all throw them off. Also, hot dogs are beef, sometimes chicken.''

''Okay,'' said Bandari, ''then forget about veils. Even forget about the poor Muslim children who are brought there and raised to be prostitutes. That island is mostly fat rich Americans who think they are safe from the poor who they have robbed.''

A yawn from Ozal. ''Manhattan is also fat rich Americans. We'll go instead to Manhattan.''

''I will tell you what these people think of Manhattan. They saw how that bunch bombed the World Trade Center and they said, 'What has this to do with me? Who cares what they do in the big dirty cities which are full of poor people and blacks who sell drugs. Let them blow up the whole of Manhattan if they can. I will watch it on television and then go out and play golf.' ''

Ozal snorted at the mention of the World Trade Center. ''Egyptians did that one. Even their crazy blind sheik was Egyptian. Show me one time when a group of Egyptians ever did anything right.''

Bandari bridled but before he could speak Ozal had pulled a map from his pocket and opened it on the chart table. One of the soldiers winked at Bandari. This was the one who had started to boast that Ozal knew how to punish the West. His smile said, ''*Now you will see.*''

The map was of the United States and many locations were marked in red pencil. Bandari saw other places that had circles around them and the circles were connected by lines. The circles seemed to mark only very small towns, not a single big city among them.

''This line and that line,'' Ozal told him, pointing, ''are pipelines for natural gas. They supply almost all the natural gas that is used by New York and by most of the northeastern states. Both pipelines are totally unprotected. Both are regulated by high-pressure pumps that were bought from the Germans, made special. To replace just the pumps would take more than a year.''

The Egyptian sniffed. "Ozal, the Avenger. He turned off their gas. That's how you want to be known?"

Ozal looked at him sternly but continued. "And here," he said, pointing elsewhere on the map, "these marks are two bridges, both vital. One crosses the Ohio River near Cincinnati, one crosses the Potomac near Washington, D.C. Between them they handle almost all railroad traffic in the eastern United States. Would you believe that neither is guarded?"

He traced his torn fingers over more of the map, pausing at symbols that looked like small bells. "In these places are telephone switching stations," he said. "These stations—and there are only nine—control almost all telephone communications in all the large cities of the United States."

Ozal folded his arms and smiled down at his map as if it were a son he was proud of. Bandari was not even a little impressed.

"This is it?" he asked the one-eyed Algerian. "This is your great scheme to punish the West?"

"A few well-placed bombs and they're crippled, Bandari. No fuel, no phones and no trains to bring them food."

"No phones and no trains. This is teaching them a lesson? For this they won't call you Ozal, the Avenger. What you'll get is Ozal-who-made-their-lives-less-convenient. What you'll get is Ozal, the Annoyer."

The Algerian thrust out his chin. "That's better than Bandari, the Scourge of Golf. Bandari-who-made-their-palm-trees-go-limp. Bandari-who-caused-them-to-pack-up-and-move-when-they-noticed-their-hair-falling-out."

This last shocked Bandari. "That's all that will happen?"

"I'm not certain about the limp palms."

"Don't joke about this. Are you saying this device only makes people sick and only with the passage of time?"

Ozal relented. It was not quite a joke. "It depends," he said, "on how much they get. Take a dosage of four thousand rads, for example, and your brain boils away in one hour. Take only one thousand and your bone marrow goes so you bleed to death in one day. Blood leaks through the pores of your skin, Bandari. It even comes out through your eyes.''

Bandari was blinking, impressed by this knowledge. ''How far does this spread and how quickly?'' he asked.

''Your Russian warhead? I would have to devise a bomb strong enough to smash it and expose the plutonium core. I would have to weaken the casing of the warhead to be sure that it ruptures during the blast and try not to boil my own brain while I'm drilling it. We don't have plastique but I could make nitroglycerine. I would need five liters of sulfuric acid, another five of nitric acid, plus the glycerine, baking soda, beakers, eye droppers and a thermometer. We can buy all these things in Las Palmas, I think. Also we need plenty of ice.''

''Ozal . . .''

''Also maybe some urea crystals and one hundred kilograms of ammonium nitrate. These last make some interesting special effects.''

''Ozal . . . you didn't answer. How far and how quickly?'' he repeated.

''The blast won't be so powerful. It will kill everyone, say, within fifty meters if it catches them out in the open. But the radiation kills every man, every bug, in an area the size of ten soccer fields. The dose goes through walls, you can't hide from it. If we have a nice breeze it kills more.''

Bandari was stunned into silence.

''You know what's the best part?'' Ozal poked him as if he were sharing a joke. ''The bomb is one thing. Everyone knows a bomb. But hours will pass before anyone knows why everyone seems to be sick. There are some, down wind, five miles away, who won't start feeling bad for three days.''

''I must think about this,'' Bandari said softly. ''So many. I think it's too much.''

''Too much? Okay. I'll make something smaller. You say there's a woman you especially want? Your Algerian lives on this island?''

"A woman and . . . and another young woman. Those two, I think, are enough."

"Then we go there and get them. We shoot them or maybe we blow up their house with a bomb that won't kill so many others. My price, Bandari, will be your one nuclear warhead plus two warheads more when we're back in Suez."

"One warhead I'll give you. Suez you can't touch."

"One warhead, one Stinger. That is my price."

"No Stinger. That's Tarrant. I don't have a Stinger."

"One warhead . . ." Ozal's expression became sly, "unless I happen to find that a second one is hidden aboard this fine yacht."

Bandari glanced over at Ozal's two soldiers, both of whom lowered their eyes. He knew in that instant that they'd found both containers in the two weeks he'd allowed them to live on the boat.

"Done. I agree." He took a deep breath. There were more where they came from but as for these two he was suddenly glad to have them out of his hands. Any guilt from now on would be Ozal's.

"Done," said Ozal. "One little bomb for these women, your enemies. It will give me good practice on this island of yours."

"But the warheads you will use somewhere else. You must swear it."

"Manhattan and then Tel Aviv."

"What you do is your business, not mine."

"Maybe first Tel Aviv. I will think about this. Does Manhattan or Tel Aviv have the most Jews?"

The soldiers looking on exchanged nervous glances because they knew the mind of Ozal very well. They knew that he was teasing and toying with Bandari. He was joking a little so Bandari would forget that Ozal did not actually swear. They felt sure that if he had only two warheads he wouldn't try for either of those cities. He'd use one on Cairo, the west end of Cairo, in the big army barracks where they ruined his fingers and robbed him of one of his eyes. But first, as he promised, he would do a little practice.

He would use the first warhead on this island in America.

Twenty-three

The bodies were found after only four days.

A local man had gone out to set crab traps an hour or so before dawn. One trap became snagged in the boat Kessler sank. It seemed to be floating just under the surface, moving this way and that with the tide. A cushion of marsh grass had kept it from settling and being obscured by the mud of the bottom. Shining his flashlight, the man could make out the jagged hole that had sunk it. He did not suppose that the sinking was deliberate; he had once cracked the hull of a dinghy himself when a thirty-pound battery slipped from his hands. Whoever sank this one must have waded ashore, most likely to the cabin whose outlines he could see, and decided that the boat was not worth trying to salvage.

The boat was worth something to the crabber, however. Salt water had probably ruined the motor but the fiberglass hull could be patched. After a little sanding and cleaning he could sell it and make a few dollars. He was rigging a tow line when he heard a loud hiss. Before he could pull his hands from the water a set of jaws lunged at his face. He got one elbow up which probably saved him but the teeth clamped onto his armpit. He shrieked and he kicked and he tore himself loose, leaving a large strip of flesh in those jaws.

In shock, he managed to reach his throttle and steer for a shrimp trawler out on the waterway. The shrimp boat's skipper called the harbor police while his crew packed the injured man's wound. A Coast Guard helicopter came and lifted the man to Hilton Head Hospital where the surgeons barely saved him from bleeding to death.

According to the account in *The Island Packet* newspaper, the wound left no doubt that an alligator had caused it but attacks such as this were almost unheard of, even for this time of year. Although the month of March was their mating season and male alligators were known to be aggressive, most of their posturing was aimed at rival suitors. Females would attack to protect their eggs and especially after their young had hatched, but that wouldn't happen until April at least. Most unusual of all was that the attack took place well out in a saltwater swamp. Alligators normally lived in lagoons where the water is brackish at most. Now and then they will enter a saltwater swamp in order to kill parasites on their bodies and sometimes to help heal a wound.

When a human was attacked, whether fatally or not, the suspected attacker was hunted and killed. Such a hunt was undertaken in an area of swamp branching out a quarter mile from where the boat had been sunk. Four alligators were spotted in the immediate vicinity. The presence of four—even one would be surprising—suggested that there must be a considerable food source nearby. These creatures were shot and hauled out for study. Human remains were found in all four. The authorities ordered the entire swamp dredged.

Three bodies were discovered. Skeletally, at least, they were largely intact because their arms and legs had been wrapped in blankets. Their limbs for that reason were not easily torn free. The alligators had ripped away large bites of flesh but only from the buttocks and shoulders of each man. A spokesman for the authorities pointed out that an alligator's appetite is relatively small and its digestion is extremely slow. A ten-foot beast will normally eat only two to three pounds in a week. Nor can an alligator really chew. Therefore whatever it can't readily swallow must be left to soften and decompose until the creature can pull it apart more easily. These were in no hurry; the meat would still be there; the crabs could take their small share in the meantime. The crabs concentrated on the throats and faces because slits had been cut in each of the blankets as if done to deliberately give them access.

The dredging also produced two weapons, a Czech submachine gun and a pistol. It produced two cheap wallets, both of them empty, as was a bottle of single malt scotch. The bottle, they reasoned, could not have been there long. The label and price tag had hardly faded and almost no silt had worked in through its neck. The price tag might help them learn where it was bought. Gleneagles was a brand not sold every day.

The most shocking find was on the bodies themselves. It told the authorities that in all probability these murders had been drug-related. One man was Caucasian, his hair was blond, he was dressed in tennis attire. This led them to suppose that whoever had done this might have lured this man to a tennis game. The Caucasian's teeth had been badly neglected. What dental work there was did not encourage the hope that recent dental records could be found. The other two men were probably Hispanic. These two, from the look of them had never seen a dentist in their lives. All three had been shot but only two had died quickly. The Caucasian had been wounded by a burst from behind, perhaps while attempting to escape. What made it clear that drugs were involved was the fact that the throats of all three had been cut and their tongues pulled down through the incision. It was a signature well known to drug enforcement authorities, called a Colombian necktie.

The triple murder made headlines statewide. A national magazine ran a story whose title, predictably, was "Trouble in Paradise." But the Hilton Head paper, *The Island Packet*, made it clear that these killings occurred more than ten miles west of the bridge. No evidence had been found to connect this event to the island. It took place, in fact, much nearer to the Interstate, which had long been the route by which drugs and guns were transported north from Miami.

The cabin where bloodstains and bullet holes were found had been rented by a man whose description

seemed to fit the blond Caucasian. He had certainly used
a false name and false papers. The renting agent, now that
she thought of it, said that the man had an odd sort of
accent. It seemed Southern, she supposed, but a generic
Southern of the sort that one hears from actors on TV
who have never been south of New Jersey.

That description also seemed to fit the man who had
rented the jitney they found in a swampland. It had come
from an RV dealer in Savannah. These rentals were some
help but not very much in establishing how long these
men had been dead. It might have been three days. It
might have been eight. A state trooper noted that the cabin
was near the scene of a false alarm to which he'd responded four nights earlier. But the woman who had made
that call said, when interviewed, that she knew nothing of
the cabin and had heard no shots fired that evening. The
trooper, all the same, checked the tires of the car she'd
driven to a farmhouse near the cabin that night. They did
not match the tracks that were found in the dirt. The tracks
were many, some seemed oddly placed, but they seemed
to have been made by the same mid-sized vehicle, very
likely a Toyota Camry.

''Nice touch,'' said Elizabeth when she read the account.

''Which one? The twin Toyotas?'' Kessler asked.

''That, too,'' she told him. She didn't mean the cars.
She meant the Colombian necktie. Nor did she quite mean
those words as a compliment. She understood quite well
why he'd done it, but it troubled her all the same.

He had stayed at the Players Club for two more days
after the bodies were discovered. He waited and watched
and listened for gossip. The girl's misadventure was no
longer a topic, at least among the guests on whom he'd
been eavesdropping. The murders off the island were all
that they talked about. He confirmed, to his surprise, that
the girl was still there. He said that he'd caught a glimpse
of her twice, both times after sunset when she came out
onto her terrace, both times in the company of either Nadia or Jasmine. She apparently took all her meals in her
room. She did not join the others on the courts or on

excursions but Martin had expected as much. They would certainly wait for her bruises to fade and would probably also spend time making sure that she knew what she could and could not tell her schoolmates. Elizabeth thought it was much more than that. She had probably been told about her parents.

After those two days Martin decided that it was probably unwise to stay on there. Someone would notice, if someone hadn't already, that he'd never been seen playing tennis. He was also anxious to get rid of his Toyota but he knew that he couldn't do that without moving lest anyone wonder why he'd suddenly changed cars. Nor did he ask to move in with Elizabeth. To be seen as a couple would not be smart either. He rented a condo that overlooked Harbour Town in a complex known as Ketch Court. He turned in the Camry for a Mustang convertible. He made a bundle of his new tennis clothing and dropped it in a bin at the Bargain Box, a charity center run by one of the churches.

Elizabeth came to his condo the first night he moved in. She brought with her a bottle of Chardonnay and some cheeses and a duck that she'd roasted at home. As he set the small table that was out on his balcony he heard her in the kitchen emptying ice trays in order to keep the wine chilled. He went in to tell her, don't use the bottom tray unless it's a very good vintage. She looked at him blankly but then realized immediately that the third tray was where he kept most of his diamonds except for those few he wore sewn in his belt. She suggested that he ought to leave some of them with her in case he ever had to disappear quickly. This was nice to hear her say. It meant that she'd be there for him. But the night was too pleasant to talk about running.

They sat on his balcony looking down at the lights of the yachts that now filled almost every slip of the harbor. It was nine in the evening. Other tenants were out on their balconies as well. Tourists were still standing waiting for their tables outside the Crazy Crab Restaurant of Harbour Town. Others were walking in and out of the shops or strolling the footpaths around the marina. It was a scene that was peaceful and pleasant or lonely depending on whether one felt part of it. Looking in lighted windows of comfortable homes had always left Kessler feeling wistfully sad. He assumed that was true of most men like himself. He felt sure that it was true of Elizabeth.

Elizabeth did not ask if and when he was leaving. She seemed content that he was near, not too close, and had shown no interest in moving into her house, nor had he attempted any physical initiative beyond a kiss on the cheek.

On that night of the killings he had also kept his word and had tucked her into her bed by herself. He sat with her telling her stories from his boyhood until she drifted off to sleep. Once or twice she reached a hand out to make sure he hadn't left. She needed him then. She needed him mostly to spend the evening persuading her that no, she wasn't a psychopath. Damaged, yes, but hardly a monster. She could stand to narrow her mood swings a little but this was a suggestion that he kept to himself.

Her mood swung back to coolness a few days later when she learned of the Colombian neckties. This surprised him but not greatly because he knew where her head was. Elizabeth in her Black Angel mode could probably have done that while they were alive. Her coolness, he realized, meant only one thing. Elizabeth was wondering what the girl must have thought when she read the accounts in the newspaper. How would Cherokee feel about her hero, Martina, when she realized that the woman who she wanted to hug hadn't chased those men off after all? Well, she'd feel what she feels but he, Kessler, couldn't help that. Elizabeth finally realized that she wasn't being fair, which was one reason why she showed up with the duck. They had mostly consumed it under the stars when she got to her secondary reason.

"There's a tournament coming up. A big tennis tournament." Elizabeth said this while sipping her wine.

"At the Van Der Meer Center? Don't be foolish, Elizabeth."

She shook her head quickly. "No, not there. It's here. It's the Family Circle Classic here in Harbour Town."

Ah, yes, thought Kessler. Women's tennis, professionals; he had seen the posters. Already the stadium at the tennis club here was putting up tents for the tournament sponsors and adding more seats built on scaffolds.

"Are you telling me this because you want me to take you?"

"Um . . . actually Jonathan called. He has tickets for the tournament. He asked me to go."

Kessler looked away. He said nothing.

"Martin . . . I'm asking if you'd mind if I say yes."

"Why should I mind? We've no claim on each other."

"Like it or not, yes, we do."

Kessler grunted, not flattered. She reached out to touch his arm.

"That came out wrong and I'm sorry. Martin, this is a tournament that everyone goes to. I'd just like to do something normal right now."

"So do it. You now have my blessing, Elizabeth."

"Can you understand that? That I'd like to feel normal?"

"I have news. I'm as human as you are."

"No, we're different, Martin. Very different."

"How so?"

"For starters, you think everything is a game. I'm not criticizing, Martin. I envy you sometimes. I don't think you've ever had a single regret, not once in the ten years I've known you."

"You don't think there is much that I would change if I could?"

"Like what? Tell me one thing you'd change."

"Never mind."

"You see? You can't."

"You're being stupid, Elizabeth."

"Then tell me. I'd really like to hear."

"In Bucharest . . . I moved left instead of right."

"I beg your pardon?"

"If I had dodged to the right instead of to the left you would not have been shot and we wouldn't be having this conversation."

Her lips parted. She said nothing.

"By now you would have two children at least and you might, you just might, have had them with me. Don't tell me I don't have regrets."

She fell silent for what seemed several minutes. She was watching the couples who were strolling the paths.

"You really do love me," she said at last, very softly.

"Always quick on the uptake," he muttered.

"I mean, do you? In your heart?"

"Yes, *like it or not*. Like it or not, yes I do."

"Except now you're going to sulk. You're going to tell me to go."

"No, I'll ask you to stay. That way you'll go."

The wrong thing to do with Elizabeth was to manage her. Kessler knew this as soon as he spoke. She promptly stood up and took off her shoes which she threw one by one down into the harbor. The second shoe bounced off the roof of a yacht before making a splash in black water. Heads turned on the boats and on the walkways. Next she stood and began to unbutton her blouse.

Talk about mood swings. "Elizabeth, stop. What on earth do you think you are doing?"

"I'm staying."

The blouse came off and went over the side. It floated down onto the pedestrian path causing several young women to stop and look up. They soon found the source because next came the bra.

Kessler hissed, "That's enough, Elizabeth. You have had too much wine. This is not how a lady behaves."

"He loves me," she called to the girls down below. They answered with laughter; one pumped her fist; another made a sound like a choo-choo.

Kessler was mortified. "What was it you said? That you needed to do something normal?"

"This is normal for horny. Sure you want me to go?" Elizabeth did not say this softly.

"If he does, come down here," rose a young male voice. It came from the boat where she'd just thrown her shoe. A young female voice on the walkway below asked, "Don't you have anything in size 6?"

Kessler set down his wine and he picked up Elizabeth.

He said, "Say good night to your fans." This brought groans of disappointment but a burst of applause as he carried her through the sliding doors, Elizabeth now blowing them kisses.

In the morning, thought Kessler, he must try to remember how he managed to manage Elizabeth Stride.

Twenty-four

The men in dark suits had gathered again in the sound-proofed room at Fort Meade. The chairman pointed a remote control at a screen that lit up with a face and biography. "Meet Martin Kessler," he said.

"It was Peter's wife, Lauren, who picked him out of the files. You'll recall that he made an impression on her. She was fascinated because she had always assumed that Kessler was a fictional character."

The man who was Peter nodded and smiled. "You'll also recall I said much the same thing . . . about him being not quite real, I mean. It's because they had made him a comic book hero well before they sent him on a two-year tour with the GDR Embassy in Washington. We have a few examples of those comics in his file."

The chairman found the button marked *Scroll* and advanced to a frame that showed a montage of comic book covers. The covers were titled *Reineke Fuchs* in type that resembled a lightning display. Underneath, translated from bold Germanic script, was "The heroic true adventures of Martin Kessler in defense of his Socialist motherland." Each cover showed Kessler in an action pose, considerably more handsome, his scar more pronounced, each cover more lurid than the last. In one he was hurtling down a mountain on skis while firing a pistol at those trying to stop him. Two of his attackers lay face down in the snow. So there was no mistaking who the attackers might be, all their jackets said CIA on the back. But Kessler was wearing his Olympics Team uniform, complete with the medal that he in fact almost won.

"This was ten years ago?" asked one man at the table.

"His Washington tour? More like twelve or thirteen."

"Well, how can you know that it's Kessler's voice on that call to Lawrence Tarrant and his wife?"

"Because we kept Kessler's voice print. We kept all of their voice prints. Kessler's is a positive match."

"Do we know where he is now?"

"Well, we think that we might. At least we know where to look."

The chairman clicked his remote several times until Cyril Pratt's face appeared on the screen. He clicked it again to show a new montage, this one concerning reports of three bodies that were found a few miles from Hilton Head Island.

"I leap to the assumption," said one of the suits, "that you think the blond one among them was Pratt."

"Oh, it's definitely Pratt. We showed that photo to the real estate agent from whom he rented a cabin, and also to a dealer who rented him a minibus. For now, however, we'll keep that to ourselves. We don't know who the other two are but they're not Hispanic, I promise you. Pending a report from our own pathologists, they are probably the Muslims Kessler mentioned to Tarrant. Both men had short Muslim beards. He also mentioned a girl and an Algerian. The girl, we assume, is Bandari's niece but I'm afraid we don't have a photo."

"Why would you think it's his niece?" someone asked.

A shrug. "If it's true that Bandari killed his brother and his wife, their daughter is all there is left. Pratt hunted female Muslims, remember."

"The Algerian," asked another. "Who would that be?"

"We're not sure. But Kessler's inference seemed to be that the girl and the Algerian are in the same place . . . which brings us to Hilton Head Island."

The chairman winced slightly when Peter got to this part. His expression told the others that what followed was guesswork but probably worth hearing with an open mind.

"You'll recall," Peter told them, "that Bandari said a woman had called him. A woman who frightened him out of his wits. I think that woman was Elizabeth Stride."

A few smiles appeared on the faces at the table. The man named Charles rolled his eyes to his aide and muttered, "Oh, for heaven's sake, Peter." Peter glanced at the chairman who said, "Never mind him. Continue."

"We know that Kessler was involved with Stride during that Martin Ceausescu business. After that they both disappeared from the scene although Martin resurfaced a year ago. In Boulder, Colorado of all places." The screen showed a newspaper photo of Kessler. He had broken the fingers of a local securities salesman. "We know that he was traveling with a woman at the time. That woman answers Stride's description."

"What description? Dark hair and dark eyes?" asked Charles.

"And slender. Mid-thirties, which is what she'd be now."

This brought a smirk from the aide Charles brought with him and a pained expression from Charles. He said, "Peter, for God's sake, she doesn't exist. There *is* no Elizabeth Stride."

"An open mind, Charles," the chairman reminded him.

"I can keep one on Kessler, the comic book Marxist, because at least we know that Kessler exists. Elizabeth Stride is pure invention. She's an Israeli practical joke."

"A rather deadly one then, by all accounts."

"Her toll is what . . . thirty? How can anyone believe that?"

"Maybe now thirty-three. Charles, why do you doubt it?"

"Because Mossad credits her with at least two reprisal killings that were done on the same night three countries apart. That argues for two Elizabeth Strides but we've run across at least ten, all nut cases. The Black Angel legend says she's an American from Houston but no one by that name was born in that city within five years of the age she's supposed to have been. Do you know where they got the name, Elizabeth Stride?"

"Um . . . offhand, I don't. Where did they?"

"It's the name of one of the five London prostitutes who were murdered by Jack the Ripper. Don't you see? This is Mossad's sense of humor at work. We now have a modern-day Elizabeth Stride slashing victims all over the Middle East and becoming an Israeli folk hero. She has died, by the way, at least four times that we know of. She was shot to death in Bucharest, beheaded in Riyadh and knifed in Paris . . . in fact that time I think she was scalped. Oh, and having run out of colorful ways to die, she expired last year somewhere in Kansas while pedaling an exercise bike."

"Ah . . . would you believe there's a woman whose name is E. Stride now living on Hilton Head Island?"

"Who says so?"

"She's in the telephone book."

"Why on earth would you look in a telephone book to see if there's a listing for Elizabeth Stride?"

"Actually I was looking for a listing for Kessler. On an impulse I looked under Stride."

Charles threw up his hands. "Do you want to know something? Our critics are right. Why do we need these intelligence services when all we need do to locate foreign agents is consult a Hilton Head telephone book?"

"In fact you'd be surprised at who else is on that island."

"The Ripper's four other victims, no doubt."

"Do you remember Roy Willis, the DEA agent-in-charge from New York?"

"That's the one who resigned to become a Black Muslim?"

"He converted to Islam. It's not the same thing."

"Has he taken to wearing bow ties and short hair and calling the white man the devil?"

Peter hooded his eyes. He said nothing.

"Very well," Charles sniffed. "He's a brown Muslim, then. What's he doing on Hilton Head Island?"

"I'm not sure I know. Perhaps finding himself. He's been there for several months now at some tennis academy. I'd been thinking of asking him to take a look at this Stride and find out if she happens to hang out with a German, a German with a scar by one eye.''

"What the hell for? Why Willis, I mean?''

"Because I know him and I trust him and he's there.''

"You'd trust a man who turned his back on his agency just to join a bunch of damned—''

"That is *not* what he did,'' Peter said through his teeth. "And for your information—''

"Let's move on,'' said the chairman with a tapping of his pen. The chairman, named Roger, looked oddly at Peter. "If you trust him, then ask him. Why haven't you done so?''

"He'd have told me that this is none of his business. I think now I can persuade him that it is.''

Charles snorted. "Persuade him of what? That his oath of allegiance is still binding on him? Don't waste your time on religious fanatics. We've no shortage of men who will do as they're told.''

The man named Peter paused to measure his words lest the first ones he uttered tell Charles he's an ass.

"We've a shortage of men who know and understand Muslims. Roy Willis, who is no more a fanatic than I am, would detest a Pratt or a Tarrant.''

The chairman raised his pen. "Let's wrap this up, please.''

He looked over his glasses at the man named Charles. "For the record,'' he said, "what Willis does with his life and his conscience is nobody's business but his own.'' He waved the pen to avert further comment. "We need to find Kessler because we need to ask him what he meant about Tarrant wiping out cities. I don't really care about Elizabeth Stride except to the extent that she can lead us to Kessler. You can laugh at Kessler's comics but the man is no clown. He's resourceful, he's clever, he's elusive as hell. If he spots our people before they spot him, he's gone and we're back to square one. Roy Willis has been working at a tennis club, you say?''

"As a maintenance man,'' Peter answered and then shrugged. "Don't ask me why. I don't know.''

"After New York City, I'm not terribly surprised. Perhaps laboring in the vineyards brings him peace.''

"We need him, if he'll help us, because he knows the island and because being black there, he's largely invisible. Put a rake in his hand and even Kessler won't see him.''

The remark struck the chairman as faintly racist itself although no less perceptive for that. He nodded agreement. A flick of his finger told Peter to see to it at once.

"There's also the matter of Bandari," said the chairman. "His boat, the yacht *Alhambra*, stopped to refuel in the Canaries. This was yesterday noon. One refuels in the Canaries if one is crossing the Atlantic. We expect that he intends some sort of rendezvous with Tarrant. We've lost him but we'll find him when the yacht nears our coast.''

"Sir?" The young aide to Charles raised his hand. "Any luck in unscrambling that call Tarrant made?''

"Almost none but it's clear that they argued. Tarrant tried a later call but Bandari's not answering.''

"Thank you, sir," said the young man. His question had drawn a raised eyebrow from Charles. Charles made a mental note to remind his young aide to speak only when asked in these meetings. The young man, however, was glowing inside.

"This meeting is adjourned," the chairman said, rising. "Peter, please stay. I'd like a word with you, please.''

Peter took his seat as the others left the room and the last of the aides closed the door. He felt sure that he knew what was coming. The chairman drummed his fingers as he often did when about to say, "*Enough of this nonsense. What's really on your mind?*''

But instead he cocked his head toward the door. "Charles . . . has his good qualities," he said.

"One supposes he must.''

"He cares about his country. You'll at least give him that.''

"He cares only about his part of it, Roger. The part that's white and has money.''

"Well . . . Charles is Charles," the chairman answered.

"All the same, I don't think he wants anyone destroying our cities."

"Charles couldn't give a damn about any of our cities, give or take a few restaurants he likes."

"Peter . . ." The chairman was sorry he mentioned him. "Roy Willis is the reason I asked you to stay."

"Would you like to know what Charles thinks about cities? He considers them a relic of the pre-computer era. He would not give five cents to revitalize a city."

"That may be but let's talk about Willis."

"This *is* about Willis, but know this about Charles. He sees most major cities as vast welfare ghettos that, as such, are financially and culturally unsustainable. Inner cities, to Charles, have but one useful purpose. They give us a place where we can quarantine our poor against the day when the welfare spigot turns off."

The chairman began to see a flicker of relevance. "Peter, why did Roy Willis resign?"

"As you said, it's a matter of conscience."

"Yes, but why quit? And why Islam?"

Peter glanced toward the door. "Did you hear Charles's reaction, that country club bigot? He hears that a good man found meaning in his life and all he can see is that Farrakhan crowd preaching hatred of whites . . . to say nothing of Jews . . . who, by the way, can't get into his country club either."

"Your restraint was noted. But what *has* Roy decided?"

"He was DEA. He'd seen enough drugs."

"And enough dead young blacks in the cities, I imagine."

"Enough alcoholism and pregnant teens. Enough fathers who desert their families. Enough lives without purpose or meaning or hope. Shall I tell you something about Muslims, Roger?"

The chairman's only interest was in one Muslim in particular, but good manners required that he let Peter speak.

"It isn't just Willis. It's not just all those athletes, those boxers and football and basketball players who have taken names like Mohammed and Kareem. Over two million

Americans have converted to Islam and they're not all black people either. They are people who now have a sense of belonging to something that's bigger, more important than themselves. Roger, when was the last time you saw that among whites? You'd have to go back to Pearl Harbor."

The chairman, sadly, was inclined to agree.

"There are converts to Islam who used to deal drugs. There are women who used to be prostitutes and drunks. Look where they came from and look where they are. They work, they raise children, they don't cheat or steal. They help each other, they trust in each other, and they'll fight if they must to protect each other."

"Trained to do so, I gather, by men like Roy Willis." The chairman drummed his fingers before Peter could answer. His eyes said that this time he means it. "Then what is he doing in Hilton Head, Peter? And why did you say you don't know?"

"He's . . . sort of on loan. Roy and one or two others."

"On loan to do what? To protect? To fight?"

"To protect certain women from creatures like Pratt."

A grunt from the chairman. It was as he'd suspected. "So Willis is not some convenient acquaintance who might do a little snooping as a favor to you. Why the smokescreen, Peter? You're afraid of what? That it's Willis who murdered Cyril Pratt and the others?"

Peter took a deep breath and blew it out slowly. "If he did it, I would not call it murder."

Now a sigh from the chairman. "Which brings us to Kessler who you—and you alone—have managed to identify. Am I to believe that you've actually done so or is Kessler as much of a fiction as Stride?"

"The voice was Kessler's. Depend on it, Roger."

The chairman stood up. He paced before speaking. "A Martin Kessler, an Elizabeth Stride. These two would not stand high on any list of people who would flock to the banner of Islam."

"I wondered myself. I don't know their motive."

"Kessler seemed to tell Tarrant that he didn't much care what Tarrant did in any part of the country but one.

From that we might conclude that Kessler lives on that island. Does Willis know Kessler or not?''

''I don't know.''

''But we care, don't we? And you care especially. You care because the cities Tarrant seems to be threatening are where your Muslims are making their lives. What am I to deduce from that, Peter?''

''That I'm a closet Muslim? I'm not.''

''Would . . . sympathizer be too strong a word?''

''It's precisely the word. I admire these people. I applaud what they've done.''

''Excluding, I trust, their more extreme measures.''

''Islam, like Christianity has its moderates and its extremists. Their terrorists, like ours, are a deviant minority.''

''Would they turn them in?''

''Not to us. But they'll stop them.''

The chairman drummed his fingers. ''Well, I'll give you two days. See Willis, find Kessler, and learn what you can. The problem with electronic surveillance is that we hear a lot of talk that's just talk. We hear crackpots boasting of impossible schemes, taking credit, for example, for planes going down when we know that the real cause was icing or wind-shear. That in mind, let's remember how Tarrant insisted that he didn't know what Kessler was talking about.''

''You're willing to assume there's no substance to the threat?''

''No, I'm not, and that's why you get only two days. After that I'll have our people scour that island for Kessler and question every Muslim and German they find there. They'll also pick up this woman, E. Stride, unless she turns out to be eighty years old.''

The DEA man was aghast. ''On what charge?''

''Three murders, Peter. Three dead bounty hunters. You'll agree that there's probable cause.''

''And if I find Kessler? If he tells us what he knows?''

''Then those three go back to being drug-related murders. Kessler is left to stay or go as he pleases, even though there's that matter of a Colorado warrant. Neither

Willis nor his Muslims will be bothered again."

"Two days, you said."

"I suggest you don't waste them."

The man named Charles had rebuked his young aide in the car as they drove through the gates of Fort Meade. The aide was contrite. He said that he had forgotten himself in his zeal to be helpful. In the future he would remember his place. But that future, he knew, was looking very bright indeed.

He could now tell Tarrant many things of great value. So many that they ought to be rationed. He had already shown Tarrant how to code his scrambler so that the NSA computers could not translate more than gibberish. He could now confirm it but that wasn't worth much because for that he had already been paid. He could also confirm that they'd sequestered his wife but that she hadn't told them much that could hurt him. Most of what Clarisse knew, she'd heard from the German. Most of what she could tell them of his other activities were things they already knew or suspected. That was, after all, why he was under surveillance in the first place. Tarrant already paid for that knowledge as well but not much because this is Washington, D.C., and he would have been surprised if he were not.

These old men had nothing, only hints and suspicions, but nothing for which they could order his arrest. What they did have, however, was the name of the German who had certainly killed the Englishman, Pratt, and had then placed that call to Tarrant. Tarrant would pay a great deal for that name and a printout of his file with his photo and the knowledge that he was probably on Hilton Head Island.

Of at least equal value was the news about Bandari, who was now sailing West and not East as he'd claimed. The aide could only guess why. Pratt having failed, he was going after his niece, who was apparently somewhere on that island. If the niece was on Hilton Head, so must be the woman who placed the other call that so frightened Bandari. But who was she? This Stride, who may or may not exist? Or was she the Algerian who the German had mentioned? Or might they be one and the same?

He didn't know. What he did know was what this ought to be worth. A new Porsche just for starters. And a promise of a job in the next year or so running one of Tarrant's offshore firms on Grand Cayman. But that was in the future. Tarrant needed him right here, taking notes in meetings for an arrogant old bastard who had twice held him back from promotions.

Twenty-five

The Family Circle Tennis Classic, held in March of each year, had become a rite of spring on Hilton Head Island. It attracted the first major influx of tourists after a winter of relative quiet. It was a time when the island was ablaze with azaleas and the sun was reliably warm. Every Harbour Town boat slip was filled with yachts, many leased for the occasion by the tournament sponsors.

This tournament was a singularly civilized affair compared, for example, to New York's U.S. Open. Security, while present, was entirely discreet and the players were far more accessible to the fans. For residents, parking is not even a factor because the tournament, for many, is a leisurely bike ride away. For some, like Elizabeth, it's a five-minute walk, first to Martin Kessler's harborside rental and then a short stroll to the tennis club grounds.

She appeared at his door in a sleek white jumpsuit topped by a flat-brimmed straw hat, also white. The hat had a band of metallic gold ribbon that gathered to a fist-sized flower in the back. The jumpsuit was trimmed with gold buckles and zippers. This was, apparently, the all-new Elizabeth. Happy, fun-seeking, in love with being loved. Kessler shielded his eyes as if blinded by the glare.

"You don't think this is overcorrecting?" he asked. "I mean, I'm not suggesting that you get your abaya but . . ."

She ignored him. She looked at his knees. "You're wearing shorts?"

Yes he was. It was spring so he'd bought a pair of madras shorts that more or less went with his baggy golf jacket. She asked him to put on long pants.

"What's the matter with shorts? It's supposed to get hot."

"It's just that . . . some men can't wear shorts."

In her mind she had seen an impossible picture. They were walking through the tournament grounds. Armed men appeared, who knew who, who knew why. Martin reached for his pistol, blazed away, but the armed men didn't even bother to duck because Martin looked so ridiculous in shorts. Martin grumbled but he changed into slacks. She also made him leave the pistol that this time was under the jacket.

They spent the morning wandering the grounds watching qualifiers battle for a place in the tournament. A few, noted Elizabeth, seemed no older than Cherokee but some, twice her age and with sun-damaged skin, were still struggling to make a precarious living after years on the women's pro tour.

The established professionals, the seeded players, would not start their matches for another two days although several had come early to practice. There were four practice courts adjoining the clubhouse. The clubhouse had a raised front porch that provided a view of the practice sessions. On its second floor, reached by an outside staircase, was a lounge reserved for the visiting players.

A crowd had gathered at the foot of the stairs and along an opening in a low chain-link fence that bordered the entrance to the practice courts. Here, the players had to pass through the fans. Most did so with grace, most would stop to sign autographs. Several young girls wore tournament T-shirts already well covered by the signatures of players scrawled on them and on their skin underneath with red or blue Magic Markers. Two big-name players were already on the courts hitting low baseline drives with their coaches. Word spread and even more people gathered. Elizabeth recognized Amanda Coetzer and Arantxa Sanchez-Vicario. She stood by the low chain-link fence for a while admiring their power and discipline. Martin, however, was admiring the aromas that were drifting their way from the food tents.

"You smell that? Kielbasa with garlic, fried onions and peppers. What would you say to a big gooey sandwich?"

"Yuck. It's too early. But you can bring me a Sprite. I'd like to stay and watch awhile longer."

Martin gave her a squeeze and began picking his way through the crowd that had filled in behind them. Between the porch and the fence was a narrow path that served as a shortcut between the food tents off one end and the courts where the qualifying matches were played off the other. A constant flow moved in either direction. But suddenly a young voice said "Oh, there's GiGi," and the flow almost came to a stop. Elizabeth looked up. At the top of the stairs she saw GiGi Fernandez about to descend to the practice courts. A crush quickly formed at the base of the stairs as the girls in their T-shirts squeezed into position. It was then that Elizabeth saw the straw cowboy hat, the one with blue feathers in its band.

"Cherokee, stay with us, please," came a voice from the opposite end of the porch. Elizabeth knew that voice in an instant, the accent with a faintly Arabic sound. She turned and saw the same tall woman whose face was in Cyril Pratt's clippings. She was with another woman, younger and black, who could only be the one they called Jazz. Elizabeth lowered her eyes; she looked away. She should not have raised them to look for the hat again but she did and now she saw Cherokee's face. The face, rather sad but mostly healed of its bruises, was now brightening at the prospect of meeting the player whom she said in the car was her idol. She waved as if to answer, "Just give me a second," and even swapped grins with young faces around her. Every face was now turned up toward the tennis star; every face, that is, except Elizabeth's.

But for that, the girl would never have seen her. No part of Cherokee's brain would have wondered why this woman by the fence had no interest in GiGi Fernandez. Her glance swept over Elizabeth's face, it lingered for the smallest part of an instant before—gratefully—moving away. But the grin on Cherokee's face now seemed frozen and something within her made her stop and look back. For the second time, they made eye contact.

Elizabeth told herself that this was impossible, there was no way in the world that this girl could know her. She turned away and began to move in the direction that Martin had taken. Stupidly, wrongly, she looked up once again. The girl's eyes were locked on her own, she was staring, and her lips were mouthing, "Martina?"

Elizabeth coolly looked this way and that as if wondering who this girl was addressing. She then pretended to hear a voice calling her. She mimed an acknowledgment, waved to no one in particular and started shouldering her way through the crowd. Behind her she heard Nadia Halaby's voice saying, "Cherokee? Cherokee, get back here." Elizabeth could now see Martin; he was turning away from the sandwich counter, two soft drinks and a hoagie in his hands. She did not look at him, she kept her eyes straight ahead but she grimaced to show him that something was wrong.

"Behind me. Block her," she hissed as she passed him.

"I see her," he answered. "Keep going."

With that he stepped into Cherokee's path and the sandwich and sodas flew into the air. Greasy sausage and onions spilled onto her shorts as his hip knocked the girl to the pavement.

"Oh, my goodness," he said. "Are you hurt? I didn't see you." He bent down and held her, pretending to steady her, and positioned his body so she couldn't see past it.

"I'm okay. I'm sorry." She twisted from his grip. Kessler did not dare delay her further because he now saw the women, they were coming fast, and he feared that they might recall seeing his face at their school. He turned it away and caught sight of Elizabeth who was quickly disappearing from view. He saw that she had removed her white straw hat to make herself harder to pick out in a crowd. But removing it caused someone else to recognize her. An elderly couple was coming this way. Kessler didn't know them but they seemed to know Elizabeth. The woman began to smile a greeting. The smile turned into a look of bewilderment as Elizabeth rushed past without so much as a nod.

The two from the tennis school reached the girl's side. Kessler retreated to the sandwich counter where he busied himself wiping grease from his hands. Passersby now blocked the girl's view of him but he could hear what the women were saying to her.

"Where the hell were you going?" the tall one demanded.

"No one. I mean nowhere. I mean I thought I saw Monica Seles."

"You run off again," said the other through her teeth, "I'll whale your ass good, little lady."

Kessler heard this, relieved but confused. Confused because he could not understand how this girl could have spotted Elizabeth. Even if she did get a glimpse of her face that night, what she saw was dark hair and dark eyes. Perhaps Elizabeth was talking to someone and the girl recognized her voice. Even so he found it hard to imagine that Elizabeth could be taken by surprise, even spooked. But ultimately Kessler was very much impressed that the girl was saying nothing to give her away. He found a trash can and disposed of his napkins, then quietly faded into the crowd before Nadia could think to apologize to him or offer to buy a new sandwich.

"I am so damned stupid," said Elizabeth, seething.

Elizabeth was still berating herself when he found her waiting at the entrance to his building.

"Perhaps there's no harm done. Don't be hard on yourself."

He told her how the girl had covered her tracks, perhaps out of loyalty to the one she called Martina, or perhaps, and more likely, because she couldn't be sure.

"What's so dumb is I *knew* it. I knew that if Fernandez showed up at this tournament, that girl was sure to be near."

"Is it possible that you—"

"Don't say that in my heart I was hoping I'd see her. It isn't true so don't say it."

Kessler, no fool, did not.

"Damn it, Martin. You said they'd be moving her."

"My fault. Absolutely. Blame me."

"I'm sorry. I'm just—"

"Let me drive you home. Get out of that jumpsuit, put the hat in the garbage, put on something that's a little less like shooting off rockets."

"The woman, Nadia. Do you think she saw me?"

"Not even your back. She cared only for the girl. Nobody looked at me either."

"I lost it, Martin. I panicked."

"The truth is, my darling, you were quick, you were smart. Panic is not someone who picks an escape route and sets up a block on her way."

"Every eye at that clubhouse was looking up the stairs. Every eye but mine. I was looking at Cherokee."

"That's all that happened? That's how you stood out?" She nodded. "She felt me, Martin. She knew."

Now we're speaking of psychic connections, thought Kessler. There is no denying that a bond had been established, but mind reading took it a little too far.

"Elizabeth, let me tell you about girls that age. They have the attention span of a radish. What she cares about at this very moment is getting GiGi Fernandez to write on her body."

Elizabeth frowned. She knew better.

"Let's go home. This time I pick your outfit," Kessler told her.

The girl known as Cherokee was thrilled beyond measure. In the instant when she looked into that woman's eyes it was as if an electrical spark had jumped between them. The face was saying, "Good to see you're okay," but then it said, "Damn it, stop staring at me."

It was dumb to go after her. She shouldn't have done that because Nadia and Jazz would have wanted to know who she was. They would never have guessed that it was Martina. But if Nadia had stopped her and spoken to her she just might have known her by her voice.

Cherokee had to remind herself that she had not heard Martina speak either. At least not today. Yet she had heard her voice in her heart and in her head just as clearly as she had in that cabin that night and all the way back in her car. A part of her head tried to tell her she was wrong. Look at her eyes and her hair, you dummy. Martina's were dark, even darker than yours. That woman had eyes like little gold buttons and her hair was a sort of reddish brown. But you don't forget eyes just because they change color. Color doesn't change the life and the strength in them. Color doesn't change kindness. It doesn't change love.

"Just look at your shirt. You look like a salad." Nadia had bought a can of club soda and was using it to wash that man's sandwich from her clothes. But at least they weren't taking her back to her room where all she'd done was cry for most of a week over pictures of her mother and father. They were letting her stay. She had promised to mind them. And she had to stay for as long as it took because there was now someone else she had to find in this crowd.

They walked with her back to the practice courts where they let her watch GiGi Fernandez for a while. She no longer cared about autographs. Next Nadia wanted to look at a match where a girl who she'd taught once was trying to qualify. Cherokee cheered for her while asking God in her mind to please let her win in straight sets so they could leave. God answered her prayer. Now she could do some more walking and looking.

An hour later she had almost despaired of seeing that elderly couple again. She said another prayer, she prayed as hard as she could. God answered by pressing on Nadia's bladder so she'd need to go to the bathroom. Two large public toilets, big ones mounted on trailers, had been set up at one end of the Stadium Court. Nadia and Jazz stood in line in front of one of them. God had made them pick that line because there on the next one was the elderly woman she was looking for. Her husband was standing next to a tree. He was reading the draw sheet while he waited for her.

Cherokee said, "I'll take that line. It's faster." Jazz started to say, "No, stay here with us." She squirmed and grimaced so that Jazz would believe that relief was all she had on her mind. But Nadia was giving her a skeptical look. She asked Jazz to stand in that line as well. Jazz did, but not before two other women got on to the line in front of her.

A volunteer attendant was directing the traffic, letting each woman enter as another came out. Cherokee watched the old woman go in and offered a final prayer that she'd be thorough. She was genuinely squirming by the time her turn came. This prayer, like the others, was answered but barely. The woman was washing her hands as she entered.

"Ma'am . . . excuse me?" God would forgive her for one more little lie. "There was a woman who I think you might know. I spilled food all over her beautiful jumpsuit." She gestured toward her own stains as proof. "She was so upset . . . I guess she ran off to change . . ."

The woman smiled. "Oh, so that's it. I wondered."

"Do you know how I could call her? I mean I'll have it dry cleaned or I'll pay for a new one. I really feel awful that it happened."

The woman reached for a paper towel. "Well, you're sweet. But I'm sure she knows it was an accident. Um . . . speaking of accidents, have you . . ." She had noticed the fading discoloration that surrounded Cherokee's eye. Cherokee flicked a hand to convey that it was nothing.

"I've got to at least apologize to her. I could send her a card or some flowers."

"Tell you what. She's my neighbor." The woman touched her cheek. "I'll stop by her house the first chance I get and tell her how badly you feel."

Cherokee wanted to scream.

"But I suppose there's no harm. She's in the telephone book. Her name is Elizabeth Stride."

Thank you, God. "That's *Stride*? As in walking? Is she listed by her name or her husband's?"

"As in walking, yes, and no husband; she's a widow."
The old woman reached for the door.

"Is she really? I mean . . . she's so beautiful and all.
Does she date? Because I have this uncle . . ."

"Young lady, I'm sure I don't know."

"I'm sorry. You're right. I'm being so stupid."

"Well . . . I'm sure your heart's in the right place, dear.
But as it happens I do think she's in a relationship. A
doctor named Jonathan something or other."

Cherokee thanked her and held the door for her. When
it closed she snatched a paper towel from the wall and
scurried into one of the stalls. She used her red Magic
Marker to write down the names on the towel. That done,
she sat and said a prayer in her mind. So many lies, so
much deceit. She promised to think of a suitable ransom
such as giving away her very best clothes to a student
who had not had rich parents. Then God might forgive
her for going too far. God, the merciful, God, the compassionate will take her intentions into account.

Elizabeth Stride. A strong name. A good name. The
first part made you think of a queen and the second fit a
woman who moved like the wind. It was a brave name.
But a kind name. One that couldn't be cruel. Cherokee
knew that she couldn't have done what the newspaper said
had been done to those men.

But a doctor could have done it. They weren't bothered
by blood. The man, the one who stayed outside the cabin,
must have found the three men who Elizabeth scared off
and killed them after she and Elizabeth were gone. The
man who'd been with her was this doctor named Jonathan.

"Cherokee, honey?" Jazz's voice startled her. "Are
you going to be much longer in there?"

"Two minutes." She gave the roll of paper a spin, then
grimaced when she realized that she'd lied again in doing
so. So she said another prayer, not to God but to her
parents. Her parents were surely in Paradise. She asked
her father . . . no, better her mother . . . if it was okay to
love Elizabeth Stride. Or at least if she should try to be
her friend.

Her father would have said, "Stick with Nadia and Jazz because you know where they stand. They'll protect and guide you according to Islam. From your own mouth you don't think this woman is Muslim." But her mother who was not a Muslim herself . . . except in her heart where it counted . . . would say, "She's my kind of woman. Go for it, Aisha. Don't worry, your father and I will be near."

And she did. She said that in Cherokee's mind. Her mother had answered her prayer.

Twenty-six

The Tuareg, Ozal, was nearly finished with his bomb when the boat was still a night out at sea.

The easiest part was the nitroglycerine that he made from the chemicals they bought in Las Palmas. Sulfuric acid mixed with nitric acid and then the glycerine added drop by drop. He used Bandari's galley for the mixing and measuring but his soldiers had to do the delicate siphoning because the fumes caused his ruined fingers to swell and they caused his good eye to run. Very gently they drained off the acids leaving only the nitrated glycerine remaining. This they mixed carefully with sawdust and an alkali, which was ordinary baking soda. They tamped all this—lightly—into trays used for muffins. The trays then were packed in ice. One thing they had forgotten was litmus paper to test if the acids were completely withdrawn and they should have lit a drop or two to see how it burned. But Ozal wasn't worried. He'd done this before and the soldiers had made very good pupils.

The easiest part was the timing device which was made from a clock and some batteries. The hardest part was the artillery shell. The casing had to be scored very carefully so that it would fragment when the nitro was detonated and scatter the plutonium sleeve. This part was done while Bandari napped lest he realize that the bomb would be nuclear after all.

As it was, Bandari did nothing but complain. It made him half crazy if the soldier was whistling as he stirred the ingredients in a big copper pot. "Why is he whistling? Does he think he's making soup? He is going to kill us all with his whistling."

He got even more crazy when the soldier was silent. "What's happening down there? What are you not telling me? Did he spill it and it's melting a hole in my hull?"

Ozal tried to calm him. He explained the whole process. He said there was almost no danger of explosion as long as they kept it from getting too hot and as long as Bandari kept his mind on navigation and didn't run into a tanker in the dark.

"Almost? What is almost? Why did you say almost?"

"Bandari . . . shut up and steer."

"And how do you know you can get them with a bomb? You have guns. Why can't you just shoot them?"

"It's a bomb because I make bombs. Now shut up."

"And that smell. It's practically peeling the paint. What if the Coast Guard should show up and board us? What will I say is that smell?"

Ozal was not greatly concerned about the Coast Guard. They would rarely board without probable cause and this yacht was one of hundreds that were coming this way. At most they might radio and ask what was aboard. What was aboard? Drugs, of course. And bubonic plague. Oh, and two atomic warheads, I almost forgot.

A ridiculous country. Its borders were a sieve. Any boat could sail into almost any little port and no one would ask if you'd stopped off at Customs or if anyone aboard had a passport or visa. They would only ask, as did Harbour Town, "What's the length of your vessel and how long will you stay?"

"Three days," Bandari told them from ten miles out.

The marina office answered, "We can guarantee two. After that we're solidly booked for the tournament."

Tournament? What tournament? Fishing, perhaps. "Two is enough. I take two."

They assigned him a slip. That was all there was to it. Bandari told them he would be there by nine in the morning which was then still six hours away. He used those six hours to try to vent out the smell but it clung to his curtains and cushions.

"Why two days?" Ozal asked him. "What takes two whole days?"

"To find out where the girl and the woman are living."

"What, you don't know this now? How come you don't know this already?"

"All Tarrant told me is it's a big place for tennis but also there are Muslims who live there. Muslim women on this island should be easy to spot."

Ozal stared at him. "How? You think they play tennis in hijab? Or maybe they play with a racquet in one hand and the holy Koran in the other."

"We will find them," Bandari insisted.

The motor yacht *Alhambra* had found its slip in the circular harbor at Harbour Town. Bandari backed it, stern in, in a section for big yachts in the shadow of a complex whose sign read Ketch Court. Ozal was surprised at the number of tourists who were strolling the quays and gawking at boats. He had not imagined such crowds. He was pleased, however, to see many fine yachts even larger and grander than Bandari's. That was good. Their own boat would not attract too much attention. The throngs worried him, though.

"How *will* we find them?" he asked Bandari.

"Leave that to me," said Bandari.

We don't need, thought Ozal, to know exactly where they live. All we need do is narrow it down. All we need do is find the big place for tennis. It's enough that they are there and downwind of the bomb.

"I am going ashore," he announced to Bandari. "I'll pick up some maps and a telephone book so we can locate this big place for tennis."

"No, you'd better let me. I look more like a tourist."

"Being fat with short pants? This makes you a tourist?"

Bandari stuck out his lip. "What, you think you're more typical? Show me a tourist with one eye and such fingers. Why don't you wear a kaffiyeh while you're at it and walk with an assault rifle under your arm?''

Ozal grumbled at this but Bandari was right. He wished that he had thought to purchase an eye-patch. He retreated to the galley where he fashioned a headband, cutting strips from a clean terry dishcloth. He covered his hands with the thick yellow gloves which his soldiers had worn while they were cooking the nitro. They were stained and they stank but they helped him to look as if he might be a mechanic. He wiped the galley floor with a smelly old shirt, then wore it to complete the illusion. Bandari groaned when he appeared back on deck.

"Give me some dollars. I have only pesetas."

"Now you look worse than ever. I order you to stay."

"Give me dollars," he said, "and shut up."

If Bandari had not tried to give him an order, Ozal might not have stayed ashore as long as he did. He might not have bought a newspaper along with his maps. He might not have sat down in a red rocking chair—such chairs were left out for the tourists to use—and would not have learned several important things.

The first was that the bodies of those first three had been found. It was still in the paper, even now a week later. The authorities, it seemed, still did not know their names but they could only be the Englishman Pratt, and his helpers. Bandari didn't know this. How could he know? They have been out at sea for six days.

Bandari would faint if he knew how they died. Throats cut ear to ear and their tongues pulled down through. A few bullet holes added to their bodies for good measure, then fed to the crabs and the alligators. This woman who phoned him and made all those threats was more than just talk after all. Ozal, however, was not going to tell him. Telling him might put some steel in his spine but it also might turn him to jelly.

He would surely not tell him the second thing he learned. In the same newspaper item a subheading appeared. It said, "More Evidence Dredged From Murder Marsh Site" and there in a box was a picture. In the picture was a watch, a gold Rolex, it said. You couldn't see it was a Rolex because the picture showed only the back in order to display the inscription. And there, no mistake, written in Arabic, was the name of Gamal Bandari. "To Gamal Bandari—who has been a good friend." Very likely, the friends were that Libyan gang who were growing less friendly by the day. Ozal could not imagine how the watch got in that swamp but he knew without question how Bandari would react if he saw his own name in the Hilton Head paper.

The third thing he learned was why this place was so crowded. All the time he was ashore he heard cheering and clapping in the distance. The sound struck him as unlike the sound of a soccer match. It was much more polite and refined. On an impulse he climbed the steps of the lighthouse to see where the sounds could be coming from. It was also to get the lay of the land and to see all the boats in the harbor.

He had plenty of room to take in the view because the tourists got a whiff of him and moved quickly away. He could see what looked like stadium seats and white tents and more milling crowds through the trees. An event so big must be in the paper. He opened his copy to the section marked Sports and there it was, page after page, describing what seemed to be an annual event. The Family Circle Tennis Classic. Even the name was polite, he thought. This must be because they were all women.

And then it struck him. It came like a thunderbolt. This had to be the big place for tennis.

The more he stared, the more perfect it seemed. The wind, to begin with, was steady from the west and the west was now at his back. It would blow gamma rays all over this Harbour Town and over the courts where the tennis was played. Every seat in the stadium would be filled when it came. They would hear the explosion but they would think it was thunder. They'd look up but then they'd go on with their clapping, not knowing that they all had already been killed. Every man, every woman, every child would be finished. Everyone in those apartments, everyone in those tents, everyone in those restaurants and shops. The only survivors would be those who

were upwind. Even those, however, would soon die as
well because downwind was the only way out of this place
unless you went upwind by boat.

This was big. So big.

He would telephone first. He would tell them exactly
what was going to happen but he'd let them have no more
than ten minutes' warning. He would tell them who he
was and why he was doing this. He had done it to show
them that no place is safe, not even this haven called
Hilton Head Island where the blood-sucking rich come to
play in the sun. He had done it to show all the women of
Islam that there was no place to hide if they ran from their
duties. He had done it to show all enemies of God that
they could not escape the revenge of the poor.

Which was pig shit, of course.

It's the kind of nonsense Bandari would spout, thinking
half the world's Muslims would applaud him.

What it was, was a war. It was a war against a world
which, if God really existed, he would have had the good
sense to destroy before this.

Above all, it was practice for Cairo.

Twenty-seven

On that morning Lawrence Tarrant had swallowed a Valium. He could have done with two but he took only one because he needed his head to be clear.

His pilot had called from Washington National confirming that his plane had returned from Grand Cayman, had refueled and would be ready to depart at his pleasure. The pilot, who called on an unsecured phone, advised that his baggage was already on board. The baggage, in this case, was a certain associate whom Tarrant could no longer put off.

That call was followed by one from an attorney who announced that he had been retained by Clarisse who would that day be filing for divorce. The attorney would not tell him where his wife was then staying; he said that any contact would be solely through him. He proceeded to list the grounds she would cite and certain demands that she would make in the interim, among them that Tarrant should vacate her home taking nothing but his personal belongings.

Tarrant listened long enough to be satisfied that her grounds were all of a personal nature and made no allegations of criminal activity. No longer interested, he broke the connection. His primary reason for abruptly hanging up was the arrival of a messenger in his driveway. The envelope that the messenger carried would contain the file that his overly ambitious young friend had promised him. The file on the German named Kessler.

That in hand, he buzzed his chauffeur to say that he would be leaving for the airport in fifteen minutes. He used that time to make copies of the file and to scan its contents as he did so. The copies would go to Lester Loomis and his men who were to meet him on Hilton Head Island. They were four, including Loomis, all good at their work. If Kessler was there, they would find him and kill him more slowly than Kessler had killed Pratt. They would also be watching for Bandari's boat because that island, Tarrant could no longer doubt, was where the damned fool must be going. He would see to Bandari himself.

But first must come that meeting he dreaded. The man who was waiting aboard his plane was at least of his own sort, not a Libyan colonel. This man was an American, a powerful banker, the product of excellent breeding and family. But his breeding wouldn't stop him from making a phone call if what Tarrant had to say didn't satisfy him. It would do him no good to lay the blame on Bandari. That phone call would tell the two Libyan colonels that Lawrence J. Tarrant could not be relied upon. Such a call, if he made it, would cost Tarrant a fortune to say nothing of making it extremely unlikely that Clarisse would have need of a lawyer.

Outside, his chauffeur pulled up and signaled. It was time to leave for the airport. Tarrant made one more call on the unsecured line, this one to the offices of Tarrant Associates in downtown Washington, D.C. He informed his receptionist that he would not be coming in; he would be leaving for Grand Cayman immediately. There, for at least the next several days, he would be in conference with a Mr. Bandari. He would be taking no calls until their business was concluded.

"Bandari," he repeated. He spelled the name for her. "We'll be meeting on his yacht when it gets there."

The receptionist was a decorative if rather dim woman who knew virtually nothing about his business. The call, in any case, was not really for her. It was to tell whoever had a tap on this phone that Grand Cayman must be where Bandari was headed and that that was where he himself was headed as well. The flight plan that his pilot had filed did not mention a stop on Hilton Head Island. That was where he would deplane. The banker would go on. This banker, tall and thin like himself, would pass as Lawrence Tarrant to anyone watching when the plane arrived at Grand Cayman.

In his car Lawrence Tarrant could now take the time to examine Kessler's file more closely. The more he read, the comics included, the less he was sure what to make of this man. Parts made perfect sense to him. Others did not.

Kessler's father, it seemed, had been third in command of East German counter-intelligence. The father, during World War II, had done the same work as a Nazi. Captured by the Russians at the end of the war, he then spent several years in a Soviet prison camp before being released and repatriated. He promptly joined the Communist Party for, one assumes, exactly the same reasons that had led him to become a Nazi before that. A smart man did not swim against the current. His alternative to joining the party in power would have been to remain a political neutral—and therefore live a life with neither travel nor privilege—or to become, if he were stupid, a critic of the system and end up as a trash collector in Leipzig.

The father died of a stroke in 1985 but not before bringing up his son in his footsteps. The son, who grew up knowing only one system, was apparently a good deal less cynical at first. He believed—it said here—in the Marxist ideal but he became disillusioned over time. A slow learner. He saw that an essentially humanistic philosophy had evolved over time into a self-serving racket for the party elite. Even so, he had stayed in counter-intelligence. His file said he stayed because he enjoyed the game. More likely, thought Tarrant, his father pointed out that he, the son, was now one of the elite so shut up and don't rock the boat. In any event the son stayed on until the system disintegrated under his feet. After that, together with a former Israeli agent—a note said ''See Stride'' but there was nothing on him here—Kessler helped himself to a share of its leavings and pursued the good life with new vigor.

A renegade after my own heart, thought Tarrant. In an avalanche every snowflake pleads not guilty. As to why such a man would want to help female Muslims—even assuming he'd eventually run short of funds—the answer had to be that he would not. The answer has to be that Pratt was quite right when he said he was concerned about attracting competition. This Kessler clearly wanted the million dollars himself that had been offered for that other woman down there. Well, Kessler could have had it and welcome to it, if he only hadn't made that call to Clarisse.

Tarrant's jet was airborne. It was over Virginia headed southwest and climbing. Very soon, somewhere over the Carolinas, his pilot would discover an electrical problem and would make an unscheduled landing on Hilton Head. Tarrant had until then to try to satisfy this man that their project was able to proceed.

He thought it best to tell him about the German named Kessler on the chance that the banker had sources of his own. This Kessler, he assured him, was about to be silenced. He was, however, no immediate threat because his interest was solely in collecting a bounty now that Pratt was out of his way.

"Pratt told him about you? And your business with the Libyans?"

"He was trying to bargain for his life. He failed."

"Yes, but how did Pratt know in the first place?" asked the banker. "And why in God's name would you have told him a thing?"

"I didn't," he answered. "Bandari must have boasted. Bandari needs to feel important, even in the eyes of a creature like Pratt."

"But not you, you'll assure me. You said nothing yourself?"

Tarrant, again, thought it best to seem candid. He acknowledged that Pratt had heard him speak of that shipment, but only in the vaguest of terms. He had mentioned the warehouse but not its location, and certainly not what was in those containers. As he said this he could barely contain his relief. That the banker had focused on the state of Pratt's knowledge had to mean he knew nothing of that group at Fort Meade, and the fact that they were looking for the German as well, or that Bandari had gone into hiding.

"Is the shipment indeed in that warehouse, Lawrence?"

"The brother was given no time to move it. It's under armed guard but it's there."

"Yet Bandari stalls you when you tell him to get it. Is it possible that he's already given the warheads to those lunatics he's been working to cultivate?"

"No it isn't. He knows that I'd kill him."

"Well, let's see then. What's left?" The banker paused for a sigh. "I'll pass over his nonsense about the need to do this legally as the recognized head of his family. Is it possible that he's getting a case of cold feet at the thought of depopulating a city here and there?"

Cold feet, thought Tarrant, but not for that reason. He chose not to mention the Algerian woman who had threatened to lop off his hand.

"Because if that's his concern, you can put him at ease. Our own lunatics have no such intention."

Tarrant blinked, not sure that he followed.

"Oh, they might set off one but not in a city." The banker drew a cigar from his pocket. "They have chosen a vineyard town somewhere in France. Our friends, you'll recall, have a thing about wine."

Tarrant must have stared in a dim-witted manner. His expression brought a smirk to the banker's face as he snipped and lit his Corona.

"Very well, I'll narrow it down just a little. It's a town near Bordeaux but that's as much as I can tell you. When it happens and you see what labels are affected, you'll want to snatch up a few cases for your cellar. You won't see them again in your lifetime."

Tarrant wanted to smack the cigar from his mouth and choke him to get him to shut up about grapes. But the fact that the banker was toying with him offered further proof that he had no suspicion that their project was nearly in shambles.

"You really haven't figured this out?" asked the banker as he blew a stream of smoke toward the ceiling. "Our friends might be brutal but they're not suicidal. NATO would grind them to dust in a week. Think money, dear boy, and it will all become clear."

Tarrant's eyes widened slowly. "They're going to try blackmail?"

"More or less," smiled the banker. He patted Tarrant's knee. "Our friends intend to inform the UN that they've infiltrated a terrorist group. The plotters are that Algerian bunch, the Islamic Salvation Front. They're the ones, you'll recall, who tried to hijack an airliner and intended to explode it in the sky over Paris. Since then they've had to settle for planting bombs in the Metro for want of the means to do something more dramatic."

"For want of six nuclear warheads, for instance."

"Terrorism is theater. The bigger the better. 'Wide slaughter,' you know, and all that."

Tarrant controlled his impatience with effort. "Are you saying that these warheads will be used or that they won't?"

"Don't you see? That's the point. They need never be used. The devices will be planted in cities throughout France and one at NATO headquarters in Brussels. France is the terrorists' primary target because of their support for the Algerian regime. The Libyans will offer to prevent their detonation but of course they'll want something in return."

"Such as the unfreezing of all their seized assets."

"That and an unrestricted market for their oil. Right now they have to sell it at a discount. They'll also want commercial airline flights resumed and an end to being pestered about that Lockerbie business."

Tarrant was not at all sure that he liked this. From his point of view there was more to be made from an embargo left firmly in place. He was also beginning to understand why the banker was speaking so freely. No doubt he was carrying a recording device. His intent was not entrapment so much as enwrapment, so that Tarrant could not, at some future date, try to claim no knowledge of this.

"Will the UN believe them?"

"Of course not. Would you?"

"I would . . . want to see proof. A confession, perhaps, and by someone still alive whom I could interview."

"Oh, they won't provide that yet. It would spoil their fun. Our friends will say, 'Well, we did try to warn you,' and the French will lose that village plus a few surrounding vineyards that they think of as national treasures. This will happen in mid-April by the way, after Ramadan, which is why we have little time to lose. After that, should the vineyards fail to get their attention, I suspect the next target would be a nuclear power plant, because France is trying to go 100 percent nuclear in order to reduce their dependence on oil. But my personal favorite is Cannes. The Film Festival is held there in May. Film stars and tourists all packed cheek by jowl. Once again our friends will warn them; they'll say, 'This is what we've heard. We can make some arrests and get them to talk but, remember, there's the danger that they'll then turn on us so it needs to be well worth our while.' By then the UN should be ready to deal."

Tarrant wondered about that. More likely, there would be a French ultimatum. They'd give Qaddafy one hour to produce those devices or he could kiss his own capital good-bye. The Algerians would also carve a chunk out of Libya as a payback for trying to frame them. Other Arab leaders would make use of the confusion to settle disputes with their neighbors. They already have designs on each other's oil but it was water that was becoming more precious by the day. They'd fight over oil if they had the will. They'd fight over water because they'd have no choice.

"It's inevitable, you know," said the banker.

"What is?"

"Total war in that region. Isn't that what you're thinking? All it takes is a spark. Just a spark."

"And that spark . . . what you're saying is, why leave it to chance?"

"Exactly, Lawrence. Exactly."

So the master plan went beyond mere extortion. It envisioned the entire Mideast occupied; every NATO nation carving out its own zone and Israel tripling in size. It envisioned establishing a NATO protectorate to administer the Western world's oil supply. Corporations would move in. And the bankers who funded them would end up controlling everything.

"Our friends need those six shells," said this prince among those bankers. "You must not disappoint them . . . or me."

"They'll have them."

"And your German must be silenced, as you put it, at once. It's no good if he ruins the surprise, is it, Lawrence?"

"Give me three days for Kessler. Three more for the shipment. I will have it or Bandari is a dead man as well."

"Um . . . 'as well' would include you, I'm afraid."

"Oh, that's clear," Tarrant told him. "That's perfectly clear. But I intend to collect my twenty-five million."

The banker seemed satisfied, although guardedly so, because this was a man who understood greed. But in Tarrant's mind the amount now seemed modest when compared to the hundreds of billions at stake here.

The banker was right. This is how it would start. Not with invasions by the great superpowers but with terrorist acts so atrocious that the West would have no choice short of massive response. And it wouldn't be the work of the terrorists we knew. Not Hamas or Hezbollah, not Iran or Iraq or especially that pipsqueak, Qaddafy. It need only seem that their hand was behind it.

If providing these shells was worth twenty-five million, one would think not to do so should be worth even more. In the long run he'd be doing the Libyans a favor if he sold them to the French instead.

And the banker was right to ask who would believe this. Few believed that Hitler, who specifically promised it, would actually try to exterminate a whole race. No one believed, much more recently than that, that a Japanese cult had the means and intention to kill a few million commuters. And they weren't even doing it for God in those cases.

No one would believe it. So they'll have to be shown. At least one of those devices would be used.

"This is right to do, you know," the banker said quietly. He stared at the glow of his cigar.

Tarrant was startled. He said, "Um . . . I'm sure."

"The alternative is chaos. Islam rising and all that. As Christians we're bound to prevent it."

"Absolutely."

"Read your Bible. Jeremiah. It's all there, you know."

"Oh, I will. And it's there. I've no doubt."

Tarrant's answer, once again, drew a pat on his knee. The banker seemed pleased that he understood. But Tarrant felt a twinge. He would not have called it conscience. People suffer and die one way or the other but the business of making money goes on. And yet he still wondered about men like these bankers. He himself was not troubled by the rightness or wrongness of what they intended to do. It was wrong. Accept it. Then go do it.

But to claim that it's right? That we're doing them a favor? Tarrant was uncomfortable with that sort of thinking.

Lost in reflection—what to do about this—Tarrant gazed out the window of his plane. His eye caught the glint on another small jet that was headed on a similar course. Beyond was the coastline and the gray-green Atlantic. He could not make out any yachts from that altitude but he prayed that he was right and Bandari's was down there.

"A penny for your thoughts," said the banker to his ear.

"They're worth twenty-five million. Just be ready to move it."

"We've no doubt that you'll do the right thing."

Twenty-eight

Roy Willis had come early to Hilton Head's airport, driving one of the Van Der Meer jitneys. The man he was to meet there had made the pointed suggestion that they meet in the parking lot, not in the terminal. He'd be coming alone, no escort, no staff.

"Yeah, but *why* are you coming?" Roy had asked when he called. "Seems I heard that you're not DEA anymore."

"Do I need a reason to see an old friend? Maybe hit a few tennis balls? Talk over old times?"

"Okay, then, why *else* are you coming? If this is about those three stiffs in the swamp, all I know is what I've seen in the papers."

"Well, the truth is I'd like you to look at some photographs but it's mostly an excuse to come visit. Believe me, Roy, I could use the vacation."

Willis didn't believe him. He knew more than he was saying. One other thing he had trouble believing was that Peter would be traveling alone. This was because he'd been watching the cars that had entered the lot since he got there. One car had two men in it. They parked and they sat. They did not have the look of either tourists or locals. A second car came. Two more men like the others. They did the same. It struck Willis as unlikely that all four men were simply waiting for out-of-town guests to arrive.

Peter's plane landed. A few minutes later he emerged

from the terminal. He wore a yellow windbreaker and a baseball-type cap, a garment bag hung from his shoulder. He spotted the jitney and waved. Willis scanned the three cars. The men had not reacted. None of them started an engine.

"Those men. Are they yours?" Roy asked as he slid back the door of the jitney.

Peter followed his eyes. "No, they're not," he said, frowning. "Let's go. We'll see if they follow."

Willis hesitated. "Do you have a camera?"

"As it happens, I do." He reached into his bag. The camera was a Nikon with a telephoto lens of a type that was used for surveillance.

"Just what every vacationer carries," scowled Willis. But he took it and shot half a roll through his window. The angles were catch-as-catch-can. "What the hell. Why be cute about this?" he said. He started the jitney and moved it forward, stopping again at the terminal entrance. Once there he rolled his window down and shot the rest of his roll. All four men could now see what he was doing. All four tried to cover their faces, too late. Willis took his time pocketing the film when he finished. He put the jitney in gear and drove toward the exit. The men in the cars watched him go.

"And here I thought you'd learned to relax," remarked Peter when he saw that they hadn't been followed.

"Old habits," said Willis. "And speaking of pictures, where are yours?"

"Pick a place to pull over and I'll show you."

They had stopped in the lot of a Piggly-Wiggly Market. Willis climbed out from behind the wheel as Peter spread his carry-bag across his lap and pulled a large envelope from its pocket. Willis felt fairly sure of what he was going to be shown. Three bodies, now identified, two of them Muslims. He could think of no other reason that Peter had called him. The man had assumed that there must be a connection. Or at least Willis thought so. He was wrong.

The first photograph that came out of that envelope

caused the hair on his neck to rise. He struggled not to show his surprise. The face he was looking at was one that he knew. He had questioned this man in the Players Club parking lot when he saw him peering into another guest's car. And that guest, as he had later determined, was none other than the late Cyril Pratt.

"His name is Martin Kessler. Do you know him, by chance?" asked Peter, who was watching his eyes.

Roy answered with a shrug that he hoped was convincing. He yawned in an effort to improve on the effect. "Not offhand. What about him?" he asked.

Peter drew another photo, this one of Pratt. "Then I don't suppose you'd know this one."

Willis felt his cheek twitch. Another shrug.

Peter pulled out more photos, one after another. These were morgue photographs of three men or what remained of them. "As you've said, you wouldn't know a thing about these beyond what's appeared on the news."

"Those drug dealers, right?"

Peter sniffed. "If you say so." He brought out more photos. "And therefore you wouldn't know these fellows either."

In fact, he did not. The next photos shown were of a man in a business suit and a second man, darker and stockier.

Peter watched him as before. "You don't know them? Truly? Well, let's see if some names might ring a bell. The fat one's name is Gamal Bandari. The one with no lips is named Tarrant."

"I've . . . heard the name Bandari. Who is Tarrant?"

"Bandari's niece is in your charge, am I correct?"

"If she is, that's nobody's business."

"It was certainly Pratt's. Isn't that why he came here?"

"Peter . . . who is Tarrant? And who is this Kessler?"

In reply, Peter reached for the photo of Kessler and slid it back over with Tarrant's. He explained that Kessler had called Lawrence Tarrant—the man was an arms dealer among other things—and told him that Pratt and the others were dead. Kessler warned him against sending anyone else to this island or ever again bothering a certain

Algerian—who, we felt certain, was Nadia Halaby—and especially a certain young girl. The leverage with which Kessler backed up his warning was his knowledge of certain other plans Tarrant had made.

He reached for the photos of Bandari and Pratt and arranged them in a square with the others.

"Bandari works with Tarrant. Pratt worked for Bandari. Pratt came to this island in quest of a bounty on the girl, or on Halaby, or both. Are you really going to make me go through all this, Roy?"

"Not if you'll cut to the chase."

"How is it, incidentally, that a man you've never heard of has appointed himself as your champion?"

"I don't know," Roy answered. "That's the truth."

"And your word that you had no part in it yourself?"

"Part of what? Killing Pratt?"

"And his two Muslim thugs. Kessler didn't do that without help."

Roy thought of the woman who the girl had described, but Peter did not seem to know about her. "The answer is I would have but I didn't."

Roy's friend seemed relieved. "He was tortured, you know."

"Tortured by Kessler? What for?"

"Well, let's see. To get answers to questions, I would think. Would one of them have asked where this girl could be found?"

Willis looked at him evenly. "If I were you, I'd bet no." This Kessler knew that all along, he now realized. If anything, he used her as a lure to get Pratt.

Peter apologized. He hadn't meant to be snide. "If you're right, we can rule out that he's after a bounty. But he did learn something about Tarrant and we think it involves a terrorist attack. A very major attack. It involves the poisoning of entire cities. We suspect that New York is the primary target. More specifically, northern Manhattan."

This last was invention. It was done for effect.

Roy's expression went cold. He was rising to the bait. "You suspect," he repeated. "You don't know for sure?"

"Kessler does. I need to find him and talk to him."

Willis narrowed his eyes. "Those men at the airport. You're sure they're not yours?"

"I've already said no. I'm alone."

A doubtful sniff. "This thing's that big and you're doing a solo?"

"Roy, read my lips. I cannot risk a leak and I can't risk a manhunt. I can't risk that Kessler might slip through our fingers or get himself killed if we corner him."

Roy nodded slowly. He reached for his cell phone.

"You're calling . . . ?"

"My people to let them know we're both coming. When we get there, we'll see what we can do."

Nadia Halaby stood at the window of her second floor office at Van Der Meer. She was keeping an eye on the parking lot below where young Aisha was skating in circles. Or trying to skate. She had, apparently, never used Rollerblades. She had asked that as long as she couldn't leave the grounds and since Nadia couldn't take her back to the tournament, could she at least try to learn to skate on some blades another student had lent her.

Nadia saw no harm in it. She couldn't say no. They might also go back to the Family Circle matches later but for now she was waiting for Roy to return. It had been almost two hours since he went to meet the man who had once been his boss in New York. She wished that he had called from the airport.

She hoped that she knew what the meeting was about. Three dead men, their throats cut, a drug-related killing. These could easily account for his coming to the island. Knowing that Roy was now living down here, she supposed it seemed reasonable that this Peter would ask him what he thought or might have heard about the three. Or perhaps it was an excuse to just look in on Roy and see how an old friend was doing. Perhaps that was all there was to it.

Nadia winced as she saw the girl stumble and fall. So graceful on the tennis court, so awkward on skates. She would have already left some skin on the pavement were it not for her knee pads and wrist guards and helmet. Right now she was scrambling to avoid a jitney that had just turned into the lot. Nadia straightened. That was Roy at the wheel and he seemed to have brought that man with him. Roy pulled up to Aisha and rolled down his window. From his gestures he seemed to be telling the girl to keep her weight forward, knees bent. Now he seemed to be introducing her to the man who rode with him. She could not think why he would do that.

Nadia heard a knock on her door. Jasmine opened it and entered. Nadia told her, ''Roy's back. He's got company.''

''I know. He called me ten minutes ago. He had to stop and get some film developed. He couldn't say much because the guy was there with him. All he'd say is the meeting was interesting.''

''Did you know this Peter yourself?''

''Heard Roy talk about him is all. He's still DEA but he's on some new task force. He's more into terrorist activity these days.''

''Where's he looking for terrorists? Here?''

''Hey, we're Muslims, right? So we must all be killers.'' Jazz poked her. ''Relax, he doesn't care about us. Look at Roy. He seem worried to you?''

Jasmine had approached her and looked past her shoulder. She saw that Roy and Peter had emerged from their car. Roy was gesturing again, he was pointing to Sam. Sam, dressed in his coveralls, knew Peter as well. They walked toward each other; they shook hands. Jasmine's attention now drifted to Aisha. The girl was resting against one of the jitneys, her own eyes on the men who were walking away from her.

''She looks different. What's different about her?'' she asked.

''She's not Cherokee anymore. She's just Aisha.''

It took Jasmine a moment to understand. ''No more braid. She cut her hair short?''

''Don't ask why. She just did it. It was after I told her that we're sending her away. She leaves tomorrow morning, first thing.''

Jasmine grunted. "Poor kid. How'd she take it?"

"A few tears. Some were mine. We're all she's got left. But I promised we'd come see her in New York."

Jazz gave her shoulder a comforting squeeze. "The Nasreens will take care of her. They'll love her to death."

Nadia smiled, almost. They were still at the window. They watched as Aisha pushed off from the car and began a tentative glide toward another.

"What's she doing?" Jazz asked. "Why's she skating like that?"

"Like what? It's her first time. She's learning."

"The hell she is. I've seen her on blades. She could skate up a wall on those things."

Jazz pushed her aside and opened the window, prepared to tell Roy to go back and stay with her. But Roy was nowhere in sight below and the girl had suddenly picked up speed. Jazz called out her name but she did not look back. Instead she leaned forward and lowered her head and made a dash for the parking lot exit.

Jazz stuck out her head. "Cherok . . . Aisha? Aisha, get back here." But the girl had leaped over a wide grass divider and was making a bee-line for the parkway.

"I've been suckered," hissed Nadia as she snatched up her keys. "Get your car. Get Roy. You two cover the main road."

"No, wait. I saw her. She turned left on Coligny."

"Left? That's only Sea Pines. You're sure she went left?"

"Well, you *know* she's not heading for the bridge on them skates. You think she's gone back to Family Circle?"

Nadia paused for a moment. She wondered. Her mind was replaying that last time Aisha bolted. She said then she thought she saw someone she knew. "Does Aisha know anybody in Sea Pines?" asked Nadia.

"I don't know but you better get after her quick. Me and Roy, we'll get our cars, work our way in from the gates."

"Check her room first," said Nadia. "See what you can find."

"Like what? An address book?"

"Or maybe a note." She snatched up her car keys. "If she left one, let me know on my car phone."

Elizabeth could hear, from her yard on Marsh Drive, the sounds of the tournament a few hundred yards distant. Martin was there. She insisted that he go. He annoyed her by agreeing that he shouldn't waste a ticket.

She had wanted to go with him. She had wanted to be with him. She had gone so far as to search her wardrobe for an outfit that would have disguised her sufficiently in the event that the girl might be there again today. She had settled on a sweatshirt, big dark glasses and a kerchief. But the outfit she'd worn when the girl saw her yesterday should have been an effective disguise in itself. It wasn't. She would never be able to enjoy the matches because she'd spend all her time searching faces in the crowd for one that would be searching for her own. And so she decided to stay home. She'd catch up on some overdue gardening instead. Her outfit was more suited to that purpose anyway. She slipped on an apron that had pockets for tools and a pair of green gardening gloves.

Her property had a long semicircular driveway with flower beds at each end near the road. The mums that she'd planted in those beds last fall had no sooner bloomed than the deer had discovered them and reduced them to stalks in one night. On this morning she had made an early trip to The Greenery where she sought their advice on what the deer would not eat. They suggested a border of wine-colored vinca against a background of Dusty Miller. The vinca would flower ten months of the year. The lacy and silvery Dusty Miller would repel, they said, the most ravenous doe and keep its color all through-out the next winter. With luck, thought Elizabeth, she would be here to see it.

She was on her knees planting a second tray of vinca. Now and then a few tourists would laze by on their bikes. There was also the occasional jogger. Most would greet her as they passed or they would comment on the day or they would tell her that she had a most beautiful yard.

The Koran, for some reason, came into her mind. There was a verse within it that had always intrigued her. Book 4, the Book of Women, Verse 86. "If a person greets you, let your greeting be better—or at least be sure to return that greeting because God keeps count of all things."

The Koran is filled with gentle thoughts such as that one. And the Book of Women spelled out certain rights that were greater than a man's in some ways. It required that Muslim women be treated with honor. A Muslim woman could not be forced into marriage; she could not be divorced without fair compensation; she could not be deprived of a family inheritance. It took the women of Europe another twelve hundred years before they finally won these same rights. In the meanwhile, unhappily, a few Muslim men decided that these rights were not what God really meant. They proceeded to take them away.

Lost in that reverie, and busy with her planting, she barely noticed the skater. Girls on blades, lean and fit, coasted by all the time. This one had entered off Plantation Drive and turned left, away from her house. By the time it registered in Elizabeth's mind that this one was darker than most, she was gone. Elizabeth stared after her. The road was now empty. She tried to recapture the fleeting imprint that this skater had left in her memory. There was no long braid, she was quite sure of that. No cowboy hat with feathers. Elizabeth chided herself for even wondering. No way would that other girl be out skating alone. No way could Cherokee have found her. It was only her thought about that verse from the Koran that caused her brain to try to make a connection.

But even as Elizabeth formed that opinion, a tickling began at the hair of her neck. She now had a sense that the girl was behind her, having entered Marsh Drive at its opposite end in order not to be seen. And this was dumb, thought Elizabeth. She refused to give in to it. The girl was not there; she would not even look. She went back to her work with her trowel.

"That's . . . going to look pretty," came the small voice behind her.

Elizabeth froze, still unwilling to turn. She heard the voice take a breath.

"I'm sorry. I mean . . . I don't know you or anything. I just wanted to say it looks pretty."

Nadia could not get her car into Harbour Town. The police were redirecting all vehicles to parking lots further away. It was just as well; Jazz was probably right. Aisha would not have gone through that whole act just to sneak off and watch a few matches. Nadia made a U-turn on Lighthouse Road and picked a new direction at random. She saw several young people on skates but not Aisha. She grabbed at her phone when it chirped.

"There's no note," Jazz told her, "but I found something else. You might check out number 30 Marsh Drive. The name there is Stride." Jazz spelled it.

"What is it you found? Did she have an address book?"

"It's a cheap paper towel from a restroom dispenser. And she used a Magic Marker to write on it."

Nadia blinked. Once again she thought of the day before when Aisha had carried a red marking pen with which to collect players' autographs.

"I'm close to Marsh Drive. I'll go look."

"It also says 'Jonathan.' After that it says 'Doctor.' But the only doctor in the phone book named Jonathan lives over in Shipyard; he's a surgeon. His full name is Jonathan Leidner."

A surgeon, thought Nadia. She felt a vague chill. In her mind were the incisions in the throats of those three. She signaled a turn onto Plantation Drive. "Do you have an address for this doctor?"

"Yeah. Want me to check it out?"

Shipyard Plantation was two miles north and Aisha had turned to the south. But she might have done that because she knew Jasmine saw her. "Where's Roy? Out looking? Ask him to drive up there. If that's where she went he might catch her en route."

"Roy still has that guy with him, remember."

Nadia had forgotten but she didn't think it mattered.

"That's okay. He'll help look. You stay put while I check out Marsh Drive."

This was not the way Aisha had imagined their meeting. She could not think of what else to say. The woman whom she felt sure was Martina only mumbled a thank you and kept jabbing at dirt. But the knuckles of the hand with the trowel had gone white and the muscles of her shoulders were like springs. She was angry and not in the least glad to see her. She had not turned around or looked up.

"I'm . . . bothering you. I'll go if you want."

The woman said nothing. She reached for a plant.

"I mean . . . it's just that I'm being sent away in the morning and I'm taking a last look around."

Still nothing but her head cocked a little. Aisha swallowed. She tried again.

"The thing is . . . I never knew this street was here. I mean . . . no one I know knows this street is here. No one I know knows a single person on it."

She realized how stupid that had to have sounded if by any wild chance she was wrong. In her mind she asked her mother, who had promised to be watching, to tell her how else to make this woman believe that she hadn't told anyone else.

"This street you don't know," said the woman, still not turning. "How is it that you happened to find it?"

Aisha felt a thrill in her chest. The voice was kept low and a little bit throaty but it was the voice that she knew.

"I . . . sort of met your neighbor. She was at the Family Circle. I think she sort of mentioned that you live on Marsh Drive."

The woman sighed. It was almost a growl. It said she understood but didn't like it a bit. She stood up, slowly, and at last she turned. She seemed so much smaller than Aisha remembered her. But the bulk, she realized, had been mostly her abaya, and that night she, Aisha, had not been standing on skates.

The eyes were as different as night to day, and yet only their color had changed. Their shape, her mascara, the

lines at the corners, all these were exactly the same. The
heart and the soul in them hadn't changed either. All that
was missing was the kindness she'd seen there.

"You say you're leaving. Where will you be going?"

"There's this group in New York. The Nasreens."

The eyes flicked up at the mention of the name. She
seemed to want to ask a question about it. But she didn't,
thought Aisha, because she was afraid that a question
would reveal too much of herself. Now, however, the eyes
flicked again, this time at her hair, what was left of it.
She didn't speak; she didn't ask *"Why did you cut it?"*
But Aisha did see her lips start to move as if she wanted
to ask that question.

"I don't need to pretend I'm an Indian anymore. I was
trying for a *stack* ... one like yours ... but I butchered
it."

A tiny light came and went from her eyes. She was
maybe, thought Aisha, just a little bit flattered. And she
was rubbing her mouth with the back of her hand like you
do when you don't want to smile.

"When I come back ... and I will when I can ... do
you think you might talk to me then?"

"I'll be long gone myself, very likely."

"Oh, but why?" she asked quickly. "I mean, you don't
have to go. You can stay here, you both can, no one's
ever going to know ..."

"We both? What *both?*"

"I mean ..."

"I know what you mean. How did you know about
him?"

She groaned in her mind. Her big mouth again. But at
least this big wall between them was crumbling. Martina
was no longer trying to pretend that she was just plain
Elizabeth Stride. "From your neighbor," she said. "I
guess she's seen you together. But it's true that Nadia and
Jasmine don't know that."

"How is it that you're out alone, by the way?"

"I snuck out. I needed to see you just once."

She was not pleased by that. "Won't you be missed?"

"I'm already in trouble. Jazz saw me take off. But I took the long way. I wasn't followed."

Elizabeth glanced back over her shoulder toward the road that led into Marsh Drive. She looked through the trees at the traffic on Plantation. "They'll be out trying to find you. They mustn't find you here."

Aisha followed her eyes. "Omigosh."

"What is it?"

"I saw one of their cars. Can I hide in your house?"

Elizabeth looked as though she wanted to hit her. "Get in there. Go quick. Stay away from the windows."

Aisha ducked low and pushed herself off. On her way to the door her cheeks felt hot, but a part of her was grinning inside. She had not seen a car that she recognized.

It was one more deceit for which she would have to do penance. But the lie would give her time to talk to Elizabeth. She had so much to ask her, so much to tell her, so much that only the two of them could share. She would ask if she could write to her and if she would answer. She would ask if Elizabeth ever came to New York and if she did would she visit. Elizabeth might say, "*You don't have to go. You can stay here with me and I'll protect you. My friend Jonathan and I didn't let them take you then, we won't let them take you now either.*"

No, Aisha thought sadly. She won't say that. But she might say, "*I'll write. We're friends. We're a team. I know you'd sooner die than betray me.*"

She might say, "*Don't worry about your Uncle Gamal. One day he'll be arrested for the things that he's done and then all this pretending will be over. Maybe we'll even play some tennis, you and me.*"

She might say, "*But for now, let's go into my bathroom. We'll see what we can do about your hair.*"

Roy and Peter had driven to the main Sea Pines Gate in case the girl had doubled back in that direction. Peter didn't seem to mind the waste of his time. "This girl we're looking for . . . the one you thought couldn't skate . . ."

"Just one of the kids here. No big deal."

"What are the odds I can guess what her name is? She's Bandari's niece, am I correct?"

Willis grunted. "She's not your concern."

His friend did not pursue it. He seemed more interested, at least for the moment, in the guards that were checking each car at the gates. "It's a sad thing, you know," he said. "We're looking at our future."

Roy threw him a questioning glance.

"Gated communities," said Peter. "Four million Americans live in them now. Within a decade that number will quadruple."

"If they can afford it, God bless 'em."

"Want to hear another dismaying statistic? Do you know what this country spends every year just on private security guards? Not on metal detectors and all that stuff, mind you. Just on guards like the ones in that gatehouse."

"Three times what it spends on police. I know."

"You don't think this is sad? What kind of a country will we have in the end if we wall everybody else out?"

"We could use a few walls in New York City."

"But you're building them, aren't you. Not of wire or brick. You're building little enclaves only Muslims can enter."

"That's not true."

"Could I live there?"

"Fat chance you'd want to, but sure. You'd be welcome."

"Would I have to convert?"

"We just talking?"

"Just talking."

"We might give you a few things to read, is all. Beyond that, we'd expect you to pitch in where you can and above all don't do any crimes. The only difference between our laws and yours is that nobody breaks them and walks."

"You'd . . . police any terrorists that arose in your midst."

A weary sigh. "Yeah. Them, too."

This was not a new discussion. They had argued it before. He didn't blame Peter—his job is counter-terrorism—but it's not something Muslims think about much. Muslims know there are always a few nuts running loose. But their numbers don't equal the tiniest fraction of what lives all around us every hour of the day. Mere children who'd kill you for the change in your pocket or because you didn't drop your eyes soon enough. Merchants and landlords; it's not so much that they'd cheat you, it's more that it wouldn't occur to them not to. We grow our own monsters. We don't need to import them.

The next subject would be that self-policing is bad. It leads to private armies and vigilante justice. No reformer, once successful, has ever failed to become a tyrant. No group of armed citizens, starting out with good intentions, has ever failed to become a criminal organization. Well, maybe. But tell me, do you like street gangs better? Do you like seeing millions of lives turned to shit getting hooked on liquor and drugs? How about seeing your wives and daughters grabbed off the streets by thugs who drive by and tell a henchman, "Get me that one."

Peter knew all this. He was not unsympathetic. But he hated what he saw as the unraveling of a nation and the return to a tribal society. But it was not an unraveling. It was a ground-up rebuilding. A tribal society was at bottom a family. You want family values? Here they are.

Roy's cell phone broke his train of thought. He grabbed it. It was Jasmine. She was calling to say where Nadia had gone. She was asking him to check in the other direction, the road up to Shipyard Plantation. Roy scribbled two names and addresses on a pad. He had broken the connection and started the jitney when he realized that Peter was staring, mouth open, at the notes he had jotted on his knee.

"What you just wrote there . . . does that say Marsh Drive?"

Willis nodded distractedly. "But it's not where we're going." He signaled a turn toward the circle.

"Is that name you wrote 'Stride'? Is that *Elizabeth* Stride?"

Willis had no first name. Just the second. "You know her?"

"I'll be damned, I'll be damned." Peter's eyes began blinking. "And that other name under it . . . that's a German name . . . Leidner."

Now it was Willis who stared. He said, "Talk to me, Peter." But his brain had already made the connection. Maybe, just maybe, they had found Martin Kessler. If they had, then this woman, this Elizabeth Stride, had to be Aisha's new friend, Martina.

Willis snatched at his cell phone. He punched Nadia's number.

If Aisha had looked up sooner than she did, the car need not have been an invention. She would have seen Nadia, driving slowly on Plantation. Nadia had spotted her through that same stand of pines.

Her first thought was that Aisha must be asking directions of a woman who happened to be tending her yard. But even at the distance of two homes away she could see that there was some kind of tension between them. She pulled over on grass and walked back to look, bringing her cell phone in hand. She approached by trespassing on one of those homes because its property was bordered with a row of azaleas behind which she could avoid being seen. Her phone chirped. It startled her. For a moment she was sure that the woman had heard her. The woman looked around and then so did Aisha but neither was looking her way. When Aisha moved slightly, Nadia could see the small lawn post that displayed the number 30. She dropped to a crouch and hit the button to receive.

"I spotted her, Jazz," she said in a whisper. "She's at that address on Marsh Drive."

"Not Jazz, it's Roy," came the voice in her ear. "Don't go near that house or that woman."

"I'm going to have to. Now she's going inside."

"Nadia . . . you listen. Aisha will be fine. Get back, I'll explain when I see you."

It dawned on her finally. She whispered, "Martina?"

"We have things to think out. You get home."

Twenty-nine

Tarrant's jet had touched down twenty minutes after Peter's. On advice from the tower, his pilot had taxied to a service ramp where he might check out his claimed electrical problem before continuing on to the Grand Cayman. Tarrant pretended to want to stretch his legs. His briefcase in hand, he wandered away toward the terminal proper where he waited for a second commercial flight to land and then blended with the incoming passengers. He exited the terminal entirely confident that his arrival had gone undetected. That confidence, however, was soon undermined by his man, Lester Loomis, who climbed out of his car when he approached.

"Two men in a jitney? A Van Der Meer jitney?"

Loomis nodded. "Black man had the camera. He met a white passenger. Older man in a baseball cap, yellow golf jacket. The black made sure we knew he was taking our picture."

"Um . . . why would he do that? As opposed to on the sly."

"My impression? He did it on a just-in-case basis. He didn't stick around to see who we were meeting and our guys were all careful not to act like they cared. But this means if you plan to ask us to hit Van Der Meer, forget it. For that you're gonna need some fresh faces."

"Never mind Van Der Meer. You're here for the German. And remember, I need him alive."

"This kraut . . . he's a bounty hunter, you told me?"

"I don't know that but I think it. The woman he'd be after does in fact live at Van Der Meer but she wouldn't know what he looks like. That's probably why they take pictures of strangers."

Loomis frowned. He seemed doubtful. "But you say he's been down here a week at least. If he's hunting her, he'd be where he could watch her."

"Your point?"

"I'll say it again. We can't go near Van Der Meer. If he's there, send in somebody else."

"If he's there," replied Tarrant, "he'll eventually come out. Let's not get ahead of ourselves." Tarrant opened his briefcase on the trunk of Loomis's car and drew out the three sets of the file on Kessler.

Loomis read the first page. "We're after a comic book hero? No shit?"

"You might keep in mind that he killed three armed men."

Loomis sniffed all the same. He studied the photograph. "How recent's the picture?" he asked.

"It's at least ten years old but he was spotted more recently. I'm told there's been very little change in his appearance."

"Still got that scar?"

"And the same curly hair."

"The scar should make it easy. We'll find him," said Loomis.

Tarrant had reached for his file on Bandari when a beeper went off in his briefcase. He flipped his cell phone and punched out a number that he knew to be a pay phone on the Washington Beltway. A young male voice answered, that of the aide.

"They know you're en route to Grand Cayman," the aide told him. "They know the Egyptian is heading there too. Are they right or is that what you want them to think?"

Tarrant smiled within himself. He ignored the aide's question.

"I ask because my boss might be planning a raid. He's beginning to wonder what that boat might be bringing. I were you, I'd think twice about meeting Bandari."

Tarrant's inner smile faded. He was wondering for the first time himself. "Your advice is noted. It's all right. I won't be there."

A satisfied snort. "I didn't think so."

Tarrant moved his thumb to break the connection but the aide said, "Oh, before I forget, did you know that Bandari's watch has been found?"

"His watch? What watch are you talking about?"

"A Rolex. It was dredged from the swamp where they found those three bodies. His name is engraved on the back."

Tarrant groaned inwardly. He remembered the watch. It was the one that Mahfouz had extorted from Bandari. The damned fool had given a watch with his name on it to a man he was sending on a criminal errand.

"Any more such surprises?" he asked.

"That's it. I have to get back to my office. I'll beep you if anything else pops."

"You do that." Tarrant clicked off the phone.

He drew a second folder out of his briefcase and produced a Ministry of Development brochure in which Bandari's photo appeared. He opened a copy of *Yachting Magazine* that he had bought at the airport that morning. He had marked an ad that showed several models of Italian-made luxury yachts. He pointed to the yacht in the middle.

"The yacht is a Benetti, it's seventy-eight feet, it's a twin of the one pictured here. Its name, *Alhambra*, is lettered in script on the transom."

Loomis whistled. "Big boat. You think it's here now?"

"Or a day out at most. You or I would dock it well away from this island and continue by car or by launch. But Bandari, lately, has not been thinking clearly, so don't be surprised if he breezes right in. I want you to board him as soon as you find him. You can say you're from Customs or the Coast Guard, whatever."

"I'm sure we'll think of something, Mr. Tarrant."

"Bandari's not a fighter but watch out for his crew. There are three; they are led by a man name Ozal. I need

Bandari. I don't need the crew. Take them out but do it quietly. Try to do it below decks.''

''You're saying don't blast them in front of an audience. We appreciate that advice, Mr. Tarrant.''

Tarrant heard the sarcasm. He showed his teeth. But the mention of blasting brought a nagging concern that the warehouse in Suez might be empty after all.

''Don't put any holes in that boat, Mr. Loomis.''

Nadia Halaby, with the greatest reluctance, backed away from the hedge that concealed her. She had watched young Aisha skate into the house but the woman had stayed near the road. The woman had gone back to her gardening chores but she seemed to be keeping a more vigilant eye out for anyone who entered Marsh Drive.

Roy had assured her that Aisha was safe there, that the woman hadn't saved her to do harm to her now. Harm to someone seen lurking in the shrubs near her home was another matter entirely, he said. Her greatest urge was less to fetch Aisha than to go to that woman and speak to her again. She had so much to offer her . . . loyalty . . . friendship . . . and so many questions to ask her. This time Martina couldn't threaten her and hang up the phone. But Roy had said to stay away and he must have his reasons. Nadia made her way to her car and drove to the Players Club where Roy had said he would be waiting.

There in the parking lot she saw Roy's jitney. Jasmine was standing at the jitney's open door. She touched a finger to her lips and cocked her head toward the jitney's front seat where the man named Peter had a cell phone at his ear. Roy sat across from him, listening closely. Roy, using gestures, appeared to be telling his friend what to say and his friend raised a calming hand in response. Jasmine watched Nadia as she parked and approached. She shook her head and twirled a finger toward the sky. The gesture said, ''*You're not going to believe this.*''

''What's happening? Who is he calling?'' Nadia whispered.

''Guy he works with. Roger something or other.''

"Is he telling him about that woman who helped us?" Nadia tried to brush past her to stop it.

"Hold on. No, he isn't." Jasmine held out an arm. "This Peter . . . he already knew who she was but Roy made him swear he'd say nothing about her. All he wants is to talk to this guy she was with when they took out Pratt and got Aisha. He's a German, name's Kessler, but that's not his name here. He's that doctor named Leidner I told you about."

"Then why the call? What else is he saying?"

"He's also telling Roger that we didn't do those killings. Roger thought maybe Roy did those three in the swamp. And he's trying to find out about some men at the airport. He thinks maybe this other guy sent them."

Nadia started to ask what men, what other guy, but these were the least of the questions she had. Nor did she much care what he wanted with the German but Jasmine made her listen all the same. Jasmine told her about an arms dealer named Tarrant who was in business with Aisha's uncle, Gamal, and how they were selling some powerful bomb to some terrorists who planned to wipe out most of Harlem.

Nadia blinked. "You said Harlem?"

"Well . . . that's Peter's story. I thought maybe someone was looking to wipe out the Nasreens. But Roy thinks he's jerking our chain about Harlem so we'll help him sit down with this German."

Nadia wasn't so sure. "If the uncle is behind this, what's so hard to believe? He might have found out that's where Aisha's going."

Jazz rocked a hand. "Then why wait for her to go? If this business about these big bombs isn't bullshit, why not wipe out her part of the island right here?"

Nadia rubbed her eyes. She could only sigh. "What did Roy learn about the woman she's with?"

"Full name is Elizabeth Stride. Ring a bell?"

Nadia shook her head slowly.

"Think back where you come from, not here. Peter says there was a woman named Elizabeth Stride who wore full niqab and worked with a knife. Peter says she was called the Black Angel back then.''

Nadia's lips formed the name. Her eyes grew wide.

''You heard of her?''

''. . . Yes.''

''Well, that's her on Marsh Drive. Even Peter had trouble believing it at first but when Aisha went straight to that address, that clinched it.''

It was almost too much for Nadia to absorb. Her mind was whirling with the stories she'd heard, some true, some unlikely, all ending in death. Muslim men, some said dozens, who had died clutching their throats. More men running screaming through Beirut or Riyadh, spraying blood from a stump where a hand had once been. And not only the men. Women suffered as well. How many thousands were harassed and searched on the chance that they might have been Elizabeth Stride. In Kuwait they were pulled from their cars and arrested for driving while wearing a veil.

''How . . . how could Roy tell me to leave Aisha there with her?''

''What he told you is don't you go near her by yourself. What he's thinking is she might hurt you but not Aisha. Most of all he needed time to think this out. He says that this woman might be psycho, big time, but like it or not, we owe her.''

''Jazz . . . I've got to go back there right now.''

''Wait till Roy's done with Peter. I'll go with you.''

Thirty

Aisha waited nervously in Elizabeth's kitchen but Elizabeth did not appear. Nor did she continue with her gardening work. Aisha could see her through the laundry room window, just standing, arms folded, thinking and watching, as if not knowing what to do next. Aisha didn't know what to do either.

She wanted badly to look through the house for the things it would tell her of Elizabeth Stride, but to do so would be almost like stealing. Then there were her skates. They would track up the floors. In the kitchen, however, not meaning to snoop, she noticed a magnetized grocery list that hung from one side of the refrigerator. Elizabeth had written such ordinary things. Milk . . . bananas . . . coffeemaker filters . . . and what looked like ingredients for a meat loaf. She was not sure why it surprised her, exactly, that a dangerous woman bought such ordinary things.

Aisha was about to turn away when a bit of blue color caught her eye. Looking closely, she recognized a piece of blue feather that she realized must have come from her hat. It was on the refrigerator, also held by a magnet. The same magnet held tickets to the Family Circle tournament. She did not know what to make of the fact that Elizabeth had held on to the feather. It meant, she hoped, that she liked her a little. A bit more, at least, than she had let on outside.

Outside she'd been cool, even stern when they talked.

Aisha understood that perfectly well. She also understood that, to make matters worse, Elizabeth felt unable to use the tickets for fear of running into her again. Perhaps it would help to apologize for that. And to tell her that keeping the feather was sweet. Anything so she'd talk and maybe loosen up a little. Aisha tore a piece of paper from the grocery list pad and scribbled her New York address. She would take it outside, say nothing of the feather, just give Elizabeth her forwarding address and insist that she please use those tickets.

"Uh-oh."

She was coasting down the driveway, too late to turn back, when that lady from the restroom came walking down Marsh Drive with a miniature poodle on a leash. She nodded to Elizabeth and smiled when she saw Aisha. She said, "I see you two got together. That's nice."

The poodle barked at Aisha because of the skates but she stopped when Aisha offered her hand to be sniffed and told her how pretty she was. The dog wagged her tail and turned back to the street, more intent now on taking her walk. The old lady followed. She said, "Have a pleasant day." Aisha waved good-bye and said to Elizabeth, "Um . . . it *is* a nice day for a walk."

Elizabeth sighed. Her expression said, "*Why not?*" She picked up her trowel and slipped it in the apron. She gestured with her head in the direction that was opposite from the one the old woman had taken.

"You're leaving tomorrow, you said?" asked Elizabeth.

"For New York. Here, I wrote the address."

Elizabeth hesitated but she reached out a hand. Aisha grinned when she did so. She skated backward as Elizabeth walked. Elizabeth looked at the piece of paper that she recognized as a leaf from her grocery list pad.

"This address . . . it's in Harlem?"

"Yes, but near Central Park."

"Wouldn't you . . . stand out there? I mean more than down here."

"Jazz says maybe not. Jazz says I'm no snowflake. There are lots of black people who are lighter than me."

"This Jazz is a Muslim. A convert, I assume."

"Pretty much. She knows that it's helped her be better than she was but she still has some problems with Islam."

"Better than what? What was she?"

"She's . . . been to jail a few times. Before she found Islam, not since."

"I see."

Aisha grinned as if at a private joke. "You know what Jazz says? She says they ought to call it *Hislam*. The men make all the rules. The women come in second. But no one's had much luck in getting Jazz or Nadia to take second place to any man."

Elizabeth's expression softened. It was almost a smile. Aisha thought that she'd try to help it along.

"You know what else she says? You know how in a mosque the women sit behind the men? That's so the men can't see a woman's butt when she's bending over for prayers. It's so they won't be distracted or have lustful thoughts. Jazz says this proves that the early Muslims realized that men are fundamentally weenies."

The smile did broaden. Elizabeth walked on. They were moving toward a path that led to Harbour Town, although Elizabeth had no intention of going there.

"But it's changing, you know," Aisha told her. "It's slow but it's changing, especially here. Even back in Egypt more and more Muslim men are becoming a lot like my father. And like Nadia's father. I met him once. Neither one would have dreamed of ever beating a wife or having a daughter sewn up and stuff. I guess I need you to know that."

Elizabeth nodded. She said nothing.

"Women still go covered, the Nasreens especially, but that's partly so everyone knows that they're Muslims. That way no one ever bothers them when they're, like, out walking but they dress as they please when they're with friends and family. It's not such a bad thing, Elizabeth."

"Um . . . the Nasreens. I've been meaning to ask. Are they named for anyone in particular?"

"Uh-huh. A woman doctor. She died."

Elizabeth felt a burning on the skin of her face. It was a burn that she'd thought was long healed. "Was her name Zayed? Nasreen Zayed?"

"Yes it was. How did you know that?"

Elizabeth didn't answer. She was staring at the pavement. "There was a woman, a teacher, who was murdered with her. Does the name Rada Khoury mean anything to you?"

"Murdered with her?"

"Yes. By some men less . . . progressive than your father."

Aisha seemed confused. "When did all this happen?"

"A long time ago. Fifteen years, give or take."

"Then I don't get it. Rada Khoury isn't dead. Nasreen Zayed died but it wasn't that long ago. She wasn't murdered either. She died of a plague—it was cholera, I think—that broke out in Southern Jordan. She's considered a martyr because she didn't have to stay but she did and she saved a lot of lives."

Elizabeth listened, stunned into silence. A feeling of gladness fought with disbelief. She walked on, seeing nothing, only faces from her past.

Aisha told her that she knew these stories because Nadia had told them to her. Both these women's pictures hung framed on Nadia's wall. Nasreen had started an underground railroad after saving one woman whom the Saudis had imprisoned.

An American, thought Aisha, but that might have been legend. After that first woman there were dozens, maybe more. Rada Khoury, true enough, was condemned through a fatwah because she wouldn't stop teaching family planning. She was sentenced to death, but Nasreen helped her escape. She got her out of Jordan and into France through a sister network that had been started by Nadia Halaby.

Nadia funded her network with her winnings from tennis and with money donated by sympathetic Muslims, Aisha's own parents among them. Nadia, by then, had a price on her head already because of her work with Algerian women. The network she started pushed its way up to a million and that was why she decided that she'd better move here. Rada Khoury, meanwhile, was now living in France where she managed Nadia's network. But she came to New York a few times each year, escorting new runaway women and children. When Nasreen got sick and died a few years ago, it was Rada who proposed that the New York branch be named in her honor.

Elizabeth had to struggle to control her breathing as the meaning of all that she was hearing sank in. If true, and it must be if Aisha was telling it, it meant that the Israelis had lied from the beginning. They had used the story of her friends' deaths to recruit her and to help stoke her hatred of Muslim men.

She had left the road and was walking through pine trees, not knowing it or rather not caring. She heard Aisha's voice ask, "Elizabeth, what's wrong?" but the voice came as from a distance. Aisha followed with difficulty, her blades sinking in the soft ground. "Elizabeth? You look funny. Are you sick?"

She reached out a hand. It touched the girl's shoulder. She squeezed it.

"Listen . . . Aisha," she said softly, "I think I'd like to be alone."

"No way. Wait a second. Let me take off my skates."

Elizabeth did not wait. She walked on ahead toward the shouts and the cheers that rose from the tennis courts of Harbour Town. She barely heard them as roars of a crowd. They were more a part of the thousand other voices that echoed through her mind as her brain tried to sort what was real and was not.

"Elizabeth . . . wait. I'm coming with you."

Lester Loomis had instructed two of his men to begin making rounds of the restaurants and bars showing photographs of Martin Kessler. The work might be slow but there was no other way. Armed with a listing of restaurants and a map, they would begin with those restaurants nearest to Van Der Meer and widen their search from that point. Loomis, meanwhile, had begun making calls to the marinas that were listed in the yellow pages. On his third call he smiled and broke the connection.

"You were right. The schmuck's here," he told Tarrant.

The marina office at Harbour Town had confirmed that the yacht *Alhambra* had docked that morning. He opened a map on the hood of his car and marked the location for Tarrant. "He's in slip B-4, which the office said is here, stern in against these condos." Loomis circled Ketch Court.

Tarrant showed his teeth. He said, "Let's go," and had reached for the car door when the beeper in his briefcase sounded again. Tarrant almost ignored it. He could imagine no message that was nearly as urgent as the need to get his hands on Bandari. But he opened his briefcase and saw the number that had called. The young aide would not stay by that public phone if he didn't call him back within ten minutes. Tarrant punched out the number on his cell phone.

"You're on Hilton Head, right?" said the aide when he answered. "If you are, you're going to like what I've got."

"Never mind where I am. Come on, talk to me."

"Kessler's using a new name. It's Leidner," said the aide. He then spelled it. "He's posing as a doctor. Doctor Jonathan Leidner."

"A doctor? Why a doctor?" asked Tarrant, scribbling.

"Who knows? All I know is Peter . . . who's there too, by the way . . . called Roger to tell him that he thinks they've identified Kessler. But he also asked if Roger sent any operatives. It seems he saw four suspicious characters hanging around Hilton Head's airport. Roger said he did not and then he called my boss. He played it cute; he asked my boss if he'd sent any men to a certain island. My boss admitted, 'Yeah, he has,' but he's talking, remember, about Grand Cayman Island where he thinks you're headed right now."

A satisfied grunt. "How long ago was this?"

"The call to my boss? Ten minutes."

"You said *identified* Kessler. They haven't located him?"

"By now? I don't know, but they could have."

Tarrant said, "You've done well; this is worth a bonus. Keep me advised." He broke the connection and reached for the phone book that Loomis was holding in his hand. He found the listing for Jonathan Leidner. The address was a house in the Shipyard Plantation. On the map it was not far from Van Der Meer.

"Call your men back. We've found him," he said to Loomis.

"What you've found is a house. So have they. Let's go slow here."

Tarrant ignored him. He was studying the map. Shipyard was also on the way to the marina. Bandari was tied to a dock; Kessler wasn't.

Bandari could wait ten more minutes.

Nadia and Jasmine had missed them by seconds. Their delay was caused by a dispute with Roy Willis over whether to risk a confrontation with a woman as dangerous as Elizabeth Stride. Willis had argued that the girl would be safe; that Stride didn't save her to harm her. But he did want their help in finding Martin Kessler, who was far more important for the moment.

"To you, not to me," was Nadia's reply. She walked to her car. Jasmine followed.

They saw the red Bronco parked at 30 Marsh Drive and the flower trays left with their planting unfinished. These suggested that Aisha and this woman were inside.

"You go knock," Jasmine told her. "I'll be covering you."

"Covering? What's that mean? Did you bring a gun?"

"You bet your ass. It's the one from your office."

"Jasmine, damn it. Keep that thing in your—"

What stopped her was the woman back from walking her poodle. The poodle had paused at the flower trays. The woman seemed to take note of the Van Der Meer jackets that both Nadia and Jasmine were wearing.

"Are you looking for Elizabeth? I don't think she's home."

"Um . . . I'm picking up my daughter," Nadia said quickly. "Young girl, dark hair, she's on skates?"

"Ah, the matchmaker, yes. I believe they took a walk."

"Matchmaker?" Nadia blinked.

"Ooops. I don't think I should have said that. But they can't be far. They went that way."

"That way?" She was pointing where there wasn't any road. "Could you . . . guess where they might have been going?"

"Harbour Town, I guess. It's up through that clearing."

"So you . . . must know Elizabeth," Nadia asked.

"Not really. She's quiet. But she seems very nice."

"So I'm told. That way?"

"Through those trees."

Thirty-one

Ozal had at last gotten rid of Bandari. They could now start assembling the bomb. He had told Bandari that he must go ashore and start looking for the girl and the Algerian.

"Look for them? Where would I look for them?" he asked.

"Over there where there is tennis." Ozal pointed toward the crowd. "This is not only a big place for tennis, it's the biggest place on the island for tennis."

"But here there are thousands. I'm to find them in so many?"

"All these thousands are pink but those two are like coffee. Take your binoculars with you. Besides, Bandari, you know your own niece. If she's here you will spot her, but she won't spot you because you said it's been eight years since she's seen you. When you see her, come and get us, we will follow her home. That way we'll know where to bring the bomb."

Bandari did not think this was much of a plan. Ozal said they would then simply steal a tourist's car and explode it in front of her house. He said not to worry, if you don't see her here, I have maps of all the places on the island where these people go to practice their tennis. But Bandari agreed to get off the boat because the stink from the galley was making him sick. Ozal's two soldiers were sick from it already. One of them had vomited over the side and the other had not managed to make it that far before spewing his breakfast all over the quarter deck in full view of many passing pink faces. Ozal, not surprisingly, looked not so good himself and his breath was like that of a goat. Bandari would go, and he would look for young Aisha, if only to get some fresh air in his lungs.

The soldiers, once Bandari had vanished from view, went to get a wheeled cart from the dock. The cart was the type most marinas provide for hauling provisions on board. They pulled it down the ramp and down Bandari's slip where they parked it at the boat's boarding ladder. Ozal threw them a grommeted tarp. The tarp was for making a tent on the cart so that all these pink faces couldn't see what they were doing and also to tie it all down when they were finished. Ozal stayed on board to direct them. He told one to climb aboard and carry up the ingredients. The other, the more nauseous, would stay on the slip where at least he could vomit in the water.

Ozal was afraid that he knew why they were sick. He hoped that the sweats and the throwing up of breakfast were a case of nerves, nothing more. But he knew that these symptoms, including his own, might well be the first signs of radiation poisoning. He had tried to be careful in scoring the casings. His ruined fingers did not always cooperate. If the casings are leaking, however, so be it. It would be too bad if he never brought that second bomb to Cairo, but if he was going to die a martyr, let it be here. He would strike such a blow against this godless place that his name would be remembered for all time.

The soldier on board first brought up the timer. The timer was simply the parts of a clock attached to a detonator he had devised. The detonator—the charge that would set off the nitro—was made from the powder of parachute flares, of which the boat had an ample supply. Next came the nitro, still packed in ice to keep it under ten degrees Celsius. Once in place, he told the soldier to scoop out the ice so that it wouldn't dampen the charge when it melted. This was also to allow the nitro to warm up. Even if the detonator should fail to ignite the sun would eventually do the job on the nitro.

On top of the nitro they piled several bales wrapped in

plastic, each weighing about twenty kilos. One of the soldiers dropped one of the bales because his hands were now slippery with sweat. He gave a little shriek and a few faces turned but Ozal quickly calmed him and said no harm done. To those watching, he said, ''Butterfingers,'' and shrugged. They smiled back at him and kept going. To the soldier, he whispered, ''Don't worry about the bales. You could shoot them full of holes and the worst that will happen is you'll have a big mess to sweep up.''

This was true. He didn't lie. The bales contained a mixture of four parts ammonium nitrate and one part urea crystals which were soaked in fuel oil and then wrapped in newspaper. This concoction, essentially a commercial fertilizer, was perfectly safe unless you ate it. If packed correctly and exploded correctly, it produced a powerful shock wave, however. Not as big as the van-load from Oklahoma City but enough to take a few roofs off these buildings and blow people as if they were leaves.

With the last of the bales in place and tied down, they covered the package with the grommeted tarp, which they fastened with shock cords underneath the cart. That done, they weighted the package down further with two cases of soft drinks in cans. This was, in part, to make it look like provisions—but also to see how high the cans would go when shot up like rounds from a mortar.

''We're too late,'' said Loomis, his phone at his ear.

The driver of the car bearing Loomis and Tarrant had no trouble getting into the Shipyard Plantation. Any driver needed only say, ''Lunch at the Golf Club,'' and the guard at the gate would hand him a pass giving no further thought to that visitor. Signs showed them the way to Gloucester Road where the phone book said Kessler/Leidner was living. The car with his two other men were there already; they were watching the house from some distance away. The driver of that car had called Lester Loomis to warn him to keep his distance as well.

''He says that same jitney, the one from the airport, is sitting in Kessler's driveway right now.''

Loomis listened further while repeating for Tarrant.

"Same two men . . . the big black and the older man he
met. The older one's this Peter you were talking about?
. . . They're talking to some guy who came to the door
. . . little guy . . . my guy says he looks kinda Jewish . . .
My guy says it's definitely not Kessler."

Tarrant cursed as they approached. He peered ahead.
He could see the white jitney. Two driveways before it
he could see the car from which the man was reporting
to Loomis.

"My guy says this guy is pointing . . . like he's giving
directions . . . the black guy is nodding like he knows
where it is . . . the old guy is turning back to the jitney
. . . he's waving like 'Thank you.' They're leaving, I
think. Guy's watching them go . . . guy steps back inside
. . . guy seems in a hurry to get in."

"He's told them where to find Kessler. We'll follow."

"Wait a second. Let's think. Would this Kessler have
a roommate?"

"So what if he does? What's the difference?"

"Would Kessler live with someone to save on his rent?
I'm asking; you know this guy better than me. Hey, didn't
that file say he had a Jew partner? Guy named Stein or
something like that."

Tarrant remembered the reference. Not Stein. It was
Stride. But the partner named Stride was certainly a Jew
if he worked for Israeli Intelligence.

"Guy ducks back in the house. Say he's going to the
phone," Loomis told him. "Say he's dialing right now
because he wants to warn Kessler. Say he sent those two
off on a goose chase."

Tarrant nodded. He agreed. "Go find out."

Tarrant watched as Loomis and his man approached the
house. The other two men had held their positions to warn
them in case a patrol car appeared. The jitney was well
out of sight.

Loomis tried the front door. The man hadn't locked it.
Loomis opened it slightly and listened. He turned and
gave Tarrant an I-told-you-so nod; at the same time he
reached for his pistol. Tarrant wanted to stop him; this

was no place for guns; he wanted to lean on the horn but dared not. Loomis had entered, his man close behind, both moving with stealth through the doorway. Tarrant watched and listened for what seemed much too long although his watch said that barely two minutes had passed. At last there was Loomis. He opened the door. There was anger on his face toward the man who came out with him. Tarrant knew at once that there had been trouble because Loomis was holding what looked like a washcloth and was wiping both knobs of the door.

"What happened, damn it?" Tarrant demanded as the two climbed back into the car.

"You were right, is what happened. He was trying to warn Kessler. Let's get out past the gatehouse and I'll tell you."

"We heard Kessler's partner from outside the door." Loomis studied his map as he explained. "He was on the kitchen phone, he was asking whoever was on the other end to page Doctor Jonathan Leidner. I had to stop him; I showed him my gun; I took the phone out of his hand and hung up. I asked him where Kessler was but the guy played dumb. He said he didn't know any Kessler. I say, 'Okay, then where's Leidner?' He said he didn't know. I smack him and I press *Redial* on his phone.

"This woman answers; I hear like an office. She says 'Family Circle Tennis Classic. Can I help you?' I told her to cancel that page for Doctor Leidner and I asked her, by the way, where was this Family Circle. She said it's in Harbour Town which is . . . hey Ralph, hang a left . . . no more than five minutes away."

"Um . . . Loomis," Tarrant asked him. "What else happened back there?"

"It's a pro tennis tournament. It goes on all week. There's a calendar in the kitchen that has 'JL-FC' written in for today and tomorrow. That's gotta mean Jonathan Leidner-Family Circle."

"Mr. Loomis . . . I asked you what happened."

"Guy ran for the door. We couldn't help it."

"You shot him?"

Loomis cocked his head toward his driver, named Ralph. "Choke hold. Something popped. I don't know. He wasn't breathing. We shoved him under a bed."

Tarrant closed his eyes. He mouthed an obscenity.

"Shit happens, Mr. Tarrant. I don't like it either." Loomis gestured with his hand as if to say, *Let's get over it*. "We can beat it to death or we can wonder why Kessler would be interested in a bunch of girls playing tennis."

"Your point?"

"The tennis is in Harbour Town. Bandari is in Harbour Town. Kessler picks the one day when Bandari shows up. You believe in coincidence, Mr. Tarrant?"

Tarrant hesitated. He shook his head slowly. "How could Kessler have known that he was coming?"

"Who knows. A little birdie. You got yours; he got his. But I'll tell you one thing. I'll make you a bet. When we find him he'll be watching Bandari, not tennis."

Roy Willis, with his pass and his Van Der Meer jitney, had no trouble parking on the tournament grounds in a space that was reserved for sponsors. He asked Peter for one more look at Kessler's photo before entering the crowd to try to spot him.

He put aside those of Lawrence Tarrant and Bandari, who were not a concern for the moment. According to Roger, the man Peter had called, they'd be meeting in Grand Cayman where surveillance would soon be in place. The photo reinforced his mental picture of the man he had seen in the Players Club lot. He was now twelve years older but little had changed. The face bore an expression, even back then, of a boy who was planning a prank. Kessler's housemate had said that he was dressed in white slacks. His shirt was green with a Shipyard golf logo and he had on a hat with a dark plastic visor. They had thought it unwise to alert the housemate by showing him either their credentials or the photograph. Better to claim that they were simply two friends and that Jonathan was supposed to have met them for lunch.

"We could stake out the toilets," Willis suggested.

"There's one major bank of portable toilets. He'll need one sooner or later."

"I think I'd rather wander than stand in one place. Let's concentrate on green shirts."

But what they saw within minutes of beginning their search were two faces conducting a search of their own. "There's Nadia," said Willis, craning his head. "Jazz is with her. They must not have found Aisha."

"Or the lethal Elizabeth Stride, it appears."

Willis threw him a look. "You made me a promise."

"Give me Kessler and I'll keep it, my friend. That's the deal."

"Then let's go. We'll all look for him together."

It was too bad, thought Kessler, that Elizabeth dared not come, but her decision was not without its benefits. He could roam around freely, come and go as he pleased, not get stuck at a match in which he had little interest when Elizabeth wanted to stay to the end.

Also, he could wear his new madras shorts which Elizabeth thought looked ridiculous on him. They did not look ridiculous. His legs could use a little tanning, perhaps, but so could all these fans who drove down for the day. And he could wear his baggy golf jacket which Elizabeth would have complained about as well. This time, in fact, it did conceal a pistol, but only because it would really raise eyebrows if he'd worn his ankle holster with shorts. Best of all, he could order a big gooey sandwich without Elizabeth telling him he was plugging up his heart and should order some tofu instead. Elizabeth owed him a new sausage sandwich to replace the one he had to spill on the girl.

He was waiting his turn at the same sandwich tent, having passed those that offered only salads or hot dogs or pizzas or cups of frozen yogurt. Nearby was a clearing in which several large trailers were parked. They were all painted white; they all bore signs. One said *Administration*. One said *First Aid*. Another seemed to be for the use of the professionals to cool off and maybe even to shower. He saw one of the professionals, a young qualifier, limping toward the one that provided first aid, with her tennis shoe unlaced. Sprained her ankle, perhaps, or got a blister. His head had turned just enough to catch sight of the people who were waiting behind him on line. He was startled to see, two places behind him, Elizabeth's Jonathan Leidner. White shoes, white pants, green shirt and a hat. The hat was the type that Cyril Pratt wore, except Pratt's had no plastic sun visor.

Kessler felt a small tickle running up his spine. A part of his brain was attempting to annoy him by suggesting that this Jonathan might actually be stalking him. That this man had somehow found out the name of his rival for Elizabeth's affections. But Kessler knew that this was certainly nonsense. Her Jonathan was here because he had tickets. He had, after all, invited Elizabeth. This Jonathan had no way of knowing what he looked like unless, of course, he had been driven by jealousy to follow Elizabeth for the last several days. Which would have been pathetic. Totally childish. Never mind that Kessler had done that himself.

Kessler's turn came and he ordered his sandwich. He asked that they pile extra peppers and onions. Off to one side was a condiment counter that had relish and mustard and slices of pickle. He moved to it, intent on creating a sandwich that would give mortal offense to Elizabeth's idea of what was fit for human consumption. He was only halfway through arranging the pickles when he realized that Jonathan was standing at his side. Jonathan brought with him a diet cola and a prepackaged garden salad to go. He was choosing a dressing from several on the counter. Kessler knew even before he reached that he would choose the one that boasted "Fat Free." What on earth could Elizabeth have seen in this man? Real food right in front of him and what does he order? A can of flavored water and some plants. Kessler, almost not realizing that he was doing it, pulled out a Swisher Sweet and lit it. He exhaled a stream of fragrant smoke in the direction of Jonathan's salad. No reaction from Jonathan. Just one annoyed grimace. He picked up his salad and walked off.

Okay, that wasn't nice. It was pointless and peevish. He had risked provoking a confrontation with a man to whom he needed to stay invisible and who, being a surgeon, could not risk hurting his hands in a brawl. That was how bullies behave. Cut it out.

Kessler, biting into his sandwich, wandered off in the opposite direction. He had ordered the sandwich just in time; now a stream of fans was moving toward him, indicating the end of a match in the Stadium Court. He suddenly spotted a black face among them and recognized Roy from the Van Der Meer School. Roy's face was turning this way and that as if scanning the oncoming crowd. An older man seemed to be with him. Far off to his right he saw another black face, this one belonging to the woman called Jazz. Near her, looking in another direction, was a woman with Elizabeth's coloring and carriage. He knew that could only be Nadia. Kessler assumed that the girl was here again and perhaps, as before, they had lost sight of her.

He thought it best not to make eye contact with any of them so he turned away and went instead in the direction that Jonathan had taken. He no longer saw Jonathan but he noticed still another man who seemed to be looking for someone. But this one, a fat man, was acting very differently. He was behaving in the manner of a man who wanted to look but didn't want to be seen. He would move about but not in the open, always with a hedge or a tent to hide behind. He held a handkerchief bunched up in his fist and would use it to dab perspiration from his forehead on a day when not even the athletes were sweating. From his clothing, a blazer, deck shoes and a cap, Kessler guessed that he came from a boat in the marina. He was surely not dressed to watch tennis.

Kessler had an odd feeling that he knew this man but also that the feeling had no basis. Too many years of watching peoples' eyes for some sign of a possible threat. Kessler put the man out of his mind. He had, more importantly, a sandwich to finish. After that he would be ready for a beer.

Thirty-two

Loomis had not anticipated the tournament traffic. All cars not bearing special tags on their dashboards were directed to lots as much as two miles distant. From these, shuttle buses would take them to Harbour Town. They were fortunate to catch a departing shuttle that stopped to let the five men climb on. It meant, however, that they would have no car at hand in the event that they found and took Kessler.

"Maybe that's not so bad," Lester Loomis suggested as a shuttle bus came within sight of the tournament. "If we take him, we drag him on Bandari's boat. That way you have them both in one place."

Tarrant answered with a scowl. He was looking at the crowd, at so many pairs of eyes. He could not imagine how this could be done. But at least he understood why Bandari had chosen to dock at this particular marina. Bandari must be betting that his niece would be here. He was betting that she wouldn't miss this tournament. He intended to snatch her and get away on his boat.

"Will you listen? This can work," said Loomis quietly. "We know the boat's here. I send two guys to board it, keep Bandari on ice. The rest of us, meanwhile, grab Kessler."

"We just . . . grab him. Nothing to it. Is that what you're saying?"

"Let's just get there. His roomie gave me an idea."

"Is it better than thinking you'll just go in and pluck

him from a crowd that must number several thousand?"

"We don't pluck him, Mr. Tarrant. We page him."

Elizabeth, her mind and eyes turned inward, had almost reached the tournament grounds before she realized how far they had walked. They had crossed the golf course at the seventeenth tee and followed a cart path that led to the clubhouse. Beyond were the trailers and the edge of the crowd. The Harbour Town marina was off to her left. She stopped, not wishing to go nearer the tournament for fear that she might, just perhaps, run into Martin. It was bad enough that Aisha knew who he was. She did not have to know what he looked like.

"We could walk down to the water," said Aisha, looking up at her. "It's quiet. We could talk. Or just sit if you like." Aisha had her Rollerblades slung from her shoulder, their laces tied together in a bow.

Elizabeth breathed a sigh. She didn't answer. Her mind was on Martin and what he would say if she told him about Rada and Nasreen and the Israelis. "*So they lied,*" he would say. "*This comes as a surprise? Mossad is in the business of deception.*" He would say, "*They've been lying about me for almost ten years. Do I have all that money the Ceausescus got for Jews or did they throw me one little bag of diamonds?*" He would say, "*You didn't need the deaths of your two Muslim women. All you needed was that warden who murdered your mother and threw you in a cell for eight months. After that all you needed was the names of Muslim men who threw bombs into buses filled with children.*"

And perhaps he would be right. But they would have been enough. She had killed fewer times than the stories would suggest but more times than she'd admitted to Martin.

"Could I ask you a question?" Aisha looked up at her. Elizabeth must have nodded her permission.

"I read in the paper . . . those men at that cabin . . . I mean, I guess I know why you said they ran off . . ."

"If you're asking did I cut them, no, I didn't."

She said it and was instantly ashamed that she had.

Who, me? Of course not. All I did was drive you home. We won't mention that I first blew out Cyril Pratt's guts and then finished off a Muslim who didn't even know where he was. But the answer was the one the girl wanted to hear. She was smiling as if to say, "*I knew it.*"

Loomis had asked a tournament volunteer where someone might go if he were paged. The volunteer showed him the Administration trailer. Loomis then sent two men to locate Bandari's yacht and report. He and Tarrant, along with his driver, took positions at the edge of the food tent area that afforded a view of the trailer.

His cell phone chirped; he cupped it and listened. His men had found the *Alhambra* right away. It was docked, stern in, among the other bigger yachts. They could see the three crewmen, one on board, two on the slip; they were loading or unloading provisions from a cart.

"You see Bandari?"

"Some kid, a dock boy, said the owner went ashore. Said he went down toward you, so look out. Said he's wearing a blazer and a sea captain's hat."

Loomis looked around him. He did not see a blazer. "The other three, can you take them?"

"No sweat. They look sick. One is puking his guts out. All the same we should wait until they climb back on board. Too many people walking by all these boats."

"Okay, sit tight. Bandari shows, call me. Right now I'm going to try to page Kessler."

Loomis told Tarrant what his man had reported.

"He said they look sick?" Tarrant frowned.

"Count your blessings."

But Tarrant, once again, was beginning to wonder what Bandari might have on that boat. He wanted to go up there and see for himself, but he dared not risk being spotted by Bandari who might then disappear in this crowd.

"Make your call," he told Loomis. "Let's get on with it."

"You know, you shouldn't wear dark glasses," said Aisha, looking up at her. "Your eyes are too pretty to be hidden."

Elizabeth waved it off. "Look, about that night . . ."

"That's their real color, right? It's not contacts?"

"Aisha . . . listen. I'm not going to lie to you. I'm . . . not someone you would like if you knew me."

The girl made a tiny wave of her own. "And you shouldn't wear a kerchief over your hair," she said forcefully. "If my hair was half as gorgeous as yours, I wouldn't walk around with it covered."

Elizabeth did not want to talk about hair. Nor did Aisha, she saw, want to talk about lies.

"Um . . . you don't ever cover your hair?" she asked Aisha.

"Sure I do. When it's appropriate. Don't you know about covering?"

Elizabeth did, of course. She knew Muslim customs. But this, come to think of it, was a much better subject. She answered with a shrug that was still another lie.

"The whole idea of covering is not to stand out. If I covered down here I'd stand out."

"I see."

"In Egypt, these days, more women go covered but it's not because they're suddenly religious, so much. Some do it so the fundamentalists won't harass them and for some it's a form of political protest. They—"

Aisha stopped. She cocked an ear toward a sound in the distance. She said, "That's Doctor Leidner they're paging."

Elizabeth blinked. "You know Jonathan Leidner?"

"I know *about* him. I told you I did."

"Aisha . . . you've said nothing to me about Jonathan Leidner."

"Yes, I did. I told you. I know that he's the man who was with you that night."

Elizabeth was stricken. When Aisha had told her, "*You can stay here. You both can*," it had never crossed her mind that the reference was to anyone but Martin.

"Aisha . . . have you mentioned him to anyone else?"

"No. Well, not counting that lady, your neighbor. She's the one who told me he's . . . your friend."

Elizabeth took a breath. She understood how this had

happened. She also understood the trouble it could lead to, but she did not doubt Aisha when Aisha said she'd kept it to herself. All the same it bothered her to hear his name paged because Jonathan, a doctor, always carried a beeper. His hospital, his office and his housemates knew that, so why would he have to be paged and by whom?

"Aisha, wait here for me. I want to see something."

"I'll go with you."

"Aisha . . . I said wait here."

Kessler heard the page but he thought little of it. Doctors were called in from having fun all the time. He had more than that on his mind. He was holding tickets for a stadium match—a Dutch girl, Brenda Schultz against the Spaniard, Vicario—but was suddenly reluctant to be trapped in a grandstand.

The cause of his reluctance was still another group of men who appeared and seemed to be searching for someone. First there was that whole Van Der Meer group, then next came the fat man who was sweating so much. Now came five more who first huddled, then split up, all but one wearing loose-fitting jackets like his own. Two of the five hurried off toward Ketch Court. Kessler tensed. But he saw that those two went well past his unit and toward an open passage that led to the marina. Of the three who remained, one was dressed in a suit and carried a briefcase at his side. One with him who seemed to do most of the talking was holding a cell phone in his hand.

Suddenly this seemed not a good place to be. Too many hard faces, too many searching eyes. He began to back away when the one with the cell phone nudged the man in the suit and gestured with his chin toward the edge of the crowd. All three men froze. The one with the cell phone flicked a hand to his belt as if to make sure that a weapon was still there. Kessler recognized the reflex. It was one that a professional was taught to avoid. These men had the look of mere thugs.

Kessler, interested, followed their eyes. He easily picked out the object of their attention. It was Roy, one of only a few black faces. The three men waited and watched for several seconds. Roy's head turned abruptly as if he'd been called. Another black face bobbed out of the crowd. Kessler saw that it was Jasmine, and Nadia was with her. Roy and Jazz behaved as if they'd just found each other. Kessler had assumed they were together. Jazz and Nadia reached Roy and were gesturing excitedly. Now Roy glanced around and he shook his head. Whoever Roy was looking for at first, thought Kessler, these women were looking for someone else.

As he watched, they fanned out again, but not in his direction. They were moving back toward the Stadium Court. This was all the more reason, Kessler decided, to forgo that particular match. Perhaps he'd drop in on Elizabeth instead. He could stand by her front door and peel off his clothing just as she had done the other night from his balcony. He'd see if Elizabeth had the nerve to complain.

Curiosity, however, got the better of him. These three by the food tents were no friends of Roy's. You don't spot a friend and touch your gun. Like the fat man, they watched but didn't want to be seen. He would stay for a few minutes longer.

Tarrant held his breath until the black man turned away. The two women, by their jackets, were from Van Der Meer as well. They were now in the thickest part of the crowd and had apparently not heard the page.

The question, however, was did Leidner/Kessler hear it? The place where they were standing had a clear view of the trailer. If he answered, they could take him either coming or going. But the only people he saw within fifty yards of the trailer were a woman wearing a gardening apron and a girl who had roller blades draped from her shoulder. The woman, one of the groundskeepers, probably, seemed to be giving directions to the girl, pointing her back toward the golf course. Now a man, late thirties, was walking toward the trailer but that man looked nothing like Kessler. Off to his right, through some harbor-front condos, Tarrant could see the masts of several sailboats. The report that Bandari's Arab crew seemed ill troubled him, the more that he thought about it.

"This isn't working. I want to get to that boat."

"The boat's covered. Let me try another page."

Loomis hit *Redial* on his cellular phone. He asked the trailer to try Dr. Leidner again.

"Could the two of you handle him if he does show up?"

"Ralph and me? We can take him. The question is how neatly. I'm betting he'll behave with a gun in his ribs. Those guys don't buck the odds if they can help it."

"But if he resists? With all these people looking on?"

"Then we'll say we caught him exposing his cock. They won't mind that we cracked him in the head."

Tarrant still was uneasy.

"Look, you want to go? Go. Tell my guys to be ready to board and seize that boat if you see us coming with Kessler."

Kessler watched as the man with the briefcase hurried off. He'd been able to hear little of what they'd been saying but they clearly were watching for someone to come, either to or from one of those trailers. He eased a little closer to the two who remained until only the corner of a tent was between them. He then heard the name paged a second time but the doctor was already approaching the trailer. He was sipping the same diet cola as he walked. Kessler risked a look at the two baggy jackets. Both men seemed to note Dr. Leidner's arrival, but not with particular interest.

Only then did Kessler notice Elizabeth. Several times he had scanned all the people in view. He had noted and passed over the woman in the kerchief who was busy clipping branches from a shrub. No more than her head and shoulders were showing and she seemed absorbed by her task. She paid no attention to any other activity except twice now he'd seen her glance back toward the golf course. This time when she did it he followed that glance to a figure who was loitering some twenty yards behind her. He almost didn't recognize the girl either. She wore no straw hat and her hair was cut short. She was wearing a black plastic helmet of some kind. But there was no mistaking those big eyes of hers. Those eyes were locked on the gardener lady who, he realized with a start, was Elizabeth.

Elizabeth?

She had not seen him because her attention was elsewhere and because most of him was hidden by the corner of the tent. It was just like her, he realized, to blend into the scenery, but why was she here with that girl? His mind told him that maybe it was Elizabeth who paged Jonathan, but why then would she hide behind a bush pretending she was a landscaping worker? More likely, if anyone had placed that page, it was these two baggy jackets with their cell phone. But that couldn't be because when Jonathan showed up they paid practically no attention to him. This was crazy.

Her Jonathan was now in the trailer. Elizabeth's dark glasses moved this way and that as if to see who else might be coming. The two baggy jackets were doing the same. The one without the cell phone had some papers in his hand. The top page included what looked like a photograph but someone pausing to munch on a hot dog temporarily impeded his view. He decided, with this foot traffic, he could risk moving closer. First he opened the zipper of his own baggy jacket in case something else crazy happened.

Nothing did for two minutes, maybe three. The one without the cell phone slid his papers in his pocket, most of them still sticking out. Kessler was almost within an arm's reach. The temptation to lift them caused his fingers to itch but there were too many eyes at the food tents; he'd be seen.

The temptation ended when Jonathan came back out, a look of mild annoyance on his face. He climbed down a short flight of wooden steps that provided an entry to the trailer. The door opened behind him. A young woman called his name. In her hand was his diet soda. He said, "Oh, right," and turned back to get it. She said, "I'm sorry about the confusion, Doctor Leidner. But at least you can stay and see some tennis."

At this the man holding the cellular phone straightened.

The two baggy jackets exchanged glances. The one with the phone quickly punched out a number and stood snapping his fingers while it rang. Kessler could now hear him clearly.

"It isn't him," he said into the mouthpiece. "I'm looking at Leidner; it's not him."

The man listened to what must have been an argument.

"Mr. Tarrant . . . read my lips. It is definitely not him. This guy here looks nothing like Kessler."

Kessler stood very quietly. He tried not to breathe. He now knew who the man with the briefcase must be. This was looking not so crazy after all.

Lawrence Tarrant, his cellular phone at his ear, didn't know what to make of it either. The young aide had never been wrong before this; his information came straight from the top. Tarrant was torn between this urgent call from Loomis and the sight, before him, of Bandari's yacht and the man who could only be Ozal.

Ozal, with one eye misshapen and closed, was standing on a walkway below the sea wall and directly behind the *Alhambra*. Tourists strolled the perimeter above him. Ozal clearly seemed ill. Tarrant watched him pause and put a hand to his stomach and then try several breaths to make sure his lungs functioned. He rocked on his feet as he did so. Before him on the walkway was a tarpaulin-covered cart with two cases of soft drinks on top. Ozal would reach out and touch the blue tarp in a manner that seemed almost a caress. Tarrant was getting a very bad feeling about what that cart might contain.

"Listen," he told Loomis, "I want you to question him, check his ID. Find out if he's really Doctor Leidner."

Loomis protested. "What for?"

"Just do it."

"Mr. Tarrant, even if the guy is someone else, he still won't be Martin Kessler."

"Well, his name didn't come out of a hat, goddamn it. He must have some connection with Kessler."

"Like what?"

"Don't ask me. I pay you to find out."
Loomis was arguing as he broke the connection.

Kessler could scarcely believe that he was hearing his name. They thought he was Jonathan? Or that Jonathan was he? And now the one with the phone says, "He wants us to check the guy's ID."

"What for?"

"I been through that. He says do it; we'll do it."

"Hey, Loomis. Wait a second. We're showing him our faces? He'll remember when he finds out what's under that bed."

"He won't make the connection. He's going to think we're Security."

Kessler wondered what bed they were talking about but that was only in one part of his brain. Another part, deeper, was almost amused. You don't overhear your stalkers every day. But back in the more serious part of his brain he could see Elizabeth glaring at him. "*Martin, this is no fucking joke,*" she was saying.

Not nice language, Elizabeth, but of course you are right.

Indeed. Indeed. This is serious business. Take a nice deep breath and think it out.

Lawrence Tarrant, it seems, the man with the briefcase, has come to this island to hunt him. But the only way that Tarrant could have thought he was Leidner is if Tarrant had somehow tracked Elizabeth here. That makes sense, does it not? How else could this be? He had to have first found Elizabeth to then ask, "*So, who are the men in her life?*" The only answer, if he asked around Sea Pines, would have been this Jonathan Leidner. "*Leidner . . . Aha . . . that sounds German, you see. This Leidner must therefore be Kessler.*"

No . . . no, you see . . . that didn't make sense. It vaulted over how he could have found Elizabeth. If he did, it vaulted over why she was here now instead of lying somewhere with a hole in her forehead. Unless, of course, she found out they were on to her . . . which is why she was lurking behind that bush . . . to stalk Tarrant . . .

which was also impossible now that he thought of it because she would certainly not have brought the girl.

The truth, Kessler realized, was that he had no idea. The truth was that Elizabeth would know nothing of Tarrant because he had chosen not to burden her with him. But if that was true, why was she here? He didn't know. He knew only this. For all his good intentions he had put her in danger. If they knew who she was they would kill her.

Kessler's instinct was to cut this off at the source. He had seen the direction Tarrant had taken. He could find him and finish him; these two could wait. Except these two were now moving to intercept Leidner.

Elizabeth, stay there. Don't come out from your bush. Look here. Do you see me? It's me with short pants. Don't worry, I won't let anything happen. Don't worry, it's not your young doctor they want.

Elizabeth?!? I said stay where you are!!

So naturally, therefore, she's coming, thought Kessler. Much worse, she's coming unarmed.

Thirty-three

Roy Willis, this time, heard the name "Leidner" paged. His first thought was to curse himself for not thinking of that first instead of wading through thousands of faces.

"Yes, but who could be paging him?" Peter asked, himself surprised.

"My guess? Stein, his housemate, to tell him we were there."

Willis raised a hand to gather Nadia and Jasmine but they were already pushing through the crowd toward him. Jasmine mouthed, "*Kessler. We heard*," as they approached.

"Let's go talk to him."

Gamal Bandari peered through his binoculars. He had taken a position behind a hedge near a row of portable toilets. He had still seen no one whose skin was like coffee and no one who might be his niece. Lots of young girls but most of them blond.

He was about to give up, to go back to Ozal and tell him that his plan was impossibly stupid. Suddenly he saw faces that were browner than brown. He saw two of them converging in a sea of mostly white. He raised the binoculars to his eyes. He saw one woman, black, and one taller, not so dark. They were moving toward a man, also black. With the black man was a white man, considerably older, whose jacket was yellow, not blue like the others. Bandari wondered, almost idly, why three wore the same jacket. They met. They turned. They were coming his way.

He began to feel ill again. He did not know why. There was something about them that frightened him. He moved the focusing knob of his binoculars. At last, as he did so, he realized with a start what his brain had been trying to tell them. Those jackets. On the front. Over each of their hearts. Those jackets bore the name "Van Der Meer" and underneath they said "Tennis University."

It was them. It had to be. The tall one, not so dark, had to be the Algerian. Bandari's heart began to beat loudly. He lowered himself further to be hidden by the hedge. He would wait, let them pass him, and watch where they were going. After that he would run and get Ozal.

As the two in the baggy golf jackets reached Leidner, Kessler stepped out in the open. Their backs were to him; he was facing Elizabeth. He waved an arm vigorously; he caught her eye. Elizabeth stopped and looked back at him, surprised. She pointed her chin at the two men with Leidner and then spread her hands in a questioning gesture as in, "*Martin, what the hell's going on?*"

He could think of no gestures that could adequately communicate, "*These two think your Jonathan is me.*" But he could say with gestures, "*You get back. Let me handle this.*" He did so and then he patted his waist so that Elizabeth would know that he is armed. He knew, he supposed, that she would not find this gladdening but he hoped that she would wait and not interfere. These two, he felt sure, would ask her Jonathan some questions and then let him go on his way.

The two, however, were not being subtle. Jonathan stopped for them politely enough and acknowledged that yes, he was Dr. Leidner. He drew the line however at producing his wallet. Kessler heard him ask, "Did you two just page me? Never mind my ID; let's see yours." At this, the second man put a hand to his chest and shoved him back up against the trailer. The first said, "We hear you been flashing your dick."

Elizabeth shouted, "Hey! Get your hands off him."

She was pretending to be a meddlesome bystander. Nice touch. He'd seen her play that role before. Even so, Kessler groaned in his mind.

Both men turned their heads to see who had challenged them. What they saw was some woman, dark glasses and kerchief. And behind her, they saw, to Kessler's dismay, the approach of a girl wearing skates on her shoulder. Kessler saw no recognition, no alarm on their faces. Only annoyance at some woman who should mind her own business. The first, called Loomis, snarled, "Keep moving, lady." The second said, "This guy's a pervert."

These words were barely out of his mouth when the second, looking round him to see who else might be nosy, looked squarely into Martin Kessler's eyes. This time there was clear recognition. He mouthed the word, "*Shit*," and spun Leidner around. At the same time he clawed for his weapon.

Kessler's Walther leaped into his hand as he muttered a "Shit" of his own. He had the man beat but he had no shot because the doctor was now in between. The second man now recognized him as well and reached for his weapon in turn. The doctor was stunned at the sight of these pistols and also at the sight of Elizabeth Stride, who was bounding toward him like a deer. Kessler could see that she had something in her hand, much too wide for her knife but it was metal and pointed. The second man saw her; he brought up his gun.

Kessler had no choice. He had to swing his sights from the man holding Leidner to the man who was turning on Elizabeth. The thing in her hand was a gardening trowel. He did not want to shoot him because he didn't want shooting with so many people to see it. Already he heard rising voices from the crowd as the first of them saw what was happening. He shouted, "Don't do it. I'll kill you."

In that instant he saw the flash from the first one's pistol and he felt a hammer blow to his stomach. The impact dropped him to one knee. Through his shock he saw that the second man had wavered between himself and this woman who was almost upon him. He saw Elizabeth lead with a kick that almost knocked the gun from his grip.

He saw that before the man could recover she had buried the trowel in his throat.

Screams came now from the crowd behind Kessler. The man holding Leidner swung around to shoot Elizabeth but the doctor was clawing at his arm. The man with the trowel still stuck in his throat was staggering blindly; he tried to pull it free. The man, Loomis, smashed Leidner in the mouth with his elbow. Leidner tried to hold on but he fell. Loomis stomped him on the side of his head. With Leidner down he turned again on Elizabeth. Kessler now had his shot. He fired but he missed.

What ruined his aim even more than his belly wound was a blur of movement from off to one side. It was not Elizabeth; she had thrown herself down; she was rolling and juking to avoid being shot while she tried for the pistol of the man she had stabbed. The blur was the girl who appeared out of nowhere. As she ran, she stripped a pair of skates from her shoulder and heaved them at the man who was trying to shoot Elizabeth. The heavy skates whirled, still tethered by laces. One caught the man, Loomis, full in the face. The other continued and pulled his head with it. His head and the skates slammed into the trailer. Kessler fired before he could bounce.

Bandari had been waiting behind his hedge for the Van Der Meer people to pass him. They seemed to be heading toward those trailers to his left. When they passed he would cross to the cover of the food tents. Beyond was the passage through some buildings to the harbor. At last they went by and he bolted from cover. But before he reached the tents he heard the first gunshot. The sound had come from those trailers.

The first movement he saw was a young girl running. As she ran she hurled what looked like boots through the air. They struck one man in the face and knocked him backward. Another man was stumbling in the manner of a drunk. His fingers were holding some object to his neck. Still another in a green shirt was down, not moving, and a woman on the ground had snatched up a pistol. This woman, in a head scarf, had only started to point it when a second shot came from yet another direction. With that shot came a great spray of blood on the trailer. Red against white. It made people scream. The head of the man knocked against it had exploded, the one with the boots around his neck.

Bandari was frozen. The first thing he feared was that this might be Ozal. Ozal and his soldiers had come ashore. They had tried to set up their bomb in this place and they had been caught by police. Bandari had to see. He moved closer through the crowd against many who were running away from the shooting.

He saw another man, this one wearing short pants. This man was bent over. He was holding his belly. He had a gun in his hand. He was waving that gun at the woman and the girl as if telling them to run, get away. But the woman moved toward him; she too had a pistol. Her eyes were hidden behind big dark glasses but her face was darting this way and that as if she was looking for someone to shoot. He heard her say to the man, "You've been hit."

Now the man swiped at her. He did not want her near him. He turned and went after the man who was staggering, the one with the thing in his throat. He reached with one hand and he jerked the thing free. Bandari was horrified by what he did next. He plunged the thing into the man's throat again. He ripped as he pulled it back out. From the throat came an arc of arterial blood like the stream from a man who was carelessly peeing. The man fell backward. He hit the ground writhing. The man in short pants stuck the thing in his belt, not bothering even to wipe it of blood. The man on the ground twitched again and was still.

Bandari was transfixed. His legs would not move. But he saw now that none of these men was Ozal, nor was either of Ozal's soldiers among them. The man in short pants snatched the gun from the woman. He threw it at one of the men who was down and then he pushed her away from him. He seemed to be pushing her toward the girl who threw the boots. That girl was standing, her hands to her face, as if in horror at what she had done.

Thanks to her, that man had no top to his skull.

At this moment, the voice of a woman screamed, "Aisha!!" The scream came not from the woman in the head scarf. It came from the tall one in the Van Der Meer jacket. The name struck Bandari like a slap in the face. The girl's head looked up at the sound. And now Bandari saw her. The face. Leyna's face. The girl who threw boots was her daughter.

His brain tried to tell him, "*Gamal, get away.*" It told him that this other one must be the Algerian, not the tall one wearing the Van Der Meer jacket, this one here in the head scarf and glasses. This one must be the Algerian whore who had threatened to cut off his hand. His legs were trembling but were coming back to life. He wanted to run as many others were running, jumping over still others who had dropped to the pavement. But a man's voice yelled "Freeze!" and he stopped.

"I said *freeze*. Drop the gun."

Bandari looked around him for the source of this command. He saw the black man and the black woman. They were both holding pistols; they were both in a crouch. Their pistols were aimed at the man who killed the others. He saw them but seemed to pay little attention. His interest was more in the woman and Aisha. Now he seemed to be threatening them. He seemed to be telling the woman especially that if she didn't go he would shoot her.

The black man fired. But into the air.

He shouted, "Kessler? Last chance. I said drop it."

The older man, yellow jacket, didn't want him to shoot. The two blacks were ready to shoot all the same. But then Aisha came to life. She darted between them. She was waving her arms. She was shouting, "Roy, don't! He's a friend."

Kessler couldn't tell how much blood was his and how much came from the man he had finished. The bullet, at least, had not struck his rib cage but it probably did not miss a kidney. It was bad but he was thankful that the pain was not crippling.

Most eyes in the crowd were on the girl for the moment. She was yelling and waving, trying to shield him. His hope was that Elizabeth would see and take the chance to back away and fade into the confusion. She could, just maybe, seem an innocent passerby who had nothing to do with these killings. But Elizabeth, always stubborn, was doing nothing to cooperate. She must have known why he snatched the gun from her hand and why he let it be seen that it was he, not she, who ripped that man's throat with her trowel. But Elizabeth was more interested in grabbing the girl in case those two from the tennis school shot. She was even looking down at her Jonathan with concern. Kessler didn't blame her but he couldn't help thinking that just once he would like to be first on her list.

The girl did not cooperate either. She resisted; she seemed to have seen something else. Her eyes, already big, were now opening wider. She was trying to get away from Elizabeth.

''Uncle Gamal!?!'' She was looking past Roy. ''Uncle Gamal, is that you?''

Kessler saw the man who she must have been addressing. He was standing erect where all others were crouching, one hand to his mouth. Kessler knew this man from the Cyril Pratt tape. He's the man who had murdered Aisha's mother, and surely, the man who brought Tarrant and his thugs to this island. That whole bunch from the tennis school turned and looked as well. Kessler saw Nadia, momentarily stunned, now begging Jasmine to give her the pistol. Too late. The uncle was running for his life. His binoculars bounced, they hit him in the mouth, but he ran with his hands to his face as if thinking that what they couldn't see, they couldn't shoot.

Kessler saw policemen. They were moving up carefully, reluctant to act before they knew who was who. Only Elizabeth was looking at him. Her eyes were saying not ''Sit down, I'll get help.'' They were saying, ''Let's get that fat fuck.''

Kessler backed away toward the end of the trailer. As he did he pointed his pistol at her knee. He mouthed,

"*You will stay*." His eyes said, "*Don't make me put a hole in you, Elizabeth*." She was not intimidated but she realized at last that he could get away now or not at all. She turned her back to him, ready to cover. When she did Kessler slipped behind the trailer, unseen.

Lawrence Tarrant and Loomis's remaining two men had taken a position at the edge of the marina. They stood near a ramp that led down to the slips. Bandari's *Alhambra* was three slips away. Bandari would have to pass within reach whenever he returned to his boat.

But now Tarrant heard the shots in the distance. There were two, well spaced, one seemed louder than the other. By the second he saw people running. He muttered the name of Lester Loomis with a curse, sure that he must have shot Kessler.

"I told him, damn it, to take him alive," he hissed to the men standing with him.

"That was two guns," said one. "Two different directions."

"I better go look," said the other.

A third shot echoed as this man disappeared. Many tourists, the curious, were hurrying toward it, while others with children were hurrying away.

"Mr. Tarrant. Over there," said the man who stayed with him. He gestured with his chin to an overweight figure who was scrambling down over the stone sea wall and jumping five feet to the walkway below. Tarrant saw Bandari. He fell as he landed. On rising he almost knocked over the cart that the one-eyed Ozal had wheeled there. Bandari grabbed Ozal by the front of his shirt. He was waving, gesticulating; his meaning was clear. He wanted Ozal to get on board at once. He wanted his boat moved immediately.

"We take him or we wait?" asked the man.

Tarrant chewed his lip. The man with him was armed but Tarrant wasn't. There were four men on that boat if they took it but he did not seem to have any choice. Ozal, however, seemed in no great hurry. He seemed to be telling Bandari to wait until they could load the provisions on that cart. Bandari, to Tarrant's surprise, was agreeing. He was nodding as if to say, "*Yes. Do it now.*"

"We wait," whispered Tarrant. "But we move if they start to cast off."

What he'd seen was, indeed, Bandari agreeing but not to the loading of provisions.

"No, no," said Bandari when he got to the cart. "I don't care about your bomb. We must go while we can."

"You have seen them? The girl and the Algerian whore?"

"They have also seen me. Get aboard."

"But the bomb is now ready. They will come, we'll be gone. But the bomb will be here and it will kill them."

Bandari hesitated. "You can do this with your bomb?"

"I need only to set the timer. The timer plus one more ingredient."

Bandari had cared about nothing but fleeing, but to him this idea made some sense. It would not kill the girl and those people with guns—that would be too much to hope for. But a bomb going off might help him escape. It would cause great confusion and panic. A bomb going off meant no one would notice that any of these boats might have gone.

"Go do it," he said. "I will now start the engines. Tell your men to prepare to cast off."

"Go start."

Bandari noticed that the soldiers looked ill. "They are sick?"

"It's the flu. Go start," said Ozal.

Bandari nodded. So that's what it was. Ozal's soldiers, like himself, were dripping with sweat and Ozal looked the worst of them all. But the main thing now was to get out of sight and be ready to move this boat quickly. He climbed the boarding ladder and then up to the bridge. On the bridge was the shotgun that Ozal kept for dolphins. He would feel much safer with a shotgun.

Kessler had no trouble catching sight of Bandari because of the way he was dressed. He kept one arm pressed hard against his belly. The hand of that arm held his Walther out of sight inside the folds of his jacket. The jacket was maroon. It hid most of the blood.

Bandari, he hoped, would lead him to Tarrant because Tarrant had gone this way as well. He saw Bandari, not bothering with the ramp, climbing over the sea wall and jumping toward his boat. He counted three others but not Tarrant. He gathered himself, not sure what to do. If Tarrant appeared he would finish them both. But he could not wait long. His strength might go quickly. He did not wish to settle for only Bandari.

A flash of color caught his eye to his right. He saw another of those four baggy jackets. This man was moving away from the harbor and back to where the shots had been fired. He was alone. Kessler realized that Tarrant would have sent one man back to see what those gunshots were about. Kessler traced the direction from which this man had come. That way, he hoped, he'd find Tarrant.

One of the soldiers was still on the slip. He did not look, to Bandari, as if he would have enough strength to even free the lines from their cleats. The other, on the quarter deck, looked worse. But Ozal, who had gone to the galley for some reason, knew how to make them jump when he spoke.

Ozal, below, was banging pots.

Bandari shouted, "Will you hurry?"

"Two more minutes."

More banging, then quiet.

He heard Ozal on the stairs. Ozal was calling to his soldier on the slip to help him climb down the boarding ladder. Bandari looked out. He was so sick he needed help? It was then that Bandari saw in his hands what he knew to be one of the warheads.

"What are you doing? Are you trying to kill us all?"

In response came a smile. "You believed that it was flu?"

Bandari stared down at the face of Ozal. The Tuareg, as hurt and sick as he was, had a look of great joy on his face. Bandari had seen that look on other Muslims. He had seen it on the faces of volunteer fighters who believed, and who hoped, that martyrdom was at hand. Bandari squealed as the realization dawned that the sickness indeed was not flu. He snatched up the shotgun. He scrambled to the steps leading down to the deck.

"Ozal! Put it back. Put it back or I shoot."

The Tuareg barked an order at the soldier on the deck. His order, in Arabic, was, "*Take this fool's weapon.*"

The soldier tried to obey. He reached for it but feebly. Bandari pulled the barrel away and clubbed him in the face with the stock. The soldier reeled backward. He fell over a deck chair. He sat feeling teeth with his tongue. Bandari, once again, aimed the shotgun at Ozal. The Tuareg scoffed. He said, "You won't shoot. You're a coward." He turned to back down the ladder.

This insult was more than Bandari could bear. Even so he was afraid to pull the trigger. The noise would bring those people to the sound of the shot. Ozal was on the ladder; he was halfway to the dock. Bandari turned the shotgun in his hands and swung it as if it were an ax. Ozal saw it coming. He raised an arm but not quickly enough. The stock grazed his temple and slammed into his shoulder. He fell; his hands lost their grip on the canister. It bounced to the deck of the boat. Its lid flew off and the thing like a football rolled free from its packing. Bandari saw at once that it was all marked and scarred. Ozal had done something to the warhead.

Ozal had fallen to the slip with a crash, taking with him the soldier who was helping him. He struggled to his feet and was cursing Bandari. Now his face showed no joy, only rage. He stood breathing heavily as if judging his chances of fighting his way back aboard. But then a new light came into his eyes. He stumbled to the cart on which his bomb had been assembled. Bandari realized he was going to explode it, nuclear warhead or not. Bandari, frantic, ran to his bow and cast off the first of his spring lines. He shouted for the soldier whose teeth he had smashed to throw off the stern lines as well. Ozal, by this time, was calling to the tourists, those walking the paths above the sea wall. He was calling them in English, saying, "I am

Ozal. Come and see the surprise I have prepared for you. Come.''

Tarrant saw Bandari trying to cast off his lines. He had seen Bandari clubbing people with a shotgun and so had half the people who were strolling the promenade. These tourists were no longer looking toward the shots, they were looking now at the one-eyed Ozal who was haranguing them from that cart. Tarrant saw Ozal pull up one side of the tarp and fiddle with something inside. Bandari, meanwhile, had run back to his bridge where he started his engines with a sputtering roar.

"Now or never," said his man. "We can take them."

"With an audience gathered? Don't be stupid."

He saw Bandari try to gun his cold engines. They coughed and trembled; they did not yet have strength. Bandari gave them more throttle; they sputtered and quit. Nor did Bandari apparently realize that a stern line still held him to the dock.

Ozal, his hands still under the tarp, saw and heard what Bandari was trying to do. He turned and yelled something to Bandari in Arabic. Tarrant didn't know the words but they were surely not a warning that the boat was still tethered. Their tone was too mocking for that. His words were barely out of his mouth, however, when a great spark flew out from the cart. Ozal yelped. Then he cursed. Wringing his hands which seemed burned by the spark, he reached back inside to repair what had shorted.

"Oh, Christ," Tarrant muttered. It was just as he'd feared. "Let's get the hell out of here. *Now.*"

Tarrant's man made a grunt and started to move forward. Tarrant reached to stop him. Not that way, you idiot. But the man wasn't walking; he was falling on his face. Tarrant tried to catch him, he thought the man must have tripped. It was then that he felt the pistol jammed under his jaw. He heard a voice behind him that he knew must be Kessler's, a voice that seemed forced, one that sounded of pain.

"Move with me or die. Your decision."

Thirty-four

Elizabeth had furtively picked up the pistol that Martin had slapped from her hand. Aisha saw her do it and knew her intention. She knew that she hoped to slip away in the confusion. Aisha helped her by pointing in another direction and shouting that her uncle had run off that way. Roy heard her, as did Nadia and so did the police. They all turned their heads and it was enough. Elizabeth was melting into the background, the pistol already in the pocket of her apron.

Neither Roy nor Nadia nor Jasmine was fooled. They had seen which way the uncle had gone and were now sure that Kessler, wounded, had followed. Their immediate interest, however, was in Aisha, but she too was backing away. Nadia ran toward her. A policeman shouted, "Stop." Now Peter was waving his arms at the policemen. He was saying, "Don't shoot," he was saying his name, he was reaching very carefully into his jacket in order to produce his ID.

But this same policeman nearly shot Roy because Roy swung his pistol on a man who had come running but who now was trying to slip away as well. Roy had seen that his jacket was like those of the others. More than that, he had seen the expression on his face, not fear, not shock, but a snarl of dismay. Roy ordered this man to stop, raise his hands, lie face down on the ground or he'd fire. The two policemen saw Roy's combat stance and realized that he must be an officer himself. They swung their weapons toward the man in the jacket. The man in the jacket surrendered.

Nadia had turned, distracted by these shouts. When she looked back Aisha was gone. She could see two directions that Aisha might have taken. One would have followed Elizabeth Stride and the other her uncle, Gamal. Nadia hissed at Jasmine to get her attention. Once again, she asked Jasmine to give her a gun. Jasmine brushed past her, shaking her head.

"The uncle can wait. Let's find Aisha," she said.

Elizabeth had reached the circular harbor having failed to spot Kessler or Bandari. But she did hear the voice that rose from the marina and she did see the crowd that was gathering at its source. The voice was muffled; she could not make out the words. Her thought was that Martin might have fallen from his wound and someone was calling for help. In her mind she upbraided him for getting himself shot. She remembered the vision that had gone through her head of Martin in a shoot-out at this very tournament, looking perfectly stupid in shorts. This vision, and her anger, and her fear for his life crowded out what her brain was trying to tell her—that the words of the man who was shouting were English but the voice had a Mideastern accent.

"Over there," said Aisha who appeared at her side. "That's an Arab voice shouting over there."

"You get back, damn it. Get back, stay with Nadia."

"It could be my uncle. Let's go see."

Bandari, realizing that a stern line still held him, put his engine in idle and scrambled back down to the quarter deck. Ozal didn't turn; he did not see him coming. Ozal was too intent on haranguing the crowd but his voice was now shrill with pain and frustration. The pain, Bandari realized, was coming from his fingers that were now raw and bloody from the chemicals that burned them and from the sparks that had leaped from the detonator he built.

The soldier on the dock had pulled out his scarf and was wrapping it over his head and face so that he would die as a Tuareg. He was doing it with difficulty in the manner of a drunk. Bandari saw vomit on his shirt. He hissed at him, ''Soldier! Cast off this line.'' He hoped that Ozal couldn't hear. Ozal did; he glanced back; he showed little interest. He was much too absorbed by relating in detail what awaited these people in hell. He did notice, however, his man with the scarf and proceeded to try to unravel his own. Bandari lunged at the cleat on his deck and furiously tried to free the line from that end. But the line was too tight because the boat had strained forward. He pulled on the line with all his strength in an effort to produce enough slack. He still could not manage. With his foot he prodded the soldier still on board, the one whose teeth he had broken. But that one waved him off as he would a fly. He was too busy reading a prayer book with one hand and holding his jaw with the other. It was then that he heard his name called from the crowd that had gathered to listen to Ozal.

''Uncle Gamal!?!''

It went through him like a knife. He knew at once it was the voice of his niece. It called out again as he struggled with the line.

''Why have you done these things, Uncle Gamal? Why have you murdered my mother and father?''

He wanted to shout out that it was none of his doing. All these sins were on others, not him. But when he found her face at the edge of that crowd, he saw rising behind it the face of that woman, the one in dark glasses and head scarf. The woman who must be the Algerian whore was stepping up to the concrete sea wall, one hand in the pocket of her apron. Her eyes locked on him, her mouth showing teeth, she was preparing to jump to the walkway.

Bandari gasped. He let go of the line and ran to the place where he thought he had put down the shotgun.

''Keep moving,'' said Kessler, his gun at Tarrant's spine. Tarrant had gone rigid and tried to pull back when he saw the black smoke rising out of the cart. He held his briefcase before him as if it were a shield.

''I'm telling you, damn it. That thing is a bomb.''

''Move or die. Last warning,'' Kessler told him.

To Kessler it looked more like a revival meeting. Maybe even a magic show for the tourists. The man with one eye was making smoke and fireworks and seemed to be preparing the crowd for his finale by wrapping his face as he spoke. Kessler feared, however, that Tarrant could be right. This could be the bomb that keeps killing.

The girl appeared. They both heard her shout. They heard her anguished accusal of her uncle but Bandari was nowhere in sight. Suddenly his head popped up and then his hands. He was spreading the hands in denial. His boat, its engines having been restarted, was straining on the one line that held it. Suddenly, on the sea wall, there was Elizabeth. Bandari saw her. He clearly knew her because his eyes went wide and he stood up and ran from the quarter deck.

"How would he know Elizabeth?" Kessler asked Tarrant.

"Listen . . . shoot that one. The one by that cart."

Kessler shoved him forward. "Answer my question."

"How do I know? Who the hell is Elizabeth? Shoot the Arab before he can set off that bomb."

This now struck Kessler as a reasonable suggestion but he wanted to be close for a one-shot kill because each bullet he had might be needed. A more immediate concern was Elizabeth. Elizabeth had not seen him. She was about to jump down and he wanted her out of this. All that stopped her was the girl who was trying to follow and Elizabeth was trying to push her away.

"You!" Kessler shouted. "Both of you. Get back." He avoided speaking her name.

She followed the sound; most other heads didn't, but Elizabeth knew his voice in an instant. He repeated, "Yes, you. I'm talking to you. Get away before that thing explodes."

Puzzlement, concern appeared on her face. She gestured toward his waist. She mouthed, "*How bad?*" A toss of his head said, "*It's nothing.*"

Elizabeth mouthed, "*Bullshit,*" and drew a gun from her apron. She gestured to Tarrant and shrugged a "*Who's that?*"

You choose the worst times for conversation, Elizabeth. He tightened his grip on Tarrant's collar then pointed his pistol at the sky and fired. One shot was enough to get everyone's attention. He shouted a warning that the cart was a bomb. Some of them started backing away but the rest seemed in need of a second opinion. Several were peering through video cameras recording the rantings of the man with one eye. Even Elizabeth stayed where she was, although at least she shielded the girl with her body.

This man with one eye had glanced over at Kessler but otherwise barely reacted to the shot. He gave no sign that he recognized Tarrant. He raved on, apparently quoting the Koran, describing the torments of hell. He was saying something about garments of fire and hot water that was going to be poured on their heads. For this, Kessler grumbled, he had wasted a bullet.

He dropped his sights across the one-eyed man's forehead. But no sooner had he started to squeeze the trigger when Bandari rose up from behind his railing and now he was holding a shotgun. He was raising it to aim it up at the crowd. Kessler knew that his target could only be Elizabeth. He shouted "Bandari" and fired. He missed. The bullet only blew off some chromium trim. Bandari, however, yelped and ducked down. Kessler couldn't see him but Elizabeth could. She was looking down from the sea wall. He saw her pistol as its sights tried to find him. It was wandering as if she could not get a shot.

"He's got cover," she called. "Go and get him, your side."

At her words came a blast from Bandari's shotgun and a part of the boat's aft railing exploded. Elizabeth held her stance so it wasn't at her. That blast, and the next, got the crowd finally running. The next caused more railing to fly through the air. Bandari seemed to be shooting his yacht. It was Tarrant who understood why.

"He's shooting at that line, at the cleat that's holding it. If he frees it he's gone with that boat."

"Then move."

This time Tarrant went willingly. On the boat would be safer. As Tarrant ran he called up to Elizabeth. Tarrant knew her or he didn't but she did have a pistol. "Will you shoot him?" he pleaded. He was pointing toward the Arab. "He's trying to blow us all up."

Kessler shouted to her, "No! Get away. Just go home."

She seemed to realize what he'd been trying to do; to give her the chance to stay out of this mess. Her eyes said, "*Forget it. It's too late for that.*" Even so, she hesitated, reluctant to shoot. The old Elizabeth would have fired in a heartbeat but this one had Aisha clinging to her side and also there were too many targets to cover. Bandari had managed to climb back to the bridge but he still might stick his head out and fire that shotgun. She also had to cover the two young Arabs who were down and any more baggy jackets that might suddenly appear. Add to these, behind her, two black faces who were coming.

Kessler gave Tarrant a shove toward the boarding steps. He swung his Walther on the man with one eye. A roar from the engines spoiled his aim as he fired. The stern line broke free. It lashed the air like a whip. Kessler fired through a great cloud of exhaust. He saw the Arab double over, clutch his groin, and sink to his knees well away from the cart. The bullet hit too low for a killing shot but Kessler had no time for another. The boat was moving. Tarrant scrambled aboard. He held up his briefcase as a shield from the shotgun until he reached the safety of a bulkhead.

Bandari, however, was too busy to shoot. Kessler caught a glimpse of the Egyptian's head and the furious pumping of his shoulders as he steered. The boarding ladder was being dragged from the dock. Kessler summoned what remained of his strength and leaped for the ladder himself.

Bandari's fear had advanced to hysteria. He tried to tell himself that it could not be possible that Tarrant had suddenly appeared on that dock. Bad enough his niece, bad enough that Algerian, bad enough that Ozal has gone thoroughly crazy and everyone is shooting at everyone else. That man, please God, was definitely not Tarrant. Just some tall, skinny man in a suit with a briefcase. But he

did know that other man, the one in short pants. That was
the one he'd seen back by those trailers stabbing another
with some great wide knife.

Bandari forced himself to take a deep breath. Tarrant
couldn't be here. It could not have been Tarrant. Next
he'll be seeing Libyan colonels.

But if it were, now he'd die. Every one of them would
die. And he, Bandari, would be safe on his boat as soon
as he hit open water. They would die and all the warheads,
at least those in Suez, would be his to sell to the Libyan
colonels. Half price, he'll give them. Even colonels like
a bargain. They can't be so mad if he gave them half
price.

Bandari slammed his throttles forward. Again, too
much power. The engine coughed and bucked. Again it
almost stopped. He eased the throttles back while trying
to steer. Now the wheel got away from him, only for an
instant. His port side raked the hull of another large yacht.
In correcting from that he bounced off the slip and struck
a small speedboat that was idling in his path while its
owner tried to watch the excitement on shore. The owner
fell into the water on one side, the speedboat was pushed
to the other. The speedboat kept going, its motor still running, until it crashed sideways into a piling.

Bandari ignored both collisions. He cut his wheel left
and then right toward the channel. As he did so he glanced
back toward his slip. He could not see the man whom he
thought looked like Tarrant or the man with short pants
who was shooting. The thought seized his stomach that
they might have jumped on board. But no. They could
not have. For there on his quarter deck was Ozal's other
soldier still holding his prayer book and bleeding from the
mouth. The soldier looked almost too sick to move but
would surely have reacted if those men had tried to board.

Above the sea wall he saw those two blacks who were
dressed in blue Van Der Meer jackets. They were waving
at people, telling them to run. That woman with Aisha
was throwing Aisha down while looking back over her
shoulder at something. Bandari grazed another piling
while trying to see. She was looking, he realized, down

at Ozal who was crawling painfully back toward the cart while pressing one hand to his gut. Those shots that were fired. One must have hit Ozal. Ozal reached the cart. There were flames coming from it. Bandari wondered, Why didn't it explode?

This question had barely formed in his mind when the cart erupted but not like a bomb. It was more like a rocket, like a holiday flare. The cans shot up no higher than the roofs of the buildings ringing the harbor. They fell back to earth. People easily ducked them. The cart did a dance; it hopped up and down. Bandari heard the loud hiss from many boat lengths away. Ozal, for a moment, was swallowed by the smoke. But now, there he was, stumbling back out of it. His hair and his clothing were on fire.

A woman, the black one, seemed ready to shoot him but the man, the other black, seemed to say let him burn. Ozal was screaming, not in pain, more like rage. Bandari watched in horror as he bounced off the sea wall then turned and lurched down the now vacant slip. Bandari could see that his blindness was total. His soldier who had stayed tried to help him but couldn't. Ozal was reeling. His legs were all that worked. But one leg took a step and found nothing beneath it. Ozal tumbled headlong off the dock. Another billow of steam rose up from the surface as the water extinguished his flames. Ozal waved feebly as if in slow motion. He rolled over once and was still. It was finished. He was floating face down in the harbor. Above him the cart was a single huge ember. The plastic was melting onto the dock and the wheels were splaying outward as their axle burned through.

Bandari cursed God for his terrible luck. He cursed the braggart, Ozal, for his dud. He thought of Avram who had once said to him, "*God enjoys a good joke. Remember that, Gamal. He enjoys playing jokes on little people who mock him.*"

Well, the joke, this time, is on Ozal, not on him. On Gamal is only bad luck. The woman, the girl, and their protectors are still alive. He almost wished he'd let Ozal use that warhead but at least he was right on that score. Ozal would have muddled it. They would all now be dy-

ing. Instead, at worst, he has a terrible headache and he's
sick to his stomach from all that has happened.

The channel was clear. No police yet, no Coast Guard.
What he needed to do was get into open water so that he
could dispose of the canisters on board. The authorities
wouldn't be able to arrest him because he had diplomatic
status. They would make a big stink about those warheads, however, and Cairo might revoke his protection.
Better to be rid of them as soon as he was clear. After
that the authorities could ask all they wanted. Until he got
home they would have to protect him. He'd be safe from
Tarrant and that woman as well. He would say that Ozal
made him come here by force. Ozal, the terrorist, the
maker of bombs. He would say that he sabotaged the
bomb Ozal built and that's why so many lives had been
spared.

For that they will say that Bandari is a hero. For that
they should give him a medal.

Elizabeth had thrown herself upon Aisha. Roy Willis
grabbed Jasmine but Jasmine fought him off as she tried
to get Aisha's fleeing uncle in her sights. It was then that
the great flaring bomb erupted and the heat from it seared
Jasmine's eyes.

Elizabeth was up as soon as she realized that the force
of the bomb had been spent. She saw the *Alhambra*, by
then in the channel. She could see neither Martin nor the
man with the briefcase but she knew they had scrambled
on board. She could not imagine who that man might have
been. She would follow, she decided, in one of these other
boats. She would take one at gunpoint if she had to.

Roy Willis, nearby, had had much the same thought.
But Willis had his eye on the unmanned speedboat that
was pounding a piling in the wake Bandari left. He picked
up Jasmine, threw her over his shoulder and shouted for
Aisha and Elizabeth to follow. Jasmine asked him what
was happening. He told her what he saw. She insisted,
"I'll be fine. You get him."

Elizabeth had spotted the speedboat as well. She hesitated, one eye on Aisha's knee, deciding whether to kick

it so that Aisha would be unable to follow. But like Martin who had aimed at her own knee, she couldn't. She hissed, "You stay here. Don't you move."

"No way. I'm staying with you."

Elizabeth didn't argue. They would get to the boat. Once there she could throw the girl over the side. It would teach her to do as she was told.

Thirty-five

Kessler stood, his back pressed to a bulkhead as he tried to assess both his strength and his chances. Bandari, on the bridge up the stairs to his left, had given no sign that he knew they had boarded him. He could not see them from there, nor could he hear them above the roar of his diesels. Or at least Kessler hoped so. He was less than eager to climb those narrow stairs when a shotgun was waiting at the top.

He had forced Tarrant to sit on the deck, his back against the same bulkhead. Toward the stern, also sitting, was Bandari's other crewman. He should finish them, he knew, and not have them behind him. But that would make noise and besides he had questions. Also these two were being strangely calm.

The crewman had barely reacted to their boarding. He sat looking back at the Harbour Town waterfront, his expression serene although his face was deathly pale. He sat against the railing with his knees drawn up, his arms hugging his belly. Blood was drying on his mouth. His jaw hung crookedly. The man had been beaten, maybe shot, and seemed unarmed. Kessler could see little of whatever he was looking at. Black smoke still rose and spread from the cart, obscuring almost all movement on shore.

"Those people," he asked Tarrant, "are they all dead or dying?" His mind was on Elizabeth in particular.

"I don't know. It depends. I don't know what was in it."

Tarrant's manner was subdued. He'd seemed genuinely aghast when the bomb flared up and the cloud of black smoke began to roll inland.

"You. What was in it?" Kessler spoke to the crewman. The crewman offered a weak smile in response. Kessler raised his Walther, he aimed at this man's chest. "I will ask one more time. What was in it?"

The man smiled again, more broadly this time. Slowly, deliberately, he unfolded his arms and picked up an object he'd been holding in his lap. It was silver, scraped and dented, shaped like a small football but with several little sockets and plugs on its surface. He rolled it toward Kessler. As it rolled, it wobbled. It veered to Tarrant's feet. Tarrant sagged when he saw what it was.

"Well? What is it?" Kessler asked him.

"It's a nuclear warhead," Tarrant answered with a sigh. "An enhanced radiation device."

Tarrant reached out a tentative finger. With it he traced where the thing had been scored. Kessler blinked, not knowing what surprised him the most; what the thing was or how Tarrant was acting. He seemed not so much frightened as tired.

"So? Meaning what? Was one like it in that bomb?"

Tarrant raised his eyes to those of the crewman. The crewman dropped his own. He muttered something in Arabic. He glanced up toward Bandari's bridge and he spat.

Tarrant seemed to understand. He picked up the warhead. He examined it with an odd look of wonder.

"It's not killing them. It's killed us," he told Kessler.

Ozal's soldier smiled again when he saw the man's face, the man with the blood dripping out from his jacket. Ozal's soldier could see that he did not yet believe it but he would know soon enough that it was so.

The soldier knew Tarrant by the sound of his voice. This was the man who offered Stingers to Ozal. This was also the man whom Bandari had feared and whom he cheated by stealing two warheads. This Tarrant was now asking him questions.

He ignored them at first. But Tarrant was polite. There

was no harm in answering because the answers wouldn't help them. These two and Bandari would soon be in hell. All he asked in return was that Bandari should suffer. These two must avenge the betrayal of Ozal by Bandari, that cowardly pig. Tarrant promised that it would be done.

Tarrant asked him, "Are there any guns on board?"

"Only the shotgun; the one on the bridge."

"What of these warheads, are the rest still in Suez?"

The soldier shrugged. "We have only this one and the one still below."

"You were going to use a damned nuclear device just to kill Bandari's niece?"

The soldier answered with a wave of dismissal. "For the girl we don't care. This place was for practice."

After this, he told Tarrant, next would come half of Cairo because that was where they tortured Ozal. After that, to Suez to get more of these things. After that, Tel Aviv and after that . . . you would have seen. You should look for yourself at the maps Ozal had made. After that, America's turn would have come.

Poor Ozal.

He did not die as gloriously or as painlessly as he'd hoped but at least there was the water to cool him in the end. Ozal did his best. It was not his fault. His hands were not up to such delicate work especially in devising the timer. And the nitro was too cold; it did not have time to heat up. Bandari had kept sneaking more and more ice on it because he was afraid for his boat. All that blew was the primer, all that burned was the chemicals. In the end it was like striking a very big match.

God wouldn't hold a grudge.

Ozal did not make the wide slaughter that he promised, not here and not in West Cairo as he'd hoped. But God, right this minute, is telling Ozal that he's not going to hold that against him. Ozal had killed plenty in his years of making bombs. A thousand young men keep his picture on their walls. They sing songs about him at weddings. God, he feels sure, will be satisfied.

*   *   *

"You're sure about this?" Kessler stared hard at Tarrant.

"I would save a bullet for yourself if I were you."

The boat, at that moment, lurched from under his feet as Bandari gave his engines full throttle. Kessler slid down the bulkhead and crashed to the deck. The trowel in his belt cut into his thigh and a gush of fresh blood oozed from his wound. He recovered quickly before Tarrant could jump him but Tarrant, he saw, had no such intention. He sat there, still holding that thing in his hand, one elbow resting on his briefcase. He hefted it.

"You'd think the damned thing would be warm," he told Kessler.

Kessler still did not believe it. But maybe it was true. If so, what he found even harder to believe was that a man like Tarrant would accept that he was dying so easily.

"You're so ready to die?"

"No, I'm not. Not quite yet."

Tarrant gestured toward the crewman who was trying to vomit. There was nothing left inside him to come up. "And you saw the other one back on the dock. In two or three hours we'll be like that ourselves. Well . . . not you. I imagine you'll bleed to death first."

Kessler feared that Tarrant was right about that. But Pratt lasted quite a while with worse wounds than this. Hard to count on it, though. You can never tell with bullets. He decided that he might as well do what he came for. Finish Tarrant, do it quietly, then climb up those steps and put one big hole in Bandari.

After that . . . he wasn't sure . . . perhaps he'd take a long boat ride.

Give Elizabeth time to get away from this island.

The borrowed speedboat cleared the harbor channel just as the *Alhambra* picked up speed toward open water. Roy Willis had the wheel. Elizabeth sat with him. Willis had flipped on the VHF radio to hear any traffic from other boats in the area. There was much, mostly asking what had happened at Harbour Town. Elizabeth was counting the cartridges in her clip and listening both to the traffic and to Willis. Willis was telling her all that he knew of the man Martin dragged to that boat.

On the bench seat behind them were Jasmine and Aisha. Jasmine's eyes were burning even more from the spray but she claimed that she could see enough to shoot. Aisha found a cooler. There was beer and ice in it. She used melted ice and the padding from her helmet to make a cold compress for Jasmine. She had jumped aboard with Willis. She had helped him to free the boat from the pilings. Elizabeth, on boarding, was about to throw her off but Willis had insisted she'd be safer with them. Elizabeth was now hearing why.

All those people at the tournament, all those tourists in Harbour Town might be poisoned by that strange flaring bomb that went off. It was set there, thought Willis, to do its damage downwind. He did not know what was in it, perhaps nerve gas, perhaps toxins, perhaps even radioactive material. For all he knew, they were already poisoned but at least were no longer downwind. He knew of this bomb indirectly from Kessler. It surprised him that she seemed to know nothing about it, not even that Lawrence Tarrant existed.

Getting back to this bomb, Willis informed her, Kessler had apparently learned of it from Pratt. It was Pratt who identified Tarrant under torture. Kessler called Tarrant at his Maryland home and warned him against ever coming to this island. Tarrant's phone had been tapped by government agents because Tarrant had long been a dealer in contraband and his primary client was Libya. Tarrant worked with Bandari, whose Ministry of Development was laundering Libyan money through Egypt. When and why they branched out into weapons of terror was something that remained to be learned.

"Why here?" she asked him. "What's here that's worth this?"

Willis shrugged. He asked quietly, "You?"

"I'm in the book, damn it. They could have knocked on my door. And Pratt, by the way, was not tortured."

"Okay."

"If anyone's the target it's you and your people."

"Could be."

"You want torture? You get me to Tarrant and Bandari. I'll get answers from them in five minutes."

Elizabeth regretted those words as she spoke them. She could feel the chill from the bench seat behind her. She berated herself but she blamed Martin Kessler. A phone call to a man like Tarrant was lunacy. If he knew where he lived, why didn't he finish it? That's exactly what she would have done if she knew. But there, with that thought, she knew why he hadn't told her. She understood, in the same flash of insight, why he stabbed a dead man with her gardening trowel.

Damn you, Martin.

But for now all she wanted was to get him off that boat. She knew what he intended. To kill everyone on it and finish this once and for all. Her hope was that he would have already done it by the time this boat reached that one. They'd pick him up, get him somehow to a doctor. These Muslims must know one. One who was discreet.

"Elizabeth?" Aisha's voice. Trembling. "I'm so sorry, Elizabeth."

"Honey," Willis told her, "there's no way it's your fault."

"Yes it is. She was gardening. She was home planting flowers."

"Aisha . . ."

"I got that doctor beat up and I got that man shot. And Mr. Willis, that's my uncle who's responsible for this and you're sitting here blaming Elizabeth. I want you to stop it. You stop it right now."

Elizabeth wanted to turn, to reassure her, but she kept her mouth shut, her eyes locked on the *Alhambra*. She saw one head. A thin man. Not Martin. On the bridge she could see the silhouette of another. From the shape it could only be Bandari. If they were still standing, Martin had to be down. She tried to tell herself he wasn't dead, only down. He's Martin Kessler. He's Reineke the Fox. No arms-dealing maggot or piss-ant Egyptian could ever defeat Martin Kessler. Not even in those fucking short pants.

"Can't this thing go faster?" she snapped.

Tarrant saw the speedboat. A half mile and closing. He also saw that Kessler had picked up a cushion and had folded it over his pistol.

"You're going to kill me?" he asked. "What's the point?"

"So you don't outlive me is the point. Put down the briefcase."

"Well, don't do it. Not yet. I would like a few more minutes. I want that insect to know what he's done."

Tarrant called Bandari's name before Kessler could prevent it. The boat made a violent swerve in response. Tarrant smiled as he steadied himself.

"I think he knows we're on board."

At this he hefted the football-shaped warhead and lobbed it up the stairway and into the bridge. He smiled again at the sound of banging as Bandari tried to kick it away. His manner turned suddenly from satisfaction to alarm. He threw himself to one side. In that instant a section of handrail exploded. Bits of shot and wood peppered his pants. Kessler leaned in; he snapped a shot at Bandari but Bandari had ducked out of sight.

"That had a purpose?" asked Kessler, glowering. "I thought you didn't want to be shot."

Tarrant checked his legs. There were a few small punctures, none serious. The warhead came bouncing down the steps.

"Who was that woman, by the way?" asked Tarrant. "The one on the sea wall with the gun?"

Kessler didn't answer. In his mind he was counting the shots he had fired. He had four bullets left, maybe three. That's one each plus a third he might use for himself. He could scarcely afford another miss.

"That was the Algerian, Halaby, I take it. So you're working with them? You're not here for the bounty?"

Kessler knew that he was referring to Elizabeth but he did not bother to correct him. This was no time for chats or for games with Bandari. He knew he'd be better off finishing this one before he did anything else crazy.

"Low on bullets or blood. Which is it?" asked Tarrant.

Kessler raised the Walther. It stopped at Tarrant's heart.

"Kill me, you kill that woman," Tarrant said quickly. "You'll also be killing the niece."

Kessler blinked. "How so?"

"Here's my trade. I can tell you how to save both their lives. In return all I want is the time to take that warhead and shove it up Bandari's ass. You have about ten seconds to decide."

Kessler was alarmed. "There is what? Another bomb?"

"It's no bluff, Mr. Kessler. Agree or shoot."

"Bandari's all yours if you're telling the truth."

"Take a look off our stern. You'll see for yourself."

Kessler pushed himself up to see over the transom. He supposed he should not have been surprised, but he was, to see a small boat in pursuit. It was closing fast, maybe two hundred meters. Willis at the wheel, looked like Jazz in the back, Elizabeth was standing, braced against its port rail as if she were preparing to jump. He saw the girl reaching toward her to steady her. The boat was turning in across the wake of this one in order to make its approach. What possessed her, he wondered, to bring that girl with her?

"I would tell them," said Tarrant, "to stay out of our wind. We're trailing a cloud of plutonium behind us. If they cross it they're going to be as dead as we are."

Thirty-six

Elizabeth's chest heaved with relief. She now saw Kessler. He was alive. He was waving an arm at her, waving her off.

"What's he want?" asked Willis.

"Never mind. Keep going."

The radio blared with a voice, very loud. It was ordering the *Alhambra* to cut its engines and stop. Bandari's yacht swerved again as he looked to his rear but he showed no sign of complying.

"We've got company," said Willis, glancing over his shoulder. Elizabeth turned. She saw a Coast Guard patrol boat coming up fast. The marina office must have called to report that the *Alhambra* had made a run from the harbor just before the explosion at its slip.

She looked back at Kessler. He was waving more violently. He was saying, with gestures, move off to the side. Move off, well away, don't come close.

"He wants us off his beam?" asked Willis, confused. "He wants us . . . damn. He wants us out of his wind."

Willis cut the wheel sharply.

Kessler heard the voice of the Coast Guard commander. It came from Bandari's radio on the bridge. He heard Bandari wail that it wasn't his fault, none of it. His boat has been hijacked by criminals. At this the door to the bridge slammed shut. Kessler could no longer hear.

"Why doesn't he stop if we're criminals?" he asked Tarrant.

"He's still trying to think up his story," Tarrant guessed. "What he really wants is to deep-six this warhead." The warhead was still dancing all over the deck.

Kessler saw at least that Elizabeth had obeyed him. Elizabeth or more likely Willis. Their powerful little boat was coming up fast but it was staying fifty meters off to their side.

"Far enough, you think?" he asked Tarrant.

"If they weren't too late. Let's go get Bandari."

Kessler pointed off the stern with his chin. "The Coast Guard," he said. "Are they entering that cloud?"

"That's their problem. Let's go. We still have a deal."

"We should warn them somehow."

"Well, you could always put a note in a bottle, Mr. Kessler. I'm sure that would make them go away."

Kessler ignored him. He raised a hand to get Elizabeth's attention. His hope was to try to tell her with gestures to go back and tell them to get out of their wind shadow. He tried but it was hopeless. She couldn't understand him. Tarrant, exasperated, took the bull by the horns. Checking first to see that Bandari couldn't shoot him, he crossed the deck in purposeful strides and seized the sick crewman by his belt and his hair. The crewman resisted, but feebly. Tarrant hurled him off the back of the boat and into its churning white wake.

"You're an interesting man, Mr. Tarrant," said Kessler.

"That should slow them down while they try to fish him out."

Tarrant was watching the bridge as he spoke. He bent over and picked up the warhead once more, then shot one final glance toward Elizabeth's boat. He climbed to the second stair to the bridge and again lobbed the warhead against the bridge door. He called Bandari's name at the top of his voice.

"Bandari . . . shit head . . . do you realize you're dying? Ozal didn't kill them with that thing, he killed us."

More shuffling from the bridge but no answer.

"But you, you asshole, are going to die hard. Look off to your right. You see that woman with the head scarf on that boat? That woman is Nadia Halaby, Bandari. She's going to board us and when she does, she's going to cut off your hands, Bandari. You remember? She promised. She'll cut off your hands and after that I'm going to cut off your dick."

Kessler hooded his eyes. "This was your tactic?"

"I know him. Just wait."

"After this he'll do what? He'll thank you and throw down his shotgun, you think?"

"He's a worm so he'll try to make a deal. Wait and see."

Kessler, once again, had failed to correct him regarding the identity of the woman in the boat. This time it was deliberate. He was getting an idea.

Bandari saw the woman he was now sure was Halaby, the one who had called him that morning in Cairo and promised to cut him to pieces. He was weeping with fear; he didn't know what to do. The Algerian trying to board him, the Coast Guard trying to stop him, and now Tarrant and his henchman down below with a gun. On top of all this maybe Tarrant was right. He was feeling so sick he was weak in the head.

"It is not true we're dying," he bawled toward his door. "There are drugs to be taken. I know this."

No answer.

"There are showers, special soaps to wash the poison from the skin. In no time the sickness is gone."

No sound from below. Too quiet. He jumped when the Coast Guard came back on his radio. The commander was telling him to stop or he'd shoot. He looked back. The patrol boat was well in the distance. It had stopped to pull something from the water. Bandari turned down the radio's volume and set his automatic pilot control. The boat was now leaving the inland water and was aimed at the open horizon. He turned to the door and shouted Tarrant's name.

"Tarrant, you must listen. There are still six warheads.

They are still in the warehouse in Suez. The iodine is there; the cobalt is there, but Avram buried everything under cement. This was not my fault, Tarrant. It was Avram.''

''There are six? You mean four,'' came Tarrant's voice.

Bandari ran to look. He could not see Tarrant. But he could see two shadows that were cast on his deck and he saw the rolling warhead he had kept from Ozal.

''No, no. Two were extras. That one and one other. The other is hidden in a pot in the galley. These you must get and throw over the side in order to get rid of the poison. You must do this, Tarrant, so the Coast Guard can't see you.''

''Ah . . . why would I go to that trouble, Bandari?''

''Tarrant, listen, you can have the six warheads. You can have all the money; I give it to you. I ask only that we tell the same story; how Ozal hijacked me and I was only escaping. Also you must keep that woman from me. You can tell her I no longer want Aisha.''

No answer.

''Tarrant?''

''In the galley, you said.''

''In the galley in a big pot for lobsters.''

''It's a deal.''

On Bandari's radio, again came a warning, a threat to heave to or they'll shoot out his rudder. Bandari had reached to turn the volume down further when another voice cut in over the first. It said, ''*Negative, Coast Guard. Do not fire on the yacht* Alhambra. *Do not attempt to board.*'' The voice then recited some sort of code which appeared to establish its authority. ''*Stay well aft and well abeam to starboard. Await instructions. I say again, stay aft and stay windward of that boat.*''

Bandari's spirits rose. He didn't know who spoke. He knew only that it had to be someone important who must have learned that he himself was important and who knew that he must be protected. This was all the more reason to get rid of those warheads.

But it also meant he didn't need Tarrant.

* * *

Kessler saw some activity in Elizabeth's speedboat. The girl in the back was half-standing and rummaging while telling Elizabeth what she seemed to have found. She reached down and produced what looked like a horn. Elizabeth took it. Kessler saw what it was. A battery-powered megaphone, called a loud hailer.

He waved frantically as Elizabeth brought the hailer to her lips. He told her with gestures that she was to say nothing. She did not understand but she lowered the device. She spread her hands in a questioning fashion. Kessler answered by putting a finger to his lips.

"What's that about?" asked Tarrant who was watching.

"No use letting Nadia upset our friend further."

"Well, may I be excused? I need to find that other warhead."

"Yes, go do that. A deal is a deal."

"What are they doing? What's going on?" Elizabeth had seen Tarrant disappear from the deck and emerge minutes later with two silver containers. Martin had to be crazy to let him out of his sight.

Willis hadn't been looking. His ear was cocked to the radio traffic, waiting to hear more from Peter. That was his voice that had overruled the Coast Guard.

Elizabeth watched as Tarrant stepped back toward the transom. He seemed to be shielding the containers with his body in a way that would keep the patrol boat from seeing them. He was looking up toward the bridge. She saw Bandari gesture as if giving instructions. Tarrant nodded. He moved forward along the port side of the yacht until he was hidden from her view. He reappeared seconds later without the containers.

He stood at the stairwell calling up toward the bridge. He had picked up his briefcase as if all were normal. Her sense was that some agreement had been reached. Tarrant started to climb up the stairs but then stopped. He hesitated, then raised his free hand. She saw Kessler belt his pistol and show his hands as well. They both waited now at the foot of the stairwell as if they were obeying instructions. Elizabeth didn't like this at all.

At that instant she heard Bandari's voice on the radio. He kept his voice low; it was almost a whisper. He was calling the Coast Guard commander. He told the commander, *"Do not talk, only listen."* His voice sounded barely under control. *"The man in the suit is the boss of the hijackers. The one in short pants is an assassin. It's these two who provided the bomb that went off. But it is I, Gamal Bandari, who has saved many lives by removing the part of the bomb that would have killed them."*

"Does that mean no one's dying back there?" asked Willis.

She shushed him.

"Now this man has found these parts," Bandari's low voice continued. *"This man is now boasting that he has poisoned these waters with warheads from nuclear artillery shells that he just now threw into the sea."*

Willis sucked in a breath. "Oh, shit."

"They have fixed these shells so that both of them leak and the leaks have already made everyone sick. I have fooled them into thinking I will be on their side. You must shoot them when you see them start to climb to the bridge. Please signal with your hand if you will do this."

Elizabeth looked back. She could see the face of the Coast Guard commander. He had raised a hand, palm forward, to Bandari. The gesture was telling him to wait. He had a headset to his ear and appeared to be listening but the radio on this boat was silent. It seemed clear to Elizabeth that he was taking instructions from a voice on a less public frequency. A seaman had taken a position on his foredeck. He wore a helmet and vest and held an automatic rifle. He was braced and ready for the order to shoot.

"Get closer," said Elizabeth. "Get this boat in between."

"Not with Aisha on board."

"I'll jump out," Aisha offered. "I can swim."

"You get down on the floor."

"Please signal," came Bandari's voice again, more

desperate. "*When you shoot from your boat I will shoot from my bridge. These men are fanatics. They want to kill everyone. They have said that my whole boat is already poisoned.*"

Elizabeth couldn't stand it. She snatched the loud hailer. "Martin? Martin!!"

He heard her. He looked.

"Bandari just told the Coast Guard he's going to shoot you."

Kessler answered by raising a calming hand. The gesture seemed to say, "Well, of course."

Bandari, however, reacted with shock upon realizing that he'd been overheard. "*Coast Guard, Coast Guard,*" he was no longer whispering. "*Those people in the boat off my beam are more terrorists. They are criminal Muslims who hide on this island and they too have weapons and bombs. You must shoot them. Shoot them now or they will . . .*"

Willis reacted by snatching his microphone. "My name is Roy Willis, I'm a former federal agent. The people on this boat are—"

The roar of Elizabeth's pistol cut him off. At a glance he saw that Kessler had seized the moment to climb the stairs and rush the bridge. He saw that Kessler had pushed Tarrant before him. He saw that Bandari must have sensed it or heard it and had turned his attention from their boat to the stairway. This woman seemed to know that Kessler would act and was laying a covering fire. Her bullets pocked the bridge, they shattered a windshield, they forced Bandari to cover his head but Willis still heard the boom of the shotgun.

"*Cease fire on that boat,*" barked the radio voice of the commander. "*Stop shooting at once or I will fire on you.*"

The Coast Guard commander, already overwhelmed, was hearing too many conflicting accounts. When Elizabeth showed no sign of lowering her weapon and seemed to be searching for a target on the bridge, he ordered a warning burst by his seaman. The seaman, also nervous, obeyed. He fired half a clip at the water in front of her, stitching the surface with geysers. Elizabeth, more by reflex than design, swung her pistol to the source of those shots. The seaman, alarmed, fired the rest of his clip. He intended a warning but his aim was short. Two or more bullets ricocheted off the waves and into the fiberglass of the powerboat's hull.

"*Stop that damned shooting. Stop it now*!!"

Peter's voice.

Willis turned his head. He saw a police boat coming up fast. Lights flashing, siren bleating, it was quickly overtaking the Coast Guard patrol boat. He saw Peter's head sticking out of its cabin. He held a loud hailer in his hand. He identified himself once more to the commander. He told the commander to use his open channel to clear all other boats within a range of twenty miles. Any craft that failed to comply was to be sunk.

"Uh-oh," exclaimed Aisha.

"He doesn't mean us," said Elizabeth. She had swung her pistol back to the bridge. She saw movement. Only shadows. She did not yet see Martin.

"No, it's not that. I'm . . ."

Elizabeth glanced at her. She saw that Aisha was examining her ribs. Her fingers were bloody. There was blood on her T-shirt. Elizabeth was horrified. She stood torn for an instant between Aisha and Martin.

"It's all right," said Aisha weakly. "I don't think it's a bullet." She peeled up her T-shirt. It snagged on the wound. "I think it's just plastic. It doesn't feel deep."

Willis saw it. "I'm taking her in."

"Drop me on that boat first, then go," said Elizabeth.

"Kessler said stay away. Now I guess we know why." Willis started a turn that would take them to the island.

She stared in anguish first at Aisha, then the bridge. She turned her pistol on Willis. "Take me close enough to jump."

She waited for him to look into her eyes so that he could see that she meant it. But before he could react, a calling voice shocked her. It was Martin's voice, very loud and electronic. He was calling Nadia Halaby. She looked up and saw him at the window of the bridge. He had found a loud hailer as well.

"*Yes, Nadia. I'm talking to you. Do I see blood on that girl?*"

She stared at him blankly. He was looking at her. She saw Aisha wave a hand at him to say that it was nothing. Elizabeth reached for her own loud hailer but Kessler stopped her before she could speak.

"*Nadia, this is no time to talk. Bandari is down; we don't need you here. You can only get all four of you killed. You must see to the girl, go back to your tennis school. You will stop for nothing or nobody, Nadia. Mr. Willis, do you hear what I'm saying to her?*"

Willis blinked at Elizabeth. "He wants you to be Nadia. Why?"

"He's crazy," she muttered. "It's not going to work."

"*Mr. Willis,*" he called, "*here is something for you. Aisha's father has a warehouse in Suez. That warehouse should be carefully searched within the hour but don't tell Cairo what you're doing or why. What they'll find there has nothing to do with her father. Look under some hardened cement bags.*"

"Aisha, do you know the warehouse he means?"

"Um . . . yes, down on the docks. It's just lumber and stuff for construction."

"*Within the hour,*" Kessler repeated. "*You could find yourself in a foot race.*"

"Martin . . ." Elizabeth spoke into the hailer. Her throat caught before she could say more than that.

"*Nadia, go home. Go back to your office. Behave now and maybe I'll give you a call.*"

Willis took a deep breath. He threw Kessler a salute and pushed the lever back to full throttle.

Thirty-seven

Lawrence Tarrant used his necktie to stem the bleeding from the pellets that had torn into his thigh. He had set his briefcase on the chart table next to him. One corner of the briefcase was in tatters. It caught much of the blast when he threw it at Bandari. His chance to throw it came when the windows blew out from the gunfire of that Algerian woman.

Kessler had followed those shots through the door and had rolled before Bandari could aim again. He came up underneath Bandari's shotgun and clubbed him to the floor with his pistol. Tarrant limped to where Bandari had fallen, took the shotgun away and would have started by blowing off both Bandari's feet had not Kessler seized the shotgun and told him to sit. Kessler wanted a moment to study the controls, and the radio, and also to find the loud hailer he'd hoped for.

Tarrant watched him with interest as he called to the Algerian and as much as told her to go on with her life. It did not seem a time to wish someone bon voyage. When Kessler told the black man of the warehouse in Suez, that at least seemed in keeping with events. It surprised him a little that he felt no annoyance that Kessler, with those words, cost him twenty-five million. A part of him doubted that they were actually there. Bandari had lied about everything else. But if they were in that warehouse he no longer much cared. His head had told him that he was certainly dying and that no amount of assistance could save him. His body was starting to agree. Kessler, during this moment of quiet, was becoming considerably downcast as well. Apparently he and this Nadia had been close. Look at him now. Staring after her.

But life goes on. At least for the moment. Tarrant finished knotting his tie and reached for the knife he'd slid into his sock.

Kessler heard a noise. A dull beeping sound. He turned to see Tarrant, a kitchen knife in his hand. Another few steps and he'd have been within reach. Kessler raised his pistol. He put down the loud hailer.

"This isn't for you. It's for Bandari," said Tarrant.

"Put it down."

"The warhead won't fit up his ass. This will."

"Put it down all the same if you please."

Kessler knew that Tarrant would have probably stuck him if only to keep him from interfering. This was terribly careless. Between being depressed and the loss of blood, his brain was not working so well these last minutes. He should have known that Tarrant would have picked up a knife while he was rooting around in the galley. Were it not for that noise . . .

"What's that beeping, by the way?"

It was coming, he realized, from Tarrant's briefcase and where there is a beeper there is usually a phone. Perhaps, he thought, he could really call Elizabeth and do it without the whole world listening in. Perhaps he might even have a few words with Aisha.

"Open the briefcase. See who's trying to get you."

Tarrant shrugged and complied. He worked the snaps and opened the lid. Kessler raised his pistol and aimed it at his face just in case there happened to be a weapon inside. There was nothing except electronics.

"Step aside. Let me see," Kessler ordered.

The briefcase contained an IBM Thinkpad with fax, a beeper, a cell phone and what looked like a built-in recording device. All these were neatly arranged in felt padding. The Thinkpad seemed to be the only thing damaged. The LED read-out on the beeper was blinking. Tarrant looked at the number. He grunted, almost smiled.

"Just someone who's now out of a job," he told Kessler.

"Call him. See what he wants."

"What difference does it make?"

"Indulge me. Pick up the phone."

All Kessler wanted was to know that it worked. Again with a shrug Tarrant pressed *Redial* and brought the phone to his ear. Kessler noticed when he did this that another light came on. The briefcase was apparently recording. He heard a dim click when the phone call was answered.

"It's me. What is it?" Tarrant said without interest. But then his eyes widened slightly, a blink of surprise. "Yes, it's me and I'm alive," he repeated impatiently. "Why are you so surprised that I'm alive?"

Kessler's first thought, and apparently Tarrant's, was that the voice on the other end of that phone must have knowledge of Tarrant's predicament. Kessler guessed that one of those baggy jackets must still be at large on the island. As Tarrant listened his expression slowly changed. What had been impatience became disbelief. Disbelief turned into amusement.

"Good job. Well done. Now go turn on the news," Tarrant said and then broke the connection. He looked up at Kessler and smiled.

"What has happened?" asked Kessler.

"Want to hear?"

"By all means."

"It seems I've been murdered twice in one day."

Tarrant snapped the phone shut. He put it back in his briefcase. He then pressed a button on the other device that Kessler had assumed was a recorder. It whirred and stopped. Tarrant reached for another button and pressed it.

"The name of the young man doesn't matter especially. He's an aide to Charles Fraser, the President's National Security Adviser."

Kessler listened.

According to the young man's breathless account, a surveillance team was already in place when Tarrant's plane touched down on Grand Cayman. A man who was thought to be Tarrant disembarked. Tall and thin, graying hair, a briefcase.

"He's . . . a banker," said Tarrant. "Long story."

This banker, whoever, was approached by two men, not those who were waiting on surveillance. He tried to duck them by hurrying to a car that had driven on the tarmac to meet him. The two men called after him, angrily it seemed. When he didn't stop, the two pulled out pistols and shot him. They proceeded to empty their clips in his head until they, in turn, were ordered to surrender by agents who'd been sent there by Fraser. They did not. There was more shooting. The two men went down. One was dead and the other was dying. The two assassins— although it wasn't yet confirmed—were believed to be Libyan nationals. Their victim was presumed to be Lawrence Tarrant because it hadn't occurred to the agents thus far that he might be anyone else. Besides, he no longer had much of a face.

Tarrant snorted. He stopped the recording where he heard his own voice tell the aide to go turn on the television news.

"It's certainly been one of those days," he told Kessler.

Nadia, with Peter, had seen the great flare, all the shooting, people running and screaming through the smoke. She had seen Aisha's uncle get his boat under way. She had seen, too late, the small boat that gave chase and was aghast to see Aisha on board.

It was Nadia and Peter who had rushed to the office and told a young staffer to alert the Coast Guard that both of those boats must be stopped. Peter made two more calls, the first to a Washington number; the second was to summon the police boat. Neither call lasted more than twenty seconds. Peter ordered her to stay when he boarded the police boat. He said he needed her there to report what she saw in the aftermath of the explosion. He said one or more federal agencies would be calling. They would need to know exactly what was happening.

She could see Bandari's boat as it rounded Land's End

and could hear a running account of the chase from the Coast Guard and from a dozen or more boats that were scrambling to get out of harm's way. She had seen the pursuit boat wide and to the right of it and then she heard Willis try to identify himself. Seconds later she heard the distant echo of gunfire. She snatched a pair of binoculars from the staffer and through them saw Jazz reach to pull Aisha down. She thought she saw Aisha clutching her ribs and she heard Willis say, "*I'm breaking off. We're going in.*" His boat then accelerated, away from the *Alhambra*, then sped toward the ocean side of the island.

She knew at once where he must be going. She threw down the binoculars and left at a run. The staffer could relay what reports Peter needed. She did not stop until she reached the car that she and Jazz had parked near Marsh Drive.

"*Mr. Kessler? Martin Kessler. Please respond if you're able.*"

The voice came over the VHF radio. Kessler glanced back at the Coast Guard patrol boat. The police boat had drawn alongside and kept pace. A man who seemed familiar was leaning out its cabin. Yellow jacket, blue cap, he held a microphone to his lips. Kessler remembered. He had seen that man with Willis. Kessler stepped to the radio and answered.

"*Mr. Kessler, my name is Peter Cobb. We've met before but you wouldn't recall. It was in Washington some twelve years ago.*"

"Ah, yes. I think so."

"*Do you really? I'm surprised.*"

This is a time for small talk? thought Kessler. But he remembered the wife. Her name was Lauren. She was sort of a fan. She also became an inadvertent source for a time but that was in the old days when he thought such things mattered.

"Your wife's name is Lauren. She told wonderful stories."

"*Well, good heavens. She'll be thrilled that you remembered, Mr. Kessler.*" A pause. "*I . . . um, think what*

I'm trying to do here is establish some level of comfort between us. The business at hand is not so pleasant. May I ask who else is alive on that boat?''

He looked down at Bandari whose eyes were closed and who had not even twitched since he hit him. ''Bandari is but he's now playing possum.'' This remark was a revelation to Tarrant who promptly brought his heel down on Bandari's ankle. Bandari shrieked. He quickly revived and crawled into a corner where he fingered the lump that Kessler had raised above his ear. ''The other man's name is Lawrence Tarrant. As it happens, I know his wife, too.''

Tarrant snorted aloud as if in amusement. Peter heard the snort that was almost a chuckle. *''Um . . . you are in control, are you not, Mr. Kessler?''*

Kessler quickly offered an apology. He realized that from loss of blood and whatever they were both getting dangerously giddy.

''Mr. Kessler, I will ask that you keep them alive. I am likely to have many questions.''

''You can tell him,'' said Tarrant, ''I'll keep Bandari alive. Alive and feeling pain just as long as I can. Ask him, meanwhile, if it's true that we're dying.''

Peter heard. *''Ah . . . give me one moment, will you please?''*

Kessler looked out. He saw Peter on the police boat being handed a headset. Peter listened a few seconds while shaking his head. He handed the headset back to a policeman.

''Mr. Kessler, I've been asked to tell you that your chances are good as long as you surrender and get the proper attention. That, however, would be a lie. Mr. Tarrant is probably correct.''

Tarrant made a face. Kessler asked, ''How much time?''

''Well . . . The man with the scarf who you left on the dock is reported to be very near death at this moment. The one you threw overboard would be but he drowned. Mr. Tarrant threw something else in the water. Is it true that these were the nuclear devices?''

''He threw only pots. The devices are here.''

"*Before you? In your sight?*" he asked with clear relief.

"The one that is leaking is here on the floor. The one still intact was left in the galley. You haven't quite answered. How long do we have?"

"*I don't know yet. I've asked. I'm awaiting an opinion.*"

"Make a guess," said Tarrant. "Is anyone else sick?"

"*Quite a few. About a dozen. Most or all were living aboard yachts in that section. We don't know of any pedestrians yet.*"

Kessler had another question although he thought he knew the answer already. "Mr. Cobb, why didn't you lie?"

"*Because I need you to stay with that boat. I need you to take it . . . the Coast Guard will show you . . . it's a sand bar some twenty-five miles offshore. I need you to run it aground.*"

"And then?"

"*I will . . . tell you as soon as I know.*"

Willis beached the speedboat within a short run to Van Der Meer. The beach at that point was largely deserted except for some ocean front homes set well back. He was helping first Jasmine, then Aisha from the boat when he saw Nadia's car burst over the dunes. He motioned for Nadia to stay with the car. She ignored him.

She ran first to Aisha and let out a gasp at the sight of the shard still protruding from her ribs. The blood immediately around it had clotted. The mass made it look like an exit wound.

"It's not as bad as it looks," Willis told her. Nadia seemed about to hit him for taking her. Jasmine stepped between them, her hand shielding her eyes. She said, "This isn't bad either. Thank you for asking. Let's argue some other time."

"Help me push this back out," said Elizabeth to Willis. She was watching the flotilla now two miles out to sea. The *Alhambra*, the patrol boat and the black-hulled police boat had been joined by a helicopter. A second and third

Coast Guard boat were approaching from the direction of Savannah Harbor.

"You heard them on the radio. You can't help him, Elizabeth." He said this to her gently. He tried to take her arm. She warned him with a look. He backed off.

"Elizabeth . . ." Aisha took her hand instead. "Come with us. To the office. He promised he'd call."

"She will like hell," Nadia hissed through her teeth. "I was grateful before but today wipes that out. This woman is no friend to any Muslim."

"This woman," said Willis, "didn't try to cook this island. Those were Muslims who did that if you haven't noticed. Martin Kessler's out there dying and it's Muslims who killed him. Don't you tell me who's my friend."

Elizabeth made a gesture. It said never mind. She took off her dark glasses and handed them to Jazz. Her eyes flashed an apology for only thinking of it now. She said, "You all go. I'll stay here."

"If you do I'm staying with you," said Jasmine. "I need a dark room real bad but I'll stay."

"Me, too," said Aisha who still held her hand.

"Except what if he needs you?" Jazz asked her quietly. "What if he's trying to call you right now?"

Thirty-eight

Kessler, his head beginning to droop, was steering while listening to radio traffic. Much of it consisted of boats being warned that a twenty-mile area was now under quarantine. The first helicopter that appeared overhead had evidently been chartered by reporters. Kessler remembered that Tarrant told his caller to go and turn on the news. This thing must be flashing all over the world now. A nuclear terrorist attack on America.

A pair of military helicopters arrived, he presumed from the Marine Air Base on Parris Island. They chased off the reporters, then hovered upwind. Both were armed with machine guns and rockets. One of them was aiming some other device at him. It was not a weapon. Perhaps a listening device.

"Mr. Kessler, are you there?" Peter's voice.

"I'm still with you."

"Reduce your speed to five knots. Steer for the patrol boat ahead and to your right. When you feel your hull run aground, cut your engines."

He felt the soft groan as the hull settled in. He found the switch marked *Main Anchor*, and threw it. He did not cut the engines; he left them in neutral. That way they at least would have electrical power without relying on batteries.

"Well done, Mr. Kessler. Good job."

"You're welcome. What now?"

"Give me a minute. I'm getting a reading from one of

those helicopters. Let's see what we're dealing with here."

The radio was silent for several long moments. Kessler could see a man in the helicopter speaking but apparently the radio he was using was secure. Tarrant used this time to switch on a television that was in a small sitting room off the bridge. In that room was also a bar. Tarrant found only fruit drinks. This apparently inspired another kick at Bandari when Tarrant returned to the bridge. Bandari barely reacted to the kick. He seemed to have gone into shock.

"Mr. Kessler . . . here it is." Peter's voice came back. His tone did not foreshadow good news. *"The device in that helicopter . . . I saw that you were watching it . . . is called a sodium iodide crystal detector. What it does is sniff gamma rays. Your boat, I'm afraid, produced a very high reading. You cannot survive it, Mr. Kessler."*

Kessler grunted. He repeated, "So, what now?"

"For now, we sit and wait. If there is anything we can drop that will make you more comfortable, make a list and I'll see what we can do. What we're waiting for is a special team called NEST. That stands for a Nuclear Energy Search Team. It's been dispatched by Department of Energy's Office of Emergency Response. NEST is trained and equipped to contain contamination. Their vessel is sailing from Newport News. It is due in about four hours."

"They come in four hours. What then?"

"Ah . . . Mr. Kessler, I see that your engines are running. I'm obliged to tell you that if you try to back off . . ."

"We know that there is nowhere to go. Kindly finish."

"My understanding is this." He paused and took a breath. *"The first thing they'll do is place a boom around that yacht and then cover it with a tent made of nylon that they're bringing. They will then pump a special dense foam into the tent. When they've finished, that foam will be several meters thick."*

"It will suffocate us?"

"If . . . that's the end you choose. There must be a cabin you can close yourself off in. I mean, at least you

*needn't be drowning in foam. As I said, however, there
are things we can drop. Medications, narcotics . . . and of
course you have weapons. Mr. Kessler, I do not enjoy
saying these things.''*

Kessler glanced at Tarrant who was staring at the radio.
Bandari hadn't moved but his color was draining. It was
shock or maybe faking. Kessler kept him in view.

*''Ah . . . Mr. Kessler, I've been handed a message. Are
we sure that's Lawrence Tarrant who is on that boat with
you?''*

"You heard from Grand Cayman? This is Tarrant. That
wasn't.''

''Then who got off Tarrant's plane? A double?''

"It's some banker. Mr. Cobb . . . could we talk about
this foam?''

''Oh. Of course.''

"So they pump several meters. What's next?''

*''After that, in all likelihood, some tests will be con-
ducted before we will attempt to remove the devices. I'm
going to ask you to leave them in the middle of the quarter
deck because a robot is going to be sent in to retrieve
them. It's a robot called ATOM, appropriately enough.
That stands for . . .''*

Kessler didn't much care what it stood for but he understood what Peter was trying to do. He was like a doctor
who explained how he'll do an operation so if you die,
you at least knew he wasn't using a corkscrew. ATOM
stood for Automated Tether-Operated Manipulator. It
sounded more like a sexual gratification device.

"Tell him to send some Jack Daniel's,'' said Tarrant.

"Jack Daniel's?''

"He asked what I need. What I need is a drink. But
this clown took everything out of his bar lest Ozal think
he's less than devout. And some ice. They've used up all
the ice.''

''I heard him,'' said Peter. *''What else?''*

"A gasoline chain saw.'' Tarrant spoke to the radio.
"We'll need one to clear the way for the robot.''

''Is he serious?'' asked Peter. *''He'd go to that trouble?''*

Kessler wondered himself. He looked into Tarrant's eyes. He saw the beginnings of a smile. "I think he wants it to dismember Bandari. No chain saw, just the bourbon, the ice and some beer. A good German beer, St. Pauli Girl maybe, and also a pack of Swisher Sweets."

"*Swisher Sweets?*"

"Small cigars. You should try them. It's a way to meet new friends. Also you might send us something for pain. Tarrant and I are both shot."

It was then that Bandari came suddenly alive. He made his lunge for the knife that Tarrant brought from the galley. He slashed at Tarrant who dodged sideways to avoid him. Kessler whistled at him loudly through his teeth. Bandari froze. Kessler tapped one finger on the Walther in his hand to remind Bandari that it was not a banana. But Bandari kept the knife. He jabbed it, feebly, toward Kessler's chest although Kessler was at least three paces away. He gestured as if to say, "*Get out of my chair. I want to get at the controls.*"

"To do what? Sail away? You haven't been listening."

"*Mr. Kessler? What's happening? Is there trouble on the bridge?*"

"My radio," gasped Bandari. "Move away from my radio. I demand to talk. I demand that you protect me from this criminal, Tarrant."

Tarrant had to smile. "You're asking *him* to protect you?"

"You want to talk, talk from there," Kessler told him.

Tarrant slapped his own forehead. "Ah! Where are my manners? I've never introduced you to the man who carved up Pratt. This is Martin Kessler. He carved up all three. He pulled their tongues out through their throats while they were conscious. Mahfouz, by the way, still had your fucking Rolex. They found it pinned to the end of his tongue."

Bandari's chin dropped. His lower lip quivered.

"Look at his belt. You see that thing in his belt all smeared with old blood? That's the tool he uses to open up throats. The tongue then flops down like a fish."

Kessler looked at his belt. It was Elizabeth's trowel. He had almost forgotten he had it.

Bandari mouthed unmistakably, "Oh, God."

"And you see, there's another thing," Tarrant said brightly. "He's a Communist. A Marxist. They don't believe in God. Nothing pisses them off more than people who do. Tell him you believe in God, Bandari, and watch him shoot off your dick when you say it."

"Mr. Kessler . . . Martin. What's happening there?"

"Mr. Tarrant is expressing resentment," he said dryly.

Bandari found his voice. He was screaming at the radio and the veins at his temples were bulging. Kessler let him scream. It might bring on a stroke. That would spare him from being entombed with this man. Tarrant, at least, might be interesting company.

Bandari was demanding an immediate rescue on pain of severed relations with Egypt. He told Peter that he was a man of great influence; a friend and adviser to the president of Egypt. Next he claimed that he had pretended to work with Lawrence Tarrant to keep Tarrant from starting a terrible war. This war was for the Libyans and for Tarrant and his bankers. He, Bandari, had thwarted this scheme by burying the weapons under cement in a warehouse owned by his brother. His brother was a good man whom Tarrant had murdered. He had also thwarted the terrorist, Ozal, in his plan to bring America to its knees. As proof, he said, he could produce Ozal's maps showing where Ozal intended to attack. And this man, this Kessler, was a murderer as well. "He and the Algerian, you just heard it admitted, they murdered three men and pulled out their tongues and used my stolen watch for a frame-up."

"Um . . . Mr. Kessler . . . are you there?"

"I'm here."

"Does that man understand the position he's in?"

"I don't think he wants to, so he doesn't."

"What warehouse was that he was talking about?"

"Willis knows. Ask him. But be careful who's listening."

"Willis is trying to get through to me now. Is that what his call is about?"

"Yes it is." Willis and Elizabeth must be back at Van Der Meer.

"*What, by the way, are those maps Bandari mentioned?*"

"Ozal's plan of attack? I don't know. I'll look. More interesting, I think, might be some recordings in the briefcase that Tarrant carried on board." Kessler looked up at Tarrant. "I assume you don't mind."

Tarrant shrugged indifferently. He was moving toward the shotgun and away from the knife. "At least let me blow off his feet," Tarrant said.

Kessler told him to behave. One thing at a time.

"As for Pratt," he told Peter, "that was me and me alone."

"*Not . . . you and a certain . . . um . . . angel you know?*"

"There is no such angel. She doesn't exist."

A pause. "*In fact, that's pretty much what they tell me.*"

"Willis will confirm it. I have your word?"

"*Cooperate, Mr. Kessler, and you have my guarantee.*"

"Talk to Willis. Call me back when you're finished."

Roy Willis was pacing Nadia Halaby's office as he waited to be put through to Peter. He had asked before that to be patched through to Kessler. He had promised to do so to make Elizabeth stay but he was told that no contact with the yacht would be permitted except indirectly through Peter.

He had taken her apron, her scarf and hooded sweatshirt and had given her a Van Der Meer warm-up suit instead. He had used Jasmine's compress to wipe the blood from her hands, the blood from the throat of the man she had stabbed. She did not resist him. She seemed in a daze. She stood, staring out through a window toward the east, toward the ocean although she could not see it from there. The flotilla was in any case now over the horizon. Several times she had whispered Martin's name.

A woman in her twenties, dressed as a housekeeper,

arrived with a medical bag in her hand. She mumbled a greeting and, asking no questions, proceeded to examine first Aisha, then Jasmine. Elizabeth blinked herself back to the present. She turned from the window and stood watching the woman as, briskly, efficiently, she injected Aisha with a local anesthetic and then put a salve in Jasmine's scorched eyes. When Aisha's injection had taken effect she removed the shard from her side with some effort, then cleaned and stitched the wound and dressed it. She gave a second injection to Aisha, this one an antibiotic. That done, she spoke briefly to Nadia in Arabic. Her manner seemed apologetic, regretful. Nadia touched her cheek and thanked her. The woman picked up her bag and left the room.

"What's wrong?" asked Elizabeth. "Why did she look sad?"

"It's nothing. We'll be fine," Aisha told her.

"Don't tell me it's nothing. What is it?"

"She's a medical student. Or she was back in Syria. She feels bad because I'm going to have a crooked scar and she didn't have the skill to make it smaller."

"I'll . . . take you to someone. A plastic surgeon."

"Elizabeth . . . who cares about a scar?"

"It's just that . . ."

"Oh, wait." She brightened. "Roy got through to that man."

Elizabeth crossed the room. She stood at Roy's side waiting less than patiently as he listened and nodded. She heard him confirm that the man on board was Tarrant and she heard him recite the location of the warehouse and its layout as Aisha had described it to him. She came close to ripping the phone from his hands until he saw her eyes and said, "Kessler's still alive."

But she also saw his eyes. Her chest heaved. "What else?"

"He's alive. All three are. Kessler's still in control."

"Damn it, Willis, will he make it? Are they taking him off?"

"Ah . . . Peter's trying to tell me what they're going to do next. It's okay. He even asked for a beer."

Now Elizabeth paced. More listening and nodding. Nadia moved as if to touch her but she let her hand drop. Elizabeth found herself staring at faces on the wall. Framed photos. All women. Most bordered in black. Among those that were not she saw the face of Rada Khoury. She was older, a bit fleshier, but the eyes were as strong and as kind as they were when they first looked into hers and poured life-giving water on her lips. And near her, among those bordered in black, was the face of Nasreen Zayed. A good face. Intelligent. Plain and simple. No nonsense. Nasreen had stayed forever young. Elizabeth wondered if those two would have saved her had they known what she would become.

"Elizabeth?" Roy had put down the phone.

She spun. "Can I talk to him? Can they patch you through?"

"Yeah, they can. But not just now. Elizabeth, let's you and me go for a walk."

Elizabeth felt Aisha squeezing her hand. And she felt light-headed, as if she might float. "Just tell me," she said.

"Aisha, you stay here. Elizabeth . . . please."

"I'll come with you," said Aisha.

"Not this time," Willis told her. "We'll be back in a while."

Bandari had returned to his place in the corner. Making hardly a sound he had slid to the floor, the knife still held loosely in his fingers. Kessler paid no attention as long as he was quiet. It was Tarrant who noticed that something had changed.

"Look at Bandari. Look at his eyes."

Kessler glanced at him expecting that the eyes would show despair. The odd thing was that they showed nothing. Not fear, not even sickness or fever. Tarrant took a step. He poked him with his foot. The eyes did not blink in response. Tarrant reached down and plucked the knife from his fingers. There was no resistance. The fingers remained limp.

Tarrant muttered a curse. His disappointment was profound.

"I think he's in Never-Never Land," he said to Kessler. "Can a mind just blink off? Have you ever seen it happen?"

Kessler shook his head no. Elizabeth had, she once told him, but he himself had not. Elizabeth had seen it in Az Zahran Prison where some women would go to a place in their minds and never again come back out.

Tarrant saw the stain that was spreading at his crotch. "Well, let's toss him down the steps before something else goes. I'd rather not be entombed smelling shit."

This man was nothing if not pragmatic, thought Kessler. Revenge was one thing, clean air was another. As if to prove it, he said, "You won't need your gun. Put it down and come help me." He tossed the knife out the window.

"If you try for me again, you won't get a second chance."

"Relax. As it happens, I don't like to drink alone."

They dragged Bandari by one arm and by his collar through the shattered door that led aft. Bandari's lips moved but they made no sound as his body swept a path through the broken glass that Elizabeth's shots had spread over the floor.

"*Mr. Kessler? What's happening?*" Peter's voice on the radio. One of the helicopters hovered low for a look. A crewman seemed ready to fire his weapon. Kessler returned to the radio and explained that the issue at the moment was hygiene.

"*Okay, but don't throw him overboard. Sit him in a deck chair where we can observe him. While you're at it, leave those warheads out with him.*"

"On the subject of warheads, you've spoken to Willis?"

"*I have, and thank you. We have people on their way to that warehouse right now. I have also explained your situation to him. He will . . . pass it along where appropriate.*"

Kessler wanted to tell him that he'd do his own passing

but he knew that every scanner on the island would be working if they thought that he would try to place a call.

"Mr. Kessler, look west. Here come your supplies."

A third Marine helicopter was approaching from the mainland. It was lowering a bundle at the end of a cable. He and Tarrant dragged Bandari down the steps to the deck and lifted him onto a plastic chaise lounge. That done, Tarrant went into the galley and came out with the canister that contained the unused warhead. He held it up for Peter to see and then placed it at Bandari's side. He hobbled up the stairs and found the one that was leaking. Again he held it up for Peter to see but this one he shoved down Bandari's soiled pants. No reaction from Bandari, not a blink. Tarrant frowned, disappointed, until he looked up and saw that this was all being photographed. That pleased him. It would make the front pages in Cairo. But he had little time to pose with Bandari. The new helicopter was almost overhead.

Kessler, meanwhile, found a light piece of line in an inflatable dinghy that was lashed to the deck. At one end was a bucket made out of canvas, a sea anchor used to slow a boat's drift. He used the line to secure Bandari. He kept the sea anchor. It had given him a thought. For now, however, he moved to help Tarrant who was trying, with his bad leg, to grab the swaying cable in order to unhook a large duffel.

Willis took the call in Nadia's office. He recognized Kessler's voice and accent at once. It said, "My Nadia, she is behaving, I hope?"

"Your . . . Nadia said she needed to be by herself. This was after I told her what was going to happen. Listen, Kessler . . . is there anything at all that we can do for you?"

"What you can do is go find her. Don't leave her alone."

"She promised she'd stay on the grounds."

"Go find her. Stay with her. You don't know this woman. I'll look out and I'll see her trying to get to this boat again and if she comes near they will shoot her."

"I'll go right now. We'll all go."

"Leave someone by that phone. And write down this number."

Willis jotted it down.

"When you find her, you tell her this is not a big problem."

"I'm afraid she already knows better than that."

"Yes, but also she knows that I'm like a bad penny. You tell her that Reineke the Fox isn't finished. You tell her I'll be walking up her driveway one day and she'd better have a nice ice-cold drink ready for me. Tell her that exactly. A nice ice-cold drink."

Tarrant looked at him curiously as he handed him his beer. They had moved from the bridge to the adjoining salon. It had the bar, plush upholstery, and the windows were intact. It had doors that could be closed against the foam. Tarrant had heard what he told Willis.

"Ah . . . you're not cracking up on me, too, are you?"

"I'll be fine."

"I can feel myself starting to glow in the dark and you're making plans for the future?"

Kessler shrugged.

"What, by the way, is that sea anchor for?"

"I'm keeping it handy. I'm a little bit nauseous."

"What's the matter with puking over the side?"

"This way I don't have to get up."

Tarrant had poured his own Jack Daniel's, drained half a tumbler, and was sorting through the rest of the duffel. At the bottom was a kit marked U.S. Marines. It contained the necessities for combat wound dressings. Bandages, sulfa drugs, morphine syrettes. There were two dozen extra syrettes on the side, more than enough to overdose both of them. There was also a pharmacy-size bottle of Nembutal tablets. Someone had written, "Take at least thirty each." And someone had added a Bible.

"Your friend, Peter, likes to cover all the bases," he noted. "Will you use the morphine, the pills or a bullet?"

Kessler didn't answer. He was thinking of Elizabeth. After all this trouble, if she did something crazy, this time

he was finished and he meant it. A slight lurch of the
yacht made him stiffen. It was only the boat trying to
swing with the tide but a part of his mind saw Elizabeth
arriving. She was riding on the back of a whale. Hallu-
cinations, he realized. Not good. As he'd feared, his brain
was not getting enough blood.

Tarrant studied a syrette. He made a face at the needle.
He blurted, "Listen, Kessler, you don't have to like me.
But I'm all you've got. It won't kill you to talk."

Kessler thought he heard a crack in Tarrant's voice. The
reality of dying was beginning to set in. Perhaps to conceal it, Tarrant picked up the Bible. He thumbed through
it as he paced the salon. He might have been seeking
comfort in scripture but Kessler somehow doubted that
that was the case.

The TV, turned low, showed an aerial picture of this
boat taken when it first arrived at the sand bar. The an-
nouncer was saying that this other ship was coming, the
one that was equipped to contain radiation. Kessler heard
him say one more hour, maybe sooner. Kessler needed to
stay conscious at least until then, at least until they covered the boat with that tent.

Find her, Willis. Find her for me.

I would like to hear her voice one more time.

Tarrant had opened the book to Jeremiah. He was looking
for the place his late banker friend referred to when he
said that the justification for a war was all there. It never
hurt, he supposed, to have God on your side, although
that crowd would have found all the justification they
needed when they saw how much money they could
make.

Jeremiah, however, did seem to say it. A great destruction would come from the north. It would come because,
down in the south, the lion has come up from the thicket
and the destroyer of the Gentiles is on his way. The destroyer of Gentiles must be Islam rising up.

"Do you believe in an after-life, Kessler?"

". . . Excuse me?"

"I asked if you believe in life after death."

"Yes . . . I suppose. Yes, I do."

"Do you really? A Marxist?"

"You know nothing of Marxism."

"Shame on me then for misleading Bandari. Tell me what makes you believe."

"I believe because I choose to believe. What is the point in not hoping?"

Tarrant sniffed. "Ozal hoped and look where that got us. Ozal and his soldiers come from a world where there's almost no hope for any kind of a life. It's the same in our own urban ghettos, for that matter. Except the people in the ghettos don't get to be martyrs. They don't get to blow themselves up on some school bus and go straight to a heaven where they get to screw virgins. Ozal and his soldiers had hope up the ass. If they get there, and we don't, there's something wrong with the system."

"You can have my virgins if we get there."

"I'm serious. Do you know what Napoleon said about religion?"

Kessler lit a Swisher Sweet. Tarrant poured another bourbon.

"He said religion has always had one very useful role. It keeps the poor from killing the rich."

Kessler nodded slowly.

"You'd agree?"

"On the whole."

"But I don't suppose Napoleon had the Muslims in mind. That's the one religion that's willing to kill."

"I . . . think you should read some more of that Bible. Everyone in it is killing everyone else and it's almost always for God. What were you going to do with those warheads, by the way?"

"That was different. It was business."

"I see."

Kessler wondered how Elizabeth would have answered. She would probably have defended the Muslims. She would not admit to hating them and maybe she really didn't. At least not a lot of their women.

He and Elizabeth, one year, had traveled through southern Spain. Anyone who visited Cordoba or Grenada couldn't help but admire what the Muslims had built there in the three hundred years they ruled Spain. Cordoba, at its peak, was the world's greatest city. Cordoba, by the year A.D. 1000, had more books in just one of its libraries than were in all the rest of Europe combined. It had baths and lit streets, running water and toilets when the English, for example, only bathed when it rained. Everyone could read, everyone studied because the Muslims believed that in knowledge is greatness.

How it all fell apart is the same old story. Weak leaders, corruption, betrayal. For a thousand years, straight downhill. But now we have Muslims who want it all back. Their revolt—and Elizabeth would be the first to say it—was against not the West but their own humiliation. They want to revive the old vigor of Islam. To understand this, simply visit Cordoba. After that, take a look at today's Egypt.

Egypt and almost every other Arab country was ruled by a government that had no legitimacy in the eyes of the people it governed. No notion of a compact between ruler and ruled. It was like the Communist system in that sense, but at least the Communists had a philosophy that included taking care of the people. There was not a single government that would not be overthrown in favor of an Islamic society. Why Islamic? Because everything else had been tried and only Islam ever brought them together. The trick is to get Islam to do it again if those people could stop fighting each other long enough. Tarrant thought they were all like Ozal, wanting to kill Westerners for the sake of revenge. But when Muslims sat around talking wild jihad fantasies, most of these were against each other, not the West. They hated each other because they hated themselves. When you got so low you had to find someone lower. With Muslims, what was handy was their women.

"We should have used anthrax," said Tarrant.

"What?"

"Anthrax. Not nukes. Pulmonary anthrax." Tarrant's voice was slurring from too much Jack Daniel's. "I read that the kill rate is ninety-nine percent. And it would have been a hell of a lot easier to get.''

''This is . . . what you've concluded at the end of the day?''

''You remember that Japanese cult? They spread Sarin in the subways? That was their mistake.''

''Look, Tarrant, I don't wish to talk about this.''

''The problem with Sarin is it works right away. With anthrax, no one would have known where it came from because they wouldn't get sick until a day or two later. The Japs who placed it would have been long gone.''

''Excuse me. I need to make a phone call,'' said Kessler.

A woman answered but it was Jasmine. With effort, Kessler forced a smile into his voice. He ignored her questions, asked with deference and respect, about his own condition and prospects. The main thing, he told her, was that Tarrant and Bandari would never cause them trouble again. Kessler asked if she knew where Elizabeth had gone.

She said that they had found her, Willis and Nadia. They found her at the beach near that boat they had taken. She was simply standing, staring out to sea. She would not or could not speak when they approached her. They stayed with her as he, Kessler, had asked. Roy Willis won't let her endanger herself.

''With Elizabeth, it's not a question of letting. The girl . . . is she with her? She will listen to the girl.''

''No. Aisha is here with me.''

''I saw Aisha bleeding.''

''It's not so bad. Just a cut. It's been treated.''

''I want to speak to the girl if you will allow it.''

''I'll allow any damned thing you want, Mr. Kessler.''

Aisha came to the phone. Her voice was very small. She asked if it was true that he was not coming back. He said, ''Don't believe all you hear.''

''Roy . . . told her what you said. That you're like a bad penny.''

''Did he tell her the rest? About a nice ice-cold drink?''

"I don't know. Is that important? I'll tell her."

"Never mind. Instead I need to trust you with something. Above all, I want you to take care of Elizabeth. You will be all she has until I see her again. And remind her that I've got out of worse scrapes than this. Tell her to show you my comic books. You'll see."

"Um . . . comic books?"

"She'll explain. Now here is what I need you to do . . ."

"Speaking of nice ice-cold drinks . . ."

Tarrant scooped some more ice and poured himself another. He then proceeded to finish what he had been saying about what those Japanese cultists should have done. Here was a man, thought Kessler, whose spiritual side seemed seriously underdeveloped. One would think he'd be considering some sort of plea bargain if there was a final reckoning waiting. One would think he'd want to be sober for the occasion.

But no, he wanted to show off his knowledge of how to depopulate cities.

He was saying now that a few grams of spores, well placed, would kill everyone in, say, a major government office. It would spread through the air conditioning system. But a subway was even better. The convection currents caused by passing trains would spread it throughout the whole system. You do this while people are going to work because the anthrax spores would cling to their clothing as well. The spores would be carried into businesses, restaurants, and later back to their homes in the suburbs. The next day tens of thousands are dropping like flies. He said that getting the anthrax should be no great problem. A dozen or more laboratories keep it on hand. Bribe a technician or just go and take it.

Tarrant's spiritual side was revealed, after a fashion, when he got to the part of who would do it and why. The Muslims, of course. They would love the idea. What the Japanese showed them was how to think big. The most dangerous terrorists are those who are motivated by ethnic and religious hatreds, not politics. Their goal, therefore, was not political control but the utter destruction of their enemies. The Japanese taught them, forget about shootings, forget about throwing grenades into buses. Using anthrax was not only better theater, it's your duty. Did God spit at the world or did he start Noah's flood? Learn from God. Divine retribution should be cataclysmic. Did you think God made anthrax for nothing?

Kessler tried to close his ears to this and focus on Elizabeth. He could see her standing at the edge of the surf looking out through those wonderful eyes.

Since it was his vision he chose to see her weeping. More likely, however, she was calling him names. With Elizabeth, a "damn you" comes close to "I love you," but for now he preferred the actual words.

"*I do love you, Martin.*" She did not hide her tears.

"*I know. But it's nice to hear you say it at last.*"

"*It's because I've been stupid. It has always been you.*"

"*And for me, for ten years, there has been only you.*"

"*Bullshit, Martin.*"

"*Beg pardon?*"

"*You're saying you were celibate that whole year you were gone?*"

You see? That's Elizabeth. Even in your mind she won't stick to the script. So, okay. We'll start over. "*I do love you, Martin.*"

"*I know. But it's nice to . . .*"

"*Except those short pants. You cannot wear short pants. Would Reineke the Fox be caught dead in short pants?*"

"*Elizabeth . . .*"

Caught dead was today not a figure of speech.

"*And about that cigar. Put it out. It stinks.*"

At this, Elizabeth's voice became unpleasant. Her voice had changed, it was deeper and slurring. It took Kessler a moment to realize it was Tarrant's. In his mind, Elizabeth shimmered and vanished. Kessler tried to call her back but she was gone.

"Swisher Sweets?" asked Tarrant. He was looking at the package.

"Do I tell you what brand of bourbon to drink?"

"It sounds like something a faggot would smoke."

Too bad, thought Kessler, that he'd asked for only beer. A frozen daiquiri would have made the picture complete.

"Do I tell you that bourbon makes you boring and nasty? You're starting to be not such good company."

"Yeah, well screw you, Kessler. You're no company at all. At least I'm . . ."

Kessler raised the Walther. He fired.

Thirty-nine

Another day had passed before men in white spacesuits were able to board the yacht *Alhambra*. They had entered through the hole that was left by the robot. The robot had secured the one leaking warhead and had placed it in a lead-lined compartment. Even so, its reading of radioactivity remained well above lethal levels.

The robot, called ATOM, was equipped with a television camera. Above the lens was a pair of small jets that blew CO_2 gas to make cavities in the foam so that the camera was able to see. The camera saw the man who had been tied to the chaise. The chaise was twisted; it was on its side. The man's body was contorted, his eyes wide with terror. This man had been thought to be dead or unconscious when the foam was pumped under the tent the day before. The foam had clearly revived him. Then it drowned him.

The robot could not see beyond the rear deck. It could not report anything of what had happened on the bridge or in the small salon just beyond. Nothing had been heard since the previous afternoon when they managed to get fragments of a telephone call that seemed to have been made from a cell phone on the yacht. It remained for the men in protective suits to explore.

They found one man dead. A bullet through his forehead. He was dressed in a suit jacket, white shirt and necktie but the odd thing was that his legs were bare. Underwear, black socks, but no trousers. A black briefcase had been left on his chest. Several maps, marked in Arabic, were folded on top of it. Near his body they found a pair of madras shorts that the other man, with him, had been seen to be wearing. The other man, Kessler, was nowhere in sight.

"He's somewhere on board," said Peter Cobb into their earphones. "Knowing Kessler, he's playing a practical joke."

They searched every stateroom, the galley, the engine room. They searched the heads and the pantry. They waded through the foam that had filled the bridge, forced in through the shot-out windows to starboard.

"He's not here," they reported. "There's no other body."

"Well, there is. We'll find him when we blow off the foam. Bring the maps and that briefcase when you come."

That evening Peter lifted the quarantine that he'd placed on the whole of the Harbour Town area. But for a few hot spots near the yacht's former slip, the readings of radioactivity were deemed safe. Remaining hot, however, were several other yachts that had been berthed in the immediate vicinity. Those were towed out to sea for decontamination by other crews wearing protective clothing and helmets. About two dozen yacht owners, crew and guests had been air-lifted to the Methodist Medical Center in Oak Ridge, Tennessee. That hospital had the country's only ER that was equipped to treat cases of nuclear radiation poisoning. A few were listed as serious, two critical. All but these were expected to survive but all would be monitored for the rest of their lives, especially those women of child-bearing age.

The tennis tournament was allowed to continue after a two-day delay. A number of the seeded players had left but their departures encouraged the qualifiers to stay. For most it was a chance that didn't come along often.

More than forty FBI agents were brought onto the island and teams from several other agencies as well. The FBI interviewed every witness and participant, beginning with those involved in the shootings that preceded the attempt to set off that bomb. The doctor, Leidner, was no help whatever. He remembered nothing of the men who assaulted him and who apparently had murdered another doctor at his house. Leidner, who had been clubbed and then kicked in the head, hardly even remembered that he'd gone to the tournament.

They identified the man who had been shot near the trailers, the one who had Rollerblades wrapped around his neck. They were questioning two others who wore similar jackets and were believed to have been in Lawrence Tarrant's employ. They identified another who had been almost decapitated by the former East German spy, Martin Kessler. There were witnesses who said that a woman had stabbed him, a woman in a kerchief and a gardening apron who hid her face behind big dark glasses.

This, however, could not have been true. The woman, who indeed had matched that description, was with Peter Cobb at the time. This same woman chased after the terrorists' yacht in the company of a former DEA agent and others. She herself was a Muslim, one Nadia Halaby, who was outraged that Muslims would do anything so stupid, so utterly contrary to the teachings of Islam. She produced the clothing she'd been wearing that day, an apron, a hooded sweatshirt and a scarf. She had no prior knowledge of this man, Bandari, or of the German named Kessler.

The FBI determined that a girl in her charge had been missing on a night some ten days before this when a man named Pratt was believed to have been killed. Pratt and two Muslims had been found a few days later. Those three were believed to have been killed by Martin Kessler who, impossibly, had now vanished from Gamal Bandari's yacht. Who was this girl and what connection did she have with the events surrounding this terrorist act? Peter Cobb was able to attest that she had none. Her name, said Cobb, was Cherokee Blye. She had come, with Halaby, that day to watch tennis. She went on that boat with Halaby because she wouldn't stay behind. Children can be willful, they do stupid things. But that was the extent of her involvement.

 *   *   *

"I feel foolish even asking," Peter Cobb said to Willis, "but have any of you heard from Martin Kessler?"

Willis shook his head. "Could there be any chance . . ."

"None," Peter answered. "Put it out of your mind. Martin Kessler is dead three times over."

"Then why ask?"

"Because he's making me crazy. Because you said he promised to come back and see Stride."

"She's gone too. We can't find her. She's run."

"But why?" Peter asked. "I've kept my word to Kessler. She's in no way involved. Only Nadia."

A sad smile washed over the face of Roy Willis. He answered, "She might have had a date."

"Don't start."

"Like I told you," said Willis, "she owed him a drink."

Peter Cobb knew well where Kessler had to be. He had seen him pick up and examine that sea anchor when they carried Bandari out onto the deck. He knew that Kessler had waited until the tent was in place and until the NEST ship started pumping the foam. The outgoing tide was steady and strong. It had nearly lifted that yacht from the sand bar. What Kessler had done was ease over the side, between the hull and the boom with the tent attached to it.

He had executed Tarrant. Peter thought he knew why. Very likely to keep Tarrant from using the radio and alerting them that Kessler was gone. Or perhaps to keep Tarrant from destroying that briefcase and burning the maps of the terrorist, Ozal. The maps were interesting; they would lead, no doubt, to some changes in security arrangements here and there. But as a serious scheme to cause economic havoc, he doubted that Ozal had the means or the manpower. It was, more likely, one of those pipe dreams that terrorists are fond of sitting around and discussing, in the hope of getting funding from Libya or Iran. Tarrant's recordings, however, were a gold mine.

Even more so was the briefcase of that banker on Grand Cayman. That one had recordings of its own. And names. Surprising names. By tomorrow they would all hear a knock on their doors.

But for now, back to Kessler.

He had swum under water as far as he was able, the sea anchor helping to pull him along. He probably surfaced more than once to get air. The sun was low. The glare on the water would have helped him go unseen. No one would have been watching the seaward side. There was nothing out there before Portugal.

Still, why would he do it? He could have died comfortably. Trailing blood from his belly he might have drawn sharks before he could let his lungs fill with water. All this for what? Just to leave people guessing? And why, for God's sake, would he change into trousers—especially Tarrant's—which he could barely fit into? The whole thing was crazy. Ridiculous.

And yet Peter felt a smile start to tug at his mouth. He remembered how Willis had smiled. Willis was smiling because he wanted to believe that Kessler and Stride were somewhere together. They were clinking their glasses in some distant saloon.

Damned if he didn't want to believe it himself.

Epilogue

A week had passed and then another.

Aisha had stayed. She did not go to New York. Nadia knew that she would have run away if she were sent there. She would have returned to the island somehow and waited for Elizabeth Stride to come back. And she would be back. Aisha knew it in her soul.

Every afternoon since Elizabeth left, Jasmine had driven her to the house on Marsh Drive. The house had not been locked since that day. Aisha searched the kitchen but could not find a key. She walked through the house checking tables and dressers in the hope of finding one there. She could not look further without opening drawers and she could not bring herself to do that. One closet in the bedroom was open, however. There was a space on the floor where a bag might have sat. But Jasmine didn't think she packed anything at all because her toothbrush and razor, her robe and her hair dryer were still in plain view in the bathroom. All that was missing seemed to be her red Bronco.

Aisha would take in her mail each day and the paper that was left in the driveway. The mail consisted only of bills and the odd piece of junk mail addressed to the "Occupant." On every second visit she would sweep off the driveway because the leaves from the big live oak trees were still shedding as new leaves pushed in behind them. She had finished planting the half tray of vinca that Elizabeth had left near the road. On every fourth visit she would water the houseplants and run the lawn sprinklers if there hadn't been rain. She would leave a note saying that this had been done. The note also said, "I must see you. It's important."

One night, her mother appeared in a dream. This had happened before, many times, but this was different. In this dream her mother was sitting with Elizabeth. They were on the big lawn that sloped to the lagoon in the rear of Elizabeth's house. Their backs were toward Aisha. Both their knees were drawn up. They didn't seem to be talking or anything. Just sitting together, almost touching. Enjoying the breeze and the warmth of the sun, watching the mullet jump out of the water, watching the egrets wade the shallows.

At sunrise, during prayer, she remembered the dream. A chill went through her as she thought about its meaning. Either her mother was there on Marsh Drive with Elizabeth or Elizabeth had gone where her parents had gone. The scene from her dream could well have been heaven. She finished her prayers and dressed quickly. She ran down the hall and rapped on Jasmine's door. Ten minutes later, Jasmine still grumbling, Jasmine's car turned into Marsh Drive. She fell silent when she saw the red Bronco. It was dirty. It looked tired. Jasmine turned to Aisha.

"You're a piece of work, kid," she said softly.

Jasmine waited. Aisha knocked. She saw lights but heard no sound. But she did smell coffee. Elizabeth was home. She peered through the beveled glass panels of the door. She saw nothing until she raised her eyes to the sliding glass doors that led back off the living room. She could see through the house and out toward the lagoon. And there she saw Elizabeth, her back to the house.

She was sitting on the grass. Her knees were folded up to her chin as they were in the dream with her mother. She was hugging her knees tightly. It made her top, a white silk blouse, ride up toward her bra baring part of her back. Aisha saw what looked like an ugly round scar. She remembered how Elizabeth had reacted to her own scar and now thought perhaps she knew why.

At Elizabeth's side was not her mother's ghost but only a small blue duffel. As she watched, Elizabeth reached for the duffel and rose slowly, stiffly to her feet. She rocked the duffel forward, then back, and then threw it. She threw it underhand as far as she could. It splashed like the mullet in the middle of the lagoon. Elizabeth sank back to her knees.

"How long have you been there?" she asked, not turning, when she heard Aisha clear her throat behind her.

"Just now."

"What did you see?"

"You're back. You came back. That's all that I care about."

"I saw your note. Thank you."

"Then you're staying?"

"No, I'm not."

"Well . . . I'm like a bad penny, too."

It was the wrong thing to say. She saw Elizabeth swallow. Elizabeth turned her head away even further as if she were trying to hide tears. Aisha knelt at her side.

"I . . . brought you something. Something from Martin. He told me to get it and give it to you."

She reached for a pouch that she wore around her neck and pulled it over her head. "These are diamonds," she said. "Martin wanted you to have them. He said he tried to tell you . . . have a nice ice-cold drink for him . . . but then he was afraid you'd be . . ."

"Too dumb to catch on?" The words caught in her throat.

"He didn't say dumb. He said sad."

Elizabeth made no move to accept the pouch. Aisha set it down by her feet.

"Jasmine and I went and got them from his freezer. Jasmine had to break in but she's good at stuff like that."

Elizabeth said nothing.

"Jasmine kept all his other things. She thought you might want them. She said the FBI would have taken them if we didn't."

Still nothing. One hand wiped an eye.

"Could I ask you a question?"

No answer. But a shrug.

"Why do you think he did that? I mean, swim away? Why didn't he want them to find him?"

"Because he's Martin Kessler." The words burst from her, angrily. "Because he never grew up. Because he's still a boy who likes to play ga . . ." She choked on the last word before she could say it and a great heaving sob rose up in her chest. She bolted to her feet before Aisha could touch her. She moved several steps to be out of her reach and stood hunched with both hands pressed hard against her mouth. She said, "Damn him." She said it twice more. The third time was only a whisper.

Aisha was not sure that she could speak either. But she had to; she had promised Martin that she would. She glanced behind her as if looking for help. She saw Jasmine standing at the side of the house. Jasmine took a step back and put a finger to her lips. She held up a hand and waved it a little. The gesture said, "*Stay. I'll be waiting out front.*"

"I have things to tell you," she said to Elizabeth. "I'll start with the easiest. I have a picture to show you."

She held it up so that Elizabeth could see it. Elizabeth only glanced. "That's my neighbor. What about her?"

It was a photo of the woman two doors up with the poodle; the one who told Aisha Elizabeth's name.

"Roy Willis took the picture. Now Mr. Cobb has it. There's a file on a bunch of Elizabeth Strides. There's a new one on you. They had to start it because word got around that another Elizabeth lives here on this island. This picture now goes with that file. Do you get it?"

Elizabeth hesitated.

"From now on anyone who looks at that file will see that you can't be that other Elizabeth. You don't have to be, either. Not anymore."

Elizabeth didn't speak for a very long moment. She started to form words several times before she spoke them. Finally, she asked, "What . . . do you think of that Elizabeth Stride?"

"I don't know. I'm not sure. I only know you."

"Aisha . . . I think you understand what I'm asking."

"Um . . . I'm Cherokee again for a while."

A sigh. "Never mind."

"No, wait, Elizabeth. I'm really not sure. But I can tell you what Jasmine thinks. Jasmine says she would have done the same thing in your place. She's not just talking; I don't know if I told you, but . . ."

"She's been in prison. You did."

"Nadia says . . . well, she thinks you're scary. But if it's true that you once cut off a man's hand, she wanted to do the same thing to my uncle."

Elizabeth looked away. She said nothing.

"And Mr. Willis . . . he likes you. The only thing he feels bad about . . . he wishes he had known Martin Kessler. Um . . . you . . . weren't with him these past two weeks, were you?"

"No. No, I wasn't with Martin."

"You know what I bet Jasmine? I bet you went to France. I bet you went to see Rada Khoury."

"I thought about that. But I didn't."

"Martin asked me to tell you something. Except not right away. He said I should make you say it first."

"That I love him?"

"I don't know. Are you saying it?"

"Listen, Aisha . . . Cherokee." A shuddering breath. "I don't think I can handle this right now."

Aisha had left her. She went into the house through the rear sliding doors. She returned with a mug of steaming coffee and handed the mug to Elizabeth. They stood in silence a while longer.

"I lost both my parents. You know that," said Aisha.

Elizabeth sipped from her mug.

"I miss them but I don't really feel that they're gone. I feel them with me. They talk to me sometimes. I know they're in heaven because they both died as martyrs. They died for trying to do a good thing."

Elizabeth thought of Pratt's tape that was still in the

duffel, now bubbling from the bottom of her lagoon. She reached to touch Aisha. "I know."

"That they did a good thing? Or that they're still with me?"

"I know . . . that they're still in your heart."

"Not just in my heart. They're here. They're not gone. Martin Kessler isn't gone either."

Elizabeth sighed deeply. "Cherokee . . . listen. It's good that you have your faith . . ."

"I'm not talking about Islam. This isn't just Islam. Martin Kessler is a martyr by anyone's faith. He's a martyr even if you don't have any faith."

Aisha reminded her of what Martin had done. "He saved Doctor Leidner, all those tourists near the bomb. He saved us when we were chasing him out on the water because that thing he found on board would have poisoned us, too. He saved all the other people who would have died if the rest of those warheads were used. If that's not a martyr, what is it?"

"A lunatic."

Aisha stared at her. Angrily. "You shouldn't have said that."

Elizabeth reached for her. Aisha backed away.

"Okay. I'm sorry. But you just don't know Martin. If he could hear you, calling him a martyr . . ."

"Then a hero. Is that better? That way it's not religious."

Elizabeth didn't know how she could explain. Martin's not a hero. He simply *does* things. He has a mind that . . . well maybe it's not actually deranged . . . it's a mind that doesn't think, it just *does*.

"*Last chance, Elizabeth. Tell her you love me.*"

"*Damn you, Martin . . .*"

"*Say it, Elizabeth. I don't have all day. Leyna Bandari has asked me to play tennis.*"

Oh, God. Don't start this, said Elizabeth to herself.

"*After that Leyna wants to cool off and go swimming but I think I've had enough water for a while.*"

"Aisha, honey . . . look, let's go inside."

"*It's Cherokee, Elizabeth. She just told you. Get it straight.*"

"Aish . . . Cherokee, I loved him. I did."

"*Past tense? What past tense? I'm here talking to you.*"

"And he loves you. He still does," said the girl.

"I know." The tears began to well again.

"So do I. If you'll let me."

"No matter what?" She dabbed at her eyes.

"There isn't any no matter what."

"*Your Ingram, your big knife, are sunk with that duffel? You're not Ozzie and Harriet quite yet, Elizabeth. Even that woman in your driveway keeps a weapon.*"

"*I'm not going to do this. I'm not talking to you.*"

"*Except I don't think anyone will come looking for you now. But they'll be spotting me like Elvis all over Europe. You wait and see if they don't.*"

"*Martin . . .*"

Forget it. She turned toward the girl.

"Is that Jasmine or Nadia who brought you?" asked Elizabeth.

"It's Jasmine. She's waiting out front."

"Let's go ask her in. I'll put on some breakfast."

"She'd like that. I'd like that. Very much."

"After that . . ."

The girl waited, her eyes wide and hopeful.

"After that . . . we'll see what we can do about your hair."

IF you liked *Haven and The Shadow Box*, you'll love *Mosaic*, an exhilerating new thriller with all the suspence you've come to expect from John Maxim.

The following is an excerpt from the first chapter of John Maxim's new novel, *Mosaic*, coming in early 1999 in hardcover from Avon Books.

Grayson knew that going back to the same place was foolish. He was breaking a cardinal rule of survival. Avoid routines; never follow a pattern. Assume that they're watching and charting your movements, waiting for their best chance to take you.

Grayson more than knew that, he'd taught it. But he needed to see that young woman again, the one who'd seemed either the twin or the ghost of the woman he had probably murdered.

For the past several months he had stayed within the gates of an Air Force base outside Washington. His bachelor quarters were in a well-secured area that required passing through several checkpoints to enter. He'd felt safe enough there but increasingly restless until he could stand the isolation no longer. So just after sunrise on a cool September morning, he put on some shorts and an old hooded jersey and studied the effect in a mirror.

He could have been anyone. People said that was his gift. He had medium brown hair, worn long, almost shaggy. A military cut would not do for his work. His eyes were non-descript, not quite blue, not quite gray. He could be almost handsome; he could be almost homely, or his face could be cold, almost cruel. General Hoyt had remarked that he'd never seen two photos that seemed quite the same Major Grayson. But today, the look that he wanted was average. Middle of the road, don't stand out from the crowd, the he's-nobody-special kind of average. The look that he saw in his mirror was that, especially with the hood of his jersey in place. Satisfied, he sat and fastened his knee brace. That done, he went out and climbed into his car and started to drive off the base.

The corporal at the gate had known he was coming; one or more of the checkpoints had alerted him. The corporal tried to stall him while he called for an escort. Grayson said that he was armed and had his cell phone and pager. He assured the corporal that he wouldn't be long and would stay within sight of the perimeter. He'd be back before anyone could miss him.

What he wanted was to run. Not run away, just run. But he had no intention of staying near the base. He wanted to drive the few miles into Washington and park near the Jefferson Memorial. From there, he would walk to the jogging path that circled the Tidal Basin. Few tourists, if any, would be out at that hour. There would be, at most, a few dozen runners spread over its two-mile length. They would all be civilians who lived normal lives and they would know nothing about him. Unlike the personnel on the base, there wouldn't be anyone pointing him out and repeating gossipy stories about him. The civilians would not drop their eyes as they passed him. The civilians would not be afraid of him.

For a time that first morning he felt wonderfully free. He had started with his hood up but it soon fell away. He had wanted to run the full two miles but the knee that took the bullet wasn't up to it yet. He jogged part way and he walked part way. The knee, even so, began to swell inside its brace. He would ice it later. It was worth it.

He had almost made a full circle of the basin and was headed back to where he'd left his car. It was then that he saw two women running toward him and he felt his stomach rise up into his chest. One of the two could well have been a ghost for all that she looked so much like Janice.

The woman running with her, a light-skinned black woman, was wearing a Clemson sweatshirt. The one who could have been Janice had the same long blond hair and, like Janice, she wore it gathered loosely in the back. She had the same way of brushing strands from her eyes, the same slight tilt of her head to the right. She was running in frayed cut-off jeans and a halter. She was the same age, mid-twenties at most. Both women were laughing and bantering with each other as they ran. They smiled and said "Hi!" as they went by him.

It, of course, wasn't Janice. Janice was dead. Up close he could see that her skin was clear where Janice's had been lightly freckled. The mouth was different in the way it formed a smile. But Grayson's stomach had not settled back because her greeting seemed more than a reflex civility. She'd made eye contact longer than was needed to say "Hi." He had nodded in response. He did not smile back. He lowered his head and kept going.

Grayson realized why her gaze had been more than fleeting. She had seen how intently he'd been staring at her. She was probably wondering whether they'd met and was simply trying to place him. Even so, he found himself starting to think that the resemblance was too much of a coincidence. He listened to their footsteps as they went by, alert to any change in their cadence. He heard the scuffing sound of a sneaker turned sideways and he knew that one had half-turned to glance back at him. His left hand moved toward the pistol that he carried.

But the sneaker had resumed its soft slap against the pavement; the two women kept going. Grayson felt like an ass. He had almost allowed himself to believe that a vengeful twin had appeared out of nowhere. He was showing signs of cracking and he knew it.

He tried to put her out of his mind but her face stayed with him all the rest of that day. It appeared in his dreams when he slept, where she began as the jogger he'd seen but the place where he'd seen her soon melted away until all that was left was her face. Grayson reached up to touch it. He caressed her cheek. He saw that her hair was no longer tied back; it was brushing the back of his hand. It was no longer the jogger. She had turned into Janice. She was wearing not a halter but one of his shirts. She was sitting on the edge of his bed, a four-poster. He realized where he was; it was a country bed-and-breakfast in the West Virginia hills, just over the Maryland border. They were where they'd made love on the night that she came to him, where they'd met several times after that.

Grayson knew that he shouldn't have let himself care for her. She was an informant. He was there to debrief her. But she had come to his room in the middle of the night and asked him to please let her stay for a while. She said she was frightened. She asked him to hold her. He did. He should not have. But that's how it started.

Some weeks later he was with her, same inn, same four-poster. They'd made love well into the morning. She snuggled against him, lightly tickling his chest. She said, "You know what? It's such a beautiful day. I'd like to take you on a picnic."

Grayson told her that a picnic was a lovely thought but it wasn't a very good idea. They might be seen together. That could put her in danger. The woman who ran the b-and-b was reliable but anyplace else was a risk. Still Janice said that she knew a magical place. It was a lake near Ice Mountain in the northern Shenandoahs. She said it was only a two-hour drive and yet hundreds of years back in time. She said her father used to take her there when she was a girl. It had trout that would practically jump into his net and deer so tame that they'd take food from her hand. In all the times that she'd been there, she said, she'd never seen so much as a footprint left by anyone but her father and herself. Nor had she ever shared it with anyone else, but she wanted to share it with him. She told him to shower while she went downstairs and ordered a special box lunch.

They went there. She was right. It was a beautiful spot. She spread a blanket and had him lie back. She took his head in her lap. He lay there listening to the splashing of fish and the whisper of the wind in the trees. She had opened his jacket, put her hand on his chest.

She said, "You know, there's something wrong with this picture. Did you have to bring a gun? The gun ruins it."

It was in a holster under his arm. He tried to push it

back out of view. She said, "Uh-uh. Come on, Give it here. I'll cover it with the blanket."

Grayson drew the Beretta. He laid it at his side. Janice folded the blanket over on top of it. She bent and kissed his forehead, ran her fingers through his hair. Within seconds, Grayson had closed his eyes, feeling only the tender warmth of her body and the gentle touch of her fingers. He could feel it when she lifted the hand that had caressed him and raised it to the level of her head. He thought nothing of it. It felt as if she were shooing an insect or brushing a hair from her brow.

But then he felt the muscles of her stomach go tight. He opened one eye and looked up at her. He saw that she seemed to be waving at someone. Her hand was moving in a beckoning motion toward someone directly behind them. He started to rise; she tried to hold him down. Her touch was no longer so gentle. His left hand, by reflex, groped for his Beretta but she'd covered it with her legs. She shouted, "Get in here. Right now."

Grayson wrenched himself out of her grip. He twisted and rolled until he was free. Now he saw two figures coming out of the trees. He recognized both; they were dangerous men. He had come to know them very well. Both men had assault rifles in their hands, but today they seemed tentative, frightened. Again, he tried to locate the Beretta but Janice had beaten him to it. She snatched it from the blanket and flipped off the safety. She said, "Give it up. Don't make me shoot you."

"Screw this, kill him now," called one of the men. "Let's bury that psycho right here."

"Damn it, no," shouted Janice. She had turned her head toward them. "Your orders are to take him alive."

At that instant, Grayson made a feint with one hand and slapped at the Beretta with the other. He remembered doing that. He was not quick enough. He remembered the muzzle blast for the pistol and hammer blow on his right knee. He remembered the ringing that began in both his ears and grew until it reached the pitch of a scream.

He would remember almost nothing that had happened after that. He knew only that the ringing in his ears began to fade and he found himself standing, holding onto a tree limb. His Beretta, for some reason, was in his right hand. The two men were on the ground, not moving. One had crumpled backward, his legs folded under him. The other had fallen forward on his face. Grayson looked around him. He did not see Janice. For a moment he thought that she must have run off. He tested his leg; he tried to take a step; the leg seemed unable to move forward. He looked down to see how badly he was hurt. He saw what was stopping it, Janice's body. She was lying facedown, her long hair across his feet. The back of her head was blown off.

Grayson had dreamed of that day many times. Those that tormented him the most were the gentle ones of the morning of that day, he and Janice in the four-poster bed. He would rather have dreamed about the shooting itself in hopes that it might finally tell him exactly what had happened, what he'd done.

There was no question that he had killed Janice. He had hoped that one of those two men had shot her by accident while trying to fire at him. But the evidence—the pathologist's report—left no doubt. Although one of the men had emptied half a clip, all the bullets that hit flesh had come from his pistol. And Janice was unarmed when he shot her.

In some dreams he'd find himself looking into her eyes and seeing, not affection, but betrayal. She would claw at his weapon, he would push her away. Lights would flash and he'd wake up alone in his room, aiming a pistol that he wasn't holding at people who weren't there either.

This night's dream, too, was over, but the images remained. Not fully awake, his mind tried to tell him that Janice had survived. But he quickly realized that the Janice who lived was only the woman he'd seen jogging. Grayson found himself wanting to see her again. He didn't know why; the wish made no sense. He would not, he decided, indulge it.

Even so, when dawn came, he drove back to the basin.

*   *   *

Grayson knew that the woman was not likely to be there just because he was hoping that she would. But there she was, coming toward him again, her friend, as before, keeping pace. Grayson's throat went dry, but when he got within range, he managed a nod and a wave. The one who looked like Janice smiled again and said "Oh . . . hi:" She said it with a hint of pleasant surprise as if she had been thinking about him as well.

Grayson smiled back, but his heart was in his throat. He continued without speaking to her. That was it. Enough. He'd got it out of his system in time not to make a fool of himself. But, again, her face stayed in his mind all that day and, again, he went back the next morning.

That day, the third time he saw them approaching, he noticed the black woman nudge the other with her elbow.

"*Go ahead*," she mouthed.

"*Will you stop*?" mouthed the other.

Grayson realized that the one who looked so much like Janice must have expressed an interest in him. Her friend had urged her to do something about it. But the blond one lost her nerve and kept going, just as he had the morning before.

They'd assumed, he supposed, that he was someone important, maybe because of the cell phone on his belt. A young congressman, perhaps, or a presidential aide. They had looked at his hands and had seen no rings. They had looked at the brace that he wore on his knee and assumed . . . whatever . . . that perhaps he'd played football or had torn up his knee on a ski slope.

He was almost disappointed that they didn't stop. If they had, he might have taken a chance. He might have invited them for coffee. The black one, the matchmaker, would have said yes. Then she, at some point, would have made herself scarce so that he could be alone with her friend. They would sit and talk and, maybe at the end, he'd have asked if she'd care to see a movie or something.

"Why didn't you, Major?" asked the Pentagon shrink.

"You're kidding, Doc, right?"

"What's the harm in a movie?"

Grayson shrugged. He wet his lips. ''For one thing, she would have asked what I do.''

''And?''

''Almost anything I'd tell her would have to be a lie.''

''Well . . . yes, but so what? If you told her the truth, she'd assume it was bullshit. This is Washington. Everything's bullshit.''

Grayson grimaced, then nodded. He almost smiled.

''Let's have the real reason,'' said the shrink.

''Doc, she's a ringer for Janice Novak. Don't you think that would be a little sick?''

''It . . . might raise an eyebrow. But there are other women who don't look like Novak. You don't try to meet any of them either.''

''I'm bad luck for women. You know that.''

''I know that you've talked yourself into believing it. You're afraid of what, that you'd put them in danger? That those people would hurt them to get back at you?''

''Doc, they killed the woman who ran that bed-and-breakfast.''

''Ah, yes. I'd forgotten. She was also one of ours?''

''Her late husband was. Died of cancer, left her strapped. We looked for ways to use her place, help her out. All that did was get her murdered in a terrible way. The slashed up her face with a bread knife.''

The shrink took a breath. ''And . . . you blame yourself.''

''Who else? My mistake got her killed.''

''Which mistake?''

''I could have told Janice that she was discreet. Lots of b-and-b owners are discreet. But the word I used to describe her was 'reliable.' That was how Janice knew. That woman was probably packing up our box lunches while Janice was on the phone to her friends.''

''But you had no reason to think she was a plant.''

''I got suckered in a lot of ways, Doc.''

''Major Grayson . . . Roger . . . let me ask you a question. Is this how you plan to live the rest of your life?''

Grayson sucked on his lip. He did not have an answer.

"You used to have friends. You had lots of friends. You withdrew from all of them. Why?"

"It's the other way around. They withdrew from me."

"You must have had calls . . . invitations from some."

"Doc, you don't kill three people and get asked to dinner parties. It makes one hard to seat, as my grandmother used to say."

The Pentagon shrink had to smile.

"But I'm dealing with it, Doc. I'm doing my best."

"No, you're not. All you've done is crawl into a hole. It's time you gave yourself a good kick in the ass. It happened. Get over it. Move on."

Grayson thanked him for his sensitive words of encouragement. The shrink ignored the sarcasm.

"Don't you think it's time you told someone the truth of what really happened that day? And don't say it's all in your report."

"Doc, I honest to God don't remember."

"This blackout, then. This siren in your ears. Has that ever happened before?"

"Only in sports. I've had my bell rung. But I didn't kill anyone I was playing against. If I had, the coach would have mentioned it."

"Well, when you remember, and I think you will, I want you to call me and tell me."

"Sure."

"And I mean just me; it would stay between us. Don't let this thing fester by keeping it inside you. You've got to find a way to let it end."

"Doc, I'm not the one who won't let it end. Those people have put a bounty on me."

The psychiatrist sighed. "I know, there is that. I assume, by the way, that you did change your route. There's no sense in asking for trouble."

Grayson answered with a grunt. It avoided a lie. He'd gone back that way because . . . and he knew this was stupid . . . he needed to see someone smile at him.

They were there, same place, same time, and they were waiting. His sense was that they were waiting for him.

They had stopped just past the new Roosevelt Memorial and were looking out over the Potomac River where a race of small catboats was in progress. The blond one was sipping from an Evian bottle. She looked up, saw him coming but had to look twice because Grayson was wearing a warm-up suit this time. As he drew closer she waved and said, "Hi! Look at this." She was pointing toward a pair of catboats that had become tangled in each others' rigging. One was being pulled over on its side.

Grayson looked away. He jogged on.

Grayson, you putz, he muttered to himself.

He had done a rude and cruel thing and he knew it. He glanced back and saw that they had lowered their heads. The blond one was probably kicking herself and her friend would be saying, "Forget him. He's a jerk."

Grayson answered in his mind, *Yes, I am and I'm sorry.*

Let me tell you, he thought, just how big a jerk I am. I'm wearing this warm-up which is too hot to run in because it's easier to reach my gun if I need it. I wanted to see you, I wanted to meet you, but then all these voices started whispering in my head. What if I really am being stupid and what if she's not what she seems? Maybe she's been trying to get my attention so her friend can stick a knife in my ribs from behind. Or more likely these two are exactly what they seem, but perhaps someone else has been watching us. Maybe the price they'll pay for being friendly is to get in the way of a bullet.

So what did I do? Stay home? Change my route? No, what I did was strap on my speed rig, come over here just to see you again, and behave like . . . you said it . . . a jerk.

One thing, though, he thought. The shrink was right. He could not live the rest of his life this way.

Grayson was considering leaving the service.

"Is that so? To do what?" asked the Pentagon shrink.

"I don't know. Do some traveling. Disappear for a while."

"And then hope to resurface as a butterfly somewhere?"

"Doc . . . we've been through this. I'm not a bad man."

"I know you're not, Roger. A poor joke. Forgive me."

"I'm not a killer. I'm not even a hurter."

"Roger . . . I know. Tell me more about your plans."

"Not plans yet," he answered. "Just some thoughts on what else I might do for a living."

"Such as?"

"You'll laugh."

"Not 'til after you've gone."

"Well, I think I'd like to teach at a small college somewhere. Maybe do some drama coaching on the side."

"Drama? Not sports? What qualifies you for drama?"

"What I've done, what I teach, is basically acting."

The psychiatrist smiled. "You know, you're quite right. I'd never thought of working undercover as acting but that's pretty much what it is." He sat back. "The groves of academe, I understand the appeal, but what in a standard curriculum would you teach? Your specialty has been rather narrow, don't you think?"

"Psychology isn't. I have two degrees. Psychology is what I know best."

"Everyone's but your own. You really should give it time."

"This assignment the general wants to talk to me about . . . is it something you recommended?"

The shrink shook his head. "I knew nothing about it. I merely suggested that he try to keep you busy; find you something in line with your talents and interests while your mind and body are healing. All he said was that he had just the thing."

"I'd be working with Prentice Teal. Do you know him?"

"I know him. He's . . . an unusual man."

"He does black budget stuff. That's not my cup of tea."

"You say you want to teach? Spend a month or two with Teal. You'll learn things that are not in any textbook I know of."

Edgar Award Winner
STUART WOODS
New York Times Bestselling Author of
Dead in the Water

GRASS ROOTS 71169-/ $6.50 US/ $8.50 Can

WHITE CARGO 70783-7/ $6.99 US/ $8.99 Can

DEEP LIE 70266-5/ $6.50 US/ $8.50 Can

UNDER THE LAKE
70519-2/ $6.50 US/ $8.50 Can

CHIEFS 70347-5/ $6.99 US/ $8.99 Can

RUN BEFORE THE WIND
70507-9/ $6.50 US/ $8.50 Can